Grey Masque of Death

Also by Mai Griffin

In the Grey Series

Deadly Shades of Grey

A Poisonous Shade of Grey

And Coming Soon

Haunting Shades of Grey

Watch www.uppublications.ltd.uk/maigriffin
for more information

Grey Masque of Death

Mai Griffin

U P Publications
2008

All rights reserved
No part of this publication may be reproduced or transmitted by any means, electronic, mechanical, photocopy or otherwise, without the prior permission of the publisher

First published in Great Britain in 2009 by
U P Publications Ltd
25 Bedford Street, Peterborough, UK PE1 4DN
Head Office: 80 Lincoln Road, Peterborough, UK PE1 2SN

Cover design copyright © G. M. G. Peers 2008

Copyright © Mai Griffin 1997, 2009

Mai Griffin has asserted her moral rights

Extracts are taken from "Anon - A Book of Unknown Quotes" a private publication copyright © G. M. G. Peers 2007

A CIP Catalogue record of this book is available from the British Library

ISBN 978-0-9557447-2-3

Printed in Great Britain by the MPG Books Group Bodmin and King's Lynn

FIRST EDITION

www.uppublications.ltd.uk/maigriffin

**With grateful thanks to
Valerie and Jean for their encouragement**

All characters are fictitious ... although the
creation of Sarah and Stephen Grey.
was inspired by my late parents to whom
the Grey series is dedicated.
Mai Griffin 2009

In Life and Death there is no Black and White,
No core construct that always must be right,
No path or light that clearly shows the way
But filters through a Deadly Shade of Grey.

In Death's dark realm, where none of us may stray,
The light glints through a Poisonous Shade of Grey.
A Glimmer glimpsed, beyond a heart's endeavour,
Where lost souls wander in their dark forever.

Now mourners gather to share a lasting glance
Where grief full memories perform a final dance
and movement stills as with departing breath
the music plays the last Grey Masque of Death.

Anon

Chapter One

Margaret Heywood-Dunn gripped the arm of her chair in awed anticipation. Firelight flickered over her thin pale face – the skin over high cheekbones was drawn tight by the pull of grey hair which, twisted into a bun at the back, gave her eyebrows a permanent lift. A younger woman sat opposite – stiffly upright with eyes tightly closed. As Margaret fidgeted, with growing impatience, Irma started to sway gently back and forth. A frown of frustration creased the girl's brow and her head tilted as if striving to hold on to faint, faraway sounds. Margaret had been warned that the attempt to communicate might fail – there were no guarantees – she was therefore prepared for disappointment and sighed heavily. Even so, she waited in hope.

After a few minutes Irma started to breathe more deeply; both hands, previously resting lightly on her lap, began to clench and unclench. The rasping breath grew louder and low muttering came at the same time from Irma's parted lips. In all her seventy years Margaret had never witnessed such a thing before... She was gripped by chill fear.

Suddenly the noise stopped and Irma opened her eyes. She smiled, distantly, but it was enough to restore a measure of calm to Margaret's fluttering heart.

Looking towards the door Irma said, "God Bless you. How lovely to see you. Please say who you are and why you are here."

"What is it? Who is here?" Margaret turned in alarm, not really able to believe...

Irma frowned and made reassuring gestures, not towards Margaret, but as if to someone else in the room with them.

"Shush now... don't be frightened. Tell me your name? Yes – Olive ... and you have a message for Meggy? ..."

"Good God! How incredible ... is it really Olive? She is the only one who ever called me Meggy!"

"Yes – she wants you to know how much she missed you when you were sent off to school ... she was barely nine years older than yourself and you used to help with her chores so that she would be able to play with you ... a game on a board ... Chess? No, I see black and white discs!"

"Draughts, it was draughts!" Margaret cried, almost bursting with excitement. I beat her most of the time and ..."

"No, no – please don't tell me anything. If you do, you won't know, later, how much I really saw and heard and how much information you gave me yourself! "... Irma sighed and gave a small shudder before lapsing into stillness. Her eyes closed and a few minutes later opened again with a brightness they had previously lacked. "Well? How was that? She has gone now, but you did know her didn't you?"

There was absolutely no shadow of doubt in the mind of Mrs Heywood-Dunn. Irma had been in contact with 'The Other Side' and was making it possible for her to relive those far-off days of her early childhood ... the only time, apart from her too few years with poor dear Martin, when she had been truly happy.

It must have been a benevolent fate that brought Irma Rigby into her life when she was in a state of depression, having so recently lost her only close friend, Jean.

Jean Webb had been with her, more like a sister than an employee, for over fifteen years – ever since Margaret's husband had died. Because he suffered a long illness Jean, a private nurse, 'lived in' to tend him for the final three years of his life. She had been almost as devastated by his death as Margaret herself. It had seemed natural for her to stay on as a companion. Jean was ten years Margaret's junior and very fit ... it was a terrible blow when she was killed ... a wicked shame, everyone agreed, to be mown down by a drunken driver.

The tragedy had happened only three months ago, on the thirteenth of November. Jean was cycling back from the village after her Wednesday night choir practice; "The driver said she fell off in front of him! There was nothing he could do," Margaret told everyone ... "Drunken fool!"

She was so upset that she couldn't contemplate replacing her. Jean had been more than just a housekeeper.

Then, one morning soon after Christmas Edna, her daily woman, told her about Irma. "She could put you in touch with Miss Webb! I've had my old granny come back to me, through Irma, several times. A great comfort it is, and she is a very nice young woman – not weird or anything!"

At first, Margaret turned down the suggestion very firmly. The idea shocked her. She did not believe in life after death ... except for the way the Bible treated the subject, of course. Ordinary people didn't come back as ghosts – she was quite sure! But the more Edna told her, the less certain she became. The nagging thought that she might get in touch with Jean gradually began to intrigue her, and she finally agreed to meet Edna's friend.

When Irma arrived at the house, the following morning, Margaret was already regretting having invited her ... one heard that it was dangerous to tamper with 'ouija boards' and the like. Trying to contact the dead was 'Courting the Devil'! But it was too late ... Irma was standing before her, hand outstretched. This in itself was enough to repel Margaret ... it was up to her, the senior, to decide whether or not to shake hands, but she took it anyway, lightly.

With a rather aloof smile, she murmured, "How do you do, Mrs Rigby. Please come and sit down ... Edna will bring in the coffee directly, and then we can talk without interruption."

Irma, tall and slimly built, was dressed neatly, not at all flamboyantly – no flowing robes, bangles and beads, Margaret noted with relief – in fact she had a rather staid mien for a woman in her mid-forties. Gathering her calf-length skirt over her knees as she sat and placing her hands together primly on her lap, the young woman spoke. "Please call me Irma, Madam. What a pleasant room ..."

Margaret ignored the 'Madam' ... She had no inkling then, that their association would last beyond that first meeting. She didn't know how much she would come to rely on Irma, in every aspect of her life!

Chapter Two

Sunday March 8th...

The telephone suddenly rang, shattering the companionable silence. Sarah had actually been on the edge of sleep. The warmth of the fire and the satisfying memory of Polly's excellent lunch had enabled her to relax, putting the last few weeks of trauma behind her. It was Clarrie who, with a sigh of irritation, pushed herself up from the depths of her armchair to answer. It was probably for her anyway, she thought ... but it was not.

It was someone called Johnson – Jay Johnson; he wanted to speak to her mother. Sarah was astonished. She hardly knew him and had not been in contact with his wife Amy for almost a year! Her first thought, that her old friend must be ill, thankfully was not so. Saying that he was about to ask a favour, he hoped she would forgive him for springing it on her, because she might possibly enjoy herself while helping him out.

He had booked theatre tickets and a table for dinner, meaning to take Amy himself, but now was unable to go. He had not told Amy. It was meant to be a birthday surprise as she so rarely got out of the house these days. If Sarah could not take his place he would cancel – no harm done – but as he was giving her over four weeks advance notice, he hoped she would accept. He knew, apparently, that there was no-one with whom Amy would rather go than her oldest and most valued friend – Sarah's name was often on her lips – it would be a real treat for her.

At the back of her mind Sarah felt an uncomfortable sense of disquiet but thrust it aside; it was probably due to his obsequious approach, or even a fleeting return of her initial doubts about him. Jay's unblemished record over the past twenty years surely entitled him to be taken at face value although, personally, she had never felt really comfortable with him. Amy, a childhood friend, first introduced him to Sarah at their wedding reception. She had said his name was really John but he's always been known as Jay. "Two John's in the same house could have been so confusing," she burbled happily.

If only it had not been too late she would have tried to persuade the girl to think again! It was nothing she could have explained at the time – even to her own satisfaction, but as a psychic she was extremely sensitive to the individual aura that surrounds people. She had schooled herself to tune out these emanations – to explore them seemed like uninvited intrusion. Anyway, letting down her guard often led to an onslaught from the Spirit world. Souls who had passed on were always eager to contact loved ones left behind, usually with the best of motives, but that didn't render them any less of a distraction in her daily life. Only when unavoidable in those days did she use her unusual gifts – very few, even amongst close friends, were aware of their existence. Psychometry had always intrigued her. It was principally her natural ability to discern information from inanimate objects that had first alerted her to the paranormal. It had been an exciting game as a child; only in adulthood had she appreciated it fully and learned to control it.

It was consequently something she rarely practiced, but she was tempted when she saw Jay's silver card case forgotten on the table. The sudden coldness she had felt when Jay shook her hand earlier had been so disturbing that, for Amy's sake, Sarah picked it up and held it hopefully, attempting to discern more about him. Concentrating on the flat surface, she had stared at the unusual design which incorporated the initials 'J J J' expecting immediate empathy with Jay – his life, background or anything. Sarah was puzzled when something strange and shadowy enfolded her, but whatever it was seemed beyond her grasp. Considerably disturbed she replaced the case quickly just as Jay walked up to retrieve it. He remarked that it had belonged to his grandfather, James Jerome and really belonged to his father who was now ill and had no use for it. He would not want to lose it!

Over the next few years Jay was good to Amy and they appeared to be very happy, so Sarah had gradually forgotten her first impressions. In those days she was a very inexperienced medium. Her misgivings may have been due to a previous owner rather than the boy himself, who actually had a pleasant personality. Amy's continued prosperity lulled Sarah's trepidation. Now, a dull ache of dread returned. Thumbing through her diary she found she had no other commitments that day, no excuse for refusing, so she accepted. She need not worry about transport Jay said, a car would collect her and later return her to her home ... all she had to do was keep the trip secret and enjoy herself on the night.

Since moving in with her widowed daughter a few years ago she had fallen into the habit, in spite of Clarinda's protestations, of giving her own pleasure a low priority and, returning to the sitting-room, immediately regretted agreeing to go. She found it almost impossible to settle down again. Why was she filled with foreboding? There was almost four weeks to get through before the theatre date so Sarah determined to put it completely out of mind until then; however negative her attitude, she'd have to go! After all, she told herself repeatedly, theatre visits were diverting – special events to look forward to – and it would be nice meeting Amy again. Yes, she was glad she had accepted ... she would thoroughly enjoy herself!

But still the ice cold knot tightened in the pit of her stomach.

Clarrie was enthusiastic about the invitation – the outing might help to restore Sarah's usual happy outlook on life. She eyed her mother's figure – still in good shape for a fifty-nine-year-old and pointed out that it was a good excuse to buy a new dress. After glancing at Sarah's upswept waves of silver hair, she added encouragingly, "Your hair always looks nice, but you could treat yourself to a salon 'do' and catch up on old magazines!"

The year had begun on a high note. Their friend Bettina Bane's son Adam had his first birthday party on January 3rd. It had been a large gathering of adults for a tiny child but at that age a child doesn't have a huge social circle of its own! They had known Bet before her husband died almost a year earlier and had introduced her to Algy Green, a Detective Inspector in the CID. Since last May, when Clarrie met Del Delaney, they had spent many pleasant evenings together as a foursome. At the time, Algy's wife was a long-term patient in a psychiatric hospital ward ... she hadn't recognised him for many years, but he still adored her and hoped for her complete recovery. Unfortunately, she developed pneumonia at Christmas ... and, incredibly, died on the anniversary of Bet's husband's death – January 15th. So the month ended in the sad aura of funeral and memorial services.

Clarrie had never been able to believe that Algy's wife would recover ... perhaps now he would face up to the future without her ... it could really be the best thing for him, but it was far too early to say so. Sarah had invited Algy and Bet to dine with them several times since then, but the occasions did more to depress Clarrie than cheer anyone else ... she couldn't stop feeling gloomy about Del's absence. After a flying visit in December, he went back to the Middle East. Because his contract was likely to be extended beyond July, instead of piling up leave until June, he had taken a short break, hoping to persuade Clarrie to make their engagement official ... What was the point? It was better to wait until he finally returned to England, his tour ended.

When Polly heard of the theatre trip, she agreed whole-heartedly with Clarrie and together they banished Sarah's doubts. Polly, older than Sarah by seven years, had progressed from being the Grey family housekeeper and Sarah's friend for over thirty years, to being more like a member of the family. She too had moved into Clarrie's house in Mapledurham and loved every minute of life now – looking after them was a labour of love. Her own daughter Jane lived only a mile away, so she was still close enough to see her grandchildren, but living with them had been far too tiring!

After an early supper Clarrie went to her studio/ bedroom to prepare a canvas for her next commission and Polly stayed downstairs to watch television, but Sarah decided to read in bed for a while to take her mind off Amy and Jay. In spite of her determination not to worry, her mind refused to switch off.

The sky lightened with false dawn and darkened again, before Sarah found release from her churning doubts and slept.

Chapter Three

Halfway through March Clarrie also had a telephone call, from an old client, which would bring about a disturbance in her life. Some years ago she had painted several pictures for Emily Grant's family. The first was a portrait of their child which Clarrie set in the garden. Mr Grant was so impressed by the background that he asked for a picture of the house itself, from the front approach. His brothers saw the painting and also had their properties immortalised in oils.

Clarrie hardly expected more commissions from Mrs Grant but was pleased to hear that her pictures were still proudly displayed and were often admired.

"I know how busy you always are," Emily said, "but I took the liberty of mentioning you to a neighbour of mine. Miss Matthews has left her home in Wales to come to a smaller house. She misses the old place so much, that I suggested she should ask you to do a picture of it, before it's sold."

Clarrie immediately remembered another Welsh cottage she had painted and the terrifying situation in which that had landed her ... She gave a slight inward shudder.

Sensing her hesitation Emily added, "She is certainly very impressed by the work you did for me. Could you come over for lunch one day to meet her?"

Recovering quickly – after all, she had enjoyed the greater part of her holiday in Wales and the cottage painting turned out to be her best ever – Clarrie said she would be pleased to talk to Miss Matthews and would bring a more recent picture with her which strangely enough was also of a Welsh cottage.

"Oh, I'm sure hers is not a cottage. From what she says, it sounds like a rambling old place, but do bring the painting anyway – I'd love to see it myself."

A date was fixed for Saturday the twenty-first and Clarrie went back to her easel. The subject she was tackling was another landscape, started last summer. To finish it she was using sketches and photographs taken at the time. Always her own severest critic she knew it was not even nearly as good as the one she privately called 'The Haunted Cottage' which had, after all, been painted from life ... much more satisfying than using snaps however good.

She was filled with pleasurable anticipation, as always, at the prospect of another out-door commission ... but only if the weather held good. If Miss Matthews did decide to have a painting she would plan to go soon – in early spring.

As she worked she wondered if it would be within calling distance of Williams' farm where the cottage still stood – she had a standing invitation to stay with them and Gareth could show her some more of his favourite views for her to paint. It would be interesting to see them again – the haunted house too! Was it still empty, she wondered? She decided to photograph her painting of it, which they had wanted to buy, and give them an enlarged print on canvas. She couldn't part with the original ... it held too much significance in her life. Sarah also seemed to regard the painting as special ... To her it marked her daughter's spiritual advancement and she had actually asked that Clarinda should never sell it.

***

In her new village home on the outskirts of Oxford, at the beginning of April, Bertha Matthews looked from the front room window, at the profusion of plants in her small garden. When they were in flower the daffodils here were close enough to enjoy and pick easily, to carry a breath of spring inside. She visualised the sweeping slopes around her old home in spring-time – ablaze with glorious golden trumpets, but so remote. She recalled a succession of gardeners, year after year, planting bulbs within the grounds but none ever came up. Her mother settled eventually for less formal landscaping with a few trees and shrubs. The resulting open views, even from the lower windows, were a pleasing bonus. It should make it easier for that young artist she had met to find the best view of the house, unhindered by too much green growth.

A member of the welcoming committee, offering advice to newcomers, picked up her remark about missing the house where her family had lived for generations and asked if she'd like to meet Clarinda Hunter who painted beautiful pictures in oils. Bertha wasn't particularly interested in art. She had grown up surrounded by pictures on every wall in the house; most were originals and all had gone to auction. The majority had been gloomy and uninspired, but the idea of having one specially painted for her, held great appeal.

When she met the girl last week, and saw her interpretation of an old Welsh cottage, she was stunned; it was not just a scene. In it was a depth of vision verging on the supernatural, recognisable to Bertha more than most people! In choosing this distant village as her new home she had yearned for a new start – freed from the finger-pointing and gossip of families that had known hers and handed on, from one generation to another, scandalous tales of the past.

It was not her fault her ancestors had delved into black arts.

In spite of all their attempts to indoctrinate her as a child, her two Grandmothers, who were twins, had failed. The family had intermarried for generations. Themselves the off-spring of cousins, they had both prudently married outside the family but the sisters refused to be parted. Their husbands moved into the big house and when their boy and girl babies were born in the same month it was inevitable that one day they would marry.

Bertha was born a year later and as her mother nearly died in labour she was an only child. Her parents disapproved of their own mothers taking charge and keeping her so close to them but were powerless to intervene, so until Bertha was eight-years-old she knew no other children. Her only happy moments were spent with the old books in her grandfather's study, and dusty volumes about 'The Old Religion' given to her by her grandmothers.

Only when the authorities insisted that she must attend the local school did the child escape their clutches. In many ways, especially reading, she was well in advance of her new schoolmates which only alienated her from them, increasing their immediate distrust. As well as being unhappy at school she was not very robust and hated the miles she had to walk to and from the dreaded place.

The other children, sensing she was 'different', excluded her from their play and even tormented her cruelly, just to impress each other. In her fierce resentment, little Bertha stared up at the dark sky one night, fists clenched, an ancient mantra throbbing somewhere in her head ... wishing the most hated bully dead. She never saw him at school again – or anywhere else! It didn't occur to her that his family had merely moved away. Her feeling of relief was far outweighed by her sense of guilt because she was convinced that her curse had killed him!

After the grannies and her parents died, not having to earn a living, Bertha became more and more of a recluse until her doctor advised her to sell up and move while she was still fairly active ... the property should fetch a good price, he suggested, and it was far too big for her anyway. The idea had merit: it could surely not be too late, she told herself, to change her life and perhaps make a few friends.

Now, only six months later, her dreams of a happy, normal existence were shattered. It was hard not to weep. But for the nasty malicious child next door, she would have made friends. Things could have been so different.

***

The firm commission from Miss Matthews meant a lot of extra work for Clarrie during the three weeks before Sarah's theatre date, so she scarcely noticed how little the idea of a night out appealed to her mother. Polly endeavoured to ignore Sarah's apathetic mood ... as if by doing so it would go away. She even had a problem of her own which might have distracted Sarah and tried to broach the subject several times without success; she could never get to the point before something interrupted them.

Elaine, the wife of Polly's nephew Dan, was concerned about an elderly relative of hers. They both had a high regard for Sarah's unusual powers; she had helped them through an unusual and harrowing problem last year, when they were newly married. Dan asked Polly if she would discuss it with Sarah or Clarinda. Polly was not at all sure what Dan expected either of them to do about it, but had promised to do her best.

Elaine's Aunt Margaret had apparently come under the influence of a woman who claimed to be a medium. Dan said that before they knew Sarah they would have had forty fits, but now they appreciated that the woman, Irma Rigby, might be above reproach. They wouldn't care if they could be sure the woman was genuine but the change in Aunt Margaret's behaviour concerned them. Perhaps Irma was a con-artist, taking advantage of her.

It occurred to Polly that before involving the others, perhaps it would be better to find out in more detail what this woman was doing to upset the family. While Sarah was out with Amy she would telephone anyone likely to throw light on the subject. After Sarah's night out, Polly would be able to present her with a fuller picture of what was happening. What with one thing and another, even Polly was beginning to feel a bit depressed ... but at least she had reached a decision and could put it firmly out of mind until Friday night ... until Sarah was safely on her way to the theatre.

As the night of April the seventeenth approached, Sarah began to regard the theatre outing more positively. She reflected on how long it had been since she last visited Amy; apart from the funeral of Jay's mother, Dorothea, it must be at least three years. They hadn't much in common really – in fact she could perceive why Dorothea had disliked the girl – but always ready to see the good in people rather than the bad, Sarah accepted Amy as she would a young sister, with all her faults.

Amy was one of her oldest friends. They shared the same childhood memories in spite of their nine-year age difference because their parents had been a close foursome. Sarah, newly arrived from Canada when Amy was only just learning to walk and talk, had adored her ... she was a real living doll to play with!

When Amy herself rang up two days before the event Sarah was pleased. John had sensibly told her of his plan in time for her to organise her wardrobe and hair. She sounded ecstatic. "I can hardly wait to see you again darling," she gushed ... "but we can't possibly catch up on all our news unless you stay at least overnight! Why don't you come for the weekend?" Sarah hesitated and guessing why, Amy hastened to add that the idea had actually come from John. "He's in the middle of one of his boring experiments! I hardly see him these days – please say yes!"

Knowing that Clarinda was fully occupied and probably leaving on Saturday for a week in Wales, made it easier for Sarah to accept – it suddenly seemed like a good idea. There had been little light relief during the last few months ... a change of scene might do her good and she felt inclined to enjoy it.

On Friday afternoon Polly drove Sarah to the village salon to have her hair done. When they returned and Clarrie joined them for tea, Sarah talked happily about her early association with the couple. She had never met Jay's father. Just before Amy and John married he had a stroke of some kind from which he had still not recovered, but his mother, Dorothea, was at the wedding.

"I remember Mrs Johnson," said Polly, "she had a small apartment somewhere near Goring, surely?"

"That's right," Sarah confirmed. "She wanted to be nearer to the psychiatric hospital where her husband is. She died about a year ago, but never lost hope that he would recover. I probably missed her more than they did; we became close friends."

Polly and Clarrie were pleased that Sarah was having a break in routine. The Johnson place was near a quiet village south of Oxford – a picturesque, sleepy village, where it seemed that nothing ever happened. They could not have wished for a better place for Sarah to relax.

Clarrie had visited Dorothea there before she moved out and described it to Polly as one of the most fascinating houses she had ever known. She said that an air of old-fashioned quality permeated every niche, yet it wasn't heavy with antiques. Even on entering the grounds there was a pervading sense of timelessness. It always brought a poem to her mind: 'The Lotus Eaters'. She could imagine how easy it would be to languish there, letting the rest of the world go by!

In view of the change of plan and Clarrie's announcement that she was definitely leaving early on Saturday morning, Polly informed them that she would like to go away too, to Dan's in Oxford – just until Sunday night.

"Oh, of course," Clarrie recalled, "Elaine's baby is due soon ... you must be excited! I hope she is well. You're not going because there's anything wrong are you?"

Polly assured her that Elaine was fine. She was going on a whim: for a change of air! What she failed to say was that, depending on what she learned by telephone, she might even pay Elaine's Aunt Margaret a visit. Perhaps, with luck, she could deal with the problem herself, without being a nuisance to her friends.

Chapter Four

Friday April 17th...

Jay Johnson glanced at his watch: the car would be here soon with Sarah. He removed his glasses and studied himself critically in the full length bedroom mirror. He was not a vain man but as he finally adjusted his tie he couldn't help feeling smug that over twenty years of laboratory desk-work had not thickened his waist or rounded his shoulders. He looked much the same as when he had married: unlike Amy! He could hardly remember what an attractive woman she had been. He had idolised her and given in when she refused to consider having a family – she was, after all, almost thirty and he in his early twenties was not particularly eager to be burdened with children. It was only as time went by and he saw friends enjoying their sons that he felt cheated. He begged her to change her mind but her appearance was then too important to her, to risk spoiling her figure just for what she claimed was his selfishness!

    What was about to happen was entirely her own fault. She should have given him a child when he wanted one ... when he wanted her. After years of indulging her passion for titbits, she had become, literally, a white elephant, for whom he had no affection and no use. If only he'd realised how self-centred she was – but he'd been inordinately susceptible to her surface charm. She was, after all, the first girl he had really known. Always a serious student, it had been easy for his father to commandeer all his spare time to assist with experimental work in his home laboratory. Even during his late teens his interests didn't widen much beyond science. Whenever the subject of girls came up, his father urged him to distrust pretty faces and look for more lasting virtues in a wife ... "When the time is right, Jay," he'd add, as if hoping it never would be! If only he'd taken the advice to heart, the ensuing tragedy might have been averted; he and his father would not have been cruelly torn apart.

    Throughout her teens and early twenties Amy enjoyed life and was not interested in settling down until she met John. The handsome young scientist impressed her. He was brilliant – his future place in the scientific world already assured, even if only because his father headed government research projects ... secret stuff of course! She knew that much and the thought thrilled her. She was proud to be seen with him and eager to share what she was convinced would be his distinguished future. The only thing she disliked about him was his wearing glasses so, to please her, unless he was reading, John seldom wore them when they were out together. He had consequently not been wearing them on the evening the accident happened, just before they were married. Had his father recovered there might not have been a wedding because until then John hadn't realised the intensity of his father's feelings.

Knowing his parents would disapprove of Amy, who was everything his father hated and had him warned against, how could he even take her home, let alone introduce her as his future wife? Had she been a teenager he might have taken the risk, but Amy was a sophisticated older woman! Both his parents would have thought her unsuitable for their quiet, serious-minded son. Amy had always seemed so understanding about delaying the confrontation with his family that he was startled to see her standing in the drive that night as he opened the door. He would never forget what ensued: the most terrible experience of his life! He had promised to collect Amy from her nearby home as usual, but was held up: she grew impatient and walked round to meet him but at least had the good sense to wait by the car – if only it had not been locked she would have been sitting inside, out of sight.

They were going dancing; in her flowing, silver evening gown she shimmered from head to toe in the warm porch light. He stopped and caught his breath... she was so beautiful, so utterly desirable! Then he became aware of his father behind him. His one thought was to get away – to escape with Amy – time enough for explanations and recriminations later. Thrusting his glasses into his pocket he rushed out and ushered her quickly into the passenger seat and sat beside her. Just before he turned his head to back out of the driveway, he saw his father running towards them and as he frantically pushed the gear lever gear into reverse, to race away, the old man's howl rang in his ears: "NO! ...Oh my God! NO...!"

He did not stop. Nothing would have made him give up Amy. His father's violent reaction was sick and, even after all these years, beyond his comprehension: screaming as he had! At the time he'd thought he was crazy! Demented! So agitated was he that he took a curve too fast and crashed. Three weeks later when he regained consciousness in hospital he discovered how right he had been.

That terrible strangled cry had been John senior's last sensible utterance. It was as if he had gone wholly out of his mind... His mother had rushed out just in time to see her husband fling himself to the ground, with glazed unseeing eyes. She watched in dismay and disbelief, unable to help, while he bashed his forehead repeatedly on the sharp gravel until blood poured down his anguished face.

The doctor, a family friend of long standing, came immediately Dorothea telephoned and administered a sedative, but a week later, although no longer violent, he was obviously in need of special treatment and removed to hospital. Eventually he was admitted to a psychiatric ward and for the rest of her life she visited the hospital almost every week, although never able to approach him. Normally docile and silent, the mere sight of either his wife or Jay sent him into uncontrollable fits of hysteria.

Jay loved his father but had long ago resigned himself to the fact that he would never recover. His mother, almost fifty and still a beautiful woman when it happened had never looked at another man. Until the moment she died she prayed that her husband would mentally return to her one day. Her prayers were not answered. He was still in that joyless place, looking far older than his eighty seven years.

Just after his mother's funeral, Jay went to see him ... his first visit for ten years. He hardly knew what to expect. As he stood outside the door his pulse rate accelerated with apprehension. Moving the lever on the double glazed window to adjust the slats of enclosed blind, he peered into the sparsely furnished room. The withered old man was scarcely recognizable to him. He sat like a statue – only his eyes moved from side to side as though seeking escape. The doctors all agreed; it was exceedingly unlikely that his father would recover and he must accept the fact. So – there was nothing to hold him here now. For many frustrating years his plans had been put aside in consideration of his mother ... her death had released him. It was time to act.

***

Sarah had looked radiant when she swept out to the taxi – obviously set on having a good time. She had resisted all attempts to push her into buying a new outfit but her pale peach skin and silver hair were set off to perfection by her favourite blue velvet dress – it was classically cut with a draped skirt. Over it, she wore a beautiful palomino mink stole that had been her husband's wedding gift to her in 1957. In the current frenetic 'animal rights' atmosphere he probably wouldn't have bought it but, as he had, Sarah would never part with it.

After the limousine whisked Sarah away, Clarrie retired for an early night because she'd planned a six-o-clock start the following morning and had already loaded her car. Polly insisted on fixing a picnic basket for Clarrie as she would not be awake early enough to see her off. She was glad she had not burdened either of them with Elaine's problem... Polly was also anxious not to waste any time in the morning so, as soon as she was satisfied that the kitchen was tidy and spotless, she packed her own suitcase with a sensation of mounting excitement.

She could hardly wait to make contact with Elaine's family.

***

Jay Johnson had idealised his mother, Dorothea, and was filled with admiration for the courage she displayed when his father was taken from her by his sudden illness. Had she still been alive he would not have added to her sorrow – she had been a wonderful mother and always put his interests before her own. She even insisted that he and Amy live with her in Oak Lodge, at least temporarily, because of the well equipped cellar laboratory. She said Jay could carry on using and maintaining it, until his father came back. Unfortunately, his father would never return now – he would never know that Jay had followed in his footsteps and become a physicist. Like his father, Jay also rose to the higher echelon of the scientific world, the private work space had been essential to him too, although, he had to concede that Dorothea used to see much more of his father than Amy did of him! If only he had married someone more like his mother..!

A few miles away Sarah leaned back in the soft luxury of the car which had been sent to collect her. She too was thinking of John's mother, Dorothea. When hope finally faded that her husband would ever return to normal, Dorothea had handed over the house completely to the young couple and bought a small apartment. She had been sad to leave the Lodge which stood alone on sloping woodland near Nuneham Courteney; the upper windows commanded sweeping, impressive views over the Thames ... but she and Amy grated on each other's nerves. Both tried to maintain good relations for Jay's sake but Dorothea was driven to retreat too often to the privacy of her own rooms.

Learning of her mother-in-law's intention to move out, Amy had been ecstatic. She immediately rang Sarah who lived only about twelve miles from the hospital and knew the area well, to enlist her help in recommending agents or suitable districts. Of course, Sarah did more than that – she joined them both on inspection trips. It had been fun and Sarah was pleased when eventually Dorothea chose to live in Goring, within a half hour drive of her own home. Their tastes were similar in many ways and Dorothea looked forward to meeting Sarah more often. She lamented often, that If only Amy had not been so childish and shallow, everything could have been very different; Amy might have become as firm a friend to her as Sarah. Dorothea never complained to Jay, but confided in Sarah how angry she was when, within months of being mistress of the Lodge, Amy modernised it from top to bottom! She said she was sure Jay disapproved too – why had he allowed her to do it?

Sarah's thoughts and Jay's were still running on parallel lines...

Jay was lost in contemplation. He regretted not having taken more control of his home life. At first he merely wanted Amy to be happy and had been far too absorbed in his work to notice that his old home was gradually changing, almost beyond recognition. No wonder his mother stopped visiting them, she must have hated what it became.

He always kept his cellar securely locked, as his father had; that was one place where Amy would never be allowed to interfere! How he'd longed for his father's recovery! He yearned to communicate with him, especially about the old yellowed files. The pages were dry and brittle with age and it had taken him months to decipher their content. Rewriting them had at first amused him: more like science fiction he thought, than serious work! The notion that his sober-minded father might have been planning to write a novel intrigued him and he persevered. Then one day he perceived a glimmer of intrinsic sense... however shattering, the seemingly impossible was suddenly within reach!

The papers came to light one day when he was searching the attic for some replacement equipment which was stored there. They were in a cardboard box he could not remember seeing before, so he took it to the cellar to sort through it, prior to throwing it away. Neither he nor his father approved of storing papers unless they were enclosed in metal – he supposed his mother had left them there. Once he began to examine the files the more he was intrigued... and the more he studied them the more they dominated his thoughts.

All his previous experimental work was put aside. Incredible possibilities were revealed to him: things only dreamed of since that obscure clerk in a Swiss patent office had the temerity to challenge Newton's laws. Through crude electrical experiment in a Zurich Polytechnic, first putting together, and then adding to, the ideas of Gauss and Riemann, the man developed his strange theory of Relativity. He added a fourth dimension, time, to the Universal model, where Matter and Energy are accepted as being equivalent, or at least forms of the same thing. In every subsequent decade, more weight was added to the 'rightness' of Einstein's theory, until his predictions of light bending were eventually proved in outer space. Jay fervently believed that his own father was another such genius. If he had not been so tragically stricken, he would undoubtedly have consolidated his findings. His discoveries would have become known to his colleagues, the Government Ministry and then – the world. Millions would welcome the chance to re-live even one day, to undo actions which resulted in misery; some might opt to start again and do better at school. Dissatisfaction with his marriage even led him to fantasise about how different his own life might have been, if he hadn't married Amy.

As the weeks passed, the allure of a second chance grew, especially when he confirmed that travelling back would not change the atomic structure of the object sent. A hot apple pie, transported to yesterday, would not be raw apples and a bag of flour! ... A dying dog would not become young; it would still die of old age in its allotted span! He had added nothing to the axiom personally. His own experimentation had been aimed solely at convincing himself that the theory was capable of being proved. Under controlled conditions with an unlimited official budget he would have tested it within short spans of time, but he couldn't obtain backing without first disclosing his objectives. His personal resources were limited and had it not been for the other items he found in the same box he wouldn't have hesitated to make his discovery known. Rolled with the diagrams and formulae were some faded private papers. The most significant items were certificates of birth. One was his own: 1946 ... 'mother Dorothea, born 1917'. Another, less easy to read, was that of his father, John Jerome Johnson, 1905. He was still puzzled by a

1945 death certificate, for another Johnson, a woman, which almost fell apart in his hands. His grandmother, May, might have died around then.

There were also two disintegrating newspaper cuttings. One announced the glorious death of James Jerome, his grandfather, in 1917 aged thirty-four, on the battlefield. The other tore as he tried to open it out, making it even more difficult to see. It was a group photograph which, except for the clothes, reminded him of his own wedding ... but then, one wedding was much like any other! The groom was certainly his father but the bride's face was round, what he could see of it – definitely not Dorothea's. The date on the tattered border of the thin paper was illegible – it had to be before 1945 when his parents married; his father appeared to be in his early twenties. He must have been married twice, so his bride could be the Johnson on the death certificate. His first wife must have died, or he wouldn't have been free to marry Dorothea!

No matter how long he cogitated over the mystery he would never know. His father was always reluctant to discuss his past and Dorothea had never revealed that she was his second wife. He could imagine no reason for keeping it a dark secret but could hardly ask her. Anyway, his parents had always been devoted to each other – if she was determined to put part of their past out of her mind, he understood and would respect that. There was much in his own life he would gladly have wiped out and when the possibility of doing so was revealed, four years ago, he began to plan on doing just that! His present circumstances could endure, immutable, for years. Even if he could afford to divorce Amy she'd never be off his back ... she was like a leech. He would not come out unscathed. When his father eventually died he would be financially better off, but that wasn't likely to happen in the foreseeable future. In any case Jay didn't wish him dead – he'd prayed every day since his collapse, for a miracle to bring about his complete recovery so that he would be able to enjoy his own money but the likelihood of that was too remote for him to wait around!

Since embarking on the fantastic, daunting project, there had been repeated setbacks and frustration when spots of mildew hid vital numbers but, like a gleaming trophy, something spurred him on. At last he knew he could do it. If only it were possible to climb into a fictional time machine ... he could not only leave, but could return! Unfortunately he would have only one chance to get things right, so had decided to go back to December 1945. It was the perfect era; the war would be over but there would still be sufficient chaos reigning for him to establish himself, slipping unnoticed into a new life. Having his father's birth certificate would simplify things although he did wonder briefly what he would do if he came face to face with a forty-year-old John Senior or even himself as a tiny child! However, he need not run the risk. Once back in time, he could set himself up miles away, or even go abroad! He couldn't take money of course or more than a small amount of gold, but with a few year-books he should soon be able to accumulate a fortune by judicious betting at race tracks! It would be easy too, for him to gain qualifications quickly and establish himself as a scientist. Feeding his knowledge of the late twentieth century into the pipeline, as occasion warranted, he would be hailed as a genius! As soon as possible he would find a suitable house and build into it a laboratory – exactly like the one he was leaving behind. After marrying a woman of taste, whom he could love, they would make a home as beautiful as the one destroyed by Amy's lack of appreciation ... and he'd have a family – perhaps a son!

He was almost forty-six. His reflection assured him he could pass as much younger – in 1945 he would be just about acceptable as looking old for his forty years but he could not afford to postpone his plans any longer – he was ready to risk all. Even to himself, the wild gleam in his eyes held a hint of madness and he sobered abruptly.

The petulant whine of his wife's voice reached him from downstairs. "Jay! What on earth are you doing? Sarah will be here soon! I want to go over the timer settings for the video recorder with you."

With a sigh, he replaced his glasses. His fingers brushed the raised scar above his temple: his only legacy from that long ago car crash. Now that his hairline was receding it was beginning to show. Fortunately, Amy was thrown clear. Had she suffered any disfigurement it would have been one more reason for her to reproach him, even though it was to please her that night that his spectacles were in his pocket instead of on his nose.

As soon as he entered the room downstairs, Amy thrust the television magazine under his nose. It was open at the evening programme schedule. She stabbed it with a heavily ringed, well-manicured finger ... "There," she pointed, "I've marked what I want you to record ... Oh, I know you're busy, but surely it isn't too much to ask. You can set the alarm on that watch you're so proud of! You'll only have to come up twice to change satellite stations. Be quick on the second change because it's part two of a serial, you mustn't miss it."

She paused for breath – even rising from her armchair was beginning to put a strain on her. As an afterthought she said, "I didn't have time to prepare a meal for you to put in the microwave, but I don't suppose you'll be very hungry – if you are, there are sausages and a tin of beans. I'm sure you can manage!"

Before he could reply – it mattered little anyway whether he did or not – they heard the car outside; Sarah had arrived.

They went to greet her and he was amazed when he saw how kindly the years had treated her ... if only Amy had retained some pride and not let herself go – perhaps he would not have been so eager to leave. When Sarah's eyes met his he felt a strange shudder down his spine – someone walking over his grave! For a moment she seemed to look directly into his soul!

It reminded him of the first time they had met. She'd taken his hand when they were introduced and instantly withdrawn it! He'd known she was not much taken by him but it didn't matter now. The excited small-talk was soon over and, after a few more reminders from Amy about the things he must not forget, they were all outside again...

The two women were happily on their way. He was free!

Chapter Five

When Polly finally settled down with the telephone and her address book, she began to feel quite excited – just as if she were a real sleuth. She selected a few names and numbers and before dialling, wrote each separately on clean sheets of paper... this way she would know who said what! If there was one thing she had learned from Sarah it was to write everything down, in order to keep track of each tiny scrap of information however seemingly insignificant. Even the most trivial fact might later prove vital.

By the time Polly finished her final call she had a promising stack of data but when the notes were collated there seemed to be little to show for all the time she had spent talking. She discarded all but three of the contacts on her original list – most family members knew little, if anything, about Irma Rigby and, even if they voiced concern, were disinclined to interfere.

After ruling them out entirely, she was left with only three: Elaine's Great Aunt Emma, Aunt Ethel who was her mother's twin and Uncle Jack; of these three, only Ethel – who first raised the alarm – had any first-hand information about Margaret Dunn. She and her cousin had been out of touch for years except for annual letters at Christmas but this time, unusually, Margaret had scribbled only the briefest of messages on the back of her card. Her friend Jean had died and she seemed so depressed that Ethel started ringing her once a week, to cheer her. Ethel was gratified when Margaret responded by initiating calls herself.

Even though they began to establish a closer relationship, Margaret remained subdued until the third week of January when, within the space of two weeks, she met and actually engaged Irma as companion / housekeeper. Ethel said Margaret believed Irma to be clairvoyant and was firmly convinced about her sincerity. The woman had put her in touch, not actually with Jean yet, but with her parents, grandparents and even an old friend. Ethel voiced, to Polly, her disgust that any sensible person could credit such unadulterated rubbish!

Polly couldn't help smiling ... if only she were at liberty to talk about Sarah and Clarinda – both gifted Psychics, beyond a shadow of doubt – she could have opened Ethel's eyes! If Margaret had been fortunate enough to meet someone like Sarah, there was more reason to be pleased than sorry, but this would have to be checked out. Polly felt reasonably qualified to judge if Irma was a fraud but if, on the other hand, she seemed genuine, Polly would have to seek Sarah's advice. Sarah had her own ways of getting at the ultimate truth!

Margaret's mother Sophie was the eldest of three sisters. The second was Helen – mother of Jack and the twins. Both Sophie and Helen had died. The youngest sister, Emma, was in her late eighties. She was still extremely sharp-witted and insisted on living alone – she told Polly that she was slowing down a lot, but not dead yet ... when she moved out of her house it would be feet first! The twins visited Emma regularly but, as she hadn't spoken to Margaret for several years she knew only what Ethel relayed about her niece.

She was eager for Polly to call on her, however – she said she would enjoy meeting her. Being the only one left who could remember the old days she might be able to help, at least with background information.

As Jack was retired (an ex-army Major) with no ties and time to spare, he proffered his help if she needed any. He had hardly seen anything of cousin Margaret since they were children – he relied on his sisters for news – but she was family and he didn't like to think of her being made a fool of he stated, "Even if she is one, giving credence to such twaddle!"

Another staunch disbeliever, Polly reflected!

She had met Jack briefly at Elaine and Dan's wedding. He was tall – an inch or so under six feet – and broad-shouldered. Only a hint of a paunch and thinning steel-grey hair betrayed his age... he had impressed her as an entertaining talker with a wry sense of humour.

Upon reflection, Polly decided that Jack's approach might be less emotional than Ethel's so, as he was keen to assist, she'd call on him initially, to form a plan of campaign. To avoid wasting time, she decided to drive to Headington first thing in the morning and ring him from there. He lived only a few miles away, at North Leigh, so if he agreed, they could meet in Oxford for coffee.

By the time Polly went to bed, tired but satisfied, it was well after midnight. She slept soundly ... not even stirring when Clarrie left the house before sun up.

***

John leaned back momentarily against the front door as he shut it. At last, the moment he had long awaited was here. He could scarcely believe that his plan was working so perfectly. He heard the car drive away and mentally followed its progress ... it turned out of the drive then sounded momentarily louder as the lane curved back closer to the house. He did not move until the sound eventually died away in the distance and he was sure they were not coming back.

Although chafing to begin his phenomenal adventure he carried out the final arrangements slowly, with careful reference to a list compiled earlier when not agitated by the pressure of the moment. He dared not risk forgetting the smallest detail.

Mai Griffin

He went first to the bedroom where he took off all his clothes. He dressed again in three layers of everything including shirts. He hesitated about the hand-knitted pullover; it held bad memories – having worn it when he visited his mother the day she collapsed. She was smiling as she opened the door but before he had fully removed his topcoat – in so few seconds – she had gasped and fainted.

Although he hadn't for one moment been stupid enough to blame his pullover for her stroke, it went through his mind, as it had then, that she had always been superstitious about wearing green, ever since his father once set fire to himself during an experiment. The sleeves of his jumper had melted into the flesh of his arms and he still bore the scars.

Still, that was her hang-up, not his. He might be glad of its light warmth. He topped it with two thick sweaters and some dateless dungarees and struggled finally into a heavy raincoat. He filled the large pockets with his favourite trinkets and a roll of velvet containing his mother's antique jewellery.

Intending to carry the year books clutched against his chest he put them into a waterproof bag. He hesitated ... then, contrary to his earlier resolve, could not resist adding a tiny solar battery calculator: it would be easy to conceal later.

He extracted his own birth certificate from the personal papers and put it with his insurance documents ... Amy would be sure to find it there! The rest, tightly rolled, he pushed up the arm of his sleeve. It would have been easier to pack a suitcase, but attempting a double transference was too risky – anyway, Amy would miss a case. He wanted to avoid arousing the slightest suspicion that he had deserted her and was not dead.

Amy had made a scathing reference to his watch and he was indeed reluctant to leave it behind, but it would be out of place and give rise to comment in the mid-forties. He removed it with a sigh and placed it on his dressing table.

All that remained to be done was to take the dog to the garden shed. Bobby hated being confined, but he would be safe out there if the resulting damage to the main building exceeded his highest calculations.

Re-entering the house, ignoring the anguished howls which followed him, he wondered how Amy would interpret the scene – she knew he was not besotted with her pet but he had never actually incarcerated it before! He locked up again, before switching off the lights and appliances, including the video recorder! Tough luck about part two of the Best Seller but the main fuse box was in the cellar, on the dividing wall outside the laboratory. There was no way it could escape being damaged by the intense heat so the power would go off anyway!

He knew now why his father had reinforced the cellar. Partly financed by his Government employers, ostensibly with security a high priority, it provided two-way protection: from interference without and experimentation within! They couldn't have imagined how necessary its strength would be; in the aftermath of his going the generated heat was sure to destroy everything inside the laboratory: in a flash! However, he was reasonably sure the rest of the house would be safe. If it wasn't – at least Amy and her dog were safely out of it: no lives were threatened.

When he bolted himself in and closed the air vents to limit the fire damage, some of his elation evaporated and his last thoughts were sad. If only his father could understand that his theories were about to be proved; if only his colleagues could have known what he was really working on! He had often been tempted to reveal and discuss the details of his father's research, he was inordinately proud of him.

Perhaps one day, in his own golden future, he would be able to prove to the whole world what a great man of science his father had been... His one regret was that they would never meet again.

***

Amy and Sarah thoroughly enjoyed their entire evening. The meal alone was good enough to make the drive worth while, but they had excellent seats at the theatre – neither could recall a more spectacular show. They were in high spirits on the journey back, unaware of the tragedy which would delay Sarah's return home.

As the car swung into the driveway from the avenue they were immediately apprehensive. Sarah had already noted that the house, glimpsed through the trees as they approached, was in darkness – visible only because it was silhouetted starkly against the paler sky. The car came to a halt and even before the engine was switched off, they heard Bobby's dismal howls from the rear of the property. They were all alarmed. "Somebody must have broken in and they could still be hiding nearby," whispered Amy, immediately locking herself in the car, refusing to move.

The driver, Eric, went nervously with Sarah to investigate. Amy wanted him to go by himself, declaring that Sarah should not leave her alone. She gave in only when he pointed out that he was unfamiliar with the garden and also unknown to the dog! Although willing to assist, he would not risk being bitten. It certainly made sense to get Bobby first, before going into the house. If the place had been robbed the villains were unlikely still to be inside but even so, Eric said, he'd be happier going in with a dog. When he saw the small animal however, now a quivering wreck, he changed his mind and Sarah handed Bobby, whimpering, to the shaking arms of his mistress.

Eric inspected the windows and doors but could find no sign of a forced entry. He pressed the bell – partly hoping for an answer but really as a warning of their arrival to anyone lurking unlawfully. Better a thief should get away than stay and attack them!

They knocked when they heard no ring.

Amy suddenly remembered that her husband had reminded her to take her key, in case he was busy and didn't hear them arrive. So, fairly sure at last that she was not in mortal danger, she climbed out of the car, waddled to the porch and handed it to Eric, sheltering behind him as he unlocked the door. He entered first, followed by Sarah. Amy trailed behind them clicking switches to no avail; the electricity was off.

Calling fearfully, "Jay... Jay!" Amy took a torch from the hall cupboard and handed it to Eric who led the way according to her directions. Ten minutes later it was apparent that all was in order and John, if he actually was at home, must be in the cellar. Pounding on the locked door at the top of the basement steps elicited no response from below but Amy said hopefully that at the bottom there was another exceptionally heavy door into the laboratory ... it was possible Jay could not hear them. She said he always became so absorbed in his work ... anyone could have broken in without disturbing him!

Sarah pointed out gently that something untoward must have occurred. John may have fused the lights while working but that didn't explain why Bobby was locked out of the house. They had found John's wrist watch in the bedroom; Amy's jewellery box was untouched. Neither scenario was likely, either that there had been a robbery or that her husband had left the house.

When Eric announced that whatever was wrong, it must have happened about five hours ago, because that was when the electric clocks had stopped, Amy became hysterical. She said whatever he was doing should not affect the rest of the house ... he used a direct power supply.

Eric, unable to cope alone, especially in the face of Amy's mounting panic, went back to his car and telephoned the police.

It was the beginning of a long sleepless night for them all.

***

About four miles north-west of Burford, towards the source of the Thames, Irma Rigby was sleeping soundly. Accepted now, her future assured, she could afford to relax, safely ensconced under the roof of Margaret Heywood-Dunn. She was enjoying her new-found status in surroundings which were luxurious compared with anything she'd previously known. She had not had an easy life. There had been no father-figure for her to lean on until she entered her teens in 1945 when, after the war, her mother married a newly de-mobilised soldier. He was short, pale faced and timid. Other than his ownership of a small cottage, his main asset was a ludicrously small disability pension, but he helped to provide for them by doing light work while her mother took in sewing. Irma secretly scorned her stepfather... what could her mother see in him? He was not even remotely like her real father.

When she left school Irma trained as a nurse and eagerly left home when she reached twenty-one to work in a large hospital. Within three years she married. What a fool she had been to be taken in by Bill

Rigby's dark good looks. He turned out to be a complete wastrel who, although out of work, landed them in debt with his gambling and drinking. Ten years later when her recently widowed mother became bed-ridden at the comparatively early age of sixty, Irma resigned her job to care for her and, with no regrets, left Bill to his own devices.

She took on a few private patients to earn a living until her mother died, twelve years ago. In the last few weeks of her mother's life, knowing the end was near, Irma hardly left the house. She had plenty of time to think and formulate a plan for the future; she was determined to move on, and act on it. The funeral expenses had wiped out her small bank balance. Selling the cottage would have solved her problems but because it was badly in need of repair it was practically worthless in the depressed housing market. The proceeds from the sale of most of the furniture helped her cash flow but in spite of this and an unexpected endowment that had accrued on her mother's estate, she was in debt again when everything was settled.

Having closed up the cottage, securely padlocking the window shutters to deter squatters, she had since worked only where she could live-in; at least, by doing so, she had no rent to worry about! She also had time to pursue her dream. She had for years been deprived of a social life but rather than being embittered, she was full of exciting plans for the future. Still reasonably attractive in early middle age, she had every intention of enjoying herself when she eventually achieved financial security. Living with Margaret was only the first, small, step.

***

Forty miles away, many residents of Nuneham Courtenay, the nearest village to the Johnson residence, were unable to sleep as soundly. Once the serious nature of the situation at Oak Lodge became apparent a constant stream of official vehicles passed along the usually quiet stretch of road. Two constables came first, gained entry to the basement and assumed from the state of the main fuse box that there had been a fire. Being unable to gain access to the laboratory, they announced their intention of sending for the local fire brigade.

At that moment, Amy suddenly gained a measure of control and found the Research Centre's emergency number. She informed them that the Centre should be notified as soon as possible because her husband worked on highly classified material. Only his colleagues would know whether there was danger in entering – and John always stressed that in any emergency connected with his work they must be contacted first.

The constables were replaced within half an hour by two senior representatives of the law in plain clothes and a female officer who stayed with Amy and Sarah while they all waited for the experts to arrive. Her job was probably to keep an eye on them thought Sarah, but she was a pleasant girl who tried to comfort Amy while not holding out false hope that her husband would prove to be alive and well.

Thankfully, some power had been restored to the kitchen by one of the first men on the scene so, sitting a little apart, Sarah was able to think quietly as she sipped one of the few dozen cups of tea she had made for everyone during the last few hours. Most of the main fuse box was a mess of melted wire. It would need expert attention ... the electricity company must be contacted first thing in the morning.

Eric was allowed to go after making a statement and Sarah cancelled her Monday booking with him. In view of the circumstances she could hardly leave Amy alone. There was no knowing how long Amy would need her but there was nothing in her own calendar she couldn't cancel. First thing tomorrow she'd telephone home to explain. Either Polly or Clarinda would be able to fetch her when Amy had recovered from the initial shock.

An old oil lamp brought up from the cellar glowed warmly. In the low illumination Sarah became even more aware than usual of the spirit world impinging on the material one. Amy was surrounded by loved ones long passed over, perhaps even forgotten, but showing their concern. Beyond her, in deeper shadow, was a man Sarah immediately associated with John; there was a strong resemblance but he'd been younger than John when he died. He wore army uniform – a soldier of the First World War: leggings, not the style of today.

She watched him pace restlessly, in apparent agitation – gazing about, as if searching for something, or somebody: perhaps Jay! At first she was relieved... he could be alive still! Then she chided herself for jumping to conclusions. In the absence of clear communication it was tempting to make assumptions, but she was experienced enough to avoid doing so. Clearly astonished – he became aware of her scrutiny and sensed the question in her mind. His image was fading but she heard his voice... "My boy – my poor stricken son – is lost. I've waited so long! Please, please help him!" Jay's father, in his eighties, was mentally ill, so Sarah guessed that the soldier was John's grandfather, Jerome, who, knowing that nothing on earth could cure his son, was waiting to help him on the other side.

She made a mental promise to visit the old man. Where medicine had failed she could at least try to reach him and bring him a measure of solace. During the remaining night hours, as dawn invaded the darkness beyond the drawn curtains, Sarah focused all her thoughts on Amy's husband. Even though failing to contact his spirit she became convinced he wasn't alive. The transition from life to death was probably sudden; she prayed his soul would relinquish earthly ties and pass willingly to a higher plain. The swishing of the drapes broke her concentration abruptly and brought her back to the uncertainties of the moment. Amy had been dozing fitfully – yesterday's make-up still caked on her tear-stained face. Bobby, who had slept on her lap, raised his head and licked her cheek. She yawned and groaned noisily.

The young policewoman turned from the window and said that help was on the way but it might be hours before they had any idea what had happened on the other side of the locked door. If Mr Johnson were found they would be informed immediately. It would be a good idea if both ladies retired upstairs and tried to get some sleep. Although ostensibly wanting to protect Amy from further stress, the police probably felt hindered by her presence. Amy didn't need much persuasion – she even seemed irritated that it had not been suggested earlier! Bobby, after a short run in the garden, immediately sought out his mistress again and refused to let her out of his sight, so she took him with her to her room.

In spite of the continuous activity below her window Sarah eventually slept. Whatever lay inside the sealed room was, to her, academic. She knew Jay was way beyond earthly help, and transferred her prayers to seeking guidance for the living.

Chapter Six

Saturday April 18th...

After loading the car last night Clarrie had risked leaving it at the end of the drive, to avoid waking Polly with garage door slamming and engine noise. She was glad she had taken the precaution as she started the car and moved out to the road. She had heard Polly going to bed late ... perhaps she'd stayed up to watch a film; with luck she'd be able to enjoy a nice lie in. Driving away from Reading, Clarrie was glad she had not put off the trip until later in the year. Apart from isolated wisps of rising mist, where the road dipped close to the winding river, the Berkshire countryside looked new and clean in the morning light. There was a tang of new growth in the air and even the built-up areas through which she passed, seemed to have lost their winter gloom.

She didn't regret choosing the scenic route! By joining the M40 and by-passing Oxford on the east side of the city, it would take her a good four and a half hours to reach Mallwyd in North Wales, the nearest town to the Matthews' property, but she was not pressed for time. Once through Oxfordshire, the midlands were soon far behind. Driving through open countryside in the sunshine the road ahead looked like a continuous thread rising and falling through a patchwork quilt.

When even the villages became more spaced out she felt a heady sense of freedom and, after switching off the car heater, she rolled down the windows. The in-coming air was cool but laden with the fresh intoxicating fragrance of budding greenery. After Welshpool, the landscape began undulating pleasantly before it became mountainous and more dramatic. Sometimes the road dipped into pockets of woodland glowing with colour where bluebells and wild daffodils ran riot under canopies of bright new leaves. Mountain streams, which occasionally rushed alongside the highway, had also lost the cold, steely gleam of winter. Wales in autumn had been fantastic but spring held a special magic and Clarrie was almost sorry when she reached Mallwyd and neared the end of her journey.

The house was not hard to find although it was isolated. An old sign on the main road, which bore the family name, directed her along a narrow lane that was obviously little used. Its surface was poor and pitted, but the masses of uncontrolled growth on the crumbling bank of a dry ditch were a worse hazard. Even so, it was not a difficult drive. It was more worrying that the area was exactly what Sarah warned her to avoid. Her parting request was to be prudent – not to work where she might be vulnerable. Sarah reiterated her customary warning; the world is full of maniacs! It isn't like the old days, when Clarrie's father isolated himself for weeks on end, with only a tent, butane gas cooker and paints for company! Mindful of these considerations, Clarrie sought a good vantage point where she could also park the car. Any hint of trouble and she could jump into it and lock the doors!

When the house came in sight, she knew she was in luck. There wasn't likely to be a better aspect than the one before her and because the ditch veered away from the road the grass verge was much wider. It would be easy to set up anywhere along the next hundred yards without compromising the composition of her work. Pulling up on the hard shoulder she made her first real appraisal of the old, neglected property. It was the sort of dwelling which usually appealed to her as romantic ... an ideal subject, but her heart sank strangely. She felt thoroughly depressed – yet only moments ago she had been eager to start work on the preliminary sketches.

Trying to ignore the negative feelings sweeping over her, Clarrie continued assessing the area, driving farther down and returning until she was satisfied that she had selected the right view. She didn't mind suffering, to a small extent, for art, but here there would be no need. Edged by pine trees, the ditch skirted a small field where a few cows grazed. Between it and the road the ground, although rough, was fairly level. It was perfect for her requirements. On this shady patch of ground there would be no distracting slashes of sunlight striking her canvas.

The building stood at an attractive angle in the middle distance. Beyond it, to the left, it was framed by woodland on high ground and, on the right, a small river snaked around the edge of what had once been cultivated ground. She knew that Miss Matthews' gardener was being retained until the property changed hands, but obviously he had no interest in doing more than keeping down the worst of the weeds.

When she concentrated exclusively on the house itself she had even deeper qualms of unease, but slowly conceived a possible reason. Apart from the hilly backdrop, it brought to mind an eerie place she'd seen as a child – a priory: Prior's something that was it! A friend's parents took them both to visit an old, timbered, black and white house near Worcester. It was reputed to be haunted; books on black magic had been found in the attic and human bones dug up in the garden!

She remembered it vividly because she'd been frightened and refused to go anywhere near it. At last they left her in the car, gazing at it for what seemed hours while, laughing at her, they went to explore. When her mother learned of the visit she was furious. She was impressed but not really surprised that Clarrie had sensed evil; she had long suspected that her daughter had inherited her own psychic gifts which, properly used to help others, could bring great personal satisfaction.

She began to teach Clarrie how to protect herself from the evil which lurks to take advantage of the unwary. She told her that thoughts were living things; bad would attract bad! By channelling her thoughts charitably, only good influences could affect her. From then on she hadn't hidden her own clairvoyance from Clarrie, but always impressed on her that it was a purely private thing to be revealed only when a more earthly approach failed to convey a vital message.

Having explained her first instinctive aversion to the house, Clarrie was able to shrug it off with a smile. She estimated that she had four hours of daylight to plan the outline of the picture and do some preliminary sketches. She would have a good start tomorrow and take full advantage of the morning light to paint. With luck it could be quite dramatic. There might even be a few strands of mist rising from the river if she came really early.

***

After waking naturally, as she usually did at eight-thirty, Sarah rang Mapledurham and was surprised when the telephone wasn't answered ... Clarinda would have left hours ago but although she knew Polly intended going away too, she hadn't expected her to leave before nine! She didn't bother to leave a message ... there was no point.

Never mind – it was Amy who needed her now. Going up to bed earlier, she seemed resigned already to her husband's death and kept asking what would happen to her, all on her own! She made it sound as though the unfortunate man had been most inconsiderate to leave her in such a manner. Within fifteen minutes of rising Sarah was washed, dressed and in the kitchen making even more tea for the officials who had taken over the ground floor of the house. She was startled when, behind her, a key scraped and unlocked the back door. It opened and a tall pleasant-looking woman came in with a smile of greeting.

"Hello. Good morning, you must be Mrs Grey our house guest..."You shouldn't be in here making your own tea ... you go and sit down; I'll bring it in and then make breakfast. It's good for Mrs Jay to have a friend staying over."

When she could get a word in, Sarah asked with some perplexity, "Did you not see all the cars parked in the driveway?"

"Cars you say! Why no, what cars?" was her bewildered reply, "I always come through the garden gate. I cycle down the back lane – it's only about half a mile. Along the main stretch to the front it's at least three times as far. But what ...!"

Two burly policemen strode in suddenly from the hallway and were equally surprised to find that Sarah was not alone. Realizing that the newcomer was Nettie, the non-resident housekeeper, Sarah told her quickly about the night's events. The police would not allow her to clean up. Nothing must be touched – but they said she would have to make a statement. She probably couldn't shed any light on what had happened, but they wanted to ask a few general questions ... after which she would be free to leave.

Amy did not appear until almost noon. Men with worried frowns – singly and in groups, some formally attired others in protective clothing – came and went all morning without disturbing her. Sarah put those few hours without her to good use. She spent them with Nettie who had been with the family for about twenty-five years.

"When I first came here to work for old Mrs Johnson – not that she was old then of course," Nettie hastened to add, "I had recently lost my own husband and my daughter was about ten. She had a real crush on young Jay ... they called him that, J for junior, so he was Jay to me too. When he married (and what a surprise that was – he'd never been interested in girls, it was all work and study with him!) I called them Mr and Mrs Jay! Two Mrs Johnsons under the same roof would have complicated life. It was difficult anyway, after a while!"

Nettie sank into thought for a while then resumed talking without encouragement but she changed the subject. She told Sarah not to worry about lunch – it was prepared and only needed finishing off. She'd cook dinner too before leaving, as usual, and clean up the kitchen first thing in the morning. Sarah protested that she could manage alone but Nettie wouldn't hear of going home and leaving them in the lurch. Probably natural curiosity, thought Sarah! She was amazed that Amy could bear to have the kitchen and presumably the dining room in chaos overnight rather than clear and wash up herself. Personally she could never ignore the mess!

As if reading her mind Nettie resumed. "It was different in the old days. I only prepared the food. Mrs Johnson cooked. "She always left everything beautifully tidy. It was a sad day for me when she moved out, but after her poor husband was taken bad, things were never the same."

Sarah knew Dorothea's version but could not resist seeking an impartial one; the more she knew the more use she could be. With Amy out of earshot and Nettie unable to carry out her usual chores it was a perfect opportunity to obtain eye witness testimony to events which took place twenty-five years ago.

***

Clarrie didn't know the exact location of the Inn where she had booked a room but did not anticipate any difficulty finding it – so she couldn't resist starting work immediately. She couldn't bear to waste several hours of good light and was soon completely absorbed in her work, oblivious to her immediate surroundings. This was when she was happiest and lost all track of time. Eventually however, the changed length of the shadows warned her that her allotted time was well past and she reluctantly started to pack up. She turned from the scene then hesitated, puzzled. Her mind's eye held the image of a face in one of the high dormer windows – the face of a child, vivid enough for her to recall wide, sad eyes. It must have been there for a long while but failed to register ... she was so engrossed in the complexities of her drawing. Now, she looked again: nothing! The window was black and empty. Curiosity made her drive downhill again, this time going through the wide farm gate to the front of the house. In the encroaching gloom it looked strangely eerie but she overcame her irrational reluctance to approach.

It was apparent that no other traffic had approached the building for months ... the weeds in the drive were thriving. The heavy double door in the gabled porch was closed but there was a bell chain which Clarrie pulled firmly. She heard a hollow clang echo inside but no-one came, so she walked to the rear of the property. It was deserted. The face must have been an illusion ... her imagination was playing up! For the moment she refused to worry. If it had any significance, it would be revealed in God's good time! Without even one backward glance Clarrie drove away. The lane she was on had been dissected by the road that brought her here and according to the directions she had been given, the other half ended at the Inn. She decided to eat as soon as possible after booking in, so that she could get an early night and rise at dawn. Unable to dismiss the vision, her mind drifted back to her childhood glimpse of the timbered haunted house. It couldn't be all that far away. The Matthews' property was strangely similar ... they might even have been constructed by the same builder!

At the junction the traffic was heavy but eventually she managed to cross and within a few minutes entered a tiny hamlet which, tucked away from the mainstream, looked clean and quaint with a quiet charm ... it would be a worth while location to paint she thought; all the houses were of grey and black stone. The Inn was easy to find and she was soon relaxing over a good meal. The regulars at the bar displayed considerable interest in her ... being off the beaten track they didn't have many visitors. When the innkeeper heightened their interest by telling them she was an artist they could hardly wait for her to finish eating to invite her over for a drink. Clarrie accepted but warned that she meant to retire early, with a clear head! She was pleased to take the opportunity of meeting local residents who might know the Matthews' family.

The oldest man in the small group occupied the armchair nearest the fire. When he heard whose house she was painting he warned her immediately to stay well away from it, but would not say why. The others taunted him for being superstitious and told her that two hundred years ago a Mistress Matthews was hanged at the crossroads for being a witch – not the one she had passed over, that was new. At the other side of the village was a much older road – but don't go there alone at night, they warned, each immediately volunteering to show her if she wished!

An hour later she reluctantly decided to leave them to their drinks, darts and dominoes and eased away. The old man caught her arm as she came near him. "There's more to that there Matthew family than one old witch," he said darkly. "Find somewhere else to paint!"

Clarrie requested an early call and said she would forego breakfast but although they didn't usually have guests who needed feeding early, especially on Sundays, the inn-keeper's wife insisted that Clarrie could not start work without a good cooked breakfast. She also promised to prepare a picnic lunch for her to take with her. As she bathed contentedly before going to bed it was easy to dismiss the bar talk which, in fact, scarcely worried her. Any isolated place attracts ghost stories. The fact that an old woman had been living there alone until recently must have given rise to even more!

She had met Miss Matthews only once and now felt very sorry for her. No wonder she seemed nervous and retiring! It then occurred to Clarrie that it was probably the Welsh cottage painting which impressed her sufficiently to commission one of her own ... it too had a reputation for being haunted and had certainly not been unlucky for her: well anyway – not in the end! The old lady said her family house was far too big to maintain and, as she had no heirs to take it over, it was more sensible to move out and enjoy some modern conveniences. Who could blame her; it must also have been terribly lonely.

In the early stages of an oil painting, composition and planning are far more important than colour so tomorrow she could work all day, concentrating on under-painting. For the rest of the week she would work only in the mornings when, hopefully, the light would be perfect. The sun at its height would ruin the atmosphere and growing shade always distorted perception in the late afternoon so, once she started painting in full colour, it would be pointless to work after lunch. She would explore the area for more subjects then relax, eat and have lots of early nights.

Clarrie welcomed the change of environment; it could only do her good. The Inn was comfortable and the people friendly ... on the whole it had been a most satisfactory start to the week.

Chapter Seven

Polly was keen to avoid the heaviest of the traffic by starting out early – to save time she even had a bowl of cereal instead of her normal fried breakfast. The studio door was wide open indicating that Clarrie had already gone, so after a quick check that the house was secure Polly was soon in her little blue Mini, speeding away from Mapledurham. Although 5'6", large-boned and, putting it kindly, inclined to plumpness, her movements were well coordinated and she was not at all clumsy. Now that she had become used to driving again after many years of not even attempting to do so, she handled the car as neatly as she carried her own weight. In fact she didn't look the least out of place in such a small car.

During the drive she decided to abandon her original intention to return home on Sunday evening. Why not extend her visit a second night? Barr's Brook was about four miles beyond Burford – a twenty mile drive from Oxford; she could leave that trip until tomorrow but couldn't guess what time she'd get back to Headington ... it might be late so it would be better to stay the whole weekend. After all, it was to put Elaine's mind at rest that she was undertaking the investigation in the first place! She would ring Sarah later in case she returned first, but it wouldn't matter as long as Polly arrived in time to prepare lunch. Unless Jack advised otherwise she would visit both Ethel and Emma this afternoon, which would be tiring enough for one day.

Because it was Saturday the young couple would be at home but she had no intentions of encroaching on their free time; she would probably be out all day. She reached Headington at nine-o-clock and five minutes later was at their front door. Elaine was only just starting to prepare breakfast so Polly gladly accepted an invitation to join them, after she had rung Jack. He had several errands to do first but said he'd be delighted to meet her in Oxford – at ten-fifteen hours. Polly smiled at his military precision and was only mildly surprised he hadn't suggested synchronizing watches!

While they ate, Elaine outlined Margaret's background ... strictly speaking Margaret was not her aunt – she was a second cousin – but being even older than uncle Jack, the title had always been used by Elaine as a mark of respect. Margaret's Grandmother, Ermintrude, was born of wealthy parents and married Basil Heywood a family friend. He was quite well off too – owned a lot of local land and managed their joint estates after Ermintrude's father died. Elaine was unsure whether he had earned or inherited his money, but it was not important now.

Basil and Ermintrude had no sons so his three daughters promised that if they married they would retain his name and pass it on to their children – particularly if they had boys. Only Emma, the youngest of the three sisters, was still alive, aged eighty-eight. Helen, the middle daughter, married William Hall who fathered first Jack, then the twins, Ethel and Elsie, Elaine's mother. Their Grandfather would have been pleased that Jack, only ten years old when Basil died, eventually joined the army as Heywood-Hall. The oldest daughter Sophie married Howard Drake who was a lot younger. A year later they became parents of a baby girl, Margaret. When she was born, Howard was still only twenty but Sophie was thirty: old, in those days, to have a first child.

"So," Polly reiterated, "your mother, her twin Ethel, and their brother Jack are Margaret's cousins. Emma is Aunt to all four of them and Basil was their grandfather. That's straightforward enough to follow." She hesitated a moment, then risked asking, "If your Great-Grandfather was so wealthy – may I ask what happened to his fortune. It might be the reason for Margaret's becoming the target of a confidence trickster!"

Elaine laughed. "Well, not much of it came our way! Helen, my Gran, wanted to become a teacher but her father wouldn't allow her to leave home. At the end of the war in 1918, she had reached twenty-one, the magic number then, so she went away to study. That alone was enough to upset her father but he was absolutely furious when she married Grandpa William eighteen months later! I think Emma was about fifteen then and Sophie twenty-seven."

Polly scribbled hastily as Elaine explained how Sophie rejected all the suitors her father introduced, saying she would never marry. She might have wanted a career too but Ermintrude was frail and needed help to run the house ... there was a large staff to supervise. Everyone slowly accepted that devotion to duty was why Sophie had abandoned the idea of leaving home but nobody could understand why she eventually married handsome Howard, undoubtedly a fortune hunter. There were many mature single men eager to marry into Basil Heywood's family but Sophie was in a powerful position so got her own way.

"Perhaps she thought a boy would be easier to mould and manage than a man!" Elaine grinned.

"When did Emma leave home," asked Polly, "before or after Sophie's wedding?"

"You'll have to ask her, I'm afraid," Elaine answered. "Like my Gran, Helen, she must have offended their father too because, when he died, the bulk of his estate went to Sophie. As Basil did nothing in his will to protect the family fortune, Howard was sitting pretty when Sophie died. Whatever he didn't squander may have been left to Margaret." After a moment's thought she added, "But Basil did make one concession. When the old house and contents were sold, the proceeds were quartered: half to Sophie – a quarter each to Helen and Emma – enough for each to buy a place of her own."

Basil had at least given some thought to his other daughters! Polly thought. She commented that the family must indeed have been very wealthy, but it often happened that when one generation made money – the next lost it! She had also written out a tree while they'd been talking and, with Elaine's help, she filled in most of the dates.

<u>Heywood Family Tree</u>

Basil (b.1860) m. Ermintrude 1890

    dau. Sophie 1892-1960 m. Howard Drake 1920
        dau. Margaret b.1922 (widowed) m. Martin Dunn (?)

    dau. Helen 1897-1970 m. William Hall 1919
        son Jack (Heywood) b.1924 (unmarried)
        dau. Ethel (Twin) b.1927 (unmarried)
        dau. Elsie (Twin) b.1927 m. James Davies 1965
            dau. Elaine b.1967 m. Daniel Bailey 1991

    dau. Emma b.1904 (unmarried)

Polly clipped it together with the rough notes and added a few more:
It was Ethel who had alerted them to the presence of Irma. They had no idea how well off, or poor, Margaret is now – her father, Howard, had by all accounts been a bit of a playboy but she married well...

Now she prompted Elaine to finish her account.

Margaret's husband, Martin Dunn was a merchant banker and before he retired they lived in an impressively large house in Stratford-upon-Avon. There were no children.

***

By the time Polly met Jack, she felt well armed with knowledge of the family – except funnily enough, about him – but where to proceed from this point was something they would have to decide together. He was already in the small bar when she walked in, for which she was extremely grateful. The modern woman might not feel out of place in a tavern, but she hadn't been looking forward to sitting on her own with a drink. Jack rose immediately and walked to meet her. He showed her to a small table near a lace-draped window and said that coffee was available if she would prefer it to a cold drink. As it was comfortably warm he helped her out of her coat. He appeared to be drinking wine which Polly enjoyed only with a meal so she said she would enjoy a glass of fresh orange. When they were settled he could hardly wait to get down to discussing the problem.

It was clear that he intended to take a full part in the proceedings – he suggested they go immediately to speak with Ethel who was expecting them for lunch. Ethel had never married and enjoyed her role as a sort of family go-between, keeping members informed of highlights in the each other's lives. Although all were domiciled either in Warwickshire or Oxfordshire there were few family gatherings so they relied on Ethel for information. She rarely visited anyone unless invited but her telephone bill must be horrendously O.T.T. Jack said – then seeing Polly's puzzlement added, "Over the top – sorry Gertrude!"

"Oh! For goodness sake! I haven't been called that for over thirty years," Polly protested, "I'll not know you are addressing me unless you call me Polly ... and please refrain from telling me that 'Gertrude' has more class!"

"Well," Jack mused, "I see that it could easily degenerate to 'Gerty' but 'Trudy' would surely be quite acceptable? How did you end up being called Polly?"

"Would you believe me if I said I was named after a parrot?" She enjoyed his look of suspicion for a moment then assured him she wasn't joking ... "When I went as a young housemaid to the Grey family I greeted their pet bird 'Hello Polly' every time I entered the morning room and it soon started answering me back. Before long everyone followed suit – they thought it funny and I didn't mind. It was a mark of acceptance."

"Speaking of the Grey family – I understand you were drawn into this because Elaine and Dan hoped you could rope in Sarah Grey's help ... is she some sort of expert on the occult?"

Without revealing any detail, Polly explained that Sarah was undoubtedly psychic and sometimes helped the police. Seeing his cynical lift of one eyebrow, Polly informed him that personally she did believe in Spiritualism and had every intention of consulting Sarah when she returned after her weekend away. Before bothering her, however, she first wanted to discover more herself, to decide how big a threat Irma actually was.

She changed the subject and going back to names said, "Elaine introduced you at the wedding as 'my Uncle Jack Hall'. She left two things out – the 'Heywood' and the 'Major'. Don't you use either any more?"

"I sometimes use 'Heywood' but I'm not fussy about my army title – some people address me by it, some don't – although it is officially correct. As a holder of the Queen's Regular Commission I'm stuck with it for life, but I retired nearly thirty years ago, before I was forty, and have had another career since, in which my rank was not used. Anyway, with each other we need only be Jack and Polly – both short and in your case sweet!"

Jack took her hand and kissed it lightly: charming and gallant. Had Polly been younger she might have blushed. Even with his thinning hair he was still a handsome man. His well pressed sports suit fitted his slim figure well, despite the hint of a slightly expanding waistline.

Looking at his wristwatch, Jack suggested that they leave her car where it was and go to Ethel's in his – if they left straight away they could be there before noon and complete their business prior to lunch. That would leave time to drive over to Burford for the afternoon. Whether or not they actually visited the small hamlet where Margaret lived could be decided later. Conscious of being under marching orders Polly stood and straightened her dress while Jack retrieved her topcoat.

She shrugged into the matching wool garment – deep jade. It was not brand new but it had cost the earth – or at least, it felt like that to her! She had bought it in a reckless moment when she felt particularly good about life, having just moved in with Sarah and Clarrie ... she was determined they should not be ashamed of her appearance at any time. Her whole wardrobe underwent the closest scrutiny and with Sarah's advice she made several really good buys.

This particular outfit had come from *Old Gold* – a little known dress shop which 'turned around' good quality clothes – many with Designer labels. When Sarah's husband died and she gave up the big house she also gave up her opulent life style. Stephen was a highly successful painter – a landscape artist, much in demand, and they attended many functions, both official and private. Commissions took him away from home sometimes and on one of his visits to a royal patron Sarah was invited to accompany him. They were marvellous, memorable days she said, but now she had no use for more than a couple of dinner gowns. The proprietor of *Old Gold* came to collect Sarah's unwanted clothes; Polly accepted her card but never intended to use it – she had a built in aversion to wearing someone else's cast-offs ... anyway she knew that even the second-hand prices would be high. Until Sarah asked her to drive them both over to the shop because she wished to buy an afternoon dress, Polly had forgotten the place existed – but if Sarah didn't mind buying there, why should she?

As she waited for Jack to return to the porch with the car she felt good from tip to toe ... there was nothing like real leather for handbags and shoes. She had hesitated earlier about changing from the clothes in which she had left home – they were quite respectable and she had expected to return, before going to see Ethel ... Polly now looked forward to spending the whole day with Jack and was glad that she had made the effort to look nice.

What a lot she'd have to tell Sarah and Clarinda ... it would make a change. It was usually they who became involved in adventure, mystery and even danger! This time, Clarrie was set to enjoy a peaceful week's painting in Wales and Sarah was relaxing with an old friend. Yes, she thought ... now, just for once, it was she who had a job to do!

***

Sarah was having anything but a happy time with Amy who was still asleep upstairs, oblivious to the continued police activity in the rest of the house. Her absence at least gave Sarah the opportunity to gather more information from her housekeeper. Having resigned herself to abandoning work, Nettie was quite happy to sit and chat about the family she had been part of for so many years.

Nettie couldn't help an occasional sniff of disapproval as she explained how Amy and Jay met when he went to a seminar where his father was speaking. "Miss Amy usually worked in the typing pool but on that day had been acting as a hostess and guide," Nettie began. Sarah already knew that although Amy had been in her late twenties she looked a lot younger and Jay had been badly smitten from the moment he saw her, but she listened patiently.

"His mother and I realised that his whole attitude changed over the space of only a few weeks," Nettie nodded knowingly. "He became extremely fussy about what he wore and started going out more in the evenings but Mr Johnson was too wrapped up in his work to notice. His mother was really pleased when he admitted he had a girl-friend. She wanted him to bring her home so that they could meet but Jay always put her off. He admitted to me later that he knew they would consider her too old for him. That's not the only thing they would have thought!"

Sarah refused to rise to that last comment and Nettie went on ... "Anyway, the night Mr Johnson was taken ill I was in the kitchen preparing the vegetables for dinner when Jay popped his head round the door, all in a rush, to say he wasn't eating in – he was going to some kind of dinner dance. He looked lovely – really handsome with his frilly shirt front and black bow tie."

Sarah, who had never liked frilly shirts, merely nodded and waited patiently for Nettie to continue.

"We heard his father come downstairs," Nettie said, "... Jay waited until the cellar door opened and shut again before he left me. He didn't want to risk being seen in his glad-rags and get caught up in explanations." She paused for effect but Sarah again made no comment, so she went on. "Anyway, he said a few minutes delay didn't matter – he was already late! Well, he could only have reached the front door when his father came up from the cellar again – he must have forgotten something." Nettie hesitated, looking embarrassed.

Sarah guessed she had been unable to contain her curiosity. Nettie must have been eager to see John's reaction when he saw Jay's attire. "Oh, dear," she murmured, "I simply wouldn't have been able to resist downing tools and peeping round the door to see what happened when they met!"

"Neither could I," admitted Nettie with obvious relief. "Not that I expected a row or anything, but – you know – I thought he worked the boy too hard and needed to see there was more to life than his precious test tubes! Well anyway, the front door was open and Jay was facing me and his father. I was amazed to see this young woman standing in the drive beyond him. The porch light was on – she was all a-glitter. Then everything happened at once. His father sort of shrieked – Jay looked frightened and ran out of the house with Mr Johnson chasing after him yelling something like, 'Oh God, no'. He collapsed, but Jay didn't see him fall. He just drove off with his friend."

Dorothea apparently arrived at that juncture, having heard the shouting, and they both rushed out. "It was scary," Nettie shivered. "We didn't know what to do ... he was thrashing about, screaming. We couldn't hold him. When we did get him inside he just lay staring up at the ceiling and was suddenly so quiet." Nettie shuddered again at the memory and dabbed her eyes with a corner of her apron. She sniffed and continued. "Blood was pouring all over the cushions but he didn't seem aware of the damage he'd done to himself. I tried to clean him up a bit while Mrs Johnson telephoned for the doctor."

The story tallied with Dorothea's in outline, but Nettie's was far more graphic and Sarah could not restrain a gasp of sympathy when she realised what her friend had experienced.

Having paused to refresh herself with a sip of her now cold drink, Nettie added sadly, "They took him to hospital – his poor wife stayed with him for days, but he never came out of it. And as if all that wasn't enough to bear, Jay crashed his car the same night and landed himself in hospital too. It was a week before he was well enough to be told that his father was suffering from some sort of brainstorm."

Sarah, with her finely honed ability to sense fleeting thoughts, knew immediately that Nettie was troubled and had not told her everything. She attempted to draw her out – first making her feel at ease by telling her how much her support had been appreciated during the ordeal. "Mrs Johnson and I were very close ... she told me you were a tower of strength," Sarah murmured. Then she risked a direct question. "Did he say anything at all while you were alone with him?"

"Well, nothing that made sense," was the reply. "He started to mutter – raving on about his son, his father and himself, being damned forever! I didn't tell anybody... it would have been pretty extreme retribution for having a secret date wouldn't it?"

"It certainly would," Sarah agreed, "and only worried his wife needlessly, but you must have been very alarmed yourself," she probed gently.

Nettie frowned and hesitated. "Well, it was after Jay was allowed home, weeks later, when it struck me as more than a bit creepy ... but never mind, forget it. I mean ... it could only be coincidence couldn't it?"

"Unless you tell me, how can I say?" Sarah encouraged with a sympathetic smile."

"I've never told anyone before, although it was on the tip of my tongue many a time to discuss it with his mother – I felt sure she must have seen it too! But perhaps she was too worried about his father to notice. Later, his hair grew to cover it!"

Sarah leaned forward expectantly showing Nettie that she had her complete attention ... "Oh! Really! Covered what?"

"It was the scar at the side of Mr Johnson's head. I saw it when I was washing away the blood and gravel from his hair – it was an old scar, healed long ago, about two inches long, hooked at one end and crossed at the other by a short curve. When I saw Jay's wound – healing well by that time – it was the identical shape, in exactly the same place on his head! It was uncanny." Nettie mopped her forehead disturbed by the memory. "Perhaps because of that, I suddenly saw how alike they were and, over the years, I've seen Mr Jay grow more and more like his father was, when I first knew him. Talk about history repeating itself! Still," she said, brightening, "if the worst has happened now and he really has killed himself, he won't live to go mad will he?"

Sarah could not make any sense of what she'd been told. She felt it must be significant but, unusually for her, an explanation was beyond her grasp. She was again aware of an icy sinking sensation in the pit of her stomach.

The sooner she visited old Mr Johnson the better.

Chapter Eight

The image Polly had formed of Ethel when they spoke on the telephone was entirely wrong. Her strong forceful voice totally belied her appearance. She wasn't at all mannish and heavy set – she was only a few inches over five feet tall and so thin she could be described as bony. She knew that Ethel was her senior by at least a year, but to Polly she looked at least five years younger. Her hair, a coppery shade of blonde, was undoubtedly tinted but she was also surprisingly fresh skinned and had the look of one who enjoys long brisk walks in bracing air.

When Jack and Ethel greeted each other affectionately it was apparent that they hadn't been together since Elaine's wedding. Polly could not remember seeing her there at all, but ceased to feel embarrassed when Ethel immediately said she was sorry they had not met before. She said they could eat whenever they liked because lunch was cold ham and chicken salad ... she knew Polly wouldn't want her to waste valuable talking time in the kitchen! Anyway she confessed she was no great shakes as a cook and did scarcely any entertaining.

She admired Polly's outfit without a trace of reticence. "How lucky you were to find a becoming hat that is such a perfect match. I don't normally wear hats and had the most trying time finding one for the wedding ... they either didn't suit me or were the wrong shade!" She shook her head ruefully. "I wouldn't have bought the dress first if I'd known what a bore it would be to match it. I'll never make that mistake again!"

When Polly eventually asked what had first alerted her to the fact that this stranger might be trying to take advantage of her cousin, Ethel launched with the same enthusiasm into the whole saga. There was one good thing about not being able to get a word in edge-ways, thought Polly, at least she could sit back and absorb the details without polite small talk.

Margaret, perhaps in her loneliness having no other distractions, was earlier than usual sending out Christmas cards; Ethel's, anyway, arrived halfway through December. Instead of the usual chatty letter there was a note on the back of the card saying that Jean had been killed a few weeks earlier. Ethel immediately rang up and heard all about the tragedy. Margaret seemed glad to talk and they began to ring each other regularly, several times a week in fact, until early February. By that time Irma Rigby was living there and often answered the telephone. She was always pleasant but sometimes seemed reluctant to fetch Margaret: always with a convincing excuse ... but!

Grey Masque of Death

In December they considered, but decided against, spending Christmas day together ... although living not a million miles apart neither wanted to face travelling in bad weather. Margaret, who didn't own a car, would have had to hire a taxi and Ethel avoided night-driving whenever possible, so to make the trip worth while she would have had to sleep over – her many pets would have gone hungry. Anyway, Ethel said, they weren't children; Christmas day was really no different from any other when it came down to it!

Feeling she was straying from the point Polly risked interrupting. "How soon after Christmas did Irma appear on the scene?"

"Well, on the morning of January the first, when I rang up to wish Margaret a 'Happy New Year', she said she knew it was going to be more interesting even if it wasn't happy ... then asked if I believed in Spiritualism! I said no, of course, and she said I should come over and meet a friend of Edna, her daily woman. For weeks, apparently, Edna had been going on about this Irma Rigby person, who could contact the dead ..." Catching the exchange of knowing glances between Jack and Polly, she said as an aside, "Yes, I know – did you ever hear anything so ridiculous! Anyway, up to then Margaret had refused to have anything to do with her. If only I could be with her, she said, she wouldn't be as nervous and it might even be amusing."

Polly wondered who was pressing for the meeting – Edna or Irma! It was something she must try to find out. Ethel was still explaining how she had expressed the view of any sane person – that talking to the dead and seeing their ghosts was mediaeval claptrap. Jack winked wickedly at Polly, expecting her to be on the defensive but Polly had no trouble holding her tongue. Over the years she had met many who felt the same way and Sarah always advised that it was better for them to remain happy in their ignorance. Everyone doubted the paranormal until faced with personal proof ... who could blame them?

Ethel with scarcely a pause, continued. "I told her to be careful, especially if the woman asked for money. Then after letting the subject drop for a few weeks, Margaret sprang the news that Irma was moving in as a kind of 'Girl Friday' ... salaried, naturally!"

Ethel was obviously disgusted with herself for not having intervened – she wished she had made the effort to be there at her cousin's first encounter with Irma. There was little more Ethel knew so after lunch they left as soon as was decent and headed for Burford, twenty miles west of Oxford. Jack said there was no point in going to Emma's until they had a clearer notion of the questions they needed answering – anyway, she lived about eight miles north of Banbury and as they were already at Stanton Harcourt not far off the A40 it was more sensible to go first to Barr's Brook. The weather was fine and as Jack was a comfortably steady driver Polly's eyes were not riveted to the road ahead ... she was able to sit back and enjoy the countryside.

Jack's maroon Rover 2000, not new but certainly in excellent condition covered the miles smoothly. It was years since Polly had been in the area, yet when they turned off the main road to the old town it looked unchanged. Many of the golden Cotswold stone buildings dated from the fifteenth century – one housed a museum with an eighteenth century dolls' house. It would be nice to see it again. She mentioned it as they drove down the wide High Street and Jack said he was sorry there was no time to stop, he had not known of its existence. He couldn't claim to be gripped by dolls but history was one of his interests and the craftsmanship would be worth seeing ... "On our next visit," he concluded, throwing Polly into a state of mental confusion. Did he think she had been hinting that they go together? Was he making a date? How silly she was being – of course he was assuming that their business with Margaret would not be settled today, on one trip.

"Have you ever visited Lego land in Denmark?" he asked. "Personally, I was impressed, not so much by the amazing things they had devised with all the tiny blocks, but they have acquired Queen Titania's Palace," he continued when she shook her head, "which is the finest example of miniaturization I have ever seen. Everything from tiny bibles and embroidered standards in the chapel, to caskets teeming with real gems fashioned into very genuine looking jewellery ... wearable if you were only a few inches high! Many of the beautifully framed paintings on the walls are genuine old masters too ... I think Turner painted at least one." Polly expressed astonishment and said if ever she visited Denmark she wouldn't miss it.

At the bottom of the slope from the town, they crossed a single lane, triple-arched bridge over the little River Windrush and were soon within a few miles of their destination. Ten minutes after leaving the town they were winding through a labyrinth of narrow lanes. There were very few houses until they reached a small hamlet of about a dozen attractive properties. Most were set back from the road and Margaret's was the last before they went over a tiny picturesque bridge spanning what was probably a minor tributary of the Thames.

The house, Riverbank, was hidden behind a high stone wall although they glimpsed it briefly through the tall, wrought iron gates which barred access to a gravel drive. They drove on through half a mile of beech-woodland. The scar of a stone quarry was visible briefly on their right – at one point it jutted to within a few yards of the road – but even that did not spoil the beauty of the woods, where a haze of bluebells smudged the shade under the tall trees. Emerging into the open again they arrived at Barr's Brook, which was little more than a group of small, terraced cottages clustered round an ancient stone Church and a village inn. There were not many shops. Grouped together, Polly noted a Post Office, a Greengrocer and a Butcher, all closed anyway.

She thought it a quaint old place, most attractive, and was pleased when Jack spotted, next to the Lion Hotel, an 'Olde Tea Shoppe' that was open for business. He suggested they pull in for refreshment ... they might even find a garrulous native – eager to gossip about Mrs Rigby. With her apparent talents, she might be famous or at least have achieved some notoriety! A chubby teen-ager, her blonde hair tied back with a blue ribbon, came to serve them. She wore a frilly white apron over a blue nylon overall which matched the decor in the small cafe. Without consultation Jack ordered the 'Special Tea' advertised outside – then, as the girl left them alone again, he asked Polly if that would be acceptable. "I'm afraid a lifetime of having only my own wishes to consider hasn't improved my manners, dear lady; just butt in if I take too much for granted."

"Oh, I'm quite happy to have such decisions made for me ... it's nice to be looked after. I'm really enjoying myself!" Polly assured him.

There were no other customers so, when the girl brought their tea-tray and a trolley weighed down with the most delicious looking scones and cakes, they found it easy to detain her in conversation. When they entered she had been reading some brochures which Polly saw were estate agent hand-outs. Nodding towards the bench where they still lay Polly said, "They must be very dry reading for a pretty young lady ... you will pardon me, I hope, but you do seem rather youthful to be house-hunting!"

The girl laughed and said she had picked them up for her married sister Esther who was expecting a baby. "She and her husband still live with us at home and it's already a bit of a squash! There aren't many properties for sale – not places that would suit her, I mean, but I know what she doesn't want," she grinned, "anything more than her husband can afford – which applies to most of the places on these lists!"

"There are not many houses here anyway, are there?" Jack asked, "At least – not the way we drove in. We came from Burford, through the beech wood, and before that we passed only about a dozen properties, on the other side of the bridge."

"I know where you mean," the girl said, "They are well above her means, but there is a larger village and a new housing estate in the opposite direction."

"You surprise me," Polly rejoined, "I thought this village must be a place where everyone knows everybody." Seeing the girl's suspicious look – *were these strangers patronizing her* – she added, "Just as they probably did generations back! It must have been comforting to live in such security."

The waitress relaxed. Suddenly overcome with curiosity, she said as she turned to leave them, "If you are here house-hunting, I can let you have a whole pile of leaflets – they are way too expensive to interest my sister."

"That's very good of you," Jack said quickly. "Please bring them over when we've finished eating. We'd better concentrate on the tea now, before it goes cold."

In low tones, as they ate, they planned their approach ... anything they discovered before calling on Margaret would be worth while, but they had to be careful not to become the subject of gossip themselves. If an account of their inquiries got back to Irma, she must hear nothing that would either hurt or alarm her, depending on her real motive for moving in with Cousin Margaret.

***

Unaware that they were the objects of such intense speculation, so close at hand, Margaret and Irma were sitting in the garden enjoying the spring sunshine. It was not a warm sun and Irma had just tucked a shawl over her employer's knees. "Thank you dear," Margaret said, "You were right, this is much more comfortable."

They had settled into a regular pattern of living since Irma moved in. In the mornings, when not shopping, Irma flitted between supervising Edna, and the study where she typed any letters required. She took Margaret's breakfast upstairs at ten-o-clock and Margaret signed anything official. She accepted Margaret's private correspondence to post at the same time. There was a collection box which Irma always passed on her daily walk. When Margaret declared her a masochist, she laughed. She enjoyed exercise and was determined to keep fit.

Margaret received few letters to answer except at Christmas, when people who had been totally out of mind for the whole year brought her up to date with their news ... mostly births, weddings and scholarly successes. They had all been thoroughly depressing, in view of her recent loss, and she had not replied to any of them until Irma came on the scene. Edna always prepared the vegetables before leaving and Irma cooked lunch ... they had their main meal at midday because Irma insisted it was better for the digestion. The evening meal was light – sometimes only soup and sandwiches, which Margaret still found inadequate. She gave in eventually because after all Irma was a trained nurse and must know best.

It was only one of many changes which Irma was gradually introducing into her regime and, although Margaret sometimes disagreed with her, she always acquiesced finally because she knew that Irma had her best interests at heart. Irma was far more worldly wise and, in addition, there was no denying that she also had Divine Guidance.

At their first meeting, even after Edna's glowing accounts, Margaret had been disinclined to believe in 'Spirit Guides' and messages from 'Beyond'. She had no intention of displaying enthusiasm or going out of her way to seek personal proof of the woman's powers and kept the conversation general.

Irma was very open about her own circumstances. She spoke of her fatherless childhood – how her mother had struggled to bring her up. She described her excitement at leaving home – her life at the hospital and her marriage just before her twenty-third birthday. Ten years later she left her husband Bill. It had not been a happy marriage ... his true nature was not at all what she had thought. He had no interest in the arts or indeed anything he could neither eat nor drink! His unpredictable temper frightened her and when her mother became ill Irma gladly resigned her post to return home. Her poor mother died in 1979 when only in her mid-sixties ... since then Irma had taken to full-time private nursing. Irma had always had 'her Gift' as she termed it, but only with her last patient had it landed her in trouble. Having referred to her psychic ability in this brief manner, she was changing the subject but Margaret was naturally intrigued and couldn't resist asking what she meant by 'trouble'.

"The lady I was nursing was deeply unhappy," Irma sighed. "Her husband had died several years earlier after they'd had an almighty row and parted in anger." Her large brown eyes clouded sadly at the memory. "He crashed his car and the poor soul blamed herself." She paused, shaking her head at the idea ... "Of course I knew he was with her in spirit and I told her he understood – she must not feel guilty. At first she didn't believe me ... then I described him and told her a lot of personal things which only he could have told me!" Irma shrugged. "I should have known better, but I was only trying to comfort her. She might have felt better physically if only she stopped torturing herself with the past. Anyway her family refused to see it like that – they virtually threw me out, without a reference."

She declined to name the family and said that when she sought re-employment she would use her many earlier references ... it was after all only six months since she had left a previous post where her patient recovered fully. She had been sacked only a few weeks before Christmas and she intimated that her dreadful experience had sapped her of the will to move on, so she decided to treat herself to a short break. The idea of spending the festive season in a Cotswold village appealed to her and she was still living at the Inn but soon, she said, she must start earning her living again. Margaret was sympathetic, but inclined to take the girl's 'Gift' with a pinch of salt. There was only Irma's word for the whole episode, so the interview ended quickly.

As Irma turned to leave, she suddenly caught sight of the bureau in the bay window. "What a beautiful piece of furniture," she sighed, touching it admiringly ... then she glanced beyond it into the garden. Turning in surprise to Margaret, she said, "I had no idea you could see mountains from here – and what is that lovely old ruin beyond the pergola?"

Margaret had almost fainted with shock ... the view which Irma described was not this garden at all – it was the one from the window of the house where she was born – where this very bureau had stood in her childhood. Margaret had almost forgotten the scenes of her early life. She seldom spoke of such things – had not even done so with Jean!

Over the next few weeks Irma visited almost every afternoon at Margaret's insistence – her thirst for proof of the afterlife became insatiable. The more she heard, the more eagerly she looked forward to speaking with Irma. Then, one morning, Edna broke the news that Irma was in contact with an agency up north and expected to be moving on very soon. The idea of Irma's leaving to resume a nursing career filled Margaret with dismay. Inevitably she decided that the only way of holding on to her new friend was to offer her the position of companion ... as she told Ethel – it was undoubtedly the best move she had ever made.

Chapter Nine

After lunch, not that either Sarah or Amy had felt much like eating, they talked; Nettie, allowed at last to get on with her work, was bustling about upstairs. They were told that a laboratory key was among a bunch found in Jay's office desk at the Research Centre. Even so, it had not been easy to gain entry because the tremendous blast, which destroyed everything inside, had even twisted the door frame. The investigators couldn't and didn't expect to find any trace of Jay, but because the inner bolts had clearly been fastened when they melted, they were convinced he had died in the explosion. The police, satisfied that no criminal activity was involved, declared the matter to be out of their hands ... there would be an inquest of course. Watching them depart, Amy looked stunned; now, apparently, she was on her own! The Research team left soon afterwards and she almost howled with dismay ... everything was a mess – how could they just go? What was she expected to do? She was considerably relieved when informed by their leader that an officer from Personnel was on his way and would help in any way he could.

Bobby lay on Amy's lap, unwilling to move far from her. He twitched occasionally and gave little yelps in his sleep. He had not yet recovered fully from his ignominious imprisonment the night before. Now alone, the two women could talk freely. Neither had admitted to anyone else but, judging by his actions, both knew that Jay had been well aware of the danger of his experiment, whatever it was. He had gone to great lengths in arranging Amy's absence and removing Bobby from the house. Voicing her thoughts hesitantly, Amy whispered, "You don't think he really meant to do it, to commit suicide, do you? How did he seem to you? Of course the police considered the possibility too, but I heard one say, when they were looking through the writing desk, that he had found a letter ready for posting to a mail order firm. There was a cheque with it. Before he saw me standing there, he said people didn't waste time sending for things they wouldn't be here to use. After they went out I looked at it – it was for socks, shoes and ties! The form was cut from a newspaper ... Jay would never send for such things. He must have left it there deliberately to mislead. Of course I didn't tell them that, but I can't get it out of my head ... did he actually commit suicide?"

Without hesitation Sarah could truthfully say she was sure he had not. No doubt he knew he was courting danger, so his intention in leaving the letter where he knew it would be found was clear. It was to protect his wife from any inference that he had deliberately taken his own life.

Amy, her fears assuaged by this very firm declaration, suddenly collapsed in floods of tears. Her whole body shook uncontrollably making the soft cloth of her long housecoat ripple like waves in a wind, over her flabby thighs. She was an unattractive sight and Sarah resolved to encourage her to get back into shape. She was not a stupid woman and must know how much she had changed since her marriage. It was little wonder she questioned her husband's desire to remain with her! But he could merely have left home – or because his laboratory was incorporated with the house he could have set Amy up in her own place; money was no problem. Suicide was completely unnecessary and Sarah backed up her previous statement by saying so.

While the moment was opportune Sarah advised her to start going out more – even walking Bobby, going a little farther every day, would soon make her feel more fit, even if she didn't do any formal exercise, and if she also took extra care over her diet she would lose weight quite quickly.

"You are a lot younger than I am dear," Sarah pointed out, "Jay wouldn't want you to go into a decline I'm sure. Your first priority must be to improve your health."

Amy sniffed, obviously not impressed by the idea, so Sarah pressed the point. "You would find it much easier to cope with your changed circumstances. Jay told me you hardly ever leave the house – that must change, and your first trip out will be to see his father."

Amy wiped the tears from her swollen face with the back of a podgy, white hand protesting that she just couldn't – she had never met him – he didn't know her! What on earth was the point? But Sarah was adamant ... she wanted to visit him herself and only with Amy's cooperation could she do so.

It hadn't occurred to Amy before, but now she asked if Sarah thought she should immediately contact the psychiatric hospital, where her father-in-law was still a patient, to inform them what had happened; it wouldn't register with him anyway, even if they told him! After considering, Sarah decided privately that it would better suit her own purpose if she were present when he heard of the tragedy, so she volunteered to telephone on Amy's behalf. The Administrator was very understanding and promised to inform the doctor in charge of his case that they would be coming the following day and would prefer to break the news to Mr Johnson themselves – or at least be present to see if he responded in any way. When he rang back, it was to assure them that their wishes would be followed and Dr. Ellis would expect them between eleven and twelve.

Amy had no excuse for avoiding the trip and her dread of going took her mind off her greater misfortune. Having persuaded her to sort out something to wear and to collect together any relevant papers which would identify her formally to the authorities, Sarah went alone to inspect the basement. The broken cellar door still clung to its frame and had been pulled into place. It was heavy and difficult to move but Sarah, in no mood to give up easily, was soon at the bottom of the steps. The laboratory door gaped wide but the meagre daylight from above was useless – her eyes could not penetrate the gloom inside.

Remembering where the torch was kept Sarah started back to fetch it ... and stopped in mid-turn. She had heard no footsteps but coming down towards her, hand in hand, were two people. The woman was smiling happily at a man whose back was to Sarah as he led the slim, elegant young lady down the steps. Sarah was so astonished by their presence that it was a few heartbeats before she realised they were spirit manifestations ... not physically there; their ghostly tread made no sound. She was thrilled, aware that there must be a reason for her being granted this glimpse of the past.

Desperate not to miss the significance she concentrated with an open mind and found her attention drawn to the slender hand resting on the man's arm. Alongside the wide gold band was a diamond and ruby ring immediately recognizable to Sarah – the design was unusual. The exquisite antique was Dorothea's engagement ring which had previously belonged to her husband's mother.

So ... the man must be Jay's father, but how could that be? At least, up to ten minutes ago, he was still in the land of the living! She stepped back and beheld their silent, happy laughter; totally rapt in each other, they moved across her path and went into a room now ablaze with light. Everything gleamed, newly resplendent, and he appeared to be showing it to her, with pride, perhaps for the first time. He suddenly turned and Sarah saw him face to face. Her sharp cry of astonishment banished the vision and in the sudden eerie darkness she felt dizzy with fear. Recovering slowly she cast the thought away with derision. It was impossible – bizarre – but she could not forget her first impression – it had, after all, been barely a day since she had last seen him. It was Jay!

***

When he was positive that Polly had eaten well and she assured him that she was quite finished, Jack nodded to the waitress and made a vague scribbling motion in the air. The girl smiled and brought the check on a tiny tray. She also gave them the promised brochures and as there were still no other customers she volunteered to tell them anything she could about the properties, if it would help. An older woman appeared briefly at the till and called to them. "I hope my niece has been looking after you and that you enjoyed your tea," she smiled warmly. When they made their satisfaction clear she walked over and put an arm round the young girl. "Betty is a real treasure," she told them... "I shall be sorry when she goes to college – weekend help is so difficult to get in a place like this."

When she saw the estate agents' lists and they told her Betty was about to help them with her local knowledge, she said they couldn't be in better hands ... not much happened in the area without being known to Betty. "My sister is the local gossip and what she and this daughter of hers don't know between them isn't worth knowing, believe me!"

"Oh, Aunt Ida – how could you? You just wait until I tell Mum what you said about her!" Betty blushed, but giggled – not at all offended.

It wouldn't be easy for Jack and Polly to find out what they really wanted to know but Betty was totally relaxed now. When her Aunt went back to the till, she took them over to a bench seat in the bay window where they could be more comfortable – the floral covering looked old-fashioned but the cushions inside it were deep foam.

One of the places listed, Elm House, was quite near Margaret's, so Polly shuffled it to the lower half of the pile and showed more apparent interest in the others. Nothing, of course was exactly what they were seeking. Betty assumed they were a married couple ... they did nothing to disillusion her but managed to avoid the subject successfully.

When they reached the Elm House details Jack remarked that it was likely to be very exposed now. Dutch elm disease had probably killed off most of the trees in the photograph ... they must have been its most significant feature. Betty said it was still a nice garden but the house needed modernizing badly.

Polly took her chance and commented, "Anyway, it is quite lonely out there, and that narrow road isn't very safe ... wasn't a woman killed on it last year?"

"Yes, that's right," Betty agreed, "but she was riding a bike! ... You wouldn't be doing that would you?"

"What happened then?" Jack asked.

Betty launched into an account of the tragedy. The woman was a bit old to be riding a bike, in Betty's opinion; she must have been nearly sixty. Anyway, the poor lady was knocked off it by a car. The driver admitted he'd been drinking but passed a breath test. He said he didn't touch her – she just seemed to jump off in front of him, but it happened where the edge of the quarry comes near the verge and she had fallen down about six feet. Her head was injured when she hit the stony ground. The bike was written off and the car was a mess, but there was no blood on it, so in the end they said she must have wobbled off and it was an accident.

"How tragic," Polly murmured. "I believe she was killed close to her home but I would have expected anyone from such an expensive area to drive themselves or take a taxi, wouldn't you?"

"Oh, she wasn't an owner – she was companion to an old lady there ... but in any case, even Mrs Dunn herself doesn't have a car, she always takes a Teddy when she wants to go anywhere." Smiling wickedly at their lifted eyebrows she added, "Ted calls his company *Barr's Taxi Service* but with a name like that – how could people resist calling him Teddy Bear! He's a good sport ... takes it all in good part.

His wife Edna works for Mrs Dunn as a daily, so he probably gives her special rates!"

Things were certainly going their way. Polly and Jack exchanged satisfied smiles. "Well, it must be a bitter blow to Mrs Dunn ... being old and alone now, or has she replaced her companion?" Jack asked.

"As luck has it," Betty told them, "There was a woman at the Inn over Christmas who was between jobs, and Edna got to know her. When Edna discovered that Mrs Rigby was a private nurse looking for somewhere to 'live in' she introduced her to Mrs Dunn ... and another thing ..." She stopped and looked embarrassed. "Well, anyway, Edna took her up there one day and they got on very well so the old lady's fixed up again now."

"What other thing?" prompted Polly hopefully.

When Betty shook her head Polly immediately dropped the subject and said instead, before Betty dried up altogether, "It was lucky for Mrs Rigby too. Where was she before she came here? If she came for Christmas she must have no family ... How sad."

"I felt so sorry for her," Betty agreed. "She kept herself to herself except for Edna and until she started going up to the house nearly every afternoon, she used to go out for hours – walking – always on her own. Fitter than me she was!"

The doorbell suddenly clanged and two more customers came in; Betty rose hastily, so Polly and Jack thanked her for her help, asked if they could keep the leaflets. As she nodded that of course they could, they left the tea shop well pleased with what they had discovered. They would have liked to go in search of Edna – she should be easy to find through her husband's taxi service – but glancing at his watch Jack declared it was, "Almost seventeen-thirty hours – time to call on Margaret. If we dally it will be indecent to call without a previous arrangement."

Polly smiled. So! Real old-fashioned gentlemen were not a thing of the past! She decided to ring Sarah later, when she returned to Headington. She was eager to meet Margaret and Mrs Irma Rigby and followed Jack eagerly as he held the car door open for her. She fastened her seat belt quickly ... her first 'case' was proving more exciting than expected!

Chapter Ten

Sarah tried to convince herself that, although unusual, on this occasion her eyes had deceived her. Reason dictated that the man with Dorothea was her husband John. It could not possibly have been Jay. Nettie declared that father and son were exactly alike but one often said such things without meaning they looked like identical twins! ... It had, nevertheless, been barely a day since she'd spoken to Amy's husband – she recalled him perfectly. Obviously the strain of the past twenty four hours had taken more toll than she appreciated.

The fact that John senior was still in the land of the living was not significant. Projected visions of living people were sometimes seen by friends or family in places far removed from where they were known to be – although she admitted, not usually in the company of a dead relative! But his son was indeed dead and it troubled Sarah that she could not discern any trace of his spirit presence at all.

She resumed her search for the torch and eventually stood waving the broad beam round the damaged room. Everything in it had disintegrated. Walls which in her vision had been hidden by benches and cabinets were now bare, but deeply etched. Intaglio images, where the vanished furniture had partially protected them, were the only reminder of what this had once been. At the far end of the room, distorted roof joists had shifted. Rubble and earth fell through the damaged ceiling; molten glass had formed misshapen grumous lumps on the floor where work-benches had once stood; veils of tree roots swayed eerily in the failing battery light.

There was nothing more to be gained by standing in what she now perceived to be dank clammy coldness, so Sarah returned speedily to the balmy fresh air of the upper floor. She reflected how fortunate it was that the fated room had been a sideways extension under the garden, rather than a conversion of the existing wine or coal cellars. It would be a fairly simple matter to seal it off from inside. Outside, the area could be bulldozed, the laboratory filled in and the lawn re-laid ... still, that was not her problem!

Unbidden, another vision burst upon her. She was outside, watching the house from the lane ... no trees hid it as they did today, and the surrounding slopes were empty of other habitation. The building itself was run down and scarcely recognizable without its garage, conservatory and landscaped garden. A man stood before it in profile to her, just looking – hands fisted into his hips. He was just a small figure in the middle distance but he looked familiar ... she was absolutely sure it was the man she had seen moments ago with the young Dorothea!

Why was she being granted these puzzling visions? ...

If not the lost spirit of Jay, could it be Dorothea herself who was showing her these glimpses of the past? Was she, for some reason, unable to rest in peace? Sarah was glad she had promised to stay with Amy for a while – perhaps Dorothea needed her too. On returning to the sitting room Sarah stood gazing for some minutes from the wide window, half hoping that she would be granted a second chance to see the face of the mystery man. The garden was trim and cultivated, so different from the way it had appeared in her mind's eye, moments ago.

Amy interrupted her reverie. She was now resigned to the outing but complaining bitterly that she had nothing to wear. The only decent dress she could get into was a most unsuitable yellow. "Perhaps you're right, Sarah – I should try to slim down but I'll look a mess tomorrow! My fur coat will cover most of it but still, what will they think? I should be in mourning."

"Mourning is a state of mind," Sarah replied firmly. "Nobody would dream of criticizing anyway, under the circumstances ... it was a totally unexpected bereavement!" Her mind was far too occupied to be sympathetic to such trivial complaints. It occurred to her that she could give Amy something useful to do, to divert her and perhaps at the same time solve a problem of her own. "Amy," she said quickly, "before you sit down ..."

Amy, about to flop into a fireside chair, stopped with a faint air of martyrdom as Sarah asked, "Are there any family photograph albums I could look through? Nettie commented on how alike Jay and his father were. Before we see him tomorrow, I feel I should be better informed about him." Amy raised her eyebrows. Aware that Sarah was psychic and knowing her far too well to be deceived, she suspected there was more than simple curiosity behind her request!

Although she knew Sarah disliked discussing the topic, she commented anyway – "Oh, my goodness, you've seen something, haven't you? I thought I heard you coming from the basement! What is it like down there? I just can't face going to look myself ... poor Jay! What happened? What did you see?"

Sarah managed to conceal her irritation – she needed Amy's help and cooperation. Without revealing much, she admitted to seeing Dorothea. While telling Amy, she was aware of having not actually seen Dorothea's face clearly, her attention being drawn more to the ring on her finger ... and was prompted to ask, "Where is Dorothea's jewellery? Here or in the bank? When we checked yours, I can't remember seeing any of hers. Where is her engagement ring?"

Amy said her mother-in-law's small personal things, valuable or not, were packed in a cabin trunk. Jay had implied that although they would no doubt be Amy's one day, he wouldn't feel right about her using or disposing of them until after the death of his father. The trunk wasn't in the attic it was in a small box room – quite easily accessible. The ring was definitely there; she remembered threading it with several others on the padded roll inside a blue velvet travel bag. Sarah was welcome to look through it if she felt it necessary ... but she was far too exhausted to climb the stairs again. In spite of her protests Sarah insisted that they go to look together – she would not have felt right, going through Dorothea's private possessions alone, even though they had been closer to each other, than Amy to either of them.

Considerably irritated, having been forced to move, and panting heavily, Amy propped her weight on the edge of a wooden crate. She pointed to the trunk, indicating that it was up to Sarah to open it – she was finished. Only when Sarah's initial search failed to produce the jewellery pouch did Amy, alarmed, begin to take an interest. Everything else was as she had left it, and she knew exactly where she had tucked the bag away. Unable to believe that it was missing, she groped through the layers of carefully wrapped packages, treasures meaningful perhaps only to their departed owner. Soon, careless of their fragility, Amy scattered everything on the floor around her. With barely controlled fury she comprehended that Jay had removed Dorothea's jewellery. Why? What had he done with it? Why he had done anything at all without telling her, she could not imagine! If he had changed his mind about giving her his mother's old trinkets, he had only to say so!

With great difficulty Sarah calmed her. There was another possible explanation, she pointed out. He might have considered them too valuable to leave in a box room and taken them to his laboratory for security: it was, apparently, always kept locked.

"In which case, they are lost anyway now!" Amy sighed. "I'm glad he didn't suggest taking all mine down there as well! Really! It is most upsetting – especially losing that particular ring. It was so beautiful and very old you know. It had been in the family for generations. I had better check the insurance papers."

As they replaced everything, Amy peered at a silk wrapped bundle on the floor of the trunk. "You'd better lift that out first Sarah, it can go back on top. They are the photograph albums you want to see – I'd like to look through them too. He brought them from his mother's after she died and I didn't have a chance even to glance at them before he put them away." Forgetting the calamity which had probably befallen the ring, Amy was almost excited as they took the albums downstairs ... but Sarah, hoping to learn something from them through psychometry, by handling them first, persuaded her to put them aside until after dinner when they could enjoy examining them together. Sarah placed the wrapped bundle on a table near the settee, saying she would like to freshen up before they ate and gave Amy a stern look which indicated clearly how annoyed she would be if Amy opened it without her. It was only after she had left the room that Amy wondered ... What was so important about a collection of old photographs? What had Sarah actually seen, and why was she so reluctant to tell her?

***

On the way to Riverbank after leaving the village Jack slowed down when they reached the quarry. He glanced at his watch, and then suggested, "Shall we have a stroll round the place where Jean had her accident?"

"Yes, let's see how dangerous it looks." Polly agreed eagerly – ready to climb out of the car even before it stopped.

The strip of quarry closest to the road – separated from it by a grass verge barely five feet wide – was several feet below: a sheer drop. It seemed either that the authorities didn't consider it unsafe or it was too short a stretch to worry about. Jack said that local folk would be aware of it and strangers were unlikely to be on foot – there were many such roadside quarries throughout the whole area. Polly walked away a few paces and, returning, agreed that it was not a concealed hazard. There was no point in his climbing down to examine the area ... months had gone by since the accident and what could they expect to find that the police had missed at the time? The instant Polly said as much she glanced down and saw a button where the grass joined the tarmac. She picked it up; it was mottled brown and fawn, the type found on a man's suit or a raincoat. It meant nothing Jack said – it may have been there for years – but Polly dropped it into her coat pocket: just in case!

Within minutes, they drew up outside Riverbank. The road became slightly wider as it sloped down, away from the small bridge, so Jack allowed Polly to alight, then drove close to the stone wall. He would not presume to open the wrought iron gates and enter the drive. At one side was a narrower gate which opened onto a footpath leading to the front door. As they waited, having rung the bell, Polly was sure someone was watching them from the curtained bay window. The door was eventually opened by an attractive middle-aged woman who greeted them with a pleasant smile and waited for them to state their business. This must be Irma, Polly thought. She was fairly tall with sleek dark hair, worn short and well shaped. Her dark green skirt and high necked jumper suited her slim figure ... not at all what Polly had expected. But what had she expected? If genuine, the woman would be no more abnormal than Sarah or Clarinda! She privately acknowledged that she had suspected from the very first that Irma was fraudulent ... now she was wavering ... she must strive to keep an open mind.

Before Jack could explain, Margaret herself came hurrying to greet them in a flurry of excitement. "Why, goodness me – I don't believe it! ... Jack! How nice to see you. Come in, come in!" She practically dragged him into the hall and Polly followed as Irma stood aside, and closed the door behind them. They were shown into a large room which spanned the width of the house from front to back – it was over thirty-five feet long with velvet draped bay windows at each end. Polly noted the way it was furnished: in excellent taste – obviously with no expense spared, and decided that several antique pieces were probably heirlooms. It was certainly not the home of a poor person.

Jack introduced her. "This is my friend, Mrs Bailey, who was charmingly christened Gertrude, but prefers to be called Polly." Irma was very composed. After they had greeted her formally, she turned to Polly and said she understood how one could become attached to a nickname when affectionately used ... she had once nursed a ninety-year-old who, even to her Great Grand-children, was known as 'Muffin'!

When they were seated, Irma left to make tea. Margaret told them she had no living-in maid – and as soon as Irma was out of hearing distance she turned to Jack and asked him to 'fess up'. "You came here to check up on me didn't you? I'll bet Ethel has told the whole family that I'm going senile! You wanted to see for yourself, didn't you?"

"I protest that not one of us suspected the onset of senility, but we are all anxious to make sure that, in your distress over poor Jean's death," replied Jack with no trace of contrition, "no-one is taking advantage of your good nature and vulnerability." He felt quite justified in feeling protective towards someone who was not only a member of his family but a woman with no husband to care for her. "You can know very little about Mrs Rigby. She seems pleasant enough, but what makes you so sure you can trust her?"

"If I had merely told Ethel that I had engaged a new housekeeper, none of you would have turned a hair – it's only because she's psychic, a Spiritualist Medium, that you are at all suspicious! I can understand, I was dubious too at first – I never believed in ghosts".

Polly, sensing Margaret's increasing defensiveness, hastened to intervene. Without risking a warning glance at Jack she declared, "I've never seen one myself but I personally have no doubt that there is 'Life After Death' or that some sensitive people are able to contact the world of Spirit ... Jack will take much more convincing I suspect!"

She was relieved to see that she had been right to speak ... Margaret suddenly became animated and, ignoring Jack, turned instead to talk to Polly. She spoke of her own early misgivings, described Irma's first visit and finally directed Polly's attention to the veneered walnut bureau in the bay. "Irma touched that desk, admiring it – then looked out of the window and expressed surprise at the aspect. She said it was a beautiful view! When I failed to understand, she described not this garden but the view from my old home in Shropshire ... How could she know the bureau once stood in a window looking out toward a pergola and a ruin, with mountains beyond?"

Turning to Jack again she asked him, "You went there as a child – do you remember it?"

"I do indeed, but she may have known about your roots before she came here. The furniture is obviously old ... probably eighteenth century ... and with the carved base quite rare, I think. She could have guessed you brought it with you!" Jack protested. "Is that the only proof you have?"

At that moment Irma tapped at the door and came in pushing a tea trolley. She immediately handed out plates and napkins and offered biscuits before pouring the tea. "It's a little late for sandwiches," she said, "I thought these would be more acceptable." She didn't sit again but excused herself, saying she had letters to write. Margaret asked her to wait a moment and suggested that Jack and Polly might like to stay for dinner. Margaret was disappointed when they declined; she had indeed thought that if they accepted, Irma would have produced a hot meal for a change! When Irma departed again Margaret pointed out that she was pleasant and considerate – some in her position would have been nosy enough to stay.

Polly had to disagree. She was in a comparable relationship with Sarah... they had been friends for over thirty years and she never stayed in the room when Sarah had guests unless specifically invited to do so ... but she kept her thoughts to herself.

"Now then," said Jack, "convince me! What other astounding things has she told you?" He settled himself more comfortably and promised to keep an open mind. Margaret eyed him dubiously, but took up her story again.

Chapter Eleven

During the week after their first meeting, according to Margaret, Irma needed a great deal of persuasion to practise her powers but Polly noted that at least one incredible act of clairvoyance happened on every visit. When Margaret asked if she could receive any specific impressions from the other old furniture in the room, Irma had placed her hands on a small occasional table and described a 'Royal Doulton' figure which used to stand on it, until Margaret had stumbled against it as a child and the precious object was smashed ... her mother had been angry, Irma said, and told her she was more clumsy at seven-years-old than she had been at eighteen months!

An inlaid mahogany whatnot in the corner had attracted Irma – she said it used to hold a collection of early Wedgwood pieces and she later spotted two of them in a modern cabinet which stood in Margaret's dining room. There were many similar stories and even Jack began to look impressed whereas Polly felt it was all too good to be true ... but how could Irma describe scenes that had changed before she was even born? In answer to their questions Margaret assured them that even Jean had not possessed such intimate knowledge of her old family home, so there was no way she could have told Edna or anyone else. Edna was the only member of the household who had previously met Irma – Jean having died before Irma even came to Barr's Brook.

There were no photographs of the old place which Edna might have seen and discussed because while Margaret was away at school there had been a terrible fire in the library. The family albums were kept there and all were destroyed along with the most valuable books. Anyway, Margaret pointed out, in those days people didn't go around taking casual snaps all the time like they do these days.

She also asked them to explain how Irma knew her mother's actual words, spoken in anger, when she had completely forgotten them herself until reminded! That was undoubtedly the most amazing part of the saga ... perhaps they had misjudged Irma after all, thought Jack.

Margaret went to a cupboard and produced a small collection of photographs, most still loose, which she handed to Polly. "You will see that the earliest were taken in the garden, looking towards the old house. No hills are visible and neither are the ruins in the adjacent field. Whoever took them must have stood in the pergola, but it doesn't feature in any itself. There are none of Grandmother, who died before the fire, or of Grandfather who died a few months after it. The few I have of my own parents were taken when they were older, but Irma has described them both to me, as they were when they first married." Polly looked through them carefully, handing a few at a time to Jack while Margaret continued. "... What's more, she has also seen – here in this room – a young girl who was close to me for years but with whom I lost touch."

"It is a most amazing account," Polly admitted cautiously. "I have heard similar stories which were impossible to disprove. What convinced you that Irma really saw your friend?"

"Well, she gave me her name, Olive, but also described her perfectly and even reminded me that we used to play draughts together! Actually, you might remember her Jack. Olive was one of our housemaids. She came to us from the local orphanage when she was sixteen – she couldn't stay on there when she became old enough to earn her own living. It was two or three years before I left home to go to boarding school. I was seven with no playmates my own age and she was just a big kid herself. I used to help her with her chores so that she would be free to play games. Anyway, I certainly can't remember ever seeing a photograph of Olive. How could Irma have done so?"

Jack and Polly were at a loss to know what else they could ask but were reluctant to leave the subject. They both spoke together –

"Could anyone else have duplicates of the lost albums?"

"Why did you lose touch with Olive, if you were such good friends? They exchanged apologetic glances but each was glad that the other had reservations about complete acceptance.

Margaret tackled Jack's point first.

If his own mother, Aunt Helen, didn't have duplicates – and he should know more about that than she did – the only person who might was Aunt Emma. They would have to ask her themselves because Margaret hadn't seen her for years. As for Polly's question – she supposed that once she was away from home, she made more friends her own age – her dependence on Olive disappeared. She hadn't wanted to go away but Olive persuaded her that she was lucky to have parents who could give her a good education – and especially fortunate to have such a wonderful father, who enjoyed doing things with her and was still young enough even to teach her to play tennis!

Olive had never known her own father, and her mother died when she was only eight-years-old. Left all alone in the world, she'd had to face life in an institution; so a slightly shamefaced Margaret eventually left with fairly good grace. They corresponded for a few months and Olive was certainly present during her first August vacation. Margaret recalled that she was still there too during the second, after the fire, and reminded Jack that so was he, both summers, on his annual holiday. Only two years separated the cousins so she had a playmate!

Olive was more adult and aloof then anyway ... and her household duties occupied her fully. Margaret had no idea when or why Olive left. "She may have found a better paying job – I don't think

Grandpa was over generous – or she may have married, I don't know, but it's hardly relevant is it?"

It probably wasn't ... and before long Jack checked his watch. "Good Lord! Twenty hundred hours – we should not have taken up so much of your time after calling without warning!"

Polly smiled. She wondered why he didn't wear a timepiece with a digital display – he always translated the time into such military language – then she voiced her own thanks for the refreshment and the opportunity of meeting another member of the family. "We are actually related by marriage," she pointed out. Seeing Margaret's astonishment Polly reminded her that Jack's niece Elaine married her nephew Dan.

"Why, of course ... Daniel Bailey! I'm so sorry I didn't make the connection." Margaret was obviously embarrassed. "I was invited to the wedding but I don't travel far these days. If you are ever in this area again please call – we will have a lot more to talk about than we have managed to fit in today!"

"I don't suppose you know," smiled Polly, "that Elaine is expecting their first baby at the end of May ... I will bring you some snaps after the event."

Margaret was pleased and said she would look forward to seeing her again. They were soon all on their feet ready to leave the room...

Irma was in the study. The few letters she'd written were finished long ago and since then she had been trying to guess what was happening in the other room. The walls were too thick for her to hear them talking, but she heard laughter occasionally so she assumed the conversation was not too solemn. As soon as she realised who the man was, she knew he must have come specifically to discover more about her ... Jean's replacement! Well – if the family was going to be round every five minutes she would have to delay things until the dust settled. It wasn't a serious problem but it might be a good idea to convince Cousin Jack that she was genuine. He would soon let his sisters know there was nothing to worry about ... they could then go back to their knitting! When she heard them in the front hall, Irma hurried to say goodnight. She had an idea.

***

It was after nine-o-clock when Nettie tapped on the door to take her leave of Amy and Sarah. She had insisted on staying to cook – and clear up for once. It was kind of her but Amy was irritated. She said it was as if the woman was lingering deliberately – frightened that she might miss something! It was on the tip of Sarah's tongue to remonstrate with her for her lack of charity but what good would it do? Amy had always been self-centred ... she was unlikely to change at her age.

Sarah did understand; had they been alone, the meal would have been less elaborate and they would have been able to settle down more quickly with the albums. They were both eager to open the parcel that now lay between them on the sofa.

Amy grabbed the latest, which was less than half full. The first few pages contained some snaps of her own wedding which she had never seen, presumably taken by guests. Sarah automatically reached for the oldest and was immediately gripped by a sense of foreboding which, in itself, she found confusing. There was not really any mystery to solve ... Jay had blown himself up! Not knowing what she hoped to discover, she gave every page close scrutiny, trying to leave her mind open to suggestion; trying to ignore the background chatter.

If only Amy would allow her some peace and quiet for a while, there might be something ... a clue to why she should feel so strangely inadequate. At the back of her mind she struggled to remember the last occasion on which a similar sensation had gripped her ... she had a growing certainty that she had been with Dorothea. It was connected to something she had said ... perhaps the last thing Dorothea had ever said to her as she lay ill, dying ... what was it?

Amy's strident voice kept calling her attention to this or that photo: "Did you notice the ear rings I wore?" she asked. "Who on earth was this woman in the huge hat? Just look at that bow!" Ignoring her was no deterrent. "Oh, look ... there you are too, with Clarrie! She must have been about eight – such a pretty girl, I should have had her as a bridesmaid." Looking up and catching an expression of exasperation on Sarah's face she added contritely, "Oh, sorry! You call her Clarinda don't you?"

Forcing a dismissive smile, Sarah assured Amy that as long as her daughter was happy answering to Clarrie it didn't matter. As for choosing a name – it had originally been a headache but her two sisters, Clair and Linda, could be equally happy that the new baby had been named for them: neither need feel slighted! The interruption reminded Sarah that she must ring Polly to inform her of Jay's death and her change of plan ... she tried, but there was no answer. She left a message on the machine.

***

As soon as they were on their way back to Oxford Polly almost burst with curiosity. "Tell me please! Don't keep me in suspense! What Irma told you about your mother – was it really true?"

"Well ..." Jack drawled, dragging the word out, to tease her ... "it was – and it wasn't!"

"Oh, come on – *which*?"

When they had been standing at the door and Irma shook hands with Jack, saying how pleased she was to have met him, she suddenly swayed and put a hand over her eyes. "Forgive me ... but I will speak out, because you've probably heard that I'm psychic. There's a lady here with you ... your mother, I think. Yes – she is nodding ... I'm hearing the name, Helen. I'm seeing her as a beautiful young girl with long fair hair and she is cuddling a little dog. It is a darling little spaniel ... she was so fond of him. Her dear little Chaz. She says he followed her everywhere!"

Her voice trailed away and Margaret clutched Jack's arm ... "You see? Believe me, I have never mentioned Helen to Irma and I didn't even know she had a dog! In fact Irma doesn't let me discuss anything other than what she has 'seen' herself!"

"That's right," Irma said, "otherwise I could be using what you tell me – making it all up, couldn't I?" She laughed as if such an idea would never have occurred to them.

Polly hadn't been able to escape quickly enough after that. She was impatient to hear what Jack had to say about Irma's vision and urged, "Please Jack, do tell!" Jack sighed heavily and said that he was now firmly convinced ... he glanced sideways at Polly who was twisting in her seat to stare at him wide eyed. "Of what? For goodness sake, put me out of my misery!" Polly pleaded.

"Okay, okay, I'm sorry – I couldn't resist teasing you! She is right in saying my mother had a spaniel. Aunt Sophie, Margaret's mother, bought it for her sixteenth birthday – in fact I still have it!"

He laughed aloud at the expression on Polly's face. She was trying to assimilate the information and imagining how old the dog must be ... nearly eighty! Then Jack took pity on her and explained with great delight ... "It's actually a fur fabric night-dress case! And before you suggest there may have been a real pet which, to quote our friend Irma, 'followed her everywhere', there couldn't have been! She had always wanted a dog but was allergic to them until the day she died; the realistic looking model was a substitute."

"But what about the 'Chaz' ... I know children do it with toys but wasn't it unusual to give a cloth case a name?"

"It was a joke. The silk label said 'King Charles' but because it fell short of the real thing Emma made an extra one out of a cardboard disc – 'Prince Chas.' it amused everyone and Chaz stuck!"

Emma sank back in her seat, well satisfied. Now they knew; Irma was definitely a liar. All that remained was to figure out how she knew enough to be so convincing and how she planned to gain by it. She was already in Margaret's employ on the strength of her deceit – Margaret must have checked her references. Her qualifications were probably impeccable ... with no ties, she could have obtained a well paid post anywhere in the country, so how and why had she selected Margaret as a target?

Jack had been thinking about the dog. As he said, he still had it. Because he couldn't very well give it to one twin without the risk of upsetting the other, he'd packed it away after his mother's death in 1970. He wasn't sure that either Ethel or Elsie would even remember it, because it was never used after his own birth. Perhaps their mother considered it would be unfair to leave such an attractive object on her bed and forbid a child to touch it. As there was no way Irma could have seen the real thing she could only have seen his mother holding it in a photograph – one he had never seen himself. This was absolutely beyond doubt he pointed out, because if she had heard of the spaniel by word of mouth her informant would have told her it wasn't real.

Polly liked his logic. If a present for his mother's birthday, it was likely that such a photograph was taken to mark the occasion – later on it would have ceased to be a novelty. "What year would that have been?" she asked.

"Nineteen-thirteen," Jack told her after a moment's thought, "years before Irma was born ... she looks less than forty never mind seventy-nine!"

"I think you're right," agreed Polly, "so we must inquire into her background very closely – and I think I know how we can go about it. Dan's friend, Terry, is in the CID; I'm sure could be persuaded to help."

Jack agreed, but nothing could come of that until Monday. They would call on Emma tomorrow ... she might remember the dog and throw light on that aspect. Polly who had thought she would be going alone, accepted with pleasure. Going with Jack was sure to be more interesting.

It was nine-o-clock when they reached Polly's car. She had refused his invitation to have dinner somewhere and although he was reluctant to let her drive off without an escort; she convinced him that she was quite happy as long as he waited to make sure the car started. He laughed at her insistence that she was 'a big girl now' but didn't walk away until she drove out of the car park.

The second thing she did when she arrived back at Dan's was to eat with them while she related the day's events ... the first was to telephone Sarah.

Chapter Twelve

Amy had fallen silent for a moment and Sarah was beginning to succeed in focusing her thoughts when the telephone shrilled. Amy looked up hopefully and was relieved when Sarah moved from the depths of her armchair and answered it. Luckily, it was for her anyway – Polly ringing from Oxford. Before listening to Polly's news Sarah told her what had happened and said that under the circumstances she intended to stay with Amy for a couple of weeks – until she had sorted out her immediate problems. Polly was shocked and couldn't possibly relate then, her own comparatively trivial experiences. There was no way Clarinda need be involved so they decided not to contact her – she could carry on working undisturbed until the end of the week as arranged, when Sarah promised to ring them at home.

Sarah returned to her seat and resumed her search through a pile of un-mounted snaps. "Oh, dear!" she muttered, "I didn't even ask how Polly had enjoyed her day out ... but she must have, because she said something about staying in Oxford for another few nights as I will be away from home."

Amy wasn't really listening. Her attention was caught by the faded photographs which Sarah held; she gasped and looked closer. "Good grief! Dorothea, outside this house I'm sure, although everything looks so bare ... quite obviously the man must be John!" She trembled with emotion. "It gave me quite a turn for a moment – I thought it was Jay! That sweater he's wearing – why, it reminds me of the one I gave Jay for his last birthday."

Overcome suddenly with a sobbing fit, Amy struggled to her feet and announced that she just could not bear any more – she would go to bed if Sarah didn't mind. "He really loved it, it was his favourite colour, green ... Oh, poor Jay – my poor, dear Jay."

The echo of her voice faded as she went slowly upstairs and Sarah, with a guilty sigh of relief, continued to examine the contents of the albums. At every turn she was drawn back to the uncanny similarity between the two men, father and son: surely common enough – why should it disturb her? The picture on which Amy had commented was among the oldest. There were several together taken at the same time, according to the white ink legend, centre page. Dorothea's flowing script announced, 'My first look at our new home'. They were about three inches square: it wasn't easy to see the detail. She almost missed one which made her draw her breath in surprised satisfaction. The house was in the background and a small figure stood arms akimbo, his back to the camera. If her vision of the same scene had not been so recent she might have been persuaded that she'd seen this photograph before and forgotten. Anyway the snaps were monochrome – she had visualised it in full colour from a different angle. Colour! ... The man in her vision – his pullover was bright green!

So? ... So what! Why could she not just accept that being so similar they also shared the same tastes? Weariness seeped through her but she was reluctant to release the thread of her thoughts. She relaxed, allowing her mind to reason along lines which she had adamantly thrust aside when less tired. Unless they were twins, two individuals could not possibly be exactly alike. Two sightings in places miles apart, at different times, need not be of two different people, they could be of the same person: but if the different times were forty-six years apart, she was going mad! Impossible. Her thinking was muddled ... it was time to give up and go to bed; tomorrow would be a busy day.

Later, on the verge of sleep as her mind drifted, the elusive memory began to come into focus. Dorothea had asked for Sarah and she sat by her bedside quietly; knowing it was the end; wondering if Dorothea knew she was there. She could now recall the scene with absolute clarity. The dying woman opened her eyes. There was despair in every line of her face and slowly she reached for Sarah's hand. Gripping it with incredible urgency she whispered, "Do you believe in re-incarnation? Must I go through all this again? ... Please, pray for them ... they are lost!"

It had puzzled her greatly at the time. What had induced Dorothea to ask about re-incarnation ... and after it, one would have expected her to frame her plea – 'Pray for *me* ... *I* am lost'. Dorothea's sudden collapse and rapid decline baffled the doctors. Before last visiting her husband, she had been in her usual state of unperturbed acceptance. The day after, she rang Sarah to cancel their regular shopping trip, declining to fix another date – although it was a weekly highlight for them both. She said she felt 'a bit down' but assured Sarah it was probably just a cold – she would telephone again when she felt better.

A week later Sarah had been the first to make contact, to say she had been roped into some committee work and would be fully occupied for the next few weeks – until after the local music festival. Dorothea sounded normal; said she was feeling better. It was therefore a terrible shock when Amy rang eventually to say that Dorothea was in hospital and seemed totally disinterested in life.

Sarah, scarcely able to believe it, went to her immediately. Looking old beyond her years Dorothea lay wanly against her pillows and after one listless glance, as Sarah sat beside her, she closed her eyes to shut out the world. Sarah held her hand and waited until Dorothea gathered sufficient strength to speak.

Eventually she began, in a low faltering murmur. For years, she whispered sadly, she had clung to the hope that whatever had struck John down so quickly, might just as quickly be reversed, but she had to accept – without a shadow of doubt, that he would never recover. She attempted to explain, but breathing was difficult for her and her voice was failing. Sarah only caught clearly her plea for her to pray for John and their son and gave her solemn promise to do so.

In spite of the most eminent consultants and careful nursing Dorothea faded quickly ... almost thankfully. Just as she died she whispered, "How does he know? – can't know: never told him, no-one told him; couldn't be him! Sheer madness ..." Her words meant nothing to Sarah then and had little more significance now ... Dorothea may have been dreaming – unaware of Sarah's presence – but the phrases did imply that Sarah's current reasoning, although disturbing, was on the right track! However impossible she found it to accept, she was forced to question her own obstinacy ... Einstein's theories were meaningful to scientists. Jay probably saw in them a profound truth! He would no doubt have scoffed at the idea of ghosts, which she accepted as normal facts of life! Perhaps they were both right within their own experience.

Drifting to sleep at last, Sarah knew she had to discover what happened on Dorothea's last visit to her husband. What did she see or hear which convinced her that he was beyond all hope?

***

At Riverbank Irma was lying awake. The arrival of Cousin Jack had been a shock even though she had quite expected Margaret's family to check her out eventually. Because it had taken them a few months to get around to it she had been lulled into a false sense of security. It was lucky she knew something about his mother, Helen. She had better concentrate her thoughts in case another inquisitive relative dropped in! But how could he not re-assure them all that her powers were genuine? He'd certainly looked impressed – especially with that bit about the dog! One of the others might also want a private show, after that brilliant performance!

Unable to sleep, Irma planned her next séance. They had become a regular feature at the end of the day. Sitting in the glow of the firelight, Irma described, and communicated with, the procession of ghosts from Margaret's past which paraded through her sitting room. Just as masques in the middle ages were complimentary offerings to princes, Irma presented Margaret with vibrant processions of scenes from her childhood. Of course, on some nights, the place was less crowded than others ... it wasn't easy to dredge up new facts, but now completely hooked, Margaret was ecstatically happy with comparatively little. Irma's mother had been readily satisfied too. With a little initiative she could have been on easy street – set up for life. The meagre income which had seemed sufficient before Irma's birth was ludicrously inadequate by the time she started school. Even had it been index-linked to the inflation rate it still wouldn't have been anywhere near enough. It wouldn't have paid for her to go to a private school, like Margaret, but it would have provided a few of the extras her friends enjoyed and her silly mother could easily have changed things.

It made Irma furious to think of her stupidity. She didn't have to wonder how her mother would regard her present actions ... she'd have been horrified, but she had only herself to blame! Well aware of Irma's frustrations and the resentment against fate the child had bottled up for years, she often voiced fears for her daughter's future happiness. With her dying breath she pleaded with Irma to accept the situation and count her blessings, but things were different now. Irma fully intended to have her fair slice of the pie!

***

Margaret's sleep was deep and dreamless although she too had found it difficult to drift off as quickly as usual. Half forgotten memories, revived by Irma, loomed and became lucent as she probed back through the intervening years. In 1960, when her mother died, she had been thirty-eight, fifteen years married and living in Stratford-upon-Avon. Martin was marvellous: generous and so considerate. She couldn't think why she had not been head over heels in love with him from the first! She wouldn't have married him had she not been extremely fond of him but at the time she was more eager to leave her mother's home than set up one of her own. Fortunately, love grew steadily as the passing years revealed his fine qualities.

Life at her Grandfather's had been blissful before he died. She remembered the last holiday before his death very well. She returned from school for the summer of 1934, just after the terrible fire which destroyed most of the library, and helped to clear up the mess. Jack was there too with his little twin sisters who were about six-years-old. It was a shame they never knew their Grandmother as she had. Ermintrude had died years before. Had she guessed then, that her parents intended to sell the family home she would have been devastated. Returning between school terms was all she lived for – she hated being away.

She had a circle of young friends, enjoyed tennis, theatre visits and parties and looked forward to a glowing future. Her generous allowance enabled her to indulge in the latest fashions and though not a raving beauty in her early teens, she was not short of boy friends. Individual dating wasn't permitted in those days but her admirers were all tolerated by her father. It was funny really ... she would have expected him to shield her jealously – he had always been more of a companion to her than a father figure. He spent months at a time away from home but her mother renewed contact with an old school friend, after whom Margaret was named, and was not short of companionship. She appeared not to resent his absence...

Aunt Meg's appearance in their lives was the beginning of the end for Margaret. She was a hard woman who frowned on anything which made life more comfortable – or as she would put it, decadent. There were few parties during her visits and callers were made to feel less welcome. It probably wasn't all that much of a shock when her parents decided to sell the property and go their separate ways. He and Meg were barely civil to each other and Margaret could never understand why her mother did not take his side more often when Meg criticised him. Wiser now, she suspected he was an unfaithful husband ... how could a child ever really know what happened between parents?

Her father had allowed them to keep all the furniture which would fit into their new, smaller abode, a five-bedroom town house in Chester ... three stories high in a quiet, tree lined road. The houses, set back behind tiny gardens, had paved yards at the rear where some owners built garages along a service road. After the spaciousness of the family estate it was almost claustrophobic and Margaret did not seem able to get away from her mother and Meg, who moved in with them permanently. The two rooms allotted to Margaret were on the top floor ... she could move neither in nor out, or entertain friends without running the gauntlet of scrutiny. It was no wonder she accepted Martin's marriage proposal.

He was extremely eligible and at twenty-three she was beginning to feel that her chances of meeting anyone more pleasing to her were small. He wooed her in the rather aloof style of the age – brought her chocolates and flowers of course, but not until they were married did she realise the depth of his passion. He was aware that her feelings for him were not as strong and was patient and gentle with her until, somewhat to her own surprise, she fell deeply in love with him.

If they had been blessed with children their marriage could have been no happier, but the existence of a family might have made his death easier to bear ... without Jean's support she would never have managed to carry on. Thinking of Jean's death made her wonder again why Irma had never contacted her dear friend during their nightly sessions. It was such a shame; those long-dead seemed anxious to 'come through' – yet Martin, and Jean who had died more recently and were even closer to her, kept away.

As sleep claimed her at last, Margaret made up her mind to ask Irma if there was anything they could do to encourage Martin to make contact ... Dear Martin; perhaps he watched, nightly – as eager to come to her as she was to be with him again. She knew Irma would help them if she could ... what a good person she was and what a lucky day it had been when Irma walked into her life ... what a very lucky day!

Chapter Thirteen

Sunday April 19th...

Clarrie, unaware of her mother's almost insoluble dilemma and Polly's deepening involvement with Elaine's family affairs, had already set up her easel, folding stool and workbox and was waiting in the warmth of her car for the sky to brighten a little. The morning was more freezingly foggy than romantically misty ... it almost obscured the gaunt dark house. There was no point in moving until it lifted – she might as well be comfortable. Her drifting thoughts were never far from Del. Last July, his parents had welcomed her to their home in Spain, although her sudden appearance in their son's life must have been as much a surprise to them as his posting to the Middle East – a Special Correspondent.

Del's father, George Delaney, met them at Alicante airport. He was almost as tall as Del, a little portly but she had expected him, at sixty-five, to look older. His grey hair had not thinned noticeably and his tan was attractive – not heavy enough to make him look like a crop-picker. As he shook her hand formally and she met his eyes – so like his son's they unnerved her – Clarrie knew he was a man of instant decisions. He already either liked or disliked her. Most of his working life had been spent abroad, in Shipping and, like many others she was to meet in this cosmopolitan corner of Valencia Province, he was so used to warmer climes that he would have found it impossible to settle in his homeland.

She insisted that Del should take the front passenger seat and settled into the rear of the car while the two men loaded the suitcases. Their conversation was personal; she tried not to listen, but as soon as they joined her, apart from a joking reference to a friend whose luggage always went astray, they talked of how little Spain appeared to change from year to year. Behind the scenes, many things were happening. More people were at long last on the telephone, potable water came from more taps, the electricity supply was more reliable, communication cables were not struck by lightning *every* time there was a storm ...all extremely important but, deep down, Spain was still the same and they loved it.

Although listening with interest, Clarrie was unable to contribute. She had time to absorb the atmosphere as they headed north in air-conditioned comfort through the tropically hot, burnished world. Distant mountains inland, to westward, were distinctly etched in purple layers against the azure, cloudless sky as though cut from a travel brochure. The sea was often in view on their right and as the road curved to hug the bays, it changed in hue constantly, from silver to deep turquoise.

A few fincas, some ruined, some still working farms, were scattered over the landscape; clusters of habitation increased in size as the hills swept down towards them, the lower slopes dropping sometimes below the level of the road. Extensive areas were carved into flat cultivated terraces; pale stone walls draped the hillsides like contour lines, holding back rich red-gold earth where the neatly pruned vines would soon be heavy with grapes. Almond groves and fields of citrus fruit patterned the countryside like well regimented armies clad in dark green; everything glowed in the afternoon sun.

The dreary Welsh fog was painfully slow in lifting – the foliage still hung limp with clinging dampness. The dark mass of the house still looked forbidding; it needed at least a hint of warmth to banish the gloom. Gazing at the dismal scene now, Clarrie wondered why she had never ventured to Spain before; it was an artist's paradise!

Her lunch box was on the passenger seat within reach so at least she didn't have to leave the car to treat herself to some hot coffee. As she sipped it slowly, she re-lived her holiday and the drive with Del and his father to their home in Jávea from Alicante airport. They stayed on the coast road in preference to the motorway. George – he insisted on the familiarity, said they could still by-pass Benidorm and it would give Clarrie a better impression of the Costa Blanca; he understood this was her first visit.

"I already feel overwhelmed by everything," Clarrie proclaimed. "Of course, I have seen it in photographs and films, but had no idea… Is the whole of Spain as fantastic as this?"

"Well, I can't claim to have seen even a tenth of it. Retirement isn't all it's cracked up to be – we never seem able to take time off." He laughed, obviously pleased that she was impressed. "When we first came to live here it was our intention to go away for weekends to explore our own region, and to holiday at least once a year in another Province, but we've never managed it. I sometimes feel as if I'm as fully occupied as I ever was, it isn't easy to get away, but at least life here is not dull!"

Although Del said his parents expected her to stay on, to paint, after he left to take up his post, Clarrie had not presumed to take any equipment with her. She wanted to make it easy for them to accept her decision, should she decide that it would be more tactful to return home. If she arrived looking set for a painting holiday it might be awkward all round. Her departure without doing any work might offend them – it would look as though she wanted to get away. On the other hand – they might feel trapped into urging her to stay!

As if reading her mind, George said, "I hope you haven't changed your mind about painting while you're with us. I saw no easel or anything."

"I didn't actually bring any gear at all," Clarrie confessed, "but when inspiration seizes me, I expect I'll be able to buy materials. This area must be crammed with artists."

The coast road along the sparkling blue Mediterranean took them through many small towns. Pueblos and exclusive villas shared a pleasing uniformity as their whitewashed walls reflected the sun's brightness; rust brown, dark-red Roman roof tiles absorbed its warmth. Inside the thick stone walls it was probably dark and cool. Within the separate communities individual life-styles might be widely different, but the inhabitants must inevitably be closely bound and inter-dependent. George said that the friendly rivalry between villages was apparent at fiesta time when they contributed teams to each other's parades and vied for acclaim in firework displays.

When they passed through Altea, where the traffic became more congested, Clarrie had time to register a few Art Galleries and Del promised to bring her back for a day's browsing. Less than an hour later they arrived at the villa and Del's mother hurried out to meet them. Without any hesitation Grace drew Clarrie to her and kissed her on both cheeks. "As Del likes you, I'm sure we will too, welcome to our home."

The gravel drive encircling the villa was itself surrounded by rockeries, flowering shrubs and trees. It wound past a high stone wall, which enclosed the garden and George drove to the end of the building. There was a double garage under the house so that the living area was elevated and a short flight of steps led up to the front door. Inside, because the villa was on the lower slope of the mountain, every window on three sides looked out to distant views. The few windows facing north overlooked the driveway and the mountain which, dotted with trees and almond groves, appeared to be very close.

Clarrie's bedroom was on an upper floor overlooking the swimming pool and the valley through which they had just driven. Several villages were visibly joined by a web of roads. Roofs and windows sparkled in the sunshine making them look like jewels on silver chains. Later during her stay they explored them all ... and she had been enchanted. In that quiet moment she had decided she liked Del's parents who seemed equally willing to accept her ... and it proved to be a fantastic holiday.

The incredibly exotic parades she saw were icing on the cake – even without them there was so much to do and see; there always seems to be a fiesta somewhere in Spain, Grace informed her. There was finally no doubt that she and George approved of Clarrie unreservedly and before she left they urged her to come at any time whether Del could accompany her or not. Memories of those few weeks had sustained Clarrie through the autumn and the coldness of winter, but she relived that last night before Del's departure with a mixture of exultation and pain.

They had been driving high up in the Bernia Mountains all day, breathing the heavy fragrance of wild herbs and vines. Against a background of live guitar music in a tiny restaurant that, despite its remoteness was crowded with diners, they ate paella. According to Del it had never tasted better but the pressure of his hand on her arm as they left, told her that it was her own presence that made it so special. Clarrie would never forget that wonderful night.

The next morning they stopped at a bodega in the Jalon valley to buy a few litres of wine to add to George's stock. Clarrie stood beside the towering vats, in the cool, dark interior of the 'Co-operative', while Del made his selection from a tasting tray. Lifting the glass jug high above his head, he allowed the wine to fall in a narrow stream from the long spout into his open mouth ... it was an impressive display; she was amused, knowing he was showing off for her benefit! It was Rastro market day in the village so parking would have been impossible if Del had not been a favoured customer – allowed to drive into the Bodega's private car park.

Taking advantage of their luck, they wandered around the hundreds of brimming stalls, astonished by the wide variety of goods on sale. Clarrie had always loved antiques and it was difficult to tear herself away but not everything on the stalls was old so, in addition to a few bits of costume jewellery and a couple of old picture frames, Clarrie managed to buy several pairs of new shoes and handbags to match.

Del teased her unmercifully and encouraged her to buy more... "You'll never be able to take all this gear with you on one flight – you'll have to come to Spain again to collect it!" They were both quiet as they drove away. His remark had reminded them that Del was due to leave on an early flight the following day. When they returned, his parents had already left home to dine with friends; they appreciated that Del and Clarrie would wish to be alone on their last night together. After freshening up, Del finished cooking the meal, which Grace had prepared for them, and they ate outside – on the patio beside the pool. The sun took a long time to set. It was hot and humid ... they alternately lounged and swam as the sky became tinged with salmon pink, deepened to golden red – to purple and eventually became dark velvet.

With the pool and terrace lights isolating them in their own sylvan world they lay on warm dry towels ... no need for words. What was there to say? Lying in his tight embrace, Clarrie knew that he sensed her unspoken fears. She couldn't forget how soon they would be parted and the knowledge gripped her, she was unable to conceal her misery. She didn't doubt their feelings, but separation would bring pain enough; the more their intimacy grew, the more difficult it would be to live without him.

Perhaps she had been cowardly refusing to marry until he returned. Enfolded in his strong arms – Clarrie was sure she could trust

Del to remain committed to her, so why had she hesitated to fix a wedding date? They had met and fallen in love in so short a time – within days – but that didn't worry her. They were not wide-eyed adolescents, caught up in their first wild romantic encounter, they were mature adults

Now, staring into the rising mist, she acknowledged another reason for her reluctance to take that final step and knew it had been wise. Del's latest assignment had taken him to one of the world's trouble spots. God forbid that anything should happen to him – that she would lose him, as she had lost Tom. It would be impossible to survive another such tragedy. He had no doubts about her love for him and was willing to postpone marriage until the lonely months ahead were over, but he had left Clarrie in no doubt that leaving her as his bride would have caused no greater emptiness.

Clarrie sighed and climbed out of the car ... the sooner she started painting the better ... the early evocative mist, for which she had been waiting as the earth warmed, would evaporate quickly when the sun strengthened. Always an optimist, she wondered if there would be a letter waiting for her, when she returned home ... she would ring up, mid-week to find out.

***

At eight-thirty, after a good night's sleep, Polly went downstairs for breakfast refreshed and looking forward eagerly to another day out. She arrived at the kitchen door in time to hear Elaine say enthusiastically, "Your Aunt seems to be getting on like a house on fire with Uncle Jack ... they are about the same age, aren't they? And they are both alone. Wouldn't it be marvellous if ...?"

"Hold your horses, young lady!" Polly interrupted, "Don't be tempted to try your hand at matchmaking! If your uncle had been interested in a wife he would have found one by now – and I am certainly not lonely!"

Elaine flushed with embarrassment and Dan put his arm round her to give her a hug... "Because marriage suits you, my love, don't think every woman wants to be hitched!"

She smiled gratefully and began to apologise but Polly forestalled her. "I have nothing against marriage," she said, "it is certainly better than the modern alternative which seems to me to be the worst of both worlds for a woman! All the responsibility of coping with a house, a lover and possibly children without the security of knowing that her partner has enough faith, confidence and sincerity to make a firm commitment!"

Dan laughed. "You are just incredibly old-fashioned! I wanted to stake my claim on Elaine – no way was she wriggling out of my clutches without a fight ... but I can understand why it doesn't suit everybody."

Polly allowed that he might be right but at her age she wasn't wasting time worrying about it.

Jack arrived promptly and looked pleasurably surprised to find Polly ready and waiting. To the young couple's amusement and Polly's evident discomfiture he said it was a pleasure to find a lady who didn't keep her date waiting while powdering her nose! Because his remark had disconcerted her, Polly was a little distant with him for the first few minutes of their drive but, as he seemed not to notice, she soon relaxed.

He said he had been very late to bed after leaving her last night because he decided to go through a couple of trunks which had been stored in the attic since his mother died in 1970. Nine years later, when his father also died, he sold his apartment and took over his parents' house. He had done so because it would have been daunting to sort through the contents in haste. As there was no need to rush, he was enjoying discovering again, items he'd known as a child and long forgotten. Eventually he meant to sell up and move to a smaller place.

His search had been worth while, because he unearthed several forgotten photographs and he was eager to discuss them. "I came across some that would be well worth framing," he said, "but very few were old – only one has any bearing on our investigation."

He asked her to lift it from the glove compartment and his eyes left the road briefly to relish her look of delight. It was a sepia snap of a spaniel in a dog basket. Polly turned to him in astonishment. "Good Heavens! ... Don't tell me this is the night-dress case? It looks so real." Then she turned it over, read *'Dear little Chaz – on my birthday'* ... and laughed with glee. "I think we've got her! But we can't just show Margaret this ... she will need much more convincing after all the other things Irma has told her."

***

When the taxi arrived in the morning, Sarah and Amy were pleased to find that Eric was their driver again. He knew about the tragedy as, most likely, did everyone else in the county, and fussed anxiously as he settled them in the car. He lived near and said if there was anything he could do, Amy had only to tell Nettie who was his wife's friend.

He drove sedately, at an unnecessarily funereal pace and they began to fear they would be late for their appointment, but Dr. Ellis welcomed them into his office with a smile. He understood why Amy, although she had never visited before, should now feel responsible for Mr Johnson but had to admit that the hospital was merely looking after his physical well-being having long ago given up hope of a cure for his mind. Amy explained, as previously agreed, that her friend Mrs Grey was a Spiritualist Medium who would also like to see her father-in-law. It couldn't do any harm and personally, as a firm believer in faith healing, she thought it might help. Sarah said she realised it was an unusual step ...

purely experimental and hoped the doctor himself could spare the time to be present.

Not only did Dr. Ellis agree to their proposition, he was quite excited by it, and lost no time in winding up his present tasks. His secretary brought them coffee while he made a few internal calls and he was soon locking away his papers, standing purposefully, and inviting them to accompany him. Amy's cup rattled in the saucer as she returned it to the table – an indication of her nervousness. She was about to confront a man, a complete stranger, to whom she was completely unknown, even in his right mind. In his present state, he was probably harmless, but if Sarah succeeded in restoring to his memory the sight of her with Jay, which caused his stroke, how would he react? In spite of passing years, the night of his collapse was burned into her memory. On wakeful nights she still heard his accusing cries and felt incredibly guilty – yet how could his illness be her fault? It couldn't ... but as she followed Dr. Ellis and Sarah down the long echoing corridors, Amy was almost sick with apprehension.

Chapter Fourteen

As they made their way to the 'long-stay' wing, where Jay's father lived out each day in mental isolation, Dr. Ellis spoke in a low voice to Sarah. He was surprisingly willing to discuss his findings. "Under normal circumstances I would never discuss a patient," he told her. He paused to be sure his point was taken ... "But he has no living blood relatives and as I know you are motivated only by his best interests I feel justified in treating you as I would a fellow consultant." He nodded condescendingly. "There are many aspects of this case which, I must admit, have puzzled me greatly since I came here six years ago. Careful study of copious reports has brought me no nearer to understanding his problem or what caused his mental block."

He went on to say that neurological tests revealed no abnormalities in his brain and his lack of physical fitness was due entirely to his own total disinterest in survival. His own first treatment had involved hypnotherapy but Mr Johnson was a most unusual subject. The results were inconclusive and in every way unsatisfactory. It was as though an impenetrable barrier had fallen over his entire childhood. He rarely spoke at all, let alone held rational conversations.

"From his wife, we know they met during the last year of the war," he informed Sarah. "As you probably know, she was a voluntary nurse in the local hospital where he was taken for treatment." They were on the point of entering a small ante room where several easy chairs were grouped round a coffee table. Seeing the looks of bewilderment they exchanged, he indicated that they should sit, nodded briefly and continued.

"Mr Johnson was declared to be suffering from amnesia and although he soon began to function normally, his early memories were gone. He was found wandering after an air raid – it was assumed that he had been bombed out of his home. He carried a few personal items and identification papers – probably grabbed as he fled; during the war people usually kept such things at hand in case of emergency – without them he could not recall either his name or where he lived. The authorities later informed him that his mother had been killed in the air raid but he had no memory at all of that night. In fact he remembered nothing before the explosion which left him partially deaf, but at least he was communicative then." Amy eyed Sarah with suspicion. She could scarcely credit that Dorothea had never discussed such a dramatic and quite romantic encounter with her ... she had clearly told the doctor.

He continued, unaware of the effect his words were having on both his listeners, for very different reasons. "Mrs Johnson described how for several weeks he drifted in and out of consciousness. She was one of those who sat constantly at his bedside to talk to him if he woke – ready to ring for the nurse. They were all intrigued by him because the first time he came round he flatly refused to believe the war was still in progress." With a wry smile the doctor added, "He said it should be over and even accused them of joking!"

Sarah felt the sickly churn of her stomach that was becoming all too familiar. Again she sensed that she was missing something strange and ominous ... failing to grasp a truth she would rather reject. She concentrated on Dr. Ellis's words ... she must keep an open mind. It was not after all her personal conception of truth that mattered; it was more relevant to determine what John senior believed, then and now.

Dr. Ellis shook his head at the notion; after five and a half years of war people didn't joke about it! He took up Dorothea's story again ... "Apparently he rambled on for days, insisting he was at fault; the war should have been over months ago, he must have done something wrong! He lapsed into unconsciousness between these brief periods. When he eventually became more sensible he was as amused as everyone else at his silly presumption – his fault indeed! But his memory did not come back." Amy's amazement at Dorothea's silence on the subject was shared by Sarah. It was an astonishing story but, loving John as she did, she could have been afraid that a return of memory would come between them and preferred to bury the past.

Sarah wondered if the cause of Dorothea's distress was rooted in that period of their lives; but how could it matter after nearly half a century? Unless it only became significant in the light of a current event: perhaps something she discovered during her final visit to him. With this in mind Sarah asked, "When his wife came here just before she died, did anything happen to alarm her? Was she able to speak to him at last?"

Dr. Ellis re-affirmed that Dorothea had never been able even to approach her husband but otherwise, although still remote, he had definitely become more aware of his surroundings during the past few months and they were reviewing their treatment. Because his wife could see for herself the improvement in his demeanour, they persuaded her to withdraw her earlier objections to resuming deep hypnosis. He then confirmed Sarah's private conjecture. He suspected that Mrs Johnson was reluctant to confront any of his previously lost memories, but there seemed no other way of treating him. At first they were encouraged. When interrogated about his marriage he responded normally until they discussed his middle years. He then became abstruse. His answers, given with equal confidence to similar questions put to him within minutes, were contradictory ... in one breath he would speak adoringly of his wife and in the next, display total hostility towards her – verging on antipathy.

Seeking an explanation, his mind was regressed to his childhood, and the results were so puzzling that Dr. Ellis discussed the recordings with Mrs Johnson. John was confused when they spoke of his wife – he said Amy sickened him he didn't want to discuss her. He also insisted he hadn't even been alive during the war. The doctor suddenly displayed acute embarrassment, remembering it was Amy, John's daughter-in-law, to whom he was speaking! Continuing hastily, he admitted that in spite of his tactful handling, it was this disclosure which had a devastating effect on Dorothea. "If only his records had been less sketchy – and updated after his son married..." He paused and passed a hand over his brow in embarrassment. "We had assumed that Amy was his first wife and it was only to be expected that his second would resent being forgotten by him – but we realised it was far more complicated than that, when she informed us that Amy was their daughter-in-law!"

Amy's jaw had fallen slackly into the folds of her chin and Sarah felt so numb with trepidation she could hardly follow what the doctor was trying to explain ... his voice sounded so far away. "Thinking to shock him out of his delusion – unknown to his wife – we allowed him to see her before she left that day, without being seen. His animated reaction excited me until I heard him say 'mother'! From other things he also said, as he watched her, it was obvious he was totally deranged: he thought he was his own son!

***

It was a pleasant drive through Woodstock along the Stratford road. Jack drove very slowly past places of particular interest such as Rolright Stones, eventually branching off to Compton Wynyates. They could have driven more directly through Banbury, but Jack said he never voluntarily covered the same ground twice; they could return that way and if the weather deteriorated at least they would have enjoyed the more open countryside in sunshine. Polly was appreciative of all his efforts to entertain her and the journey passed very quickly. She felt stirrings of excited anticipation as they neared Edgehill.

Emma Heywood, very much an older version of her niece Ethel, welcomed them to her home. It was modest in size but centred in an extensive garden which Polly admired. The old lady said the credit must go to a friend who had a small horticultural business – apart from a little weeding she did nothing. There was far too much work to tackle alone.

"I couldn't afford it if he didn't give me special rates," Emma said, "I'd have to sell off a building plot and have neighbours breathing down my neck, but you can't let a garden go, can you – especially when there are the lawns!" She took them through her living room into the sun lounge, a built-on addition at the back of the house. Although only eleven-o-clock it was comfortably warm there. The profusion of potted plants was obviously a source of great pride and now that she was unable to do much outside, Emma tended them lovingly. The kettle was already on the boil and she allowed Polly to help by scalding the tea and carrying the tray. She said she suffered from arthritis which made her nervous with her good china. Polly followed, as Emma led the way slowly from the kitchen holding the doors for her.

In spite of her ailment she was no invalid and made it clear that she had been looking forward to their visit ... it was no trouble at all. She had dressed for the occasion in a maroon crepe dress which flowed around her small wiry figure as she moved. The long bishop sleeves and high folded neckline which concealed her throat were flattering and offset the severe cut of her silver hair.

When they described their visit to Barr's Brook and the confrontation with Margaret and Irma at Riverbank, Emma listened intently without interrupting. Jack left out the last and most interesting item about the dog ... he and Polly first wanted to ask her if she had any old family albums herself. She rose painfully saying that she had, but would have to ask Jack to get them out for her; they were packed in a box which was with others under her bed ... it might take a while to find them! She placed a pile of magazines on a small footstool to occupy Polly while she waited for their return.

In the small bedroom, crammed with furniture, Jack crawled on his knees and groped under the high old-fashioned bed for the treasures hidden beneath it. As one box after another came to light, between apologizing for the dust – her home-help never had time for everything she would like done – Emma announced what each one contained. There was an astonishing variety of items hoarded away, from an ancient knitting machine to insurance papers, old account books and letters.

At last, when Jack estimated that he had removed at least three-quarters of the solid mass of boxes, Emma declared the search over. Sure enough, there was a neat inscription on the torn lid of a battered cardboard carton ... *'PHOTOGRAPHS AND POSTCARDS'*.

As all the other items were returned to hiding, Emma said cheerfully to her distinctly dishevelled nephew, "At least you'll know where everything is when you come to sort things out – after I'm dead and gone!"

"Just don't make it too soon then," Jack puffed, "I couldn't face that again in the foreseeable future!"

The three of them were soon going through the contents of the box. When Emma had wiped it over with a damp cloth Polly noted that the knotted twine which tied it was fibrous and old ... from whatever source Irma had derived information, it was unlikely to have been here. As they searched, Emma chattered about the old days, exclaiming with pleasure as she was reminded of her childhood.

"I'm so thrilled to have these out again," she said happily. "I've thought about them often but could never reach them myself and there aren't many men I would allow in my bedroom these days!" Emma gave

Polly a broad wink which hinted that, although an old maid, she had had her moments! "Are we looking for anything in particular, by the way?"

"We hope to find a few interior shots showing furniture that Margaret still has – or outside views showing the pergola." Jack told her. "Also, of course, any photographs of your parents or sisters which we could show Margaret to prove she is being duped. She thinks all her family records were destroyed."

Emma shuddered, remembering the fire. "It was awful. A window in the library was left wide open one evening and an oil lamp blew over. Before it was put out the blaze destroyed a whole wall full of books." She shook her head sadly as she explained. "It was my father's fault, if anybody's – the maid shut the window before leaving to visit another domestic on an adjacent property and he opened it again himself – it was a warm evening. He was tired and having left the room for some reason he forgot to go back and close it before going to bed."

Polly asked if there was any doubt about the fire being accidental and Emma assured her that there was not. She said it was the same maid who raised the alarm at eleven-o-clock that night... "But for her, the whole house might have been gutted and all of us burned to death in our beds! The girls saw the flames from her friend's attic room a quarter of a mile away. The other maid telephoned for help while ours ran back screaming to wake everybody up."

Polly and Jack asked when the fire had occurred and were told that it was only a year or two after Margaret went away to school. "In fact," Emma said, "it was about a week before she returned for the summer holiday in nineteen-thirty-four." She smiled at their astonishment that she should be so precise ... "It was a traumatic year for me – my thirtieth – and Sophie, who was within two years of forty teased me a lot because I kept bemoaning my lost youth. There were other good reasons too for remembering that particular year," she added enigmatically.

As Jack and Polly looked with increasing interest at the fading images of the Heywood clan, having no idea what specific information they sought, they encouraged Emma to say anything that came to mind about the old days and she happily recounted their history. She began with a brief outline of her parents' situation.

Basil Heywood, a family friend and local property owner also managed the estate for young Ermintrude's widowed mother. That was how they came to know each other and marry. She was an only child, and sole heir, so Basil eventually controlled everything. He did it so skilfully that he could soon afford to retire and still live well. They were always considerate towards each other and certainly never had a difference of opinion in public. Emma believed their marriage to be perfect in every way.

"Father was generous to his family but on the mean side with the wages he paid to the servants," Emma admitted. "They probably stayed because although their pay was low, work clothes were provided, they lived well and were treated like human beings ... they could have done a lot worse!" Apparently Basil actually employed more people than they really needed ... he never turned away anyone in need and many people were seeking work after the Great War.

Emma's sister Sophie, Margaret's mother, married a month before her twenty-ninth birthday in nineteen-twenty, to a man so much younger than herself that her parents were horrified. Even so, Ermintrude and Basil wanted grand-children and as Sophie was considerably older than all her unmarried friends they accepted her choice with a minimum of real opposition.

Howard Francis Drake was only eighteen – five years younger even than Jack's mother, Helen, who first introduced him to the family. He was among those of her friends who often came for tennis. After Helen became of age – twenty-one in those days – she left home against her father's wishes to train as a teacher but Howard and some of the younger crowd continued to play tennis with Sophie and Emma – who was after all, nearer his age! Emma said Howard may originally have set his cap at Helen but within a year of leaving home she married William Hall so he probably decided to court Sophie.

Because their mother was in poor health, Sophie gradually took over management of the household so her father couldn't risk alienating her too. Helen and William attended Sophie's wedding – she was matron of honour – but rarely came to visit until Jack was born. Basil was so thrilled to have a grandson that the family holiday became an annual event although, because of his business, William usually stayed for only a few nights at each end of it.

Sixteen-year-old Emma was Sophie's bridesmaid and confessed to never having liked Howard. His married sister was in her own home so he sold his parents' house and moved in with the Heywood family. Emma scorned his lack of interest in earning his own money ... but supposed he did help her father by managing the outside staff. She stayed out of his way as much as possible. She thought him prissy and hated the way he was always fussing ... putting an arm around her, coming the big brother, or even pecking her on the cheek at the slightest excuse.

"I was pretty naive but I knew there was no real harm in him. He was just spineless – a big kid!" Emma flushed – looked embarrassed and then continued hastily, making Polly wonder if she could be shielding him or hiding a personal indiscretion. Emma said she endured the situation for her mother's sake until she died at the end of nineteen twenty-nine... It was then Emma's turn to fight father.

At twenty-five she loved writing – she'd had many articles published locally – and wanted to leave home to join a newspaper in

Warwick. A girl-friend already employed there arranged an interview for her and invited Emma to stay with her family as a paying guest. Her father was furious and when, in the heat of the moment, she was driven to say she couldn't stand Howard, he was even more incensed. He accused her of trying to make trouble between Sophie and her husband. Margaret was seven-years-old then and when she wasn't having lessons Emma had always been available to keep an eye on her. She was considered too old to need a nurse, so Emma's departure inconvenienced everyone! When she refused to stay, an extra housemaid was taken on – a young girl of sixteen. It was expected that eventually, as Margaret needed less attention, the girl would be given more household duties.

Polly and Jack immediately questioned Emma about the girl ... was her name Olive? They explained that according to Irma, Olive's ghost often dropped in at Riverbank! Emma thought the name sounded familiar, but hadn't met her until the following summer and didn't have much to do with her. It was a long time ago; she couldn't be sure, but thought the girl was tall and dark. It matched Irma's description of Olive, so Polly asked if Emma had ever seen the maid on family snaps. Emma was certain she hadn't. Margaret and the girl may have had pictures taken together but she thought it unlikely, because camera's were not household gadgets in those days – one usually arranged for a photographer to call ... neither Basil nor Sophie would have requested a portrait of one of the staff!

"I have a hazy idea that Margaret had a Brownie box camera ..." Emma frowned thoughtfully, "although that was later, after they moved to Chester. Of course, that doesn't rule out the possibility that the maid had access to a camera but the photograph would hardly have ended up in the Heywood collection, would it!"

"So, if such a picture exists," said Jack, "it was not through the family but via Olive that it reached Irma but how on earth could she have seen all these others? Margaret hasn't got copies."

In front of him, he had assembled a stack of photographs which depicted Margaret's ghostly visitors over a period of thirty years. While Polly scribbled her notes Emma named everyone and separated them into two piles – before and after the fire. There were no formal studies taken at home after their parents died ... no casual interior snaps and none of the pergola or the distant view, so only those taken earlier were relevant at the moment. All except one were of close family members.

Emma picked up a magnifying glass and stared at the tall heavy-set woman standing with Sophie on the tennis court, and then announced that she was *almost* family! It was an older school friend of Sophie's who had fallen on hard times at the beginning of the Great War – Emma was then about ten and Helen still at home. "Meg was an excellent needlewoman and painted beautiful water colours, so father offered her room and board in exchange for instructing the three of us: mama too."

Emma couldn't recall her surname but said Margaret was named after her. Jack suggested that Meg might have had photographs which Irma acquired – the connection might not after all be Olive, but Emma said it was extremely doubtful. "See how she's frowning – and she doesn't appear on any of the others. She hated having her picture taken and didn't approve of cameras. She made a big thing of painting scenes and people: so much more artistic!"

What happened to her? Who might have inherited from her? After all, even though more interested in art she may have had snaps of other people, if not herself! Questions tumbled from Jack. He could not recall either meeting or even having heard of Meg.

"I think Sophie fell out with her – before you were born. Meg couldn't stand Howard! Perhaps that was it. Anyway Meg definitely left before the wedding!" Emma raised one eyebrow, obviously in sympathy with Meg's point of view. "She dropped out of our lives until the house was sold in Coronation year, a year or so after father died. Margaret was about fourteen, and Howard at last got his hands on some real money." Her derisive snort expressed her opinion. "When Margaret was little he was a good father, I admit, but after she went to boarding school he spent weeks away from home. Father continued his generous allowance and did nothing to stop him. Sophie didn't seem to care either."

"What about Meg? You were about to tell us," reminded Polly.

"Oh yes – that's what I was going say. Sophie used her portion of the sale money to buy a house in Chester and Meg was still on her own so she moved in with her for company ... so whatever their differences, they never lost touch." Emma sniffed and hesitated before adding, "Meg died a year before Sophie. She had no relatives, so everything she had must have gone to Sophie and then to Margaret. If she had albums I expect you have already seen them at Riverbank."

It was a dead end but both Jack and Polly were convinced they were on the right track. They could safely assume that the fire had not destroyed the old albums entirely. Somewhere there had to be duplicates of the photographs they were examining. Many of them actually did show several pieces of furniture which still stood in Margaret's home. Emma said she was gratified if her collection had solved their problem.

"Some of the mystery is possibly explained," Polly agreed. "We will presume that at least part of Sophie's collection survived the fire, even though Margaret never set eyes on it ... but Irma knows far more than mere pictures could tell her. Olive the housemaid is the most likely link between Margaret and Irma so until their connection can established and we come up with a plausible reason for her elaborate hoax we'll have to keep a close eye on Irma ..." Her voice trailed away. She was dismayed by the near impossibility of protecting Margaret, when she was so willing to be duped. But before approaching her they would need more than unsubstantiated suspicion. They must go carefully, making quite sure they were justified. There was no need for impetuosity – after all, Irma was obviously intent on monetary gain not murder!

The stab of alarm which accompanied the mere thought of violence made Polly wonder if she was perhaps overrating her own ability to cope ... but in any case there was no urgency; she wouldn't bother Sarah with the problem just yet, but had every intention of doing so. It might have been vanity which got her into this, but at this juncture pride wouldn't have stopped her from asking Sarah's advice, had she been free to help.

Catching Jack's eye, Polly's confidence returned...

Together, they could cope with anything – even Irma!

Chapter Fifteen

In view of what Sarah told him of Dorothea's rapid decline, Dr. Ellis blamed himself for upsetting her, but protested that he was merely seeking to help his own patient. The doctor then took them down another bleak shiny corridor to one of several private wards. He adjusted the blind encased in the door's glass panel, allowing them to look in. Inside, John sat in an armchair near the window gazing down into the garden. Amy refused to enter the room until the doctor and Sarah paved the way so, leaving her outside to watch, they approached him. John looked up without the smallest spark of interest. Even when a chair was placed in front of him for Sarah, he merely turned his head to the window again.

The doctor moved from the old man's line of sight and after a few moments Sarah took both John's hands in her own and started to pray silently, her eyes closed in concentration. The sounds of hospital life could be heard faintly in the background but bird song from the eaves outside created an air of peace. Dr. Ellis, usually rushed off his feet – everyone demanding his attention – began to relax, unmindful of what was most likely a waste of time. Slowly, John turned to look at Sarah and to the doctor's complete astonishment whispered, "Who are you?" Sarah told him she was there to pray for him – he must tell her how she could help. Suddenly looking beyond her to a shadowy corner of the room he started to shake. Tears ran down his hollowed cheeks. "Why, my love ... Dorothea. Where have you been? Please don't leave me again."

Sarah was also aware of Dorothea's spirit presence – had indeed been hoping she would materialise, but not expected anyone other than herself to see her. Putting gentle pressure on his hands she said, "It was you John, who left Dorothea. She loves you very much and is waiting for you, on the other side. Your son loves you too – he has also gone before you, and will be there to help and guide you when your time comes."

With an anguished cry the old man rose unsteadily to his feet. "By God! No! Not my son. Has he gone? Then it's too late," he moaned. "We are both doomed." The doctor's initial delight in hearing his patient react normally, vanished. Seeing John so distraught – seeking to create a diversion, he went to fetch Amy while there was still a chance that John might also speak to her. It was a sad miscalculation. She walked in and stood shyly before her father-in-law ... a stranger – almost a myth to her – not knowing what to expect. His hands were pressed tightly to his eyes but hearing her footsteps he dropped them and saw her. He struggled to rise, shouting. "You, you bitch! You drove me to this. It's your fault! ... His demented screams rang after her as she fled from his room in tears.

Mai Griffin

***

Margaret and Irma had been to Church. Since Irma's arrival on the scene, Margaret's life had changed in many ways. Irma had a little car so she was taken out regularly. Ted's taxi was much more comfortable for long journeys but expensive to book for weekly shopping or Sunday Services. Jean used to ride her bicycle to the village store for small items, and used it to go to church, but Margaret's enthusiasm for worship didn't extend to such discomfort, even had she been twenty years younger! Irma pulled up in front of the house and helped Margaret out of the car. The seat was very low and the door so narrow, it was not an easy manoeuvre ... why, she wondered, should she not buy Irma a larger one? It was worth considering, if only to increase her own comfort! She actually voiced the thought as she straightened her skirt but Irma vetoed the idea flatly. She said she found it easy to drive and would be nervous in anything bigger.

While Irma closed the drive gates Margaret unlocked the front door and went straight upstairs to change. Irma had promised a roast beef lunch and she could smell it cooking. She felt a pang of guilt about requesting, when Irma first came to live with her, that they should not have so many sandwiches and salads. Jean had cooked at least once every day but Margaret admitted that she'd never produced such tasty meals as Irma.

Following Margaret into the house, Irma went to check the roast. The beef was cooked to perfection so she removed it to the warming drawer and turned up the oven heat. She spooned the top layer of fat from the roasting tin into the pudding tray, re-heating it prior to pouring on the Yorkshire batter which she had mixed before going to church. The potatoes were already parboiled and sealed with butter so she turned them quickly in the remaining fat and placed them on the top shelf. She put a light under the saucepan holding the cauliflower and draped a cover over the roasting tin with its thick rich juices – it would take only minutes to make the gravy later.

Irma surveyed the kitchen. She prided herself on her efficiency. Success in anything, she thought, was only a matter of good planning. Anyone else in her position would probably have leapt at Margaret's offer to buy her a car ... she had immediately seen not only that it would cause more consternation in the family than it was worth, but it was needless extravagance – she would only have to dispose of it later; second-hand cars seldom, if ever, fetched anything like their true value! The money was better left in the bank.

Things were going well. Today she had confided in the vicar her cherished dream of one day opening a home for the elderly. As a trained nurse, she knew how old people worried about being a burden on their families, but faced with the usual bleak nursing home they were often as reluctant to move into them as their relatives were to send them there! The Home she planned would be different – for people who were at least seventy-five percent mobile; it would be and look like a real home, not a hospital. Small: no more guests than she could care for personally – although she would have a resident nurse to help her; when she could afford it, she intended buying a property in his parish.

The vicar gave her his blessing and said if he were still the incumbent on that happy day, he would gladly call every week to conduct a service of prayer. He was sharp enough to ask if she was seeking donations and looked distinctly relieved when she said that she didn't think that would be ethical at this early stage ... she had nothing yet to show to any would-be investor.

It had been tricky, choosing exactly the right moment to approach him. She had waited for two weeks but this morning, as he stood at the church door, Irma saw that Margaret was near him speaking to Edna and her husband. Irma seized her chance and knew that Margaret could hear their conversation. It was now a question of waiting for her to broach the subject! As she too went up to change, Irma decided it would be a good time to re-open her correspondence with the bank. She was now firmly established as Margaret's companion – her future plan was unveiled and after lunch, while Margaret was resting, she would settle down with her typewriter and proceed to step three.

***

After Amy's screaming exit, Sarah waited anxiously until a male nurse arrived to help the doctor who was having difficulty restraining John, then she hurried to find her, to comfort her. She tried to make Amy understand that in spite of his final outburst their visit had been well worth while. Amy was terribly shocked but her embarrassment must be set against the positive effect of his suddenly seeing her. However hurtful, his words had at least been coherent! Amy was considerably calmer by the time Dr. Ellis rejoined them. He was pleased and highly excited by what had happened. "Naturally, Mrs Johnson, I am extremely sorry that he spoke to you as he did, but during all the years we've been treating him he has never displayed any emotion at all! Really, it is a tremendous breakthrough," he declared, "and I hope you will both come again."

Amy immediately protested but Dr. Ellis tried to reassure her; he insisted that she must not allow the incident to upset her – the man was not in his right mind! He used the phrase casually, but Amy thought it was undoubtedly a correct clinical diagnosis! They were driving away before Sarah had time to wonder about the tapes; what were the other things Dr. Ellis considered to be evidence of John's delusion? If only Amy had not been so emotional, Sarah could have taken advantage of the doctor's expansive, optimistic mood and talked things through with him. Her thoughts were not interrupted. Amy was unusually quiet; still quivering occasionally.

Later, at home, she stated that Sarah could go back if she wanted to, but nothing on earth – or in heaven for that matter – would induce her to set foot in that dreadful place again! She was shattered! After only a brief glimpse twenty years ago, Jay's father still hated the sight of her enough to blame her for his own collapse and his son's death! Why? It had not been suicide – just a scientific experiment that went wrong.

After Amy went upstairs to rest, Sarah sat again with the yellowed albums. The morning's events had shaken her too. Whatever she believed, John, in his madness, thought he and his son were one! Absurd! To be reincarnated, one would first have to be dead! But according to his doctor he claimed, under hypnosis, that he was born in 1946, the year of his son's birth, not 1905 ... and he revealed no knowledge of the war years at all. Did he really imagine them to be on a kind of macabre carousel? Sarah's dreams were even more troubled that night and for many more during her prolonged stay with Amy.

***

Completely sated after a truly delicious meal, Margaret was tired and happy as she went to her room for a few hours rest. Irma had promised to hold another séance after tea so she was anticipating more exciting glimpses of the world beyond.

Irma was going through a batch of bank statements. She extracted those connected with her special account and put them with all the correspondence she'd ever had about the 'Rigby Haven Company Ltd.' When first embarking on the scheme her first move had been to buy a limited company officially registered in London – an amazingly simple procedure. Both Companies House and the bank manager would have a fit if they ever set eyes on her private version of the company's accounts. She had added a naught to the actual amount in credit – two thousand would not have been very impressive after ten years – by dint of careful blanking and photocopying the documents appeared genuine. For years she had banked money and attributed it to a variety of well-wishers including a bishop and several doctors. The bi-annual statements had also been skilfully doctored to support the books. She hadn't the slightest doubt that they would fool Margaret. She scrupulously debited another fee for E. Francis, her accountant! That subterfuge had been one of her more brilliant strokes! Before putting away the collection in a new file cover she used the company cheque book to make out the cheque for his latest audit and signed it I. Rigby. When Margaret raised the subject Irma now had something to show ... she knew she would not have a long wait!

Although exhausted, Margaret was unable to sleep. In her first approving interest when she overheard Irma's future plans, she had overlooked the fact that if the scheme came to fruition, Irma would leave her – alone again ... but what could she do to prevent her going? Perhaps that was why Irma hadn't revealed her intentions. How near to setting up the rest home was she? She had been eavesdropping... If Irma didn't raise the subject herself, how could she ask? It was a tricky problem which kept her brain churning until it was time to dress and go downstairs for tea. While waiting for meals to be served, Margaret usually watched television, but she seemed incapable of settling and was quieter than usual, nervously avoiding eye contact as she hovered between the kitchen and sitting room.

Irma could guess what was on her employer's mind but pretended not to notice. She was keen to maintain escalating supremacy over her credulous victim, and found it difficult not to laugh aloud.

When tea-time came and they sat to eat, Margaret thought her food would choke her. For once she wasn't hungry. Irma was bright and attentive but ignored many opportunities to speak of her future plans. Margaret even brought up the subject of dreams and ambitions – her own had been to run an art gallery but she never had the opportunity to go into commerce. No matter what she said, Irma merely smiled or sympathised – it was infuriating!

When Irma took the trolley out to clear up Margaret was no nearer to finding out what she most wanted to know ... but the approach of the evening séance consoled her a little. Soon they would be sitting in the glow of a solitary lamp, and the shifting pageant would begin.

Chapter Sixteen

Since returning home after an excellent lunch at a riverside hotel Emma had been in a state of euphoria. She was enjoying the company but was even more thrilled to be involved in "Saving Margaret from the clutches of a confidence trickster".

There was so much to think and talk about that Jack had insisted on taking them all out for the midday meal. Emma at first protested ... she'd bought pork pies in case they had time to eat with her. If they didn't, what would she do with them? Jack however was not to be put off; the way things were going, he said, they would still be here at tea-time – they could consume them later! Jack and Polly were in no hurry to leave.

How right he was about still being here at tea-time Emma thought. Hours later they were still re-hashing the vexatious problem that Irma presented. Having suddenly remembered the pies, Emma tore herself away from the others to fetch them. She was not yet hungry after her unusually large lunch but Jack must be ... men always seemed ready to eat!

When she returned Jack and Polly were still shuffling through snapshots. "What, for instance, about the ornament which was smashed?" Polly sighed in vexed frustration. "No photograph would have revealed that sort of knowledge!"

"She could have made that up, hoping Margaret had lost track of it," Emma volunteered as she re-entered the room.

"Oh, I don't think so," Polly replied, "She seems far too calculating and efficient to take such a chance and Margaret herself had quite forgotten the incident until Irma reminded her by repeating her mother's exact words! It therefore follows that someone alive at the time, within hearing range, related the entire episode to Irma, along with other anecdotes."

"I agree absolutely," Jack said, "and that brings us full circle – the informant could well have been Olive. As a child-minder she would have been around in less formal moments than most servants. Now we must establish how and why!"

Among the dozens of pictures were two of the dog – in one it was again in the basket – and now, Jack showed Emma his own. When he compared them he was surprised to see that the dog was placed differently ... paws crossed with head at rest in his, whereas in Emma's the dog's paws were stretched out and it's head cocked perkily as though about to jump out.

Emma chuckled at his expression. "You must know it isn't a real dog! I tied a piece of black cotton to the back of one ear and passed it through the window so that I could lift it while being out of sight." She laughed aloud at the memory. "For one shot I lifted the dog too high – it seemed to be leaping out! It turned out to be the most successful. The photographer and I had great fun preparing them. The case was to be Sophie's birthday gift for her and because Helen couldn't have a real dog I wanted the photographs I was giving her, to be as lifelike as possible – hence the doggy bed which was a studio prop."

She searched unsuccessfully for it as she continued. "Helen was thrilled with them; there were four, which the man delivered when he came to take Helen's birthday portrait."

"How many duplicates were there?" Jack asked. "I assume that my mother must have had a complete set but you have some – and she wouldn't have returned part of your own gift, I'm sure!"

"How clever you are!" Emma cried... "There were two sets. These three are from the second – perhaps I gave the other, the leaping one, to Sophie."

"How can you be sure mine isn't one of the first set?" Jack asked doubtfully.

"Because the gift set was half-plate – bigger than these. You might find them one day. I can't believe your mother would have thrown them out... Let me think. When did I see them last ... yes – of course, they were all together in one large frame." She frowned in concentration then remembered. "It was in her bedroom – now yours I assume. The night-case was on the bed."

Jack had no recollection of it at all – in fact he scarcely remembered going into the bedroom when his mother was alive. They agreed that if Irma had seen any of them, it had to be Sophie's ... it was highly likely that the dog's name would be written on the back of hers too because they all pretended it was a real spaniel. In addition, Sophie definitely had a copy of Helen's birthday portrait in which she was actually cuddling Chaz.

Emma gave the one she was holding to Jack who hadn't seen it before. "Please keep this if you wish – and any others you would like of your mother."

Jack accepted – he was pleased to have it anyway, but said it would be something else to add to the evidence. He wanted to discuss the fire again, in light of what they had decided.

It may have been Olive who raised the alarm – Emma recalled her still being around during the clearing up. She definitely wasn't there the following year, because Helen and Emma had discussed her replacement with some amusement ... the new girl was at least six-feet tall, very brawny, red faced and pimply. They decided that any man would keep her at arms' length!

"Is that significant? Did Olive leave because of Howard?" Polly risked asking. "Was he as much a woman chaser as he sounds?"

"Sophie only told us the girl had given notice saying she was tired of country life, and ..." Emma hesitated as though on the verge of an explanation, then to Polly's acute disappointment she shook her head. "Sophie never complained about Howard's conduct. She might have got rid of Olive to avoid his being tempted, but personally I'm sure he wouldn't have been."

Again, Polly would have liked to question her; how could she be so sure? ... But Emma gave her no chance to interrupt. The more she spoke of the old days the more clearly she seemed to remember them, in astonishing detail. When Emma arrived on holiday just after the fire, Margaret was apparently already there, helping to clean the few books worth salvaging. There were definitely no photograph albums because Sophie bemoaned their loss. She showed them some heavy metal clasps – all which remained of the old leather volumes. Both Helen and Emma promised to go through their collections with a view to having duplicates made but, Emma was ashamed to admit, neither ever did so. However, Jack and Polly were undismayed. No matter what Sophie thought, Olive was there and would have had the opportunity to remove whole books without fear of being discovered ... the question was, why?

Between that summer and the next, Olive left – presumably taking her trophies with her. Could she merely have wanted a memento? She might, if she knew when she stole them that she would not be living under the Heywood roof for much longer!

***

Margaret watched quietly as Irma gradually emerged from her trance. The most significant spirit visitor tonight had been her grandmother. Margaret was only seven when Ermintrude died but remembered her as a pale, gentle lady who sat under a sunshade in the garden watching her at play. She often encouraged Margaret to talk or read aloud to her and was invariably patient with her childish mistakes. It came as no surprise therefore when Irma told her how sad the old lady was that Margaret had no offspring of her own; she wondered if she might find fulfilment in helping others in want ... so many were in dire need of comfort.

Afterwards, when Irma 'came round' fully, Margaret repeated Ermintrude's words to remind Irma, who always professed to be only vaguely aware of anything that happened when spirits took control of her. Irma laughed at Margaret's stricken expression. "For goodness sake don't let it worry you. She had a houseful of servants to look after her children! She can't possibly want you to adopt one at your age – if you'll forgive me for referring to it!"

"But she seemed to be telling me that I'm leading a selfish existence – and I suppose she's right. Are there any children's homes near here? Perhaps we could have them all for tea or something!"

Margaret felt inadequate. She always gave to charity collections and even sent garments to church jumble sales but had never actually pictured the recipients of such munificence!

"Don't give it another thought," Irma laughed. "Drop some extra money in the church poor-box or send a cheque to the NSPCC – but nobody would expect you to entertain an army of children here!"

Margaret was a little reassured and, again hoping to draw Irma out, asked if during her nursing career she'd had much to do with children. Irma's pulse quickened, sensing what lay behind the enquiry. This was her chance to stress how much more concerned she had always been for the plight of older people. "Of course I like children," she said, "I regret having none of my own, but usually they recover from most of their ailments naturally. God cures them while the doctor makes reassuring noises for the parents' benefit!" Irma laughed loudly at her own joke but when Margaret did not respond, went on hastily... "But old people are different. They need sympathetic attention and careful nursing if they are to make the most of their remaining years. I always find most satisfaction in caring for the elderly." She watched as Margaret took this in. It was obvious that she was impressed but would she take the bait?

At that moment the telephone shrilled. It was Cousin Ethel and Irma would dearly have loved to cut her off – to pretend it was a wrong number – but dared not take such a risk. Forcing a smile she handed the instrument to Margaret and left the room. They would gossip for hours, she fumed inwardly. The right moment had come and gone; she'd have to forget it for tonight, but tomorrow – tomorrow was another day!

***

The pie crumbs had been cleared and Polly washed up while Emma prepared fresh coffee. "It's high time we left," Polly demurred, "We are tiring you with all our chatter."

"Nonsense, dear," Emma protested, "I can't remember when I enjoyed a day more. I hope you'll keep in touch – I'd love a chat at any time; better still, call round. I am in the 'phone book, but you don't need to ring in advance; you'll be welcome whenever you feel like driving over. I hope you won't ever drive past without calling in"

All their deliberations had led back to the housemaid, Olive. She was the most likely link between Irma and the family, but they did come up with another possibility – Howard's sister. Emma said they might have met but she had no memory of her at all. It was possible that the woman was still alive but unless she was younger than Howard she would be at least as old as Emma. Jack knew the old family home and surrounding area fairly well so he volunteered to go there during the following week to make a few discreet enquiries. Polly said that as Sarah was not after all returning home she might do some investigating of her own. She would stay at the Lion in Barr's Brook for a day or two and call on Margaret before leaving. Irma would then realise she was under observation and might hold back ... but before confronting her again Polly wanted particularly to talk to Edna.

Emma was obviously disappointed that she could do nothing to assist them but suddenly had an idea. "Will your visit to Welshpool be a day trip, Jack? If you intend staying overnight, could you put up with a passenger?"

"Why, of course. I'd enjoy your company if you feel like coming – we are both free agents and can stay one night or two, but what made you think of it?"

"It is purely selfish, I'm afraid," confessed Emma. "I've decided, after all I've heard, to cut Margaret out of my will. She doesn't need my small contribution anyway and if she's going to be swindled I don't want anything I leave to go to Irma Rigby!" They all laughed but were a little embarrassed, as Emma obviously wasn't joking. She could write to her lawyer but said it would be much more satisfactory to call in person, as there would be things to sign. There was another point in favour. Mr Dewhurst, the senior partner was also a friend – only a year or so younger than herself. There was little chance that he would remember anything about the servants, but his father's firm had handled all the Heywood family legal business since before her parents' marriage. Jack could ask about Howard's sister and, if Emma was present to vouch for him, Brian Dewhurst might even answer!

They finally agreed to contact each other for an update the following evening. By then, Emma would have been able to fix an appointment with Dewhurst. As soon as he knew the details Jack would book hotel accommodation ... they hoped they could go on Tuesday for at least one night. Polly would also, hopefully, have heard from Dan's police contact and know whether or not he was willing to help them to uncover Irma's background.

They parted from Emma on a high note of optimism. Breaking the journey back to Oxford once, for a very light supper (after the heavy lunch and pork pie tea), Jack returned Polly to her temporary home. Dan and Elaine were eager to hear what progress had been made and it was well into the small hours before Jack left and they all went to bed exhausted ... but well satisfied with the way things were shaping and happily anticipating tomorrow.

Chapter Seventeen

Monday April 20th...

In spite of yesterday's slow start, Clarrie's day went well; already she could see in her mind's eye what the finished picture would be like – if she continued to be lucky with the weather. She could take things more slowly from now on – working in the mornings on this canvas, perhaps undertaking another at a different location after lunch – or even resting with a good book! After a sociable hour in the bar last night she had written a letter to Del who was never far from her thoughts. Today, after her work was finished she would walk into the village to post it.

She wondered as she went down to breakfast whether to ring home, but decided against it ... neither Polly nor her mother would expect to hear from her unless she changed her plans for returning on Sunday. A call she would definitely make later was to Gwen Williams. The farm was only about a half-hour drive away. When she returned to finish her canvas, after working on it for a week at home, she could break her journey to visit the family if they were not too busy. By then, the enlarged photograph of the cottage painting would be ready. Bill and Gwen had seemed so disappointed at being unable to buy the original, Clarrie was eager to give them the copy. It was another pleasant morning with a promise of sunshine and having laid her plans for the next two weeks she felt mellow as she drove off after breakfast, enjoying the change of pace.

***

Irma and Margaret were going through the post in the dining room after breakfast. Edna was clearing away as they still sat at the table. There was not a great deal of mail apart from the usual junk. Irma held one aloft ostentatiously. "Oh! Here's a letter for me today ... from the bank."

Margaret was waiting impatiently for Edna to leave them. After last night, when their séance was graced by the ghostly presence of a strange lady, there were many things she wanted to ask Irma. She had often wondered why all their spirit visitors seemed to be hers, but then, Irma could contact her own loved ones in private, at any time – she didn't hold the evening sessions for her own benefit.

Margaret would be eternally grateful that Irma had agreed to live with her. She was always passing on bits of advice and guidance from the other side. Even the alterations in her diet had made her feel better. Irma also insisted that she took vitamin tablets every day; it was very comforting to have someone who really cared for her.

At last Edna left and putting her letters aside to read later, Margaret broached the subject which was of more immediate concern. "While you were in trance last night dear, you spoke to someone who has never come through before, during our little sessions." She paused, but Irma merely looked puzzled. "I couldn't help being interested. I think it might have been your mother, but whoever it was, she seemed pleased for you. I don't wish to pry of course, but it sounded as though something might take you away from me... I do so hope I misunderstood."

Irma inwardly heaved a sigh of relief. When Margaret didn't comment on the stranger's unearthly visitation before going to bed, Irma thought she wasn't going to bite! "Well, I saw no reason to tell you because, whatever she said, there's no chance of anything happening for years – certainly not in the foreseeable future!" She continued sorting the mail, deliberately forcing Margaret to ask her directly.

Realizing that Irma didn't intend to divulge more, at least not voluntarily, Margaret fell into the trap and pressed her for information. "Who came through? Was I right? Was it your mother? And what did she mean by your wishes coming true earlier than expected?" She remembered every word of Irma's half of the exchange and was disquieted, knowing it was indubitably something to do with the planned nursing home, which Irma had not even mentioned to her yet. She suspected too that when her plans came to fruition Irma would leave. How soon was a matter of supreme importance to Margaret. Surely she would have to discuss it now.

Irma was standing, ready to leave, but with a show of apparent reluctance she resumed her seat and explained. It was her mother and yes, she had hopes, one day, of running a very special home for the elderly, but her mother was wrong; it couldn't be soon. Time means little in the Spirit World, she reminded Margaret, and there was no way she would afford a suitable place for many years to come. Margaret was reluctant to believe it; after all, she had been encouraged to accept without question the 'messages' which came to her. Finally, Irma drew from her pocket the envelope which had ostensibly just arrived. She tore it open and after a cursory glance handed the contents to Margaret with a rueful smile.

"See for yourself," she said, "my company bank statement ... less than thirty thousand pounds! All I ever seem to do is pay money out!" Irma delved again into her overall pocket and waved a cheque made out to E. Francis. Later, with the surname Rigby added, it would go to her current account. "It will be years before I even start looking for property – a pity really because prices are lower now than they have been for years, especially for larger places suitable for conversion."

Margaret perused the statement and, now being included in discussing the project, wanted to know everything. Before long, all the company files were spread before her and she was listening to Irma's description of her ideal home for the elderly. 'Rigby Haven' would accommodate a maximum of ten single ladies; each would have a sitting-room and bedroom with bathroom en-suite. There would be three general rooms – one for watching TV, a reading room with ample shelves for shared books and a comfortable lounge for meeting visitors or each other. The communal dining-room would be divided into five bays – four places in each – with plenty of plants and soft music.

Margaret pictured it and could see how such a place, run like a hotel, might appeal not only to the elderly guests but to their families who would have no reason to feel guilty, leaving them in such a pleasing environment. She reached across and studied the credit column on the bank statement. At the rate it was growing Irma would never achieve her dream. Part of her was relieved that Irma was likely to be with her for many years to come, but she felt a stir of excitement. Perhaps this was her chance to do some positive good with her money, as her grandmother had hoped!

***

The first thing Polly did on Monday morning was contact her niece Pat, who would be letting herself into an empty house and must be warned, otherwise she'd be worried. Pat was happy to hear that she could take her time about starting work and promised to check the telephone answering machine, take in milk and papers and yes – she would make sure she locked up properly when she left!

Polly knew she was fussing and eventually let Pat get on with her breakfast. She was in a hopeful mood. In her absence yesterday Dan had contacted Detective Sergeant Terry White, his friend in the CID, who was well placed to delve into Irma's background and he had agreed to do so. His initial reaction was a flat refusal but Dan eventually convinced him of the strong possibility that a crime was going to be committed. He understood that Terry would decide for himself how much information to give them but, on the other hand, Dan promised to let him have any evidence Polly and Jack unearthed.

Terry said he would call Polly personally at noon, so she made notes of their progress to date, in case he was reluctant to reveal the results of his own research. It was mainly conjecture when it came down to it but he would have to agree that the circumstances were suspicious and surely the police were supposed to be keen on crime prevention! If he could be persuaded to find out what happened to Olive Harris they might confirm her link with Irma. It seemed very likely to Polly that Irma was her daughter and that Olive must have become pregnant around the time she left her employment. There were many questions revolving in Polly's mind, which Terry would not be able to answer. Did Olive leave to get married, or was she really tired of country life? Did she leave because she was already pregnant? If so – who was the father of her baby?

To clarify her thoughts, Polly listed the alternatives, the arguments for and against each, and the possible connection with Irma. Assuming that Irma *was* Olive's daughter, they must discover why Margaret should be singled out as a target. By all accounts Olive had been well treated, was happy with the Heywood family and particularly close to Margaret. She left soon after the fire but only if she had already decided to leave would she have risked stealing the photographs ... otherwise, in the longer term, they might have been found in her possession; she had no other home. Her reason for wanting them was a mystery! Were they simply to be a reminder of her few years with a real family? No, an honest girl would need a better reason. It was true that she went to them from an orphanage but, no matter how kind, they were not her own flesh and blood.

Polly suddenly had a flash of intuition! Olive had grown up an orphan; how she must have wished that she did have a family. At sixteen she had her first glimpse of what it would have been like to grow up surrounded by loving relatives; she would want that for her own child. It was unlikely that such a thought would have come out of the blue, she was young and unmarried but if, in July nineteen-thirty-four she knew she was pregnant? ...Well! Polly couldn't wait to discuss her ideas with Jack so she called him immediately. He hadn't yet heard from Emma so they couldn't tie up the telephone for long. He heard the theory, and commented. "If you're right, did Olive feel she had a right to the photographs, even if undamaged, because her baby was fathered by a member of the family? The only candidate for that position seems to be Howard! Are we justified in considering that he was cheating on Aunt Sophie?"

The conclusion matched her own, to Polly's relief, but she pointed out that Sophie, by all accounts, was much more interested in her daughter than in Howard. He was, after all, considerably younger and went his own way with her blessing, according to Emma. Until hearing from Terry, they decided not to repeat the theory to Emma but agreed that it was a very promising line of inquiry. As she waited for Terry's call Polly's mind raced. If Howard, Margaret's father, was also Irma's that might be the key: jealousy! She could for years have been consumed with resentment because while Margaret was legitimate and enjoyed wealth and security she, her half-sister, was raised in much poorer circumstances.

Since Margaret first told them, awestruck, about the comfort she derived from Irma's spirit messages Polly had felt uneasy; were they right to interfere when Margaret was so happy? But she kept reminding herself that the most impressive messages, supposedly from the husband of Irma's last patient, were unsupported. She must ask Terry another favour; he might be willing to obtain the names of Irma's previous employers and she could contact them herself.

The telephone interrupted her thoughts – it was Jack again, to say that he and Emma would be leaving on Tuesday morning. Their rooms were booked for two nights and he would expect Polly to contact them on Wednesday night. Polly had no idea where she would be then, so it was the best possible plan. Unable to remain idle, Polly had the evening meal well in hand. The vegetables were prepared and the chicken was stuffed, so she made an apple pie for pudding. Dan and Elaine were both at work and usually met at home for a sandwich at midday but as the oven was hot, ready for roasting the chicken, Polly decided to make a quiche for lunch. It would be a nice change for them with fresh salad. It had taken her mind off the awaited call and the shrill ringing startled her for a moment. This time it was Terry. They spent a few minutes renewing their acquaintance – he asked after Sarah and Clarrie – then told her what she had been waiting to hear.

Finding information had been difficult because the woman's name was not Irma ... but through her employment record, he was sure she must be Ermintrude Frances Rigby. Polly was so excited when she heard the two first names she almost missed what he said next.... Her mother, Olive, married at the end of the war when Ermintrude was about ten-years-old. Their surname became Harris, and she probably chose to be known as Irma. Terry said he couldn't spare more time today but as soon as possible he would obtain information about where Irma last worked – he hadn't noted the details but thought it was a hospital, not a private house. Polly held her breath. Had they caught Irma out in a blatant lie? Polly's note pad – blank when she picked up the 'phone – was full of scribble by the time he rang off.

The niggling thought that Irma, in spite of their suspicions and the mounting evidence, might really be harmless, was banished. The answer stared her in the face. Irma had concealed her connection to the family, so was definitely up to no good. She was, without a doubt, plotting something against Margaret.

Looking forward even more eagerly to the next few days, Polly wished she could leave immediately. She hadn't expected results from Terry so quickly when she'd fixed on Tuesday morning. She would revisit Margaret before leaving Barr's Brook, but the first person she intended to confront was Edna ... the one who had introduced the viper to the nest.

Chapter Eighteen

Tuesday April 21st...

Polly's alarm clock went off at 6:30 in the morning so she had plenty of time to make breakfast. Like many young people these days Dan and Elaine didn't usually bother with more than toast and coffee but today, with the drive ahead of her, Polly was determined to eat properly; she might not have time for lunch! She always relished her morning bacon and egg and would enjoy them more if she ate in company. Anyway, although she knew that 'eating for two' was an out-dated concept, Elaine's baby was due in less than six weeks and yet, to look at her, you would think it was a couple of months away. She should build up her stamina; a bit more weight wouldn't hurt! As she expected, they protested noisily that they didn't have time to eat, and weren't really hungry, but showed no signs of flagging once they started and even demolished extra fried bread and tomatoes. They departed eventually with admonitions that she should be careful – keep in touch – and stay again overnight, before returning to Mapledurham.

The weather was dull and wet when Polly left Oxford on the A.40 but as most of the traffic was heading toward the city she made good time. Later, when the rain stormed down heavily, she stopped for coffee, thinking it had set in for the day, but by the time she finished her drink the sun was out. Less than an hour later she arrived at her destination. Signs of life were few. A terrace of small cottages faced the church and two elderly ladies were standing deep in conversation, one on each side of a low wall. A delivery van was outside the butcher's and a few cars were parked at the inn so she pulled in near them. She noted that she was directly under the swinging sign which depicted a lion rampant and she hoped it was not as old and unsafe as it looked!

The "Olde Tea Shoppe" was next door and Polly was looking forward to visiting it again, as soon as she'd booked in. If recognised there, it would imply that she was still interested in local property. It was as well to have a pretext for returning, small villages were rife with speculation and gossip when strangers lingered. As anticipated, she had no trouble obtaining a room and they accepted that she couldn't predict how many nights she would need it. If there was anything Polly hated it was living out of a suitcase, even for twenty-four hours, so she unpacked and hung her clothes before going out. If she had not, she would have been safely inside the tea shop before Irma emerged from the butcher's shop opposite.

Grey Masque of Death
***

Irma stood motionless for a moment, unable to believe her eyes...

What on earth was that woman doing in the village? Did it follow that cousin Jack was also still around? They hadn't hinted that they were staying in the vicinity; in fact they'd said they had to get back to Oxford. As Polly had left the Lion, Irma risked going in for a drink. Having lodged there for a while she was well known and although she didn't go back often, calling would not give rise to comment. The barman greeted her pleasantly and asked how life was treating her up at the big house. After a few pleasantries she remarked on the fact that she was his only customer and asked if the hotel was empty. He informed her that on the contrary it was half full. One woman had just this minute booked in for a few days – yes, she was on her own. He had no idea what her business was: probably just a tourist! Before leaving, Irma made sure Polly wasn't in sight, then moved quickly away from the direction of the tea shop and circled to the back lane where she had left her car. She couldn't decide whether Mrs Bailey's being alone was more, or less, significant but she had to find out why she had returned ... she would have to cultivate Edna again to enlist her help.

Edna spent most evenings at the inn with her husband. They enjoyed a drink and he played darts, so it should be easy for her to get to know Polly. There was one big snag – Irma wouldn't see Edna again today and if she met Polly tonight – there was no knowing what she might tell her. To make a special call on Edna at home would surprise her and make her suspicious ... anything of that sort was out of the question: too risky. It would be far better to bring it up naturally in conversation tomorrow ... Polly might already have mentioned what she was doing in the locality and that would be the end of it. She was probably worrying needlessly. What, after all, did Edna know about her? And what could possibly be learned to her detriment in the village?

Irma had given the same story about her background to everyone, including Edna. She had done nothing out of character since her first arrival at the inn before Christmas. Last October, sensing that the time was ripe to close in on Margaret, Irma acted. Dispensing with her usual make-up left her pasty-faced so rubbing a touch of blue eye shadow round her jaw and upper lip altered her considerably. Her patently female shape was soon hidden by a thick sweater under a man's suit bought from a charity shop; with hair powdered grey under a cloth cap, and her eyes obscured behind steel rimmed glasses, she was transformed. Nobody could possibly connect Irma with an old man who had taken a six-month lease on an isolated hideaway to write about local wildlife. The farmer, not caring about paperwork, took a down-payment in cash on the understanding that the place was acceptable with no alterations. The 'professor' bought milk, eggs, butter and bread from the farm and hardly ever went to the village.

Mai Griffin

Sometimes seen in the distance as he walked the fields with his binoculars, his presence had soon ceased to arouse interest. In the guise of a stooped old man, merging into the background, she spied and planned. Observing the comings and goings at Riverbank was easy in her bird-watcher role and she logged Jean Webb's regular bicycle rides along the quarry road. The silly woman had been so predictable she was pathetic. With a contemptuous shrug, Irma put all those thoughts aside to deal with her present predicament. With only a couple of weeks left before the property lease ended, she had expected to be free of the masquerade. Walking out and re-appearing occasionally as Professor Smythe was easy when she lived at the Lion, but had become increasingly difficult since she moved in with Margaret.

She could not hypothesise how the 'professor' could either harm her or be useful in any way so decided to stick to her usual routine for visiting the farm in disguise and not let this stupid Polly woman disturb her. Things were coming to a head with Margaret ... she was actually on the verge of suggesting that they should go into partnership with the nursing home, Irma was sure. As long as she kept cool, Jack and his sisters could do nothing. They had no idea of her origins, or her mother's connection with the family ... so how could they possibly challenge her psychic talents! She sang quietly to herself as she drove home, not doubting that she was invincible; let them do their worst!

***

Clarrie had been painting for well over an hour before the heavy drone of an approaching motorbike disturbed her. She had been so absorbed there was no time to lock herself in her car as planned should anything untoward happen! Miles from habitation, alone and defenceless, she remembered too late her mother's warnings that she should not take risks; the bike skidded to a halt, cutting off her escape route. Two leather-clad youths climbed off it slowly, removed their helmets and sauntered over. One had the grace to say 'Hi' as they stood behind her staring at the picture. Clarrie immediately rose from her stool and, trying to appear calm, walked away in the direction of the car, although she had not yet decided whether to sit inside it or pretend she needed to fetch something.

The two youngsters muttered inaudibly as they stared alternately at the house and the painting. At last they turned to where she perched on the passenger seat with the door open.

"That's real good Miss," said the taller one, the driver.

"It sure is," said the other, "are you a teacher?"

Clarrie was still not confident enough to join them back at the easel, but she answered pleasantly. "Thanks, it's nice of you to be so complimentary. I'm not a teacher, I'm an artist."

"That means you must be good if you earn a living doing it! I'm Lofty by the way and this shrimp is Len. Mind if we watch?"

"What's your name," asked Len. "Are you famous?"

There seemed to be no harm in them and she couldn't hover at the car for ever, so she shook off her nervousness and walked back to talk, taking her flask with her. "I'm afraid I haven't yet achieved fame and fortune," she smiled, "but my father, Stephen Grey, was quite well known – especially in North Wales." Seeing the flask reminded Lofty that they had cans of beer so he went to fetch them and they were all soon drinking and chatting like old friends. Clarrie felt foolish to have been alarmed, but it could so easily have turned out differently.

It appeared that Len's mother helped with 'Meals on Wheels' and one of the elderly people she visited was Gordy Bates, the old man Clarrie had met in the bar. Since she had revived his memories of the Matthews' place he'd hardly stopped going on about it, Len said. His mother dismissed his wild stories but Len was so intrigued that he had persuaded Lofty to come out for a closer look.

"Old Gordy says you're nuts to paint this miserable old ruin," said Len. "Aren't you afraid of spooks, sitting here all alone?"

Clarrie didn't say that their arrival had alarmed her far more than any ghost and also avoided saying that she had seen one! Conscious that she was losing valuable time, because although still holding the brush she couldn't concentrate in the face of their chatter, she asked if they would excuse her now. She had enjoyed talking but had to get back to work – perhaps they'd like to drop round later in the week when she would be closer to finishing.

They went with good grace but not back to the main road. They were keen for a closer look at the empty house before leaving. Clarrie saw them moving around the property and hoped they wouldn't attempt to break in ... whatever would she say to Mrs Matthews if she did nothing to stop them? She saw them move away from the main building and almost forgot them until a good while later, when they waved and shouted as they roared past her. Len, on the pillion, held what looked like a folded rug in front of him. They must have explored the outhouse and she wondered if he had picked up a trophy of his visit. If he had, Clarrie felt with icy certainty that he would regret it.

***

When she had first set eyes on 'Little Thatch', a cottage in the small Oxfordshire hamlet of Hinney Green, Bertha Matthews knew it was exactly what she was looking for. The agent's photograph, although enough to stir interest, hadn't done justice to the homely atmosphere it exuded. Overhangs of the picture-book, thatched roof, lifted like brows over closed shuttered windows – as if asleep, in a tangled confusion of flowers behind a painted fence; a Virginia creeper, having dropped most of its leaves, clung like a cobweb over one of the stained, whitewashed walls. It seemed to be rejected by its smarter neighbours and she instantly empathised with it. It was as if a chord deep within her vibrated, responding to its need. Together, she determined, they would make a new start. In the busy weeks prior to moving, her hopes were high. The dark mansion, the only home she'd ever known, no longer held her captive; she would be free of the past and the stigma of belonging to it.

The cottage was well situated. The open common at the front was a place where people gathered to talk, walk pets and enjoy Sunday cricket. In the beginning it had seemed inevitable that she would make friends. She imagined how people would stop to speak with her as she weeded her garden, and she planned tea parties to which she would invite other elderly ladies. She could sew or knit for charity and might even join one of the societies which always flourished in tiny villages. Yes, surely a stimulating new life was opening up for her.

On the day she moved in, Bertha could scarcely contain her excitement. The agent greeted her with the keys and carried Blacky's basket inside. She didn't doubt that Blacky would settle in his new home although cats were reputed to stray if uprooted. He was unusually affectionate and hardly ever left her side, but taking no chances she locked him in carefully when she went across the square to shop for a few groceries. She'd had no reason to be anything other than optimistic on that fine autumn morning... She had not noticed the low cat-flap in the kitchen door. Now she was morose, churning over everything that happened then and in the weeks which followed.

To her relief the store had been empty that day. Too many strange faces would have intimidated her. The genial store owner, eager to welcome a new customer, willingly stood talking until they heard a commotion outside. The drone of a heavy vehicle heralded the arrival of her furniture, so she hurried home to open the door. A few curious neighbours were watching and a large dog barked furiously, intent on frightening the van away again.

As she reached the cottage she was shocked to see Blacky outside in the driveway, sniffing delicately where he knew she had just walked. He was nearing the road where the container was already reversing into the narrow opening. Seeing the danger she ran forward, waving frantically, shrieking at the driver to stop. Assuming that her concern was merely for her gateposts he carried on swinging in. He was a local man who had moved the previous owner out – he knew he could negotiate the turn. Fussy old biddy! Blacky, sensing danger, was about to spring to safety when he saw the dog and froze. By the time he did move, it was an instant too late. Bertha was hysterical – beside herself with grief and anger. She could not recall what she screamed at the stupid driver who had ignored her. She did remember, vividly, the terrible anguish she suffered, losing her beloved pet. No new life for poor Blacky!

By a sudden cruel stroke of fate she was completely alone.

Little Billy who lived next door (of course the wretched dog was his!) had witnessed the tragedy and Bertha blamed him unreservedly for the collapse of all her hopes. His graphic description of the ensuing scene

Grey Masque of Death

was often repeated later, to anyone who would listen, but at the time, agog with excitement, he ran back to his own house. "She must have been crackers about that cat, mum," Billy said. "She howled and screamed at the driver something terrible." After a solemn pause, he added in an awed tone ..."Curses!" His mother merely raised her eyebrows with a wry smile. Such melodrama in a child of eight!

A week later when the driver's son died in a traffic accident every child in Billy's school carried home the tale of the 'curse'. Most adults admonished their children but told each other that there was indeed something rather strange about the newcomer. Those who had actually met her said it was ridiculous – she was harmless, even 'quite nice really', but the whispers continued. Billy's mother had two younger children to keep her occupied so made no effort to meet Bertha – she continually heard enough about her from Billy to satisfy her curiosity.

Bertha often saw him spying on her and forced herself to adopt a friendly air, but always at her approach he backed away and refused to speak. She found a bundle of old comics in the tool shed – tied ready for disposal – so when he came near the dividing fence she offered them to him. At first he backed away but greed overcame his alarm ... he grabbed them and ran into his house.

Bertha fancied she had scored a small success until the following day. She looked from her front window to see him standing in the street arm raised, shaking a bandaged fist at her. Later, by questioning his little brother who was playing outside, she heard how, in hacking through the string which held the comics together, the knife slipped, gashing his hand. He now had five stitches to prove beyond doubt that she was an evil witch! She despaired when saw him showing off his bandaged wound to the other boys and pointing angrily to her cottage.

At the end of autumn when cold, damp air blanketed the garden, spoiling the colourful dry leaves and forcing even the most tenacious of them to fall, Bertha gathered the apples within reach and sprayed the trees to discourage insects from spoiling next year's crop. The next day she saw a gang of boys climbing the trees to take the remaining red fruit and flung open her bedroom window to warn them, but they ran away with the stolen apples, laughing. As they scrambled over the rickety back gate she shouted with all the urgency she could muster, "Don't eat them – they will make you ill ... very ill!"

Several people heard her and when the children were indeed sick the following day, even her previous defenders began to wonder about her. Upset by their stares and the renewed atmosphere of hostility, Bertha retreated into her shell again. She never went out for anything that could be delivered and didn't encourage visitors. She hoped Billy would soon grow out of his obsession and others would have a chance to forget ... but would she ever be anything to them now, other than 'Old Matty'?

Mai Griffin

Child or not, he was a malevolent beast ... a thoroughly wicked boy who had deprived her of her new start. At no time in her life had any other person, man or woman, filled her with so much hate. Her grandmothers would have known how to deal with him. They would despise her for having endured his insolence for so long ... but she was not like them. She didn't want to be – but her resolve was crumbling. Bitterness was slowly consuming her and she trembled with fear.

Chapter Nineteen

While Nettie prepared lunch, Sarah persuaded Amy to accompany her on a short walk. She advised that Amy should take Bobby for at least one walk every day, not only to improve her own health but because dachshunds were prone to putting on weight and look unsightly when their tummies bulge and droop. Even as she said it she knew Amy was aware that her own stomach was already in that sad condition; if it spurred her to take more pride in herself it was all to the good.

Sarah had already had a word with Nettie about diet; less carbohydrate and fat and more salad, fish and boiled chicken were better for Amy; puddings were out, jelly in! So, even if they worked up an appetite, the benefit of the walk wouldn't be undermined. Sarah hoped Amy could be persuaded to stroll out again after they had eaten. She found the atmosphere inside the house oppressive.

As she anticipated, Amy was appalled to find that her midday meal excluded potatoes. She protested that salad and cottage cheese were tasteless and it was difficult to stop her drenching everything with salt and salad cream. The arrival of coffee with no milk or sugar was too much, so Nettie promised to shop for low calorie sweetener and substitute milk with no cream content. Sarah, resigned to the fact that as soon as she left, Amy would go back to her old habits, was consequently gratified when Amy pushed herself out of her chair declaring that she didn't feel as bulky; perhaps starving herself was working already! "Come on," she ordered, to Sarah's astonishment, "let's go now if we're going, while it's still sunny." Amy's little dachshund was equally bewildered but quite ecstatic. When he saw her holding his lead he hurtled to the front door, yapping wildly. Jay had always walked Bobby last thing at night but Amy said he would have to get used to a change of routine – no way was she going out after dark. At least, Sarah noted, she was taking on the responsibility with good grace. They strolled quite slowly, talking most of the time and hardly noticed how much ground they covered. Amy was amazed to find, on their return, that the afternoon was almost over, yet she still felt alright.

Sarah announced that tomorrow she intended to visit the hospital again and Amy reluctantly changed her mind about not accompanying her, even though she would not see John herself. When Sarah rang up, Dr. Ellis was pleased to sanction her proposed visit. He said Mr Johnson's mental state had already improved immensely; personally he had no doubt she'd been instrumental in bringing back to him a measure of sanity. Sarah was glad she had kept her promise to Dorothea, but for her own peace of mind she wanted to do more. She was stimulated by the prospect of being able to communicate with John and with that in mind it was well worth visiting him every day she remained with Amy.

The stack of old albums still drew Sarah like a magnet. While Amy thumbed through magazines or watched television, she found herself endlessly leafing through them as if they held a vital clue that she continually missed. She turned the pages unable to subdue the feeling that they held a key to the enigma. She wondered why she persisted if it was likely to be disturbing; yet still she probed for an answer. Her mind frequently drifted and she was taken aback to find herself repeatedly staring at a group study of the young family. It was askew. Had it been removed from its mount and replaced carelessly? With sudden trepidation she turned it over. On the back Dorothea had written, 'With my two Johns 1948'. The faded ink wasn't easy to read – it was blotched as though a wet sponge had rested on it; she sensed that Dorothea's tears had fallen there.

Dorothea must have been devastated to discover how deeply troubled her husband's mind actually was, but his condition had remained unchanged for twenty years. She had made a life for herself without him, so why had that particular photograph upset her? There was nothing extraordinary in it. And why should she have been so shattered by her last visit to John? She would have had to believe her husband's wild talk, to be so affected by it that she lost interest in life ... it was out of the question! Sarah didn't for a moment doubt her friend's sanity. With a deep sigh she put aside the books. Perhaps things would be clearer to her after a night's sleep and her next confrontation with the troubled old man.

The photographs bored Amy, but as Sarah abandoned them she produced from a drawer a framed studio portrait of Jay. "Look," she said, "this was wrapped with the albums. Isn't it a good one of him? He's wearing the green sweater I gave him for his birthday. It isn't here so he must have been wearing it ... when he died!" She almost choked at the thought. "He first wore it for the first time when he went to his mother's and must have taken this picture to show her. With all the panic of her collapse it was left in her apartment." Sniffing sorrowfully, Amy pointed to the corner of the photograph. "He had it taken secretly, especially for our wedding anniversary I expect ... look!"

There was an inscription written in a flowing hand. It read, *'Forever Yours – John'*.

Amy frowned momentarily ... "Poor Darling – trying to sound so formal." She explained. "It came back here afterwards with her other things but he obviously forgot to give it to me, being so upset over her being ill and dying and the funeral. I might not have found it for years if you hadn't made me go through the cabin trunk." She began to get weepy again but hastily dabbed her eyes. "Clarrie paints such beautiful portraits – do you think she could paint one from this? I know she is much in demand but this is a proper commission of course, I want that clearly understood from the start." Sarah duly admired the photograph and agreed that it would make a lovely painting. Placing it on the coffee table she said Amy must speak to Clarinda about it when she came to take her back home. "Don't even speak of going home," Amy cried in alarm. There will be a memorial service – you must stay for that at least."

Sarah knew Amy was right; she couldn't very well leave her to face the funeral alone. Of course, Clarinda was still unaware of the terrible accident and must think she had already returned home. She had planned to telephone Wales to ask if Clarinda could collect her on her way home at the weekend but, now she was committed to another week away; there was no point in ringing her. When the date of the service was settled she would call Polly instead.

As she rose to make her way to bed Sarah picked up the albums. She had definitely closed them and was bewildered to find the top one lying open again, at the same family group to which she had been drawn earlier. It was monochrome and had lost its sharpness but she caught her breath as revelation struck. Jay's father, in 1948, was wearing a pullover exactly like the one in the signed portrait standing on the table above it.

It was uncanny! It couldn't be the one Jay wore on that fateful night! No, not the same one! ... Ridiculous! They obviously had similar tastes. It accounted to a large extent for their identical appearance. Surely the book had been opened by an unseen hand to reassure her – to prevent her being side-tracked by absurd, wild theories? She must adopt a more positive attitude.

Lying sleepless later, her confidence waned; she feared she had misinterpreted the sign ... and prayed for help and guidance.

***

Margaret was impatient to finish lunch. Irma had been longer than ever doing the shopping and she fancied she could smell gin on her breath when she returned. She had nothing against the odd drink and certainly didn't imagine that Irma was on the road to ruin – she was old enough to indulge if she felt like it – but it was odd; such behaviour was out of character: disturbing. When Margaret remarked on her lateness, giving her chance to explain, Irma shrugged and said the shops were busy. It was irritating, especially as Margaret wanted to talk about the nursing home project. Although keen to be involved with it, she was conscious of the fact that she knew very little about Irma personally. She didn't suspect Irma of hiding anything, but if one went into business with anyone it was wise to make a few inquiries into their background ... Margaret was no fool.

Irma was quieter than normal as they ate. She appeared distracted by her own thoughts and Margaret felt shut out; had she done something to give offence she wondered? Slowly, Irma relaxed, appearing to sense Margaret's anxiety. By the time they were having coffee she was her old self and Margaret risked asking her about her childhood. Irma's smile froze, giving Margaret reason to regret questioning her ... but Irma's words explained her reaction. Her memories were not entirely happy. She never knew her father, she said – he died before her birth. Her mother took in sewing to earn a living and the noise of her treadle machine, whirring into the early hours of the morning, was more familiar than bird-song. There was no garden to play in even if she'd had playmates because they lived in a tiny second floor apartment. As she entered her teens, Irma explained, taking a tissue to dab her eyes, her mother married a war-weary soldier whose main asset was a disability pension. Irma knew she must not appear ungrateful to him so added hastily, "He was very kind to me and worked hard to provide for us with his carpentry business, but he wasn't a strong man"

Margaret was increasingly conscious of the contrast to her own childhood and felt almost guilty. Irma was well aware of the effect her words were having and feigned sorrow when speaking of her stepfather's death, whereas she had in fact been sanguine when it happened. She never forgave him for his lies about her real father – and wouldn't dear Margaret be surprised if she knew who that was!

Continuing the sad story of her life, Irma related how she trained to be a nurse but, not wanting to stay at home, joined the staff of a large hospital near Coventry where she stayed until she married Bill ... such a handsome man but he had been unfaithful to her. She hinted too that Bill had been violent and sometimes beat her when drunk. Untrue, of course, if he really had, she would probably have killed him. After her mother died the house became hers, she said, but it wasn't worth much. She managed to raise a little cash on the furniture but it was all either cheap stuff when it was bought or completely worn out – no priceless long-lost 'old masters' which some were lucky enough to find in their attics!

As Irma expected, Margaret assumed that the cottage was sold – the proceeds forming the basis of her company assets. As soon as she could afford it, she thought, mentally side-tracked, it might be worth doing the place up a bit before putting it on the market. The funeral expenses wiped out her small bank balance and when everything was settled, she would have been in debt again had it not been for an unexpected legacy. It was the discovery that her mother had for years been receiving a monthly income from a trust-fund which changed the course of Irma's life and consumed her with rage. During her mother's last few weeks when she was too weak even to open her own mail, Irma read her bank statement. She queried the small amount deposited on the first day of the month; it had been on every statement she could find in her search through the bureau. Olive at first refused to tell her but, wearily near to death and hoping to stem Irma's constant nagging, she eventually said it was an allowance from her father's family.

Grey Masque of Death

Irma was incredulous. Onto her mother's bed she emptied the box of cherished scorched photographs and demanded – if the whole family perished in a fire – who was there left, to give her money? Was it hush money, she entreated, because the father of her child didn't want to marry her? It was all a lie wasn't it? Irma had demanded an explanation... The handsome young man her mother had loved ... their wedding, which never took place because he, his home and his entire family went up in smoke! Irma's fury had risen as she shoved each photograph in front of her mother's haggard, white face. The dying woman's silence only fuelled her ire. *"Howard,"* she had screamed, *"Is he still alive? Where is he? His sister Sophie! Their father and mother... My Grandparents! Where are they all?"*

Olive gasped something at last, and Irma caught the words, *"Not sister ... Sophie – she was his wife..."* So that was it ... Howard wasn't free to marry – he already had a wife.

For interminable hours, as her mother slowly lost her fragile hold on life, Irma contemplated the people depicted in the tattered collection of pictures who, since infancy, she had been encouraged to believe were her family. In a way, they still were her family ... the regular allowance proved at least that they accepted her as a liability! She finally fathomed the connection between Howard, Sophie their daughter Margaret and the rest ... not like anything she had always been told. They had lived and breathed for her through the wonderful tales her mother recounted – some sad, some funny. Now they looked like strangers: hostile strangers, who had abandoned her pregnant mother and continued to enjoy their own lives of luxury – consciences quieted by a miserable monthly pittance. Well, they were going to pay their dues now!

So used was she to thinking of them familiarly, that she had assumed the family name to be Harris. She had suddenly realised that it couldn't be and her mother refused to tell her the real one. The idea, that Irma might seek them out, terrified Olive who pleaded that the past should be forgotten. She gasped as she was dying that Howard was not to blame, but Irma was way beyond listening to the voice of reason. Preoccupied with her own ghastly recollections, Irma slowly became aware that Margaret was speaking to her...

"Are you all right dear? I didn't mean to revive unhappy memories."

"I'm sorry. Yes I'm fine ... just wondering if I will ever achieve my goal!" Without giving Margaret time to respond she resumed her story hastily. When her mother died, leaving her penniless, she added for effect, she was forty-four years old but determined to stay independent. She had moved back to the Midlands and only worked where she could live in; at least, by doing so, she had no rent to worry about! Her account went down well with Margaret although it didn't add much to her knowledge of Irma who was well pleased with herself.

The part she'd left out would have been far more gripping, but the time to recount that had not yet come! In fact, Irma had actually returned to Coventry, where she was still remembered at the hospital and given a part time job. To her amazement, a few weeks later, a lawyer contacted her. Her mother had left a will – made apparently when she married, because of the property. The mysterious allowance, it explained, was no longer payable, so the capital became part of the estate.

Irma knew the sum must have appeared more substantial forty-odd years ago but even then it was not a generous pay-off considering the scandal they avoided. How could her mother have been so foolish as to accept it? They could have afforded much more to keep her quiet! The lawyer refused to disclose the source of the payment – the instruction had come from another law firm which had been informed of the demise of the beneficiary. The jargonistic clap-trap irked Irma beyond measure. She needed more information. It soon became obvious that she would learn nothing by legal means but she was not deterred – Irma became determined to find Howard if it took the rest of her life and had already formed a plan!

There was a rubber stamp on the back of most of the photographs. All were damaged, but even if only one face survived, her mother had kept it lovingly, so it was easy to piece together the studio logo and town name. Irma's every spare moment from then on was devoted to finding the family that had rejected her. There had indubitably been a fire; her mother must have been there when it happened and had probably retrieved the pictures when they were thrown out. Momentarily Irma felt sorry for her – she must have been besotted with Howard to have wanted to keep such pathetic reminders of him. Lost in thought and almost deaf to Margaret's occasional small-talk, Irma relived the moment she discovered that Howard was dead: beyond her vengeance! But here still was her half-sister, his precious daughter – the one he had acknowledged and nurtured – who would pay dearly for his sins!

***

After a gloomy, rain spattered drive, Jack and Emma checked into their hotel and had time for coffee before keeping her appointment. The middle-aged man who greeted them in the antechamber said his father hadn't been active in the firm for many years but did recall Miss Heywood. He was eager to meet her again and was present, to deal with her business personally. He took them immediately to an inner sanctum which was more a cosy living room than an office. The elderly gentleman seated reading a newspaper sprang to his feet like a two-year-old and advanced on Emma with a warm smile. "My dear lady," he cried enthusiastically, "I would have known you anywhere – you are quite untouched by the years!"

"And you are the same incorrigible flatterer you always were!" rejoined Emma, laughing. She was wearing a high-necked cream silk blouse under a dark-rose, light woollen suit which lent warmth to her pale skin but did nothing to conceal her thin build. "Ignoring my grey hair and all the other deterioration, I must be at least two stones lighter," she pointed out. "On the other hand you really haven't changed much at all." She could well be right Jack thought, as he assessed the man shaking Emma's small hand firmly, enclosing it in both of his. If he really was eighty-six he definitely didn't look it. He was slim, with suspiciously dark hair and had scarcely a wrinkle to mark his advanced age. Emma introduced Jack without delay and they were soon seated with glasses of sherry.

"I hope you haven't made any plans for lunch," said their host, "my wife is expecting you to join us." He was pleased when they nodded their acceptance – Emma said she would be delighted to see Mary again – and he continued, "Now, I know why you want to see me Emma. Do you wish to come and give me the details privately, to get the main business out of the way?"

"It won't be necessary, Brian, Jack knows all about it anyway but I've written out my requirements and if you make the adjustments necessary, I'll sign it before we leave Welshpool." She handed him a prepared sheet, which he folded and put in his pocket without even a glance. He was curious about Jack's problem at which Emma had only hinted, and settled back in his armchair to listen with his hands folded over his chest.

Emma asked him to cast his mind back to 1934 and the terrible fire which destroyed her father's study.

He didn't hesitate; he remembered it well. His memory was sharp and clear about all the details. He'd heard of the fire almost immediately because someone at the fire station, knowing he was a close friend of the family had rung him. It was almost midnight but he drove over to see what he could do to help and viewed the damage while the debris was still giving off wisps of smoke. He tried to calm Sophie who was appalled to have lost so many of the oldest books. He recalled that poor Basil died soon afterward, just before Christmas.

They explained their interest in that period and Dewhurst was appalled to think that 'young Margaret' was at the mercy of a confidence trickster. When he heard why they linked Irma to the maid, Olive, he leaned forward, slapped his knee and cried, "You are right – Olive gave birth to a girl but it's quite beyond me why she should be so vindictive. The family treated her extremely well"

It was astonishing that he should be so familiar with the circumstances of one of the domestics. Jack felt a prickle of apprehension ... were they about to discover that Howard really did have an illicit affair? Emma was aware of Jack's suspicions and for the first time voiced an opinion.

"I'm glad you were so close to the family Brian and know the real truth of what happened. I can only be certain of what didn't! Whoever fathered Irma, I'm sure it wasn't Howard. Please do tell us everything you can recollect about Olive."

Glancing at his watch Dewhurst said it was a long story; better that they should not hear it on empty stomachs. "Mary will be expecting us. She might know more about Olive than I, so let's go and join her for lunch. She made me promise not to keep you here too long. You've known her longer than I have, Emma – you know what she's like if she doesn't get her own way! Believe me, she hasn't changed."

As he ushered them to his car they exchanged frustrated glances ... on the verge of discovery, they were forced to be patient, but at least, Jack whispered, their trip was proving to be well worth while.

Chapter Twenty

Terry White rang Dan at work. At Polly's request he had traced Bill Rigby, the husband of Ermintrude F. Harris. He didn't have any form with the police. There was nothing known of him officially but he had been easy to find as he still lived at the address on Irma's old employment records and worked in Coventry. Terry asked how the investigation was going but Dan pointed out that Polly had only just left; she would be ringing them tonight or tomorrow.

Terry was beginning to take a personal interest in Irma ... she had definitely lied about working with private families. She had done some home nursing long ago, near Evesham, but only part-time hospital work after 1979, until about a year ago. Since then she had apparently done nothing. Her lying could be quite insignificant. Many people hide their origins or glamorise a humble job but combined with the genuine concern that the woman was working a scam it warranted scrutiny.

Terry also noted that she registered for unemployment benefit in Burford which meant she had been in the area, close to Margaret, for a long time before making contact. Why? He suggested, if Dan was available, that they should call on Bill Rigby together. "What about this evening? We'll have to make it early because, to be honest, I have already made a few inquiries and he's a bit of a drinker. If we leave it until after dinner, he'll probably be out at the pub, or incoherent!"

Dan was eager to take an active part in things – Polly would be pleased – so he agreed, arranged to be picked up at six-thirty, then rang Elaine to tell her. She'd be sorry she couldn't go with them but someone had to stay at home in case Polly rang, and she needed to rest anyway. All this excitement couldn't be good for her. He was glad she had agreed to give up her job two weeks before the baby was due ... perhaps by then this whole nasty business would be behind them.

***

Betty, the young waitress in the 'Olde Tea Shoppe', recognised Polly immediately and asked if she'd bought a house yet. In the hope of discovering something useful Polly consumed more coffee and stayed longer than she intended, only returning to the Inn for lunch in the nick of time; five minutes later and they wouldn't have taken her order. Betty had been happy to chat as the café wasn't busy but Polly discovered nothing more of any significance. When asked why she was seeking property in the area she took a chance and said that a friend who was psychic had told her it would be a very good place for her to settle. Betty's blue eyes had widened. "Oh, I wish I knew someone as clever as that," she said. "Well in a way I do, but not nearly well enough to ask for advice." With hardly any prompting Betty continued. "Edna Barr is convinced that the woman who went to work for Mrs Dunn after her companion was killed, is a real medium but nobody else in the village has been given spirit messages, so I can't say if it's true or not."

Polly then had to fend off questions about any proof she had ever had herself that there was 'something in it' and it was obvious that Betty had nothing else to say about Irma. By the time she returned to her room with nothing of any real interest to add to her notes it was after three-o-clock. Her early start, the drive and finally a heavy lunch had drained her of energy so, as there was nothing she could do other than hope Edna turned up in the bar later, she stripped off her outer clothing and lay down for a rest. She hadn't planned to do so but, lulled by the 'in house' radio music, it wasn't many minutes before she was sleeping soundly.

***

Mary Dewhurst was delighted to see Emma. She exclaimed over her lovely silver hair (why had hers gone such a dreadfully dull metal grey, she moaned) and complimented her on keeping her figure (just look at me, completely gone to fat). "Running around after Brian should keep my weight down," she declared, casting him a friendly glare. "Men are so idle – need waiting on hand and foot!" She stopped at last and shook hands with Jack. "You may be the exception, don't take offence."

"For goodness sake woman, do stop wittering on!" Brian interrupted her flow. "We're all starving. Where's lunch?"

It was still a good ten minutes before Mary ran out of steam and reluctantly tore herself away. She talked herself out of hearing with instructions not to say anything important until she got back; the meal was ready; it wouldn't hurt to wait. She wouldn't dream of allowing Emma to help; Brian's niece 'lived in' to assist around the house. After she left them Brian explained that Mary had undergone a hip replacement operation and because of her weight, was not good at keeping her balance. His own activities would be restricted if it were not for Paula, a widow whose children had outgrown the nest; he never left his wife in the house alone. Considering Mary's request, Emma could hardly mention Irma again so confined herself to admiring the house and grounds.

Jack spoke about his mother Helen's life after she left home and Dewhurst picked up the thread. When young, he told them, he often visited the Heywood estate with his father. He was about thirteen when he last saw Helen. "Although I knew you much better, dear lady, being nearer my age," he smiled, nodding to Emma almost apologetically for mentioning age at all, "I recall Helen vividly. She was as a real stunner and I admit I had a 'crush' on her." He grinned as he described himself as heartbroken when she married. He said he hadn't looked at another woman for at least a month!

"When I introduced you to Mary," laughed Emma. "You fell for her head-over-heels too. I think I was the only older woman you didn't fall for!" The two octogenarians giggled like teenagers as their youthful memories came flooding back.

"I always came to you for advice!" Brian wiped tears of mirth from his eyes. "We shared so many secrets; I suspect you knew me too well! You certainly didn't encourage me ... you were a career woman with no intention of being tied to a house." He sighed with mock regret. "I began to believe it when you turned down the wealthy Baron but, even so, I thought you would marry that newspaper chap – the publisher you once worked for. He hardly left your side for years! Whatever happened to him?" Jack was a little embarrassed; they appeared to have forgotten his presence but Emma didn't seem to mind answering.

"Oh, it was never a serious attachment but I enjoyed his company until he started to take me for granted! He became an absolute pain. I never went out with him exclusively, but he was very possessive. It came to a head when he walked into a restaurant, found me dining with someone else, and demanded an explanation in a voice that would have wakened the dead – I thought they were going to come to blows! Everyone in the room sat poised with forks in mid-air."

"Good God! What did you do?"

"There were several newshounds nearby so I held his arm to restrain him and said very loudly, 'What must I do to make you understand? Issue a full-page proclamation? I have no interest in you. Stay out of my life!' It was embarrassing but it worked!"

Brian whistled softly and Jack reflected that perhaps Emma should write her autobiography if she'd had many moments like that!

Mary appeared again and they went to the dining room where Paula was placing a roast capon ready for Brian to carve. She scuttled off, not expecting to be introduced and they settled to enjoy the meal.

While eating, they brought Mary up to date on the purpose of their visit. She remarked that they always received greeting cards from Margaret at Christmas; the firm still took care of her affairs. She remembered Olive far better than Emma because even after Emma left she and Brian, who were married by then, still played tennis with Sophie and Howard and sometimes Margaret joined in. Even before she went away to school she was a promising player. Howard was very proud of her. Olive usually hovered in the background, looking after her. Poor girl: she had been the object of much sympathy after what happened.

What did happen? Emma wondered and tried to ask ... were they never to get to the point? It was impossible to keep on track. Having started to reminisce, Mary was unstoppable. Assuming Emma was asking about Margaret's prowess at tennis she re-played a singles match she had once lost against the child! When they mentioned the fire she went on endlessly about the re-furbishing and poor Sophie's precious first editions ... "The photograph albums? Oh, yes, burned to cinders! It was a real shame."

By the time they succeeded in reverting to the subject of Olive's pregnancy the meal was over.

They returned to the sitting room for coffee and Mary flitted out again with more hopes that they wouldn't resume the 'quite gripping topic' without her. If they had been less pleasant and hospitable Jack would have been irritated. He looked at his watch: almost tea-time! At this rate good manners would dictate that they leave before discovering what they most wished to know.

Dewhurst at least got round to saying that Basil had instructed him to keep an eye on Olive after she left. She was only about twenty-one and alone in the world. She had been part of the household since leaving the local orphanage.

"But why was he so concerned about her?" Emma asked. "As I wasn't living at home then, I can hardly remember her at all!"

"Something had happened a few months earlier which so upset her that she didn't want to stay. Your grandfather felt responsible for her and in fact he invested a small sum of money in her name which I administered personally. I arranged for the interest to be paid monthly, and it was his wish that ..." He suddenly stopped. Mary was calling him urgently – he was wanted on the telephone. He apologised and left them alone.

Jack expressed his anxiety about the time and Emma agreed – they couldn't stay much longer. "Why don't we invite them to eat with us at the hotel tonight? We can say they will be doing us a favour as we still have so many questions to ask. If they refuse it will be an excuse to ask everything we need to know now, before we leave, no matter how late it gets!" Jack declared her a genius. As soon as their hosts returned he invited them to dinner and, although astonished, they accepted with obvious pleasure. With less pressure – less need for haste – both Jack and Emma relaxed for a few minutes while enjoying their coffee. The coming evening should pass pleasantly and with fewer interruptions might prove more informative.

***

Elaine was quite content to stay at home while Dan went off with Terry. Whether they learned anything or not, the change of scene would do him good. He was a real worrier! Now she was putting on more weight he nagged her all the time to sit and put her feet up, but there were lots of things she wanted to do before the baby came. Between working all day and not being allowed to do anything in the evenings her tasks were mounting up alarmingly. It wasn't as if they were heavy jobs, or involved climbing ladders – just sorting cupboards and doing some batch-cooking for the freezer to make sure he ate properly while she was in hospital. With him safely out for a few hours she might catch up.

Grey Masque of Death

Terry was ten minutes early but Dan was ready ... before six-thirty they were heading toward Coventry. By taking the M40 motorway for most of the trip Terry expected to arrive within the hour. They didn't know what to expect, but a mate of Terry's in that division had checked and said Rigby had a woman living in. Whether she went pub-crawling with him was not known. The house, which they had no problem in finding, was a semi-detached, rustic brick with a small square garden patch between it and the road. Not many had garages so, like most of its neighbours, the front wall had been removed and the area cemented to make parking space. As they drew up, blocking the exit of an old Ford Escort, they saw that the front door was open. Someone stood in the dim hall. Terry automatically checked the Ford's tax disc as he walked by and shrugged, "Can't get him for that anyway!"

They heard raised voices from inside. A man shouted irritably, *"Why don't you speak to her? She's not my daughter!"*

"She doesn't care what I say, I'm only her mother!"

A young girl – presumably the subject under discussion – burst out of the doorway almost knocking them over. She was over made-up, with a too-tight mini skirt. Her four-inch long ear hoops swung in a wild tangle of red hair. She took one look at them and went back inside. "Knock it off, you two," she yelled, "I'm off now and you've got visitors out here!" She wobbled out and off down the road on heels so high they imparted a permanent bend to her knees. Fascinated, they stared after her, and agreed she must be all of twelve-years-old.

A woman who could have been her older sister appeared and also watched the girl's rapidly disappearing back. "I don't know what I'm going to do with her! Who'd have children? Sorry you had to hear all that. What can I do for you?" She invited them in and left them alone with Rigby, remarking pointedly that she was 'just going up to get ready'. He took the cue and said they were going out. When Terry showed his warrant card and stated their business, their interest in Irma, the man glowered. He was taller than either of them and Dan felt slightly apprehensive as the swarthy, muscular man drew himself up to his full height and glared down at Terry.

"What the hell does she want now? I needn't give her any support at all you know! She walked out on me!"

"We are here on a different matter entirely." Terry assured him. "She has no idea we're talking to you. In fact we would rather she didn't find out."

"You needn't worry about me telling her! I haven't set eyes on her since she went back to her mother and I don't want to either! What's she been up to then?" Without disclosing the purpose of the inquiry Rigby was enticed to talk about Irma, their life together and the reason for her departure. Bill Rigby said she was never satisfied – it wasn't his fault he couldn't get work. She was always going on about his drinking but she drove him to it ... kept saying she shouldn't have married him ... he wasn't good enough for her! He got sick to death of Irma and her so called good family. When asked specifically if he believed her, he said he had, in the beginning, because she had a box full of old photographs she was always showing off to anyone who would listen.

"What do you mean, 'in the beginning'? What changed your mind?" Dan asked. It was almost the first time he'd spoken and he shot Terry an apologetic glance. Terry nodded and repeated the question.

Rigby looked smug. He said Irma and her stepfather didn't get on at all. She was always comparing him with her 'real' father. Stan was glad to get rid of her when she married Bill but even when they visited his home she couldn't resist looking down her nose at the drabness of everything, making nasty comments.

She was in a vile mood on their last visit before Stan died so Bill took him out for a drink, hoping Irma would calm down. Things were even worse when they returned – she was then angry because it was late. They should have left hours ago because she had to prepare for work; she was on an early shift. Rather than tangle with her husband she attacked Stan – saying he was pathetic! How could she leave him to look after her sick mother when he was too drunk to climb the stairs!

Bill said Stan hadn't drunk all that much, but not being used to strong liquor he wasn't as timid as usual and retaliated. After sounding off about her aristocratic family and much vaunted father being myths, he finally told her she was an unwanted child of rape! She was livid and hadn't believed him for an instant, Bill was sure. Howard was her idol and Kleg was just an ignorant peasant.

Her mother was ill – bedridden – and it seemed that even Irma hadn't wanted to upset her by repeating Stan's words. Bill thought she was so sure they were untrue she saw no point in discussing them. To her it was simply more evidence of Stan's jealousy and small-mindedness. Before leaving, Bill cornered the old man and asked if he had made up the story just to annoy Irma – how could he really know? Stan insisted it was true. Because of the rape Olive was completely 'off' sex. Luckily he'd never been a demanding bloke he told Bill, his war-time back injury had ruined him for that sort of thing. He and Olive had married for companionship. She looked after him – he provided for her and her kid as well as he could. He'd never taken to the girl but for Olive's sake he had always gone along with the deception.

Bill's marriage to Irma was actually bearable for the first week, but she fancied herself a cut above him and the next ten years were hell! In the last few months they were together (although he admitted it was petty) Bill delighted in baiting Irma about her dubious parentage. Infuriated, she never accepted that Stan had spoken the truth and when he died she jumped at the excuse to leave Bill to go home to her mother.

Grey Masque of Death

Alluding to the scene they had witnessed earlier, he said he now had more sympathy with Stan – young girls were a bloody pain in the neck!

They took their leave of Rigby well satisfied. They had confirmed that Irma, however she acquired them, did possess a collection of family photographs. Dan could understand how she must have resented Margaret if she thought they shared the same father. Her resentment might have flowered into full-blown hate if she later came to accept that Howard really had raped young Olive and abandoned them both.

Perhaps her mother, who must have given her glowing accounts of the Heywood clan, recanted on her deathbed and admitted she was raped! Dan hoped it wouldn't be too late to ring Polly when he reached home. Things were really shaping up and she must be warned what she was walking into!

Chapter Twenty-One

Bertha's days went by in increasing loneliness. The mounting tension surrounding her was almost unbearable. Billy still flaunted a bandaged hand, although his wound must have been long healed. He and his gang of young ruffians stood outside jeering, daring each other to cross the garden to grimace through her window. The more she withdrew the more of a curiosity she became, particularly to the smaller children who hovered, staring, on their way to and from school. They pointed if they glimpsed her inside and ran if she opened the door.

The antipathy of the little ones caused Bertha most grief. Some looked so adorable and she'd hoped to gain their trust by making a few overtures but they too believed Billy's hateful calumny. Billy, after all, lived next door to her and was therefore an authority on witches. If he said a sure way of avoiding a curse was either to spit at Bertha, or over her fence every time they passed, then no child would dare risk not spitting. She was hurt and embittered. Why didn't their parents stop such habitual cruelty to a harmless old lady? Bertha could not face another move; she just hoped that by ignoring them they'd tire of tormenting her and find other games.

The month dragged on and the situation didn't improve. Bertha had few callers. Those who did come, representing the local authority or church, left immediately after concluding their business, or simply handing over the parish magazine. One once asked if she was lonely and offered her a kitten, but she refused. The woman's driving motive was to rid herself of a surplus animal not to bring her comfort! The only cats she had ever owned were descended from generations of family pets – Blacky was the last. He had been particularly special ... impossible to replace.

She had been in residence almost six months and instead of happiness and acceptance had encountered only insurmountable hostility and fear. Now she was defeated – she no longer cared. Swaying quietly on the swinging garden seat, isolated with her dismal thoughts, she overheard whispers from unseen bystanders – not only the children – and knew she was an object of hate to all. What had she to live for? On the other hand – who, already claimed by death, did she long to be with again? No-one! There was no hope for her on either side of the grave!

Only one tiny spark of optimism sporadically pierced the gathering shadows in her mind ... her picture must be nearly finished. The young artist – the attractive woman who had been so pleasant, who treated her with respect – would soon come to visit her again. Perhaps she would become her friend. Perhaps she could be persuaded to stay with her, at least for a holiday, if not forever!

***

When Polly entered the bar at eight-o-clock after an early evening meal, it was already full. If all the customers were not regulars it wasn't immediately obvious. Animated conversation made a constant buzz – some remarks were aimed more loudly from one group to another – it was more like a private party than a haphazard gathering. She ordered a sweet sherry and stood holding it, looking for a place to sit. The bartender shouted to a couple seated at a nearby table for four and introduced Polly. "This is Mrs Bailey. She's a guest here – do you mind if she sits with you?" They beckoned her with no hesitation and informed her that they were Sue and Hal. Hal was on the local darts team and he told her there was a match tonight, against a neighbouring village team. She was welcome to join them as long as she cheered for 'the lions' – they needed all the support they could get!

The fact that a match was about to take place explained the presence of such a large crowd ... having a quiet word with anyone in the middle of this melee would be next to impossible. Polly looked around wondering if Edna and her husband were here yet and asked how many players were on the team. As he started to reply Hal caught sight of a new arrival and jumped to his feet with a shout. "Hey, Ted. Sit over here!" Turning back to Polly he said, "Here comes our star player, Ted Barr. There are two others with us – that chap over there with the beard and the old man at the end of the bar counter." Ted joined them and Sue asked where he had left Edna.

"She's here but the car park is full so she drove round the back."

"I take it you are letting your baser instincts take over tonight," replied Sue. She laughed and told Polly, "He never lets Edna drive except when he's in a drinking mood."

"No sane man would," he rejoined, "but don't tell her I said so else I'll have to walk home!" He dragged up another chair as Edna arrived and, in turn, was introduced to Polly. Their table was in a corner and once the men left to play it was relatively quiet.

The surname Barr, cropping up in Barr's Brook, intrigued Polly and she asked Edna if an ancestor of Ted's was a landowner and responsible for the village name. Edna laughed and explained that far from being a wealthy farmer the famous ancestor was a poor labourer who lived with his family in a small shack where the land dipped on the approach to the wood. A century ago, before the road was raised, a small brook ran across the highway. Always, in heavy rains, it flooded to a depth of several feet. "Coaches traversed it with difficulty, but those on foot got wet until Isaac Barr went into business," Edna grinned. "He was a giant of a man – almost seven-feet tall and he carried people from one side to the other, sometimes one under each arm! He charged a farthing a trip and probably made a small fortune; the floods lasted for several weeks at least twice a year."

Sue, not part of the conversation, was far more interested in the darts. She kept jumping up to cheer and almost succeeded several times in tipping over their drinks. After a while, when the competition grew more fierce she excused herself and moved closer to the action. "We sometimes play too, just for fun," Edna said, "but Sue is much keener than I am. I really come for the company and of course, to be with Ted. He enjoys it but wouldn't come out every night if it meant leaving me alone at home."

Polly considered how best to approach Edna and finally decided to be direct – if only she could be sure that her friendship with Irma wasn't deep. As soon as they were alone she mentioned casually her family associations with Mrs Dunn and said she had visited her. "I met her new companion, Irma Rigby, who I understand is a friend of yours ..." Polly managed to put a questioning note into the statement and Edna protested immediately.

"Oh, I wouldn't call her a friend! Well, in a way she was, before, but I don't have much to do with her now."

"Really? I thought you would be closer now," Polly sounded surprised. "As you actually introduced her and recommended her very highly. I thought you must have known her for a long time!"

Edna looked slightly annoyed and declared emphatically that she never said any such thing; she had only known her since she came to stay at the hotel just before Christmas. They met most evenings and got on quite well. Since being in her new post, however, Edna felt that Irma had begun to put on airs – acting superior to her – she was only the hired help, whereas Irma lived there all the time and had become very close to their employer. "To tell you the truth," Edna whispered, "I don't really like the way things are going. I feel guilty; I should never have taken her there. Mrs Dunn is so ... so trusting! Oh, I don't know, I'm probably worrying over nothing!"

Making it easier for Edna, Polly said she had heard about Irma being a clairvoyant and knew why Edna fixed the introduction. She confessed to being intrigued because she also knew someone who was psychic. "I fully accept that these things are possible but I wonder – what did Irma say to convince you she was genuine." As she expected Polly heard again the story of the family which turned Irma out without a reference. Edna said she was sorry for Irma – Christmas being so near and all – but didn't set much store by her strange claims. Then Irma started telling her things about her own family which were true.

"Ted and I kept thinking how she could have found out things ... from the church register, or poking around graves in the cemetery for names and dates. For all I knew she'd been gossiping in the village, but one night she told me something she couldn't have known unless she's truly clairvoyant, like she claims. It happened before she came and was so unimportant I never even told Ted!"

Polly's pulse quickened ... irrefutable proof of Irma's powers was not really what she was after! She managed to ask what that was, if it wasn't private. Apparently it wasn't and Edna explained how she was dusting Jean Webb's room at Riverbank last year, a week before she died, when she saw a man halfway across the field.

"He was leaning against a tree looking through binoculars, I'd never have seen him if he hadn't moved," Edna declared. "Miss Webb said she had seen him before but it didn't matter; she always drew the curtains before putting her room lights on." Edna took another sip of her drink before continuing. Thinking he was spying on them – after all, he was staring in their direction – Edna was very angry and when she saw him in the quarry later, on her way home, she shouted at him.

"What on earth did you say?" Polly asked.

"Pervert...! To be exact, I yelled 'disgusting pervert'!" Edna said she had intended to tell her husband but during the afternoon she discovered that the man was a writer who was bird-watching. She looked contrite and said she definitely never told anyone; in fact she assured Polly that merely thinking about it made her blush.

"So how does this relate to a spirit message," Polly prompted, not wanting Edna to lose the thread.

"Well, here in the bar one night, after saying all the usual stuff about Gran, and my mum being worried about my back – she knew it was playing me up anyway so I took that with a pinch of salt, Irma warned me about jumping to hasty conclusions about people. She said she could 'see' something which happened not long ago ... me on my bike alone and a man standing beyond me. She said she heard me shout and even gave me the exact words! I was so ashamed and absolutely bowled over. I had no doubts after that, she really is psychic. She must be mustn't she?" Polly thought about it for a moment and then suggested that Irma may have heard about it from the man himself. Was that possible? Edna shook her head; she thought it extremely unlikely. She didn't think they even knew each other.

"But Betty, from the café next door, says Irma does a lot of walking. How can you be sure they have never met?" Polly asked.

"I suppose they could have, she usually went off from here towards the woods – she still does I think, but he's hardly ever there – in fact the farmer's wife says she doesn't know why he rents their awful old place; Bleak House she calls it! A tent would be cheaper and probably more comfortable! He spends most of his time in the quarry, nowhere near the woods."

"What other properties are over there?" Polly was reluctant to let the matter drop. "Could she be visiting a friend?"

Edna told her it was all agricultural land for miles. There was only Hill Farm and the dingy old hovel the professor was renting. It was most unlikely that Irma would visit him and she certainly wouldn't go near the farm for love or money... "She is scared stiff of animals, even pet dogs! Anyway, he's lived there since before Irma came and come to think of it, I've seen the professor from the bedroom windows at Riverbank, when Irma was out too, and I've never seen them together!"

Polly noted that the professor observed most of his wildlife in the vicinity of Riverbank and wondered if he had been drawn to the village because he also was interested in Margaret. He and Irma could even be in the fraud together! In spite of Edna's claims to the contrary they had ample opportunity to meet, both being prodigious walkers. She must find out how he found and arranged to rent the cottage ... Betty said it had been on sale for years.

"Why did you say you wished you had not introduced her to Mrs Dunn?" Polly suddenly recalled Edna's earlier remark.

"Well, I thought it would cheer her up at first – the poor thing was so depressed after Miss Webb died – but I never expected her to get so hooked on the supernatural! In my opinion it isn't healthy. And I heard Irma talking to her about investments or something yesterday. I only hope she's not advising her to do anything risky." Edna fidgeted nervously. "The way I look at it, if Irma knew anything about stocks and shares she wouldn't be working for a living!"

Polly did not smile at Edna's view of investment banking. She was too overwhelmed with fears that they might be too late to stop Margaret being swindled. The match was finishing ... there was an anticipatory hush throughout the room. Edna began to say something but several heads turned to stare her to silence. A dart thudded on the board and there were a few sharp groans, quickly stifled. Another sharper clack when the second throw hit a wire and skidded to the floor was immediately followed by a firm thud and an instantaneous burst of cheering from local supporters. The triumphant foursome, flushed with success, came over to the table accompanied by Sue who looked exhausted, as if she had played herself.

Polly congratulated them all and bade them good-night. Before leaving she asked the barman to take some drinks over and charge them to her account. She wished the receptionist good-night as she went through the hall on her way upstairs and within minutes of reaching her room they were speaking again on the house 'phone. There was an incoming call for her – the gentleman inquired if she had retired for the night but as he had just seen her, he was putting the caller through. It was Dan. Polly had contacted Elaine after dinner and given her the Inn number, but not expected to hear from either of them tonight. She felt a surge of excited anticipation; his visit to Coventry must have been fruitful.

She listened, awed, as Dan spoke. Confirmation that Olive possessed family photographs would have contented her, but the added fact that Irma believed herself to be a Heywood and had reason to harbour a grudge against Margaret, was unexpected and satisfying.

It was too late to ring Jack, good news always keeps anyway! It was better to get straight to bed and rest. Judging by the speed at which things were developing she'd need all the stamina she could muster! Her last conscious thoughts were of Sarah. Polly was exhilarated and rather proud to be coping with the problem without bothering her. Sarah would have been willing to help but she had Amy to worry about ... what a lot she would have to tell her, and Clarrie, when they were all home again!

***

Mary Dewhurst had recovered from the initial excitement of meeting Emma again after so many years and during dinner began to be more curious about the reasons for their visit. Hearing that Jack intended visiting Howard's sister she sniffed with derision. She maintained he was unlikely to learn anything of interest from her. Mary had met her several times before Brian's retirement, on various committees; she was an extremely irritating, vague woman who probably had difficulty remembering her own address!

Emma reminded her that they must discover what happened to Howard after he left Sophie and in particular whether he left his daughter Margaret wealthy enough to make her a target for a swindler.

"Why, that's no secret," said Mary. "It was a local scandal because his sister told everyone she met. He had got through most of the Heywood money – sorry Emma dear – it must be a painful subject for you and Jack, but he owned a beautiful villa in France. He took in a succession of so called friends to live with him and the one who was there at the end inherited the property!"

Mary expressed amazement that Emma had not known and continued eagerly. "His sister Vera, who is about our age, was furious. I imagine she and her husband are not well off. Anyhow, Howard's money, what was left of it, was split three ways; thirds to her and Margaret. The remaining third went with the villa – presumably to help with running expenses until the lucky person could sell it."

While Mary occupied Emma, Brian took the opportunity to tell Jack roughly the same story. He had not handled Howard's will so didn't know the details ... if he had he wouldn't have been discussing the point at all! It was obvious that Dewhurst had a low opinion of Howard. He said he would have expected everything Howard owned to go to Margaret and Vera, his sister, "But after all, both were happily married and he had his own life to lead. I don't think he saw much of Margaret after she married at the end of the war. Her husband was quite wealthy, otherwise I expect he would have looked after her interests. He was devoted to her when she was a child. I think he bought his place in the

Loire Valley in 1937 and couldn't wait to get back to see how it had stood up to the occupation"

Jack felt that Dewhurst was withholding something but refrained from asking questions. It was better to listen – they had finished coffee and time was going too fast. "Let's order more coffee and liqueurs and sit comfortably in the lounge," he suggested. He hastened to the quiet bay he had spotted from the dining room and the others followed. Once settled, Emma launched resolutely into the topic of Olive's pregnancy. She asked again why her grandfather, Basil, should have felt obligated to support his housemaid. Emma ruled Howard out but, even at seventy-four, could Basil himself have been responsible?

Dewhurst was so taken aback, he gasped with astonishment before laughing aloud. He said he had better start at the beginning and give them the whole truth. "You must both know how Basil hated turning away anyone in need and many people were out of work during the thirties. He had a large staff already but when the head gardener asked that his son be taken on, against all advice including mine, he allowed the young man to occupy a room in an outhouse on the estate to undertake odd jobs." Before they could ask, Dewhurst told them that the man had served time in prison for assault but the old gardener pleaded that his boy was a reformed character who needed the security of a good job. He vowed he would keep him on the straight and narrow and his son did in fact appear to settle down. He worked well.

One night Olive Harris left the house after dark to fetch the doctor for Sophie. The telephone was out of order and although Sophie protested that she didn't need medical attention Basil sent the girl to the village on her bike and the doctor drove over. He pronounced Sophie's chest pains to be indigestion. As he was leaving Olive staggered across the driveway from the bushes – she'd been beaten and brutally raped after entering the grounds. She almost died, but when she was well enough she identified the gardener's son. He went back to prison but Basil never forgave himself for taking the chap on in the first place, then sending the girl out so late at night.

Dewhurst sat back, having cleared both Howard and Basil, but when they still looked expectant he gave them the rest of the story. "I tried to convince Basil that if the villain hadn't done it that night, he would have attacked her at some other time – it was inevitable if he felt that way about her, but Basil was adamant. He took full responsibility and did all he could to help her." At Basil's request a place had been found for Olive to live – just a couple of rooms – but the estate took care of the rent for many years, until she married and moved out.

If Olive had died before her daughter came of age the child would have continued to receive the allowance, any siblings having no share. It was just as well, Brian said – by today's standards it would not have stretched far! As Irma was in her forties the account was closed and the original sum on deposit became due to her.

The party soon broke up after these revelations. Emma and Jack were satisfied. They were in possession of all the important facts. They wondered how well informed Irma was. She must have received the legacy and may have felt it was meagre – but surely she would only adopt that attitude if she thought her mother had been badly treated! Jack wished he had Polly's telephone number – she should have all their latest findings as soon as possible.

He rang directory inquiries and scribbled down the number of the Lion, which was the most likely place for Polly to be staying, but then decided it was too late to call. Emma agreed it would be better to ring in the morning and, as Jack now had the address of Howard's sister, suggested that he contact her first in case she had anything else of interest to add. Emma said she wouldn't go with him – she knew she wasn't as fast on her feet as he, and didn't want to delay him.

Jack smiled, noting she was not too old to blush as she added, "Anyway I promised to meet Mary and Brian for coffee."

Chapter Twenty-Two

Wednesday April 22nd...

Jack rose early, at seven-o-clock, determined to reach Howard's sister before she went off for the day. She might be in her nineties but appreciation of Emma's remarkable vitality had disabused him of his previous assumption that old ladies could be relied upon to sit at home knitting! His alarm call from the switchboard was closely followed by a discreet tap on the door. Thank heaven for room service he thought as he enjoyed a hearty breakfast. He had ordered a taxi to be sure of finding the right address with no loss of time.

Dewhurst said the house was in a maze of streets but actually not far off the main road where there was a frequent bus service so he should have no trouble getting back before lunch. It was just after nine-o-clock when the taxi dropped him and the terraced street was so still and quiet it was difficult to believe it was actually inhabited, until he saw several curtains twitch but, at number thirty, there was no sign of life at all. Next door, in number thirty-two, a face appeared and he risked nodding to it. It stared, motionless, showing no response.

Ostentatiously, he looked along the house fronts, holding aloft his note of the address. As he expected, the woman lost no time in coming out to speak to him. "Good morning," Jack greeted her. "Can you help me please; I'm looking for Mrs Bowles."

"She won't see you if you're selling anything," the woman rejoined, waiting expectantly for him to state his business. When he merely gave an understanding nod, she continued, "I don't buy at the door either. Are you from the Council?"

When he still gave no explanation for his presence she advised him, "She doesn't let anybody in if she's on her own. You can't be too careful these days – and she is ninety-two you know!"

Jack said he thought her husband was still with her.

"Oh, he is, but he's old himself – eighty-four and not a well man. When he's in hospital she never even comes to the door except for me. I have my special knock."

"Perhaps you could give her your special knock now? It really is most important that I speak with her."

"If I did, you'd hear it! I'm not stupid you know!"

Jack was getting nowhere so he pulled out his driving license and held it for her to read. "I am a retired Army Officer, Heywood-Hall as you can see. Mrs Bowles late brother and I were related by marriage.

If you would care to verify my credentials with the dear lady I shall be pleased to step away, out of hearing!"

The woman sniffed but was clearly impressed. "No need," she admitted, "she's not on her own now. He's in, and I know he's up because he's taken in the milk and paper!"

Jack concealed his irritation and lifted the shining brass knocker. When it was answered the woman was still at his elbow. He looked at her pointedly, thanked her and waited quietly, staring at her until she retreated, He then introduced himself and was shown into a dark but comfortable front room by an extremely nervous Mr Bowles.

The old man smoothed back his wispy white hair with both hands but it immediately frothed up again giving him a halo as he stood with his back to the window. He was painfully thin and stooped. "My wife isn't down yet, I'm afraid. You'll have to wait," he whispered. He ran a finger over the surface of a small table and said, "Please overlook the dust – I just haven't been able to do much this week ... it's my back. It plays me up something terrible!"

"I understand you've been in hospital," Jack sympathised. "It must be very hard if you also have to take care of your wife."

"It is, it is. I don't know how long she'll be, because she's very slow these days. Is it anything I can help you with?"

Jack decided to explain. The man was coherent and affable ... from what Mary had said about Mrs Bowles he might be better off talking to her husband. He was disconcerted when Bowles, on hearing that he was seeking information about the old days, asked how old, because he was Vera's second husband! Her first died in 1928 and he married her in 1930. "If that's far enough back I might be of some use! I knew Vera's first very well you know, my older brother was his best man," he smiled. "There isn't much about the family I don't know."

With this assurance Jack spoke about Howard and the Heywood family. When he said that Emma was also visiting Welshpool for a few days, Bowles became animated. "Oh, I remember her although I only met her once. She was the clever sister." Realizing that Jack might be offended he said hastily, "Your mother Helen was the beauty. We used to say she could have been a film star: beat Clara Bow into a cocked hat!" Jack grinned. Emma would be tickled to hear that; she would want to know how Bowles knew her, so he gleaned a few more details.

Bowles had been a photographer on the local paper in his early twenties and had been asked to help with some illustrations for an article Emma wrote about Welsh folk lore. He sighed ... "Yes, she was the clever one alright – carried on writing, didn't she? For the glossies and books too ... I have a few here somewhere." He looked about vaguely but made no move to find them. He started saying something about Emma being quite attractive, although not in Helen's league. "She was popular, plenty of followers too, and she enjoyed life, not like –" ... but suddenly, grasping the arms of his chair, he pushed himself up. "Good grief, where are my manners? I haven't offered you a drink!"

"Please don't worry," Jack assured him, "I'd much rather talk."

He thought Bowles must be wondering why he'd come. He wondered himself really. The visit was planned before they knew the facts of Olive's rape but he was still curious to know why Howard hadn't kept in closer touch with Margaret. Everyone said he was a devoted father, but his later actions indicated otherwise. The old man probably didn't have much to relieve his boredom so Jack decided to tell him the whole story. When fully in the picture he might be in a mood to exchange information.

An hour later, they were still sitting alone. Bowles didn't remember Olive by name but recollected the scandal. The rapist's father, the old gardener, was heartbroken. He gave up his job and died within a year or two. Jack admitted that before learning the true facts he had wondered if Howard had had an affair with the maid. Bowles' reaction was startling. He roared with laughter and tears streamed down his hollow cheeks. It was some time before he finished mopping his eyes and spoke. "Howard? No way ... he wasn't interested in girls! He was a right powder puff! "

"But he ... and Sophie," Jack protested, "surely it can't be true!" He was stunned. Of course Emma knew, or suspected; it explained her absolute conviction that Howard was not a likely rapist. She may have expected him to find out but didn't want to be the one to tell him.

"It's funny, you reaping it all up again," Bowles said, "because I hadn't given much thought to those days until last year. A young friend of mine works for a photographic studio, a family firm – been operating for donkey's years and still thriving." Jack tensed, discerning that he was on the edge of a significant discovery. He was not disappointed. Bowles cleared his throat and resumed. "I occasionally did outside work for them until it got too much for me and I recommended him to take over. He told me they'd had an inquiry about some Heywood portraits. Someone sent a code number from the back of an old photograph and asked if the name of the sitter was on file. It was of course – it was Sophie!"

Jack was jubilant ... so that was how Irma found the family. Dewhurst would be gratified. He'd been adamant that Olive would not have divulged information about them to her daughter, because he had a strange letter from her just before her husband died – the only time she ever wrote. She specifically asked him, if anyone should inquire, not to reveal the name of her old employer. He thought it strange but complied with her wishes. Even when winding up the trust – writing to her lawyer in connection with the legacy, he did not disclose it.

Turning the conversation back to Howard, Jack learned that he married Sophie because he was bribed. Sophie was getting older but refusing all comers, although she did want to give Basil the grandchild he craved. Basil was determined to see his eldest daughter respectably married and persuaded her to accept Howard. She did so with certain provisos. He must agree to stay faithful to her until she produced a healthy baby. Howard sought social acceptance, so the idea appealed to him but he had some terms of his own. He wanted a regular allowance and time off! Basil consented on condition he took all holidays abroad and didn't shame the family.

"But why didn't Sophie divorce him later? Even in those days it could have been arranged discreetly."

"Why should she?" Bowles smirked. "She wasn't likely to hook up with another man! That was what started it all ... Basil found out about her and her friend Meg and was apoplectic to think such depravity was going on under his own roof! He threatened to turn Sophie out unless she came to heel and married. A scandal would have killed her mother; her own good name would have gone down the drain too. Fairies stayed at the bottom of the garden in the 'Roaring Twenties' ... they certainly did not come out of the closet!"

So, thought Jack, all was becoming clear at last. He cast his mind back to those moments when he'd detected a note of reticence in Emma's tone: only when discussing Howard's conduct: never Sophie's: not even when Meg's name came up. If Emma knew of her sister's real relationship with Meg, her old school friend she was a damn good actress! Jack thought she was probably ignorant of her eldest sister's personal proclivity. As it had no bearing on the present, it was best ignored – especially for Margaret's sake. In all probability Emma hadn't guessed but, even if she knew, she certainly wouldn't wish to be reminded.

But years later, after Ermintrude died, why did Basil allow Howard still to control Sophie's financial affairs? He voiced his thoughts, not imagining that Bowles would know the answer ... it was a rhetorical question, but the old man chuckled. "Well, that was Howard's good fortune – he always fell on his feet! He told me Basil hated his closeness to young Margaret – considered him unreliable and a bad influence – so they struck another bargain."

He spun out the pause by blowing his nose then continued. "On condition that Howard kept away and saw her for a maximum of two weeks a year, Basil gave him a lump sum and increased his allowance until the girl was twenty-one. He would then have changed his will had he lived; talk about the luck of the Devil!"

Bowles was enjoying Jack's undivided attention ... it wasn't often these days that anyone asked him for information about anything!

Jack did some rapid calculations. Margaret must have been twelve or thirteen when their grandfather died. Few expect to die young but he was seventy-four, a good age in 1934 ... a few years later he would probably have split up his estate far more fairly. Who knows! Jack's own mother might have been a wealthy heiress!

It was no use fretting over what might have been. If more people recognised their own mortality their affairs would be settled more efficiently. At least Basil did make a will. Some clung to the sixteenth century belief that doing so heralded their death, and therefore missed their only chance of having a say in distributing their own wealth!

Bowles was still chortling when they heard footsteps coming slowly down the stairs. He sobered quickly. "Please don't let on I've told you about her brother. She's never got over him turning out queer and leaving all his stuff to another man!" He went to announce that they had a visitor and they returned together.

The woman, who tottered slowly into the room leaning heavily on a walking cane, was as thin as her husband but straight backed and taller. She smiled and said it was nice of him to call, they had very few visitors. Embroiled in disjointed small talk Jack was extremely glad he had already discovered all he wished to know. In desperation, when she launched into a description of one of his 'dear Grand mama's' hats, he mentioned Brian and Mary Dewhurst. He said he'd had dinner with them. At last something clicked and the old lady said she knew Mary well. "We were on the board of the orphanage together, you know. She was a lovely woman – a tower of strength."

As she went on at length about her work with the dear children, Jack glanced at his watch and caught her husband's eye. He took the hint and interrupted her, giving Jack a chance to stand and take his leave. At the door Bowles said he hoped things would work out well for Margaret. They had no children so he supposed, being a niece, she was the only family Vera had left! Jack thanked him and gave him Margaret's address. "If you can bring yourself to write to her about her father, leaving out all reference to you know what, of course, I'm sure she would appreciate it. She will probably be living alone again soon."

Walking to find the bus stop, Jack's step was light. The pieces of the puzzle were all in place; soon they could expose Irma for what she was ... he could hardly wait to ring Polly.

***

Eric's taxi was weaving slowly through Reading's lunchtime traffic. He thought his two passengers seemed a bit more cheerful than they usually were after a hospital visit.

Amy could hardly believe that her father-in-law, after years of being little more than a wax doll, was showing signs of improvement. It only went to show, she said, that doctors didn't know everything. Her interest in him ended there; she was more concerned about lunch. What tasteless fare would be dished up today she pondered, no way would she eat another salad! When Sarah pointed out that she would be more ready to enjoy dinner, Amy immediately asked what Nettie was fixing for their evening meal, but to her frustration Sarah didn't know.

While she muttered on, Sarah reflected on the events of the morning. She no longer needed to speak, to bring John out of his dreamlike state. As soon as she sat and took his hands, he looked beyond her eagerly, hoping to see again his beloved Dorothea. He was still silent but smiled and looked serene, with a new awareness of his surroundings and this morning there had been a significant break through. When Sarah rose to go he clutched her arm and said quite clearly, "Thank-you. I know she'll wait for me; it will be different this time if I go now, before it's too late! God bless you"

Dr. Ellis was beside himself, amazed and excited. He didn't understand what had happened but immediately tried to persuade Sarah that she should see another difficult patient! If her refusal offended him she was sorry, but she was confused and alarmed by John's words. What had he meant by 'going now' and 'being too late'?

All her experience rejected the only explanation which sprang to mind ... she squashed it firmly. It was outlandish ... totally unacceptable!

***

Jack tried to telephone Polly but was disappointed. The desk clerk said Mrs Bailey had been out all morning; would he care to leave a message? He declined. There was no simple way of explaining in a few words how the situation had changed and he couldn't risk any information falling into the wrong hands. He was not sure of his movements anyway, so she wouldn't be able to ring back ... better to wait for Polly to call him tonight. Things had gone so well that he and Emma could have left today, but they would fill in the time agreeably. It might be interesting to talk to the owner of the long established studio ... Jack hoped it would be possible to order copies from the family negatives, assuming any still survived. As the studio was likely to be closed for the afternoon he rang up. It took a few minutes to progress from receptionist to secretary but after explaining the unusual nature of his business he was rewarded with the home number of the senior partner, Mr Gordon Fox., the girl informed him.

To Jack's delight, Mr Fox said he'd visited the Heywood place as a boy. He was eager to meet Miss Emma – he had all her books! They were both invited over for the afternoon and he would pick them up from the hotel as his house was in the country and difficult to find. Emma was delighted. She wondered if the owner was the young man who had helped her with the photographs of Chaz ... "Good gracious," she looked startled, "It can't possibly be him! He must have been at least twenty in 1913 – he'd have to be over a hundred years old!"

They went to lunch in high spirits, looking forward to another fruitful meeting, hoping Polly was having equal success.

***

Clarrie's work was going so splendidly she resolved to relax for the afternoon. It was such a lovely day for a drive that she paid a surprise visit to the Williams. She decided against ringing first – they were busy people and she didn't want them to go to any special trouble, as they might if she warned them of her coming. As she expected Gwen welcomed her warmly and only bemoaned the fact that her husband Bill was not at home. He wouldn't be back until late night. Gareth too was away for a few days and Gwen said they would be disappointed to have missed her.

She was in the middle of a baking session so Clarrie sat in the kitchen and sampled everything as tray after tray emerged from the two huge ovens. Two hours later when tea-time actually arrived, Clarrie refused to stay any longer; after eating all afternoon and having drunk endless cups of tea, her conscience was already giving her trouble. "Everything was so delicious I couldn't resist – now I'll definitely have to forego dinner!" It had been pleasant and gossipy – all girls together.

"Why don't you have a break? Spend some time with us," Gwen suggested. "Gareth is on holiday next week and could take you out painting again! ... Always going on, he is, about this or that marvellous view you would like!" Clarrie laughed and could see nothing against accepting. Her mother would be sure to think it was a good idea so she promised to return on Saturday for a few days instead of going home.

She was surprised when she rang Mapledurham an hour later to find no-one in. No-one had been in touch with her so she assumed everyone was just out on errands. Mystified, but unworried, she left a message on the machine and asked someone to ring back if there was anything against her not returning at the weekend. When her call wasn't returned before she went to bed at 11:30 PM. she was puzzled but still not alarmed. After all, including Pat for some of the time, there were three responsible people in the house every day!

***

After Polly had rung the local estate agents and found that most had practically forgotten the existence of the farmer's old house – although it was still on their books, she struck lucky in Witney, eight miles beyond Burford. The man there remembered an inquiry for a small isolated place in her area, about eight months ago.

He had made no secret of the dilapidated state it was in, but the woman was still interested, so they sent her the details. She had not rung back and he was reluctant to supply her name and address over the telephone. He hinted that he could look up the information if Polly called personally, but he wouldn't be there after one-o-clock... No, it wasn't early closing day, but his afternoon was full. Polly told him to expect her and left immediately. She looked at her watch as she parked her car in Witney; she had made it with half an hour to spare. As long as he wasn't tied up with a customer it would be worth the rush.

She was lucky, the agent was free to deal with her and he remembered her query as soon as he heard her voice. "Ah, yes, the lady who was less interested in property than in my other clients," he said with a smile which took the edge off his words. "I am exceedingly curious about your reasons for wanting to know. Are you thinking of buying the place yourself?"

"Not exactly," Polly confessed, "but it's occupied by a writer at the moment. I wonder who made the arrangement. If he contacted the farmer personally, who told him it was available? It could have been through your office." Seeing that her words aroused not just curiosity, but something verging on antagonism, Polly added quickly, "I'm not at liberty to say why I need to know, but if you check with Detective Sergeant White of the Reading CID, he will vouch for me."

She didn't think for a moment that the agent would bother – his mailing list was hardly top secret or confidential, but it sounded good and worked like a charm. He looked it up with no more delay and said the interested party was a Miss Kleg. The name meant nothing to Polly! He scribbled the address for her; a box number in Coventry.

Polly voiced surprise that the property appeared to be unmarketable. Even if it needed renovating there were usually investors willing to take over such places, yet none of the estate agents seemed to be pushing it. She learned that it was difficult to sell because it wasn't freehold. It was part of a parcel of land taken on a ninety-nine year lease. The owner had already indicated that the title was not for sale, otherwise the present leaseholder, the farmer, would have bought it up himself. Neither he nor anyone else was willing to spend money on the property because the lease had only another twenty years to run.

The young man frowned. "I'm astonished that he's even found someone to rent it, it needed several thousands spent on it to make it habitable when I saw it," he said. "Perhaps I'll get in touch with the farmer again; if he's fixed it up I'm sure I could find him another tenant."

After her busy morning Polly returned to the Inn and rested in the early afternoon, first writing down what she wanted to tell Jack. At four-o-clock she went out to call at the few shops within walking distance. Her friendly manner always made others relax but, other than the farmer, nobody had actually met the professor so Polly discovered little more about him; he always turned away if approached and never shopped in the village even though he didn't have his own transport. He had arrived originally by taxi, not Ted's, and in the first month had occasionally been seen returning from a supermarket, about five miles away, on a late bus. Nobody knew where he spent Christmas and few had seen anything of him at all this year. Betty's mother, Belinda Jones at the post office, said if the man sent greeting cards, he didn't send them locally. She'd evidently heard about Polly from her daughter and gossiped happily as if with an old friend, while dealing with other customers. Over an hour passed before Polly bought postcards and left the shop. She still didn't see how it mattered but the professor was an enigma and made her feel uncomfortable. It might be a good idea to visit him tomorrow. Presumably he had a tongue in his head – he communicated with the farmer!

Before going to dinner she did her telephoning. Jack said he might return to Barr's Brook at the weekend. There was too much to tell her on the phone but he was convinced that they had enough evidence against Irma to warn Margaret and wondered if Polly could extend her own visit. Polly then rang Pat to give her the Inn number and heard that both Sarah and Clarrie had left messages to say they would be away until next week so there was no reason why she should not stay on longer, to meet Jack. When she rang him again tomorrow night she would tell him of her change of plan. She hadn't mentioned the professor to Jack; he did not tell her that Olive had married a man called Kleg. Neither thought the information important.

***

Irma lay in bed swallowing her mounting panic. Edna had not admitted that Polly Bailey even spoke to her at length. She kept going on about the damned darts match, but there was an evasiveness about her which betrayed her. It was way past midnight but Irma was too overwrought to sleep. Eventually, having evaluated the situation, she calmed down. Edna knew nothing of her plans and could only repeat what she had been told by Irma personally, so what harm had been done?

Tomorrow she'd make her weekly call at the farm ... only one more visit after that and she could lay the professor to rest. She would soon be done with the whole tedious business and there was nothing the interfering Mrs Bailey could do about it.

At last, smiling, she slipped into a deep sleep.

Chapter Twenty-Three

Thursday April 23rd...

Amy was irritable. She wouldn't have minded rising early every morning and going out with Sarah if only they went somewhere other than the wretched hospital as she continually referred to it. Sarah admitted there was little else she could expect to learn from the old man, but something kept drawing her back – probably her unwillingness to admit defeat!

She suggested that Amy stay at home; she didn't mind going alone. Amy sighed and refused – at least they could enjoy the drive there and back together, she said (Sarah hid a wry smile) and her new monthly magazine had arrived; she could take it to read in the waiting room. "It's full of diets and ways to 'Keep Your Figure and Your Man', by exercising: unadulterated rubbish! It is so boring. I'm cancelling it!"

In spite of her scorn, her own revised eating regime, even after only a few days, had made her feel better. She admitted to having less indigestion – heartburn, she always called it – and was sure her clothes felt slacker over the midriff ... if only she had done it earlier, for Jay! Sarah kept re-assuring her that she did indeed look healthier, with natural bloom in her cheeks. Amy was becoming used to spending more time in the fresh air, strolling down the lane or in the garden. Once, she actually leaned over the rock garden to pluck out a weed. Whatever else, Sarah reflected, at least she could feel satisfied that her attempts to reform Amy were succeeding.

An hour later, looking into the melancholy, lined face of John, Sarah wished she felt as confident about her efforts with him. He seemed to trust her and his eyes became animated when she sat with him but, in spite of the doctor's many assurances that Mr Johnson's demeanour had definitely improved, she still didn't feel she was doing enough. Dr. Ellis always remained in the room to observe her sessions. Sarah said it must be frustrating for him when nothing spectacular happened; he did, after all, have other patients, but the doctor knew she would return home soon and was confident that he could rely on his staff to cope in his absence.

Minutes had elapsed since Sarah last spoke and the doctor caught her eye. He beckoned her to accompany him and they left the room. He had come to a decision – he would allow her to listen to the tapes made when Mr Johnson was under hypnosis. Mr Johnson's wife, when she read extracts from them, could make no sense of his ravings but the doctor thought Sarah deserved to make her own assessment.

Sarah's pulse quickened with anticipation. It was an unexpected, but hoped for, development. With luck, she would find the key – the cause of John's collapse. Dr. Ellis conducted her to his office where he unlocked a cabinet full of tapes and recording equipment. Soon she was listening to 'Tape 1 of 8'. With his notebook in his hand – it was full of numbers – the doctor occasional whizzed through sections where he told her there was either silence or gibberish, but apart from that, they hardly spoke between tapes. Almost two hours later, the final tape ended and as he re-wound them he asked optimistically if they had helped.

Sarah thanked him and assured him they had but, in fact, she was completely bewildered. She instantly rejected as delusion, the chronicle of events which surfaced from his past. And yet ... was she justified in being so high handed? She wasn't omnipotent! She therefore forced herself to be open-minded. Although John had rambled on, in a monotonous confusion of statements and random thought, there was a continuous thread of sense somewhere. No, she corrected herself – an *almost* coherent thread of *nonsense*! To accept his every word as true would be to acknowledge the impossible but she tried to apply logic to John's claims. Whatever rubbish was spinning in his head, he was forty at the end of the war not forty-five. Where had he come from? According to Dorothea he had lost his memory after being almost killed by a bomb.

Trying to suspend disbelief, Sarah understood that he imagined he was Jay. They had both been caught in explosions at a similar age – he had survived to marry and have a son; Jay had died, childless. John now seemed sane enough to understand that Jay had been killed when an experiment went wrong, in fact it was this information that had shocked him out of his stupor. He rambled on as if his own injuries, at the end of the war, had also been caused by an explosion in a laboratory ... the same explosion that had caused, not Jay's death, but his also going back in time... History repeating itself... Pure science fiction! Even so, Sarah forced herself to pursue the line of thought. She must try to follow his mad reasoning if she were to be of any use to him.

He really believed that, at this very moment, Jay was not dead. Now known as John, he was living a parallel existence in 1944, meeting a young Dorothea who, if only he had not lost his memory, he would surely have recognised as his own mother in her girlhood! A year later – next year – they would have a baby son, Jay: a reincarnation of himself, John senior!

Accepting this preposterous idea, what the old man had said yesterday as they left his room had a weird logic. He wanted to die now, to be with Dorothea. The poor deluded man really believed that if his spirit failed to escape before his son Jay's birthday, they would be trapped in a mad merry-go-round ... two souls doomed to revolve with each other for eternity!

***

Before leaving the Lion for her exploratory walk in the countryside Polly brought her notes up to date. It would be fun going through them with Sarah and Clarrie when she returned home.

It was a fine day but not very warm. Apart from a raincoat she had only her good woollen coat with her and didn't want to tramp over the fields in that, so she donned an extra cardigan over her blouse and 'V' necked jumper. She had planned to start out earlier but couldn't resist having a good breakfast. She hoped she would still be in time to catch the professor at home before he started his bird-watching... Perhaps she should have foregone eating, Twitchers were probably early risers.

She didn't meet a soul on her way out of the village and very little traffic went by before she turned off the main road to walk along the edge of the wood. The hum of traffic became more constant as the roads filled but gradually faded in intensity until it was no longer audible. A little later the solitude began to disturb her. The tall Beech trees threw cool shadows over the dirt track and she couldn't repress a shiver. She wished she had worn her warmer coat after all.

When she saw the isolated house it did nothing to lift her unsettled mood. It was shabby, square and gloomy with filthy windows. Part of the roof was bare of tiles and the garden was non-existent. A jungle of weeds and long grass struggled up, seeking light between several worn-out apple trees and a dead oak.

There was no sign of life inside and she almost turned back. If Jack returned on Saturday, as he'd suggested, they could come out together ... but it seemed ludicrous, having come so far, not even to knock at the door. What harm could it do? She could ask directions to the farm if the man looked unfriendly. She lifted the iron knocker and it fell heavily on the rusty metal plate beneath it. The echo reverberated as if in an empty cavern. There was no answer.

No-one inside could have failed to hear and Polly's natural curiosity flooded back. She walked along the broken path to the rear of the house. The dark green paint on the back door was peeling from wood which looked damp and rotten; how could anyone consider living in the place even for a weekend let alone six months. It was astounding. For the sake of propriety she banged on the least dirty part of the door and was startled when it swung away from her. For a moment she thought someone inside had opened it, but the bracket that should have held the latch was hanging off. The kitchen into which she stepped was such a mess that she couldn't credit it was in use; where did the man prepare his food? She spotted a wrapped, half-loaf alongside a tub of butter on a breadboard. They could have been there for days or months – there was no way of knowing. All was dusty and still.

Calling out occasionally, Polly walked through to a dark living area. The stone floor was bare and in the middle of the room stood a wooden table with four old kitchen chairs; one was overturned – its leg broken off. The large open fireplace bore no sign of having been used recently – if ever, but a portable stove stood near a battered armchair which was the only other piece of furniture. A fairly respectable rug covered it. That's where he sits, if he really lives here, Polly noted. Of course, the bedroom might be better furnished! The chance to find out was now, and pure nosiness overcame her scruples.

She went up the stairs – fortunately still sound. Only one room boasted a bed so she didn't waste time on the others. The low cot was bare. A swing-mirror stood on a chest in front of the window and near it was a washstand with a jug, bowl and towel rail. Hanging on the rail was a fairly clean towel. That was all – no suitcase or other luggage. Then she saw a built-in wardrobe and slowly opened the cupboard door.

***

Irma, the absent professor, was on her way back from the farm with her weekly supplies. It was a nuisance but she dared not fail to go, otherwise they might be curious about her absence and start looking for the strange old man who was barely civil to them – who collected his order with a grunt, thrust out a grey-gloved hand to pay for the goods and take his change, and never lingered to pass the time of day.

She always tried to avoid the farmer. His wife was very short-sighted but the masquerade still made Irma extremely nervous. In one more week she would be free of the eccentric writer for ever. He would disappear as mysteriously as he had arrived! Removing her gloves she took a key from her pocket and opened the front door of the dilapidated property. As she entered she was instantly shocked into immobility. At the end of the long empty corridor the door to the kitchen stood wide open ... beyond it, the back door was ajar! She could see into the empty garden. Someone had been in – and could be here still.

She walked stealthily to the scullery. The bolt should have been in place; she had never used it, knowing that the frame, to which both staple and latch were attached, was rotten – but they would have held if left undisturbed. She crept up the stairs and heard a hinge squeak in the front bedroom, the one she was using. Her unwanted intruder was opening the wardrobe. Keeping her feet close to the wall to avoid making the stairs creak, she advanced slowly up to the landing. The key in the cupboard door rattled as it closed again and Irma moved nearer to the bedroom.

Polly had expected to find clothes in the wardrobe but it almost empty and, moreover, contained only female attire. One hanger held a skirt with a suede jacket. An underskirt and cream blouse were on another with a white lace brassiere looped over the hook. It was quite beyond her – unless she had uncovered the professor's love nest! Crossing to the battered dresser she found it messy with talcum powder. A flowered cotton toilet bag spilled some of its contents ... dark blue cream shadow and a brown eyebrow pencil. The incongruity struck her forcibly as she also registered what was absent ... there was nothing in it for a man, not even a shaver.

Whether or not she guessed the truth in that instant is immaterial. It was too late to do anything about it. Behind her, in the mirror, she saw a bizarre figure ... Irma dressed as a man. Her dark hair escaping from beneath the tweed cap was streaked white and falling in clumps over her garishly painted face. Holding the broken chair leg aloft Irma was hurtling across the room.

Recognizing Polly, Irma knew instantly that she couldn't afford to let her escape. There was too much at stake; everything she had already done would have been for nothing!

Polly had no time to react. She uttered a low moan as she was clubbed to the floor where she lay inert as another heavy blow descended on her defenceless head.

***

Edna wasn't her usual cheerful self. Instead of humming as she did her chores she worked quietly and looked confused when approached. Margaret wondered what was wrong but was sure it had something to do with Irma, because she too had seemed distracted. She felt she was being excluded from something, yet how could they be conspiring against her? It was unthinkable! Now she had another problem. Irma had gone to the mobile library as she always did on Thursdays but even if she collected a few groceries she always returned before eleven. It was nearly twelve thirty! What on earth was she doing?

Edna was ready to leave. Ever since meeting Mrs Bailey she had been worrying about her evident interest in Irma ... it was as if she suspected her of something. Even though Edna had denied the possibility that Irma and the professor might know each other, she kept thinking of the first time she had asked Irma if she had ever met him. Irma bellowed with laughter! What was so funny? At the time it meant nothing. Now she thought Irma might have been making a fool of her! More to the point, she wondered if Irma had just used her to get at Mrs Dunn. She was so worried and ashamed she could scarcely look her employer in the face! Calling out to say she was leaving, Edna escaped from the house the back way. Margaret had been hurrying to the kitchen to talk to her but quickly opened the front door to confront her as she wheeled her bicycle to the gate. "What on earth is the matter with you Edna? Have I done anything to upset you? You seem intent on avoiding me!"

When Edna shook her head Margaret asked, "And where is Irma? She's usually home much earlier than this! I can't think what has got into you both."

She looked so upset that Edna went back inside with her. "I'm sorry I rushed off," she said contritely, "I don't have to go for another ten minutes really – I'll make you a cup of tea." Edna could not say what had happened to delay Irma but assured Margaret that nothing was wrong as far as she knew. Personally Edna was still very happy to be working at Riverbank and she assured Margaret that she had no family problems.

She felt so frustrated ... there was no way she could warn Mrs Dunn to beware of her new companion but she added to Margaret's perplexity by saying that, no matter what lay ahead, she could depend on her absolutely. "Don't worry," she said. "Me and Ted will always be on hand if you need us, whatever happens! You can rely on that!"

Margaret was speechless as she watched Edna ride away. What had she been inferring? Why would she need anyone else when she had Irma ... but where was Irma? She didn't have much longer to wonder. As she turned to go inside, a car pulled off the road. Irma opened the drive gates, drove in and shut them again. She waited while Irma approached.

The slightly wooden smile on Irma's face increased Margaret's concern ... and she noticed several other things. Irma's face was smudged. Her make up was not applied as carefully as usual and her whole appearance was less than immaculate. Then she saw something even more puzzling. Under her jacket she was wearing a striped shirt! Earlier, when she left ... surely she had been wearing a cream blouse?

***

Jack had no trouble finding somewhere to leave his car; it was too early for most morning shoppers. Being quite near to the 'Fox & Sons' studio, they approached it on foot and were impressed by the elegant frontage. In the dark, velvet-lined window, a single enlarged portrait hung under a picture-light in a heavy old-fashioned frame. It was back far enough from the road to provide two parking spaces which were protected from usurpers by chains. They recognised Gordon Fox's black Mercedes and alongside it was a white Fiesta ... "Probably the manager's," said Jack. "They even drive in monochrome!"

Gordon Fox's invitation for them to meet him at the studio, when he had returned them to the hotel, pleased them immensely. Apparently the archives still contained hundreds of negatives of local interest – many dating back to 1870 when his grandfather started the business. Gordon's father inherited a passion for the art – it was he who took Helen's birthday pictures. Gordon was only a little older than Emma and said he had shared her delight in the subterfuge with the toy dog. His father showed them to him with great glee. The accumulated records were gathering dust by the time Gordon took over the place himself, forty years ago, and he had invited a team of enthusiastic art students to sort through them. Anything of historical value was distributed to museums throughout the county and anything of local interest had been retained. Nothing was thrown out, he told them proudly. The Art Academy now possessed a fine collection of transparencies depicting historical costumes, vehicles and architecture.

The Heywood collection was still complete apparently and Fox had offered to go through it with them if they had time. He had told them when they met in his home, that the collection had already been assembled by a staff member, who would set up the equipment to simplify viewing. As they climbed the steps and entered, they felt as if they were walking into another era. There was a lot of polished wood and brass ... not a single glass topped table or flash of chrome to be seen.

The receptionist was expecting them and conducted them immediately to a rear office. They walked through a carpeted hall where a curved staircase led to the rooms where people sat to be recorded for posterity ... it was very theatrical. The woman described the procedure enthusiastically. There was a dressing room if customers needed to change or make up, and a nursery with toys to put children at ease. Then she said something which startled them both...

"It's funny that the Heywood name should come up again. I've been here for twelve years and hadn't heard it until recently." Concealing his satisfaction that the subject had cropped up spontaneously Jack asked in what connection. "It was a postal request," she said. "Someone had a batch of our photographs and wanted to return them to the family as they were of no personal interest. Using the codes, we identified the family and sent the name but could provide no recent address. It's a shame you didn't come first. We'd have put you in touch." In answer to Jack's instant query she said she was sorry. She didn't remember the person's name but the information went to a box number in Coventry. Emma gripped Jack's arm ... another piece of the jig-saw in place. It was amazing.

Gordon Fox appeared to enjoy the viewing as much as they and, with his guidance, they finally settled on eighteen pictures which Jack ordered in triplicate – the third set being for Margaret. Gordon promised to send them personally and by way of thanks Jack invited Gordon to join them for lunch. They finally said good-bye to him at four-o-clock, promising to keep in touch.

The drive back to the hotel was pleasant – in bright sunshine ... the fine weather in tune with their animated conversation. Jack was eager to talk to Polly. "She's returning to Oxford herself tomorrow," he said. "We'll start out as early as you feel up to it, and after dropping you off I'll meet her at Elaine's." Emma murmured that rising early was no problem. "If her friend Sarah doesn't need her," Jack added, "I hope to persuade Polly to return with me to the Lion, for the weekend." He looked astonished when Emma threw back her head and roared with merriment,

"Have you any idea how that sounds? You had better be careful how you phrase the invitation in front of the children!" Emma's thin frame shook with mirth. She sobered quickly. "Are you really going to Margaret's, to tackle Irma at this stage?"

"I'd love to, but having involved Dan's policeman friend we should get his opinion before making a move. I'll ring him from Oxford."

"I think Polly said he's with Reading C.I.D.," Emma reminded him and Jack agreed but as Terry lived in South Oxford he hoped they could meet.

Emma retired to her room to rest for a few hours. She said she needed to 'sleep off' lunch in order to enjoy dinner. "I can't remember when I have been so well fed – I swear my clothes feel tighter than they did when I arrived! Anyway I don't want to risk delaying you in the morning by being overtired. When Polly rings – please tell her I shall expect her to call on me at home soon."

Jack promised, and they parted for a few hours.

... Polly would not be ringing.

She lay on a cold stone floor, dried blood matting her hair, in an isolated, empty house.

Chapter Twenty-Four

Irma barely spoke as she rushed upstairs. She had banked on letting herself in and being able to clean up properly without being seen, because Margaret usually stayed in her room until called for lunch. She really was the most infuriating woman; always wanting to know where she was going, where she'd been, what she was thinking; anyone would think she owned her! She'd had to think quickly to explain the shirt but Margaret accepted that she had spilled coffee over her blouse and left it at the cleaners! Only Margaret would have believed such a tale!

Did she also assume she had bought the frayed shirt to replace it!

There was no way she could have worn the blouse. When changing in semi-panic, it fell into a pool of blood where Polly had collapsed near the dressing table. Irma had wrapped her in a carpet and dragged her downstairs. There was nothing to gain by leaving her in the bedroom. If anyone else broke in they wouldn't confine themselves to the ground floor and, when she returned to remove the body, time would be at a premium. Irma was undecided what to do with it but, although inside the roll and out of sight, it couldn't stay there for long. Tomorrow she would dispose of it properly. It was difficult to appear unruffled, but she managed to get through the afternoon without giving more cause for alarm. After tea, while Margaret took her usual rest in preparation for another séance, Irma busied herself with an alibi for being away tomorrow. Before Margaret re-appeared she had one other thing to do ... she picked up the telephone and dialled the Lion. "Good evening," she said, "this is Mrs Bailey."

***

During the afternoon Sarah was so uncommunicative that Amy took Bobby for a walk alone. Since finishing lunch she had fidgeted with one thing after another – asking every few minutes if they were going out or not, until Sarah admitted to not feeling like their usual stroll. If Amy had not immediately opted to go anyway, she would have retreated to her own room to think, undisturbed.

Sitting with her notes and a scribbling pad Sarah doodled as she mentally reviewed the tape recordings. John's records said he was born on May 1st 1905 and was therefore 87, although he looked all of the 92 years old he now claimed to be. When he was deluded he insisted he was born on May 1st. 1946 – actually the date of Jay's birth! Such things often happened in families so she set no store by the coincidence.

It was bizarre ... but if, by a wild leap of imagination, he actually *had* covered the last forty-six years twice, Sarah mused, he really would have lived for ninety two years! She could hardly believe she was even considering such an aberration! Yet she had seen him as a young man with Dorothea... two ghostly figures on the cellar steps.

What was Time?

Called upon for help many years earlier by a friend who felt her home to be haunted, Sarah had seen a whole family living normally, superimposed on the fabric of her friend's present day existence. When the eighteenth-century woman baked, Phyllis detected the aroma; perhaps the cook, in her day, sometimes glimpsed Phyllis, a ghost from the future! Perhaps the busy cook had also sought to exorcise the house!

It was possible that to John and his new wife, had they seen Sarah watching them, she too would have been regarded as a ghostly intruder. Years later, meeting Sarah for the first time at Jay's wedding, would Dorothea have remembered seeing her 'ghost' in the cellar? It was an intriguing thought and Sarah suddenly shuddered as she remembered Dorothea actually asking, when Amy introduced them, if they had met before – there was something familiar about her!

Sarah gave herself a mental rap over the knuckles ... successive ages co-existing unknown to each other (for the most part!) was within her own experience but hopping at will between the two was sheer science fiction! She was becoming far too fanciful and must focus on John's current predicament. He has no clear idea when his father Jerome died. His mother May, according to Dr. Ellis, died when her home was hit by a bomb in the final months of the war. This tied in with John being injured and in hospital in 1945. The date of May's death, clearly written on the page before her was April 17th. Sarah couldn't tear her eyes away from it – it was significant – why? *APRIL 17th*...! She and Amy went to the theatre on April 17th! The powerful blast which took his son this year, 1992, was on the very anniversary of that wartime bombing.

It coincided with the day and, for all she knew, the time to the split second of the explosion that destroyed his home in 1945! Sarah had assumed that, in both her vision and the old photograph, John was viewing his newly acquired property, but she fantasised again as another thought occurred to her; it could have been the ruins of his own home where May, his mother, had died and from which he alone had escaped, but he had lost his memory, so would he have recognised it?

Suppose the two explosions – although forty-six years apart – were not only at the same time, on the same day and month, but had been in exactly the same place!

Had all these coincidences torn a rent in the fabric of time?

Add to the undisputed facts, the esoteric connection between father and son – so close in life – and the scenario she continually scorned became almost credible!

Almost in a daze Sarah drew a figure of eight and at points around it made more notes...

Grey Masque of Death

1905   *John born May 1st*
1945   *John loses mother and memory in an explosion on April 17th – Meets and marries Dorothea*
1946   *Jay born May 1st*
1967   *Jay meets and marries Amy – John has stroke*
1992   *Jay blows himself up in an experiment ... also on April 17th Where the lines crossed they were both alive.*

Questions ...
Did Jay really die, or had he, somehow, returned to 1945 as John?????
What happened to the John born in 1905 if he wasn't the John in hospital now?
Was he supposed to have died in the 1945 explosion? Or worse, did John Senior believe that Jay's experiment in 1992, mirroring his own in 1945 in place, detail and timing, had caused a ricochet in time...

John certainly believed he was Jay? But if, as Sarah believed, one spirit couldn't occupy two bodies simultaneously, might the essence of Jay have fused with his father – after all there was plenty of evidence that one body could be possessed by two souls....

    With some effort Sarah tried to explain away the mounting string of coincidences but the hypothesis was riveting and if only John had died, instead of lingering in limbo after his stroke, none of these wild theories would have come to light. Whatever her own misgivings, she conceded that John, a scientist, was convinced that he was trapped in a time loop and, if he died on May 1st next year, his soul would be transferred to his (as yet unborn) grandson. It would therefore remain earthbound, attached like a magnet to the son whose existence, as a middle-aged man, was itself an aberration in 1946.

    It was giving Sarah a headache and the concept was no more acceptable to her now than it had been when she started. It made no sense. How could Jay be a reincarnation of John when they were alive at the same time, existing together until Jay blew himself up? ... Unless...! Thrusting itself to the forefront of her mind was one inescapable fact. From the day of his stroke until shortly after Jay's death, John had been a mere shell, not able to communicate with anyone... A vital spark of life was missing. Was it his soul? In the instant the thought crossed her mind Sarah dismissed it, horrified. Nothing in her wide experience gave credence to such an outlandish explanation. It was rubbish! But to help John, she decided to accept that he had good reasons for his delusions.

    She could appreciate why he thought that the chain could be broken by his death, as long as he did not die on May 1st next year. Even so, John's scenario only held up if, individually, the two men had followed the same line of reasoning. It was unlikely that they worked and experimented on the idea together; Jay was only twenty and unqualified when his father was hospitalised. After taking over the laboratory Jay would, of course, have had access to his father's files and the time-travel theories. If John had already proved them, his proud son, with the impetuosity of youth, would probably have released them to the world! Alternatively, if they were incomplete but seemed feasible to the boy, why had he not become absorbed in them much earlier? She recalled Amy saying that their life was quite normal until a few years ago, when he became totally absorbed in his work. Had something specific suddenly brought the time-travel theory to his notice? If so, what could it have been? Sarah was quite energised by this new trend of thought and could hardly wait to question Amy.

When Amy eventually returned, she was exhausted, but proudly informed Sarah that she had walked much farther than usual ... almost to the village. To keep her in a good mood, Sarah took Bobby to the kitchen, making sure his bowl contained fresh water, and then returned with a glass of orange juice to quench Amy's thirst. She listened patiently while Amy described in minute detail everything that had happened on her walk – even enduring a word-perfect exchange with another dog-owner.

When, at last, Amy stopped talking, Sarah steered the conversation round to Jay's behaviour prior to his obsessive working. Amy was evasive at first and obviously reluctant to discuss the subject, but Sarah made it clear that it was of the utmost importance. Eventually, resigned to cooperating, she supposed that his routine had changed after the weekend he found John's papers in the attic. Amy admitted to knowing they were there but had completely forgotten until she saw Jay carrying the cardboard box to the basement.

Dorothea, on the day she moved out, had given the box to Amy to be handed over to Jay. It contained very old, personal documents and notes unrelated to his government work. Dorothea had considered moving them to the laboratory safe, after the official papers were removed from it, but didn't have the combination. With all the anxiety over her husband's condition it was not surprising that she totally forgot the box until she sorted everything out for the move to her new home. Unqualified to assess them, Dorothea thought her son should do so.

Sarah asked why Amy hadn't handed them to Jay at the time and, a little shamefaced, Amy said it was marvellous being just the two of them together. Not wanting him distracted, she had put the box in the attic. He came across it several years ago when he broke some equipment and remembered there was a spare part up there. As he'd had his nose in the contents ever since, Amy pointed out that she'd been proved right!

Sarah gave her a look of despair. Amy had always been totally self-centred – her answer was in character – but it did nothing to alleviate the futility of Sarah's search for a rational solution to the problem, which plagued her day and night. Rather did it support her latest hypothesis that both men had worked on the same experiment. Had they come to the same conclusion, with the same horrific consequence?

It suddenly occurred to Sarah that there must be some scientific books or encyclopaedia on the shelves in Jay's study so she went immediately to browse. She searched for Quantum Physics and it wasn't long before she found something which chilled her.

It was no consolation at all when she read:

"While the multiverse is deterministic, we perceive non-deterministic behavior governed by probabilities, because we can observe only the universe, i.e. the consistent state contribution to the mentioned superposition, we inhabit. Everett's interpretation is perfectly consistent with John Bell's experiments and makes them intuitively understandable. However, according to the theory of quantum decoherence the parallel universes will never be accessible for us, making them physically meaningless. This inaccessiblity can be understood as follows: once a measurement is done, the measured system becomes entangled with both the physicist who measured it and a huge number of other particles, some of which are photons flying away towards the other end of the universe; in order to prove that the wave function did not collapse one would have to bring all these particles back and measure them again, together with the system that was measured originally. This is completely impractical, but even if one can theoretically do this, it would destroy any evidence that the original measurement took place (including the physicist's memory)."

John and Jay could well have been challenging the statement that it is impractical ... and, if they had, the last comment was definitely wrong. Residual memories still lurked in John's brain.

***

Not only was the light going fast but there was a definite chill in the air, characteristic of late April. Clarrie had already cleaned her brushes and was placing the wet palette carefully inside a large plastic bag to preserve the oil paint in good condition when she heard an approaching motor bike. Lofty, with Len on the pillion, skidded to a halt beside the car and greeted her with a wide grin. Len looked extremely nervous; he was clutching the same object which Clarrie had seen him carry off.

He tugged Lofty's arm. "Come on, you can chat her up on the way back! I want to get rid of this thing, now!"

Lofty didn't exactly blush but protested. "Where are your manners? You stupid wimp. That old rag can't hurt you." He was abashed and explained, with many scornful side glances at a scowling Len, how 'this idiot' was scared witless by the dark.

"If you're just going to sit here, I'm not holding this thing a minute longer," Len shouted, throwing the bundle down. "I don't give a sod what you think. I never had a nightmare in my life until that thing hung over my bed. Ugly great bats came out of it and tried to kill me!"

The boy was shaking and Clarrie picked it up to inspect it for herself. It was a black quilted bedspread – probably Burmese, lavishly covered with mirrored glass beads and golden, silk embroidery. She could understand why Len had wanted it as a wall hanging. The design was a complicated amalgam of fruit and flowers and didn't look particularly animal – there was not even one fruit bat!

They admitted finding it in the shed, wrapped in a tarpaulin, under an old mattress and other rubbish. Len saw no reason why he shouldn't take it because it had obviously been thrown out! Having hung it, he was pleased with the reflected light patterns thrown on the opposite wall by passing traffic, but found he couldn't shut his eyes without thinking of it. Half-asleep, he saw vines untwist, fruit falling, flowers withering; he felt threatened. Dragged back to wakefulness he thought he saw the images moving above him but persuaded himself they couldn't be! When at last he did sleep he swore he was attacked and only saved by his mother who heard his screams and woke him. He lay awake until morning, then took it down and went to find Lofty.

"I told him to keep off the vino," Lofty was derisive. "We're putting it back now. I wouldn't mind having it myself but the idiot thinks it will haunt us both if we don't get rid of it!"

Because it was unusual, exotic and probably valuable, Clarrie wondered if Bertha would like it back; it might have been thrown out accidentally – so she offered to return it for them, rather than risk it being ruined in the outhouse. They were only too glad – Len especially; he thought restoring it to the rightful owner would protect him from retribution. After their noisy departure Clarrie re-folded it, put it in the car and returned to the inn. She didn't give much credence to its power to create nightmares but did not take it to her room. It stayed in the car.

***

Jack and Emma, replete and relaxing over coffee, were waiting for Polly's call. They were not impatient; it was only nine-thirty. When over another hour went by, Emma started to fidget. She was keen to get a good night's sleep so she excused herself; he could bring her up to date in the morning. Eventually, just after 11-o-clock, Jack decided instead to ring her. The hotel clerk said Mrs Bailey was not in residence. She had left after breakfast and since telephoned to say she would be away for a few days. She wished to retain her room and would be ringing again on Sunday. The man was sorry, but she had not informed them of her movements. Jack was horrified. He couldn't believe Polly had gone to stay anywhere else without letting him know, but she hadn't even left a message. There was an outside chance that she was with Margaret but it was too late to disturb her.

Damn it, he thought ... he had no option.

***

At Riverbank, Irma lay on her bed, fully clothed still, listening to the strident, ringing telephone, ignoring it with a malicious smile. No doubt nosy-parker Polly had been missed by someone: probably Cousin Jack!

She could now be sure the sleeping pills were working on Margaret otherwise she would have picked up the extension ... it was barely eighteen inches from her head! When the noise stopped, Irma rose quickly, picked up a case she had prepared earlier and left the house.

***

At such a late hour there was little Jack could do, but before going to bed he called the Burford police. They were sympathetic but refused to see any cause for alarm – Mrs Bailey had contacted the hotel. If she didn't ring back as promised, then they might start making a few inquiries. They required his name, and noted that he wasn't a relative ... Why didn't he ring around her family? It was hopeless

He requested early alarm calls for both himself and Emma. She would understand, and it was better than interrupting her sleep now. She could do nothing except add to his worries; she was, after all, a very old lady and the more he could shield her from anxiety the better. He didn't really need the switchboard to wake him ... it was the longest sleepless night he could ever remember.

***

Not wishing to risk being seen on the road at such a late hour Irma let herself out of the side gate which opened onto a rough stony path. Had she turned left it would have taken her to the road but in the other direction a stone foot-bridge carried the path over a brook. On the other side she went through the deserted quarry and skirted the village by crossing the five acre field behind her ramshackle, rented dwelling. It was a little before midnight but she could see the distant church outlined against the sky. The narrow lane between the church and the field would be a good place to leave her car for the few minutes it would take to convey the body out of the house and over the field. She couldn't risk driving any nearer.

As a nurse she was used to man-handling weighty bodies and, using a 'fireman's lift', was confident of being able to carry it. She was far more concerned about being seen. Dressed as the professor, while moving the body to the car, she was less likely to arouse suspicion ... he could be collecting firewood! It would need good timing but having formulated the plan as she darted from shade to shade in the moonlight, it seemed eminently feasible. She reached the front door and let herself in, clicked on the light and placed her case on the table. The low wattage bulb gave little light but she was satisfied that everything was as she had left it – no more intruders! She turned to look in the corner where she had left the body. It was still in the same place ... she wouldn't need the injection she'd brought with her after all.

If Polly Bailey hadn't succumbed to the head injuries, Irma would have used the hypodermic syringe to keep her quiet during the journey and administered an overdose later to finish her. She hadn't doubted that the woman was dead when she rushed off at mid-day; it was subsequently that doubt had crept in. Irma kept picturing her coming round and stumbling to the farm ... or being found half-dead on the main highway; without making sure all was well she could not sleep.

All she had to do now was concoct a reason for being absent for a day. Irma chuckled as she picked up her bag and switched off the light. With this setback overcome she was on track to fleece Margaret Heywood-Dunn of all she owned. Soon she would have everything rightfully due to her and be as free as a bird!

Chapter Twenty-Five

Friday April 24th...

Jack was awake and ready to leave before his early call came. Knowing they would also be calling Emma he dialled her room immediately, forestalling them. She was at first confused, noting it was still dark outside, but he broke the news of Polly's disappearance gently and said he intended leaving soon. If she would prefer to stay he could pick her up later in the day, or tomorrow, depending on how things turned out. Emma wouldn't hear of remaining without him and promised to be ready in half an hour. He assured her that they were not in a panic – not yet, anyway! They would have breakfast before leaving and she mustn't rush; he had some telephoning to do before going down to the dining room.

There was still no news of Polly at the Lion and the police were no more concerned than they had been last night, so he called a few hospitals in the area and was assured that she hadn't been admitted. He then tried Margaret again; still no answer. It was a quarter to eight when he rang Dan. They hadn't heard from Polly since Wednesday and thought she was still at the inn. Dan said he would try to reach Terry as soon as Jack put the 'phone down and promised to ring back.

Jack was packing the last few items into his case prior to leaving his room when the call came. Terry was taking a hand in the proceedings personally and even though Polly wasn't missing officially, he'd set a few balls rolling. He couldn't actually join Jack until after duty tonight, but would cancel his weekend arrangements if necessary, in order to help. He gave Jack his office number; he'd be there most of the day and wanted to be kept informed of events. Emma scarcely touched her food in spite of Jack's pretence of eating heartily. They were worried but constantly assured each other that Polly was a sensible woman – there was probably a good reason for her silence ... her message must have been misunderstood at the hotel.

When Jack dropped Emma at her home in Edgehill she insisted on making coffee while he rang around again. In Mapledurham, instead of the machine, he was answered by a young woman who recognised his voice from the messages he had left last night and earlier in the morning. It was Pat. She had hesitated to contact Mrs Grey, not really knowing what the situation was. She rang Welshpool to ask if she should, but he had already checked out. It was a relief to Jack to be able to discuss the problem.

Pat was obviously worried about her aunt. Last time they spoke, because Sarah and Clarrie were still absent, Polly was planning to wait in Barr's Brook for Jack to return on Saturday. She hadn't implied that she was staying anywhere other than the Lion hotel. Pat was sure, in fact, that she specifically said she was extending her stay at the Lion. She couldn't check because she had rewound the tape! She asked if he thought it was serious ... did he think the family and Mrs Grey ought to be told. Unwilling to sound all the bells when it might be a false alarm, Jack told her to wait until tonight when he would be in touch again.

Driving away from Emma's, he wondered whether he'd done the right thing; perhaps what he needed most was a psychic! If he had been as convinced as Polly about such things it would be different, but he had more faith in Terry and the CID!

***

When Irma brought the morning post into the dining room she was holding a letter which she said was her own; it was company business needing her urgent attention. She explained in a worried tone. Margaret accepted Irma's offer that she should read it and tried to follow the whole convoluted problem. The letter, full of whereas's, wheretofor's, parties of the first, the second and the third part, was quite incomprehensible to her. It sounded serious, but Irma assured her it was just jargon; with her permission she would ring straight away to clarify things.

As Irma looked up the area code for Coventry, she gave a running commentary but Margaret became no more enlightened; everything seemed remote. She wondered why her head felt so heavy. She hadn't heard Irma knock on her bedroom door earlier, or the tea-tray being placed near her bed. Being woken by a hand grasping her arm had distressed her – she couldn't believe it was morning.

Now, unable to take anything in, Margaret wondered if she might be ill. She was so tired. Edna came back to clear the table and, after a long hard look at her, commented on how pale she looked. This made her feel even worse so she decided to go back to bed. Perhaps dear Irma could give her another tablet or something ... it was so reassuring having a trained nurse in the house.

As Margaret walked shakily through the hall, on her way upstairs, Irma finished her call. The woman at the other end of the line must be baffled by the strange conversation, in which she had taken no part, with someone she barely knew and had not seen for years, but Margaret always checked the bill. Irma knew that if no trunk call was debited for today, she would smell a rat! It didn't surprise Irma that Margaret was jaded – the sleeping pills had been pretty strong. Even the incessant ringing of the telephone again hadn't disturbed her. A similar dose should keep her quiet for the whole day but before administering it, she wanted to explain her own absence.

Half an hour later, while Edna was dusting the dressing room within hearing, Irma told Margaret she was sorry she had to go out but there were papers to be signed, urgently; if she went straight away she should be back before tea-time. Margaret took the tablet proffered with a drink. "Is one enough?" she asked, "My head is really bad."

"One is quite enough!" Irma nodded in Edna's direction as she entered. "If we're not careful we'll have a drug addict on our hands here!" Edna laughed – she didn't know that two more tablets were already crushed in the drink! Irma told her that Margaret would probably be asleep before she left the house but, not to worry ... if anything delayed her return and she couldn't get a reply from Mrs Dunn, she'd ring Edna at home – in which case Edna promised to return to check up on her.

"Don't worry, either of you," Margaret sighed, "I'm sure I shall soon be asleep and as long as you lock up properly, I shall be fine. Just run along now. I don't think I'm really ill – just exhausted!"

Edna saw Irma drive off in the direction of the village and thought she must be going to the filling station before heading for the midlands. Leaving Margaret on her own didn't worry Edna – before Irma came the woman was alone every day. It was a shame that she wasn't well of course, but Irma was a nurse and must know what she was doing; if Mrs Dunn and Irma were happy, then so was she.

Irma left the main road before reaching the village and took the old lane through two closed fields where the farm gates had to be opened and shut by those who passed. The surface was breaking up badly but it only led to the farm so was little used except by cattle and ploughmen. Halfway along the edge of the first field a track, just about wide enough for her small car took her back towards the church. Parking out of sight she emerged on foot and walked to the house. She'd seen no-one and was sure she had been unobserved but, in any case, nobody would even recognise her when she returned.

Before approaching the door and letting herself in, Irma stood for a while in the shelter of the trees to make sure she was alone. Inside, she went straight upstairs to change. When she emerged, carrying the body, it would be as Professor Smythe...

***

Jack spent most of the afternoon at Headington with Elaine. They were sure they had covered all the angles and were waiting for Terry to call back before Jack left for Barr's Brook. When he last rang the Lion, after lunch, they said Mrs Bailey hadn't yet made contact but as they had already told him, they were sure she would, eventually – after all, did they not have her suitcase and clothes in the wardrobe!

Jack was infuriated by their attitude. Surely the fact that she had not taken a suitcase was significant. He wished he had asked about her toiletries but would check them when he got there. He didn't want to leave before Dan came but Elaine assured him she wasn't unduly upset ... If anything fatal had happened to her Aunt Polly they would have heard from Sarah Grey by now ... she'd be among the first to know!

Jack didn't know whether to laugh or cry, he was so overwrought, but he could tell she wasn't joking. Whatever other powers 'psychic Sarah' possessed, she certainly must have charisma ... everyone who knew her thought her infallible.

Terry's call interrupted his thoughts. His colleagues in Burford were now in touch with Constable Jolly, the local man in Barr's Brook, who was waiting to meet Jack. Checking accident and hospital reports and an initial inquiry on the spot ascertained only that no-one had seen her since Thursday morning at the Lion.

Elaine urged him to go directly, every moment might be precious. He could call them later, then Dan could ring his sister Pat himself, and they could come to a decision about telling Polly's daughter and, of course, Sarah.

***

It would be a thirty mile drive to Pershore and a few more to Irma's cottage which was off the beaten track between Wyre Piddle and Upton Snodbury. An intersection of two tracks, where the highwayman Osmo Goad had been hanged in the distant past, was called Goad's Halt and the name became attached to the only close dwelling – the place where Stan Kleg was born and to which he had taken Olive and Irma.

Irma had always hated it – the address sounded more like a joke than a home! She was nevertheless pleased to arrive at last without incident. It was said that Goad lay nearby – where he was shot – buried with his head to the west. Like all such places it was reputed to be haunted and was avoided, especially after dark. The ghost never worried Irma; she used to scare her school friends with grisly tales and by pretending she'd seen him, but until this morning she had never been scared of anything!

Even thinking about the shock she suffered made her break into a cold sweat! Having changed her clothes, she had removed all traces of her occupation from the bedroom and done the same downstairs. Ready to leave at last, she approached the still form, started to pull the corners of the blanket together in order to lift it, and almost died of fright when it moved! She picked up the chair leg ready to hit the woman again but saw that she was almost unconscious anyway.

Irma's medical case was in the car; so she decided that if she could get her there, by pretending to help her, she could inject something to keep her quiet. Irma quickly realised it would be safer to travel with a sleeping woman than a dead body. Perhaps it was a stroke of luck that the woman had survived.

Vaguely aware that someone had come to her aid Polly, dazed and weak, staggered to the car, leaning heavily on Irma. Progress was slow but without uttering anything other than a few moans, Polly had been manoeuvred into the back seat, silenced by an injection and covered over. She was completely out of sight to anyone who might have come near while Irma was in the bushes, changing into her own clothes. Irma was back in the car within five minutes, so her plan went without a hitch.

Pershore was busy but after leaving the main road, heading for Upton Snodsbury, Irma encountered little traffic and even less after turning off to Wyre Piddle. She could have reached Goad's Halt more directly but under the circumstances using winding back lanes had been safer. Now, outside the silent house, she switched off the engine and sat listening for a few moments in case anyone was hovering nearby.

Satisfied that she was unobserved she opened the cottage door and returned for the semi-conscious Polly who, feeling herself yanked to a sitting position, protested – obviously in pain. She opened her eyes and saw Irma but was too bewildered to register what was happening.

Irma sounded sympathetic as she encouraged her to move out of the car. "Come along dear ... we'll have to do something about your poor head. What a nasty gash you have! I'll give you something to stop the pain when we get you inside."

Polly had a vague idea that she must be going into Margaret's house and struggled, weakly, to climb out of the car door's narrow opening with Irma gripping her upper arms. Her eyes were screwed tight shut – her head swam with waves of dull disquiet. The more sentient she became, the more panicky she felt about the way she was being dragged along a stony path. When she forced herself to lift her head and saw the neglected garden, the unfamiliar porch and shuttered windows, the memory of the other deserted house exploded in her brain. Polly recollected instantly, the professor's reflection in the mirror ... her horror when she recognised him to be Irma and the splitting agony which shot through her as the first blow fell. She fainted with shock and Irma cursed as she then had to haul her rest of the way ... Polly was no lightweight.

The place was as she had left it. The heavy wooden shutters were still securely padlocked ... there was no upper floor to worry about. The trap door to the loft was bolted but without a ladder there was no way of reaching it. If she merely left Polly sealed inside, it was exceedingly unlikely that she could escape; the old-fashioned mortise locks needed keys to get in or out and she would take both back and front door keys away with her. Polly might scream, but in the unlikely event that anyone heard, they'd think the place haunted and be more keen on flight, than on investigating. Even so, there was no point in leaving it to chance. Irma removed a syringe from her case and selected a small phial of colourless liquid. Polly came round in time to see the needle point enter her arm but far too late to take evasive action. Her eyes widened in terror as she slowly slumped onto the bare mattress.

Irma thought it unlikely that, in her weakened state, Polly would ever come round again ... and in a few weeks she would certainly be a thing of the past! There was no longer any need to panic about getting rid of a dead body; the eventual disposal could be planned properly.

Ten minutes later Irma, singing along quietly with the radio music, was heading north in the direction of Coventry sticking to minor roads whenever possible. She had no intention of going there and even diverting to Stratford-upon-Avon would take her miles out of her way but it was a necessary precaution. She didn't really think she would need an alibi but she was hungry. If remembered anywhere it might as well be a place where she could reasonably have stopped on her way back home from her urgent meeting! Anyway, Margaret would be out like a light at least until nightfall. and Edna wouldn't go back to the house unless Irma asked her to, so she might as well enjoy a few hours off – window shopping for things she would soon be able to afford.

She still didn't know the extent of Margaret's wealth but she would put it to good use ... after this latest crisis, dealing with her employer would be child's play!

Chapter Twenty-Six

When Jack booked in at the Lion he asked to speak to the manager as soon as possible. The receptionist proved to be the one who took the call from Mrs Bailey. When he discovered that Jack was the man who had brought the police down on him he seemed resentful ... did everyone think he was dim-witted, unable to record a simple message?

Jack soothed him by assuring him that his word was not being doubted but the call may have been a hoax; Mrs Bailey might be in danger. He asked for the man's help, saying he was relying on him as he had also been on duty when she left the inn after breakfast. Anything he could remember might be important.

When asked how sure he was that it had been Mrs Bailey who rang, he nodded, "Yes, very sure", then he hesitated. "There was a lot of noise coming from the bar ... but it was certainly a woman's voice," he insisted. He hadn't doubted it was her at the time; why should he?

Why indeed, agreed Jack. He then heard in detail how Polly had looked when she walked out. The clerk added that she must be in the vicinity still and was sure to turn up soon, wondering what all the fuss was about! With some asperity Jack queried the basis for his assumption. The man shrugged and pointed out that she couldn't be far away because her car was still in the rear car park. He'd told Constable Jolly and admitted with a sniff of annoyance that he'd been rebuked for not mentioning it earlier.

The manager's secretary came to the desk to meet Jack and said her boss would be available in about fifteen minutes. She knew about Polly's mystery absence and was anxious to help. She suggested he should contact Edna Barr – she had seen Mrs Bailey talking to her more than to anyone else. As she spoke her eyes went to the open entrance beyond Jack and she saw Edna across the road. Before Jack could comment she dashed out and hailed Edna frantically. She returned with Edna, introduced her, and left them alone having coffee in the bar.

As far as Edna knew, Polly was not with Margaret. She wondered why Jack hadn't rung up to ask and was puzzled when told that he had tried several times, including the last ten minutes while Edna was walking over to the inn. Edna suggested that he had the wrong number because late at night and early morning Irma was always there. The look on his face when she mentioned Irma, immediately reminded Edna of Polly's mistrust of the woman and she was afraid, without understanding why.

"Polly asked me a lot of questions about Irma," Edna confided, "and was very interested in the professor too." Edna explained that Professor Smythe was a writer and a bit of a recluse. She said Polly asked about him because she thought he might know Irma. Edna expressed her own doubts again, but wondered if Polly had actually gone to the farm. "She said she'd like to meet him but I told her it was a waste of time – he would run a mile if he saw her coming!"

She shook her head anxiously. "The ground is very rough along by the wood, you know. The poor thing could have fallen and broken a leg or something. She might be unconscious in a ditch at this very minute! If only I'd known she was missing I'd have walked over there yesterday, or this morning after work."

Jack checked the telephone number he had for Margaret and Edna agreed it was correct.. She still insisted that both Mrs Dunn and Irma must have been there when he rang up this morning. She had arrived at eight-thirty, half an hour or so after Jack attempted to call and Irma was still in her dressing gown, just coming downstairs to collect the daily paper. Perhaps the line was out of order, although it must be still possible to make out-going calls, she told him, because Irma made a business call to Coventry at about nine-o-clock. Mrs Dunn only picked up the 'phone by her bed if no-one else answered it, but she wasn't well today and had overslept.

Alerted to the implications of Margaret's having been too soundly asleep to hear shrill ringing so near her, Jack immediately wanted to know if Edna had spoken to Margaret at all today. He was reassured when Edna said she seemed fine except for being tired. He was anxious again when told that Irma had given Margaret tablets before leaving, then appalled to hear she was fast asleep when Edna left at lunch-time.

It took a moment for Jack to assimilate the fact that Irma must have gone off somewhere and Margaret might still be alone – oblivious to everything! He asked if Edna would mind going there with him, as she had a key, to make sure all was well. Listening while Edna explained Irma's sudden departure – he hoped and prayed it had nothing to do with Polly – or that if it did, they would find Polly hidden in the house and Irma gone for good ... but he feared that was too much to expect.

"Is it possible that Polly could be at Riverbank without your knowing?" Jack asked, feeling that at least he should clear up the matter, as it had occurred to him.

"Oh, no of course it isn't!" Edna reacted spontaneously. Then she thought again and allowed that she did not go into every room every day. "In fact, I haven't been into Miss Webb's suite for three weeks." Jack's hopes rose as Edna continued. "It's shut up and doesn't get dusty so I usually do it during the first week of the month. I think Irma would like to move into it as she only has one room at the moment, but Mrs

Dunn can't yet bring herself to sort and finally clear out her friend's things."

After speaking briefly to the manager Jack drove to Riverbank, with Edna still chattering excitedly beside him.

"I'll be amazed if Irma isn't back yet – she said her meeting wouldn't take long – but these days, with traffic being so bad, you can never plan, can you?"

Jack's mind was still on the lack of co-operation he was suffering at the Lion. The manager wouldn't hear of allowing Jack to enter the room of an absent guest but said he would personally check the drawers and bathroom for personal items. He suggested that Jack could contact him again when he returned.

On arrival at Margaret's house, Jack rang the front door bell and, when nobody came, asked Edna to use her key to the side entrance to let him in. While he stood at the foot of the stairs she went up to peep into Margaret's room. After a moment she beckoned for him to come up. "Dead to the world she is!" Edna told him, then grinned at the expression on his face; "Fast asleep! Just listen to her! I just thought, after what you said, you'd like to look around yourself in case your friend's been here."

The main suite was at the top of the staircase and she led him along the landing to the other end of the house. On the way she pointed out Irma's room, the closest to Margaret's. The guest bathroom used by Irma separated it from another bedroom; a reverse of Irma's which she allowed Jack to inspect. Jack asked if she would mind looking in Irma's room to make sure it was empty. After a slight hesitation Edna tapped at the door, and then went in. She emerged looking relieved. "All clear," she said, "I even looked under the bed!"

The apartment of Margaret's late companion was spacious. It consisted of a sitting room, dressing room and bedroom with bathroom en-suite. It was all beautifully furnished and when Jack admired it, Edna said he should see Mrs Dunn's! It was the same size but, "All done in pale blue and ivory with lots of lace". Jack refrained from comment – he liked the less pretty but quality look chosen, presumably, by Jean Webb. Edna followed as he searched every corner including the walk-in wardrobes. There was no sign of disturbance anywhere; he hadn't expected any but was satisfied now, having seen for himself.

"I'm not at all happy about my cousin sleeping so heavily for so long," Jack said. "I'd like you to waken her to be certain she hasn't been drugged." Reading the alarm in Edna's look, he reminded her that she had told him herself that Irma had given her some medicine.

"That was just for sleeping," she protested, "and only the one tablet – I was there when she gave it to her. Are you sure you really want me to wake her up?" Jack made it clear that he wasn't leaving the house until she did, but said he would wait for her downstairs. A few minutes elapsed before Edna joined him. She said she'd been worried herself when Mrs Dunn didn't waken straight away ... she was a bit muzzy but would be down in a few minutes.

When Margaret appeared, looking pasty but otherwise quite collected, they went into the sitting room. Edna offered to make a cup of tea and left them alone. Margaret gathered her blue brocade housecoat over her ankles as she slumped into the depths of the chair. She passed a hand wearily over her forehead and said she didn't know what was wrong with her – she felt so far away.

Jack watched closely and was convinced she had been overdosed with depressants – certainly more than one sleeping tablet. Margaret was astonished to find how late it was – and that Irma had been away all day; it was most unlike her! She listened as Jack explained his presence – and Polly's inexplicable absence! Margaret wasn't even aware that Polly had returned to the area and Jack didn't tell her that she herself was the reason for Polly's visit and that they suspected Irma of being a criminal.

Margaret was miffed that Polly hadn't even telephoned but mollified when Jack said he knew Polly definitely intended to call on her before returning home. It gradually dawned on Margaret that Jack was almost frantic with worry. She sensed that the situation was serious and invited him to stay at Riverbank but he declined; he wanted to be at the Lion – on the spot, to monitor developments. She understood and, now worrying with him, insisted that he telephone all his contacts again before leaving, in case Polly had been in touch. To please her, he first called Elaine and then P.C. Jolly, locally. Jolly said he'd be at the Lion within the hour – his house-to-house inquiries in the vicinity had led nowhere. As Edna and Jack left, Margaret comforted him ... she would ask Irma to help by holding a little séance, as soon as she returned. "Irma might be able to 'see' something and if she does, I'll ring you immediately." Margaret promised.

Jack nearly exploded with fury but held himself in check.

He dropped Edna at her home, before returning to the inn and ringing Terry White. He had refrained from doing so from Riverbank knowing Margaret had no secrets from her new companion and certainly not trusting Edna's discretion; she would undoubtedly gossip about him and Polly's disappearance. The fact that he was in such close contact with the CID was something he definitely did not want passed on to Irma!

***

The Welsh mists had held off all week. Clarrie's painting was virtually finished and she was now a familiar figure at the inn. The regulars were fascinated by the picture as it neared completion. Several offered to buy it, but old Gordy was still dubious about her doing it at all and had not even asked to see it until now. At the landlord's request she had taken it into the bar and Gordy's curiosity overcame him when he heard someone comment on 'artist's license' because she'd left out the bushes at the bend of the river where it skirted the garden. She had painted a few scattered stones there instead.

He beckoned her over to show him and for a moment or two examined it in silence. He then announced, wide-eyed, that it might be overgrown now but when he was a lad it looked exactly as she'd painted it! His voice trembled fearfully as he told the gathering, "That's the very bank where they buried all their old animals. Every cat's name is hacked into one of them stones – I know 'cause I used to do some carving for the local mason and they had me up there to help with the burying! My old dad was under-gardener then."

Clarrie was puzzled by the general assertion that the bank was overgrown. She painted stones because she saw stones, and beyond them was the corner of the building, which she wouldn't have been able to see if bushes grew on that patch of ground. It was probably a long time since any of them had been there she decided, not at all perturbed by such minor criticism. The overall verdict was quite gratifying and other commissions might arise from this one. Clarrie took it to the car. The rest of her kit was already packed because she was planning an early start tomorrow – really looking forward to her few days off.

If she wasn't held up by heavy traffic she would arrive at the farm in time for morning coffee. Next week, after the picture had dried off a little, she would return to put in a few final touches, but even as it stood she was satisfied and looking forward to showing it to her mother. If Sarah liked it she need have no qualms about presenting it for her client's approval. It was often helpful to have work scrutinised by fresh eyes while there was still time to make minor adjustments.

***

It was after seven-o-clock when Irma let herself into the house. She was surprised to hear the television on ... she had expected to have to wake Margaret herself and intended to pretend she had been home for hours! Without delay Irma went to speak to her, to apologise for being late, but Margaret barely listened. She was quite excited now that her drowsiness had worn off and was eager to tell her own news.

It was difficult for Irma to keep a straight face as she heard how cousin Jack was running around in circles looking for Polly and as for 'Plod the Policeman' – from what she'd seen of Jolly, he'd better not stray too far from his patch or they'd have to send someone else to find him! When Margaret suggested that she might trace Polly by using her powers Irma was sorely tempted, but resisted. How droll it would have been to help the searchers to find her! She couldn't do anything of the sort – not yet anyway – but if she eventually dumped the corpse well away from the cottage, it might be a clever way of dealing with it. By sticking close to home in the meantime her alibi would be unbreakable; nobody could connect her with it!

She suddenly felt so invulnerable that she promised Margaret, if Mrs Bailey wasn't found within a few days, to devote a special session to the problem. At the moment she didn't feel she could concentrate; she had so much else on her mind. Margaret was contrite. She hadn't even asked how Irma's business had fared and if all was well. With a little persuasion, looking downcast, Irma admitted that she'd had a setback; a mere thousand pounds would put things right. She wasn't worried though – she had gained some time to pay and would write to a few of the people who had already pledged their support.

Without any hesitation Margaret asked for her handbag, opened her cheque book and wrote one out for two thousand, payable to the Rigby Haven. "There you are dear," she said, handing it to Irma. "This is evidence of my wish to be part of your wonderful scheme. I could help you much more, if I was officially a partner perhaps ... unless you would rather go on alone!"

Irma broke down at this gesture. It took her by surprise as she had expected to have to ask. Her tears were of wild triumph but to Margaret they represented happy emotion. At last, Irma wiped her eyes and spoke. "My dear mother was right after all. My dreams are coming true much earlier than I could ever have hoped." And when she added, "You really are the kindest person in the world ... how can I ever repay you," Margaret took her hand and smiled indulgently.

"Don't worry about that, we have so much else to discuss now. This weekend we'll work out the details on paper and next week I will get in touch with my lawyer, Mr Dewhurst in Welshpool."

More than a little startled at the mention of Dewhurst Irma withdrew her hand more sharply than she intended, but covered herself by dabbing her eyes. Somehow she must convince Margaret that it would be better to have the new partnership handled by a local firm but for now she let the matter rest. Things were going so smoothly – she couldn't afford to rock the boat within sight of land.

***

When he ascertained that Jack was still no farther forward in his search for Aunt Polly, Dan informed the family and obtained from Pat the number of Sarah's friend, Mrs Johnson. When contacted just after ten-thirty with news of Polly's disappearance Sarah was shocked and wanted to leave at once, but Dan said that Terry, whom she knew, was going to Barr's Brook himself tomorrow morning and was willing to pick her up. Sarah was grateful and said she would be ready to leave at seven.

Even before the call came she had decided there was no point in prolonging her stay beyond the funeral. Although not happy about John – she didn't feel anything was settled – she was helpless to do more for him at the moment. She'd done everything possible to encourage Amy to make a new life for herself and Nettie was willing to live in until Amy became more used to being alone, so there was nothing to hold her there now. Assuming Polly was found soon, unharmed, Sarah would return to support Amy at Wednesday's service but couldn't promise ... she was far too concerned about her old friend to think as far ahead as that!

As well as Dan's call she had one from Pat. She and her husband had been to a party and as she didn't want to go in to work on Saturday morning they had checked Sarah's answering machine on the way home. She was able to fill in the background details and gave Sarah another piece of information. Instead of returning home Clarrie was going to the Williams' farm for a few days. Not wanting to take it upon herself, Pat hadn't previously called her at the hotel and now Clarrie was at the farm Pat couldn't ring there tomorrow, because the telephone number wasn't on the pad.

Sarah said not to worry; she had the number in her diary and would ring her daughter personally if necessary. She glanced at her watch ... after half past eleven. There seemed no point in giving Clarinda a bad night so, after packing and settling in bed, Sarah focused all her thoughts on Polly. Unlike the cold vacuity she felt whenever she thought of Jay there was a sense of warmth. The more she concentrated the more convinced she became that Polly was alive.

The knowledge comforted her and with prayers for help revolving in her mind, she was soon fast asleep.

Chapter Twenty-Seven

Saturday April 25th...

In the early morning hours Jack lay wide awake. The manager had been considerably shaken to discover that not only did Polly's room contain her clothes – her toilet bag was in the bathroom, a paper-back and reading glasses were in the bedside drawer and even her handbag was in the cabinet. He didn't examine it but agreed to call in the police; they would form their own conclusions.

Constable Jolly went in, instructing them to stay outside and through the open door Jack saw him search Polly's handbag. He came out after a quick look round and returned the key to Owen Mann, the manager, with assurances that he would make a full report but he commented that the bag contained no money so she may have taken a bus! It was clear that the urgency of the situation went over his head; Jack fumed, feeling impotent. Only by searching the room himself would he be satisfied it didn't hold a clue ... and he knew where the room keys were – on a wall near the switchboard! A few hours after midnight, he dressed again and went downstairs quietly.

Amos Blake, who did double duty at night on the telephone and desk, was slumped in an armchair snoozing but stirred when the key came off the hook. Jack's eyes were on the dozing figure rather than the board and he froze, wondering how he would justify his behaviour. Luckily there was no need! If he managed to return it as successfully, no-one would ever know he had used it.

All the guest rooms were on the first floor so as long as he wasn't seen entering or leaving Polly's room his presence in the corridor wouldn't cause comment. Again, his luck held and he was soon inside, shutting the door quietly behind him. The room had been serviced: nothing out of place; not much likelihood of finding a clue lying about, so he went straight for her handbag. It contained very little and he registered that it was exceedingly neat, not the mélange he'd thought normal! In addition to a make-up pouch and handkerchief there was a key wallet and diary with a tiny pencil attached; the absence of money and credit cards wasn't significant; she'd have taken them rather than leave them in the room even if not expecting to need them.

Fingering the pencil he remembered Polly's ball point pen – a neat gold one. It was usually clipped to her notepad which was far too large to push into a pocket ... so where was it? The writing desk held only hotel literature and headed paper. In the bedside drawer with her glasses was a mystery thriller and, beneath it, a magazine. He almost shut the drawer but suddenly noticed a bright flash at the back; it was the pen.

The notebook was hidden under the glossy journal; Jack seized and read it eagerly. Polly had written:

1. *Tuesday: Arrived late A.M. Talked to B. in café – ate in Lion. Evening – met E. in bar. I. R., takes long walks – always in same direction – nothing over there except farm (about 3 miles north – beyond wood) and old house (2 miles east of farmhouse at edge of wood). House, neglected for years, now rented by Professor/writer (ornithologist) – been here longer than I. but is that significant?*
Q. Do they know each other?
Q. Does she visit him? ... Prof. also walks a lot – so –
Q. Do they meet elsewhere? (E. says not).
Q. Did they know each other before?

2. *Wed. A.M. rang local estate agents. One in B. sent out details of Prof's place about a year ago. Wouldn't give address over phone. Had to drive over. Inquiry was from Miss K. in Coventry. She may have contacted farmer and arranged lease for Prof.*
Q. Is I. Miss K.? ... Probably too far fetched but can't ignore possible connection with prof. Too late to call J. again. Will visit prof. before ringing tomorrow. Might find out something more definite.

Jack was aghast. According to Dewhurst, Irma's mother married a Stan Kleg! Why hadn't Jack told Polly that, on Wednesday night? The man and Irma must be in league! If she had approached him Polly walked straight into trouble and Jack blamed himself entirely! He read on.

3. *Wed. afternoon. Shopped in village. Discovered Post mistress, Belinda Jones (Betty's mother!), was friend of J.W's and dislikes I. Says poor Ed Sawyer has never been the same since the accident. (Ed was driver). Her husband was with him earlier that evening, in a pub in the next village, and Ed was sober when he left. E.S. is bank employee (no point in speaking to him as I. didn't arrive until after J.W's death) B.J. dislikes I. because she has "turned E's silly head" with her spirit messages! But not "tried it on" with anyone else. B.J. suspects I. is looking for rich fool to milk. Mrs D. fits the bill!*
4. *Wed. P.M... After talking to J. Dan rang – seems I's stepfather upset her by saying her mother was raped!*

There was nothing else to discover so he dropped the glasses and pen into the handbag and replaced it. Taking the notebook with him Jack left and walked to the lobby. Unfortunately Amos was now awake and enjoying hot coffee from a flask. There was no room service provided during the small hours which gave Jack an idea.

"That looks good," he said. "I can't sleep, I thought walking around might tire me physically." Jack leaned against the door post and tried to look weary. The man said he'd offer him a drink but he'd just consumed the last drop. "Oh, I wouldn't dream of taking yours – I have the makings in my room of course, but I've used up my supply of instant and wondered if it was possible to get any from the kitchen."

In a flash, Amos rose and hurried along the short corridor to fetch some. "Can't have guests going thirsty," he laughed, "no bother!" He returned in seconds but Jack had sufficient time to replace the key. Bearing the small coffee jar like a trophy, he returned to his own room.

Thank God he knew of the connection between Irma and the professor, otherwise he'd have gone to the farm to fill in time until Terry and Mrs Grey arrived. At this stage he dared not risk doing anything precipitate. Assuming that Polly was still unharmed, she would remain so only if Irma and her accomplice didn't take fright.

He managed to doze a little before daybreak and was the first resident down for breakfast. Before eating he rang Jolly again and arranged to meet him at eight – not at the inn but at the constable's house which doubled as the local police station. From now on their activity must be hidden from prying ears and eyes. Polly's safety – even her life, might depend on it. A few days ago he would have scorned the thought; a woman plotting to cheat her employer was one thing, but committing murder to avoid discovery was ludicrous ... wasn't it?

***

Although Terry arrived early, Sarah was ready and anxious to leave. Amy had roused herself to see them off and Sarah, knowing what effort it had taken, appreciated that Amy was demonstrating her support. They drove first to Mapledurham where Sarah re-packed and tried to reach Clarinda but found she had already left the hotel. It was a pity because she was now heading farther away but Sarah decided against ringing her at Williams' farm. There was no real need to worry her yet.

Terry first met Sarah and Clarrie during a kidnapping case a couple of years ago and had a high regard for their clairvoyance – if anyone could find Polly quickly his money was on Sarah! He'd never neglect solid police work, but willingly took any advantage offered when pursuing criminals! During the drive to Barr's Brook he therefore told her all he knew of the reason for Polly's absence from home. Together they devised a plan. As his investigation wasn't official Terry would keep a low profile. His presence could be justified as a friend. If Sarah decided to meet Irma face to face he would accompany her and to lull

Irma into a false sense of security they'd say that Polly had been seen leaving the village by bus. If Irma was innocent no harm would be done; if guilty she'd think she had got away with the abduction and relax her guard.

When they booked into the Lion and Jack met Sarah for the first time he was surprised, mainly by her looks. He chided himself, aware that the image he'd formed was a cross between a Gypsy fortune teller and a stern-faced religious fanatic! She looked as normal as any other middle aged matron. Wrong again, he thought. There was nothing matronly about her slim figure and in fact she was rather elegant.

P.C. Jolly and Owen Mann were noticeably impressed by the arrival of a CID Detective Sergeant and agreed not to disclose his official status. Mann was much more obliging than previously and even provided a private office for him. At last, Jack sighed with relief, something was happening. He waited until they were alone before showing Terry and Sarah the notebook and confessing how he came by it. Neither commented on his unlawful entry into another suite; both echoed his own thought – it was a good job he found it before barging in on the professor!

Terry had taken possession of Polly's room key so they went there immediately. Once inside Jack began to speak, eager to get through the inspection quickly. They hoped to visit the farmer before lunch and personally he thought they were wasting time, but Terry motioned him to sit and keep quiet while Sarah wandered about almost absently, touching things. Jack began to fidget ... Polly could be in real trouble; doing nothing irked him. He watched impatiently.

Not having opened anything, Sarah pointed out where he had found the handbag and the note pad. She ignored the drawer but retrieved the bag and examined it. "Yes!" she nodded, "Polly had only a little cash and almost left it behind. She came back for it." Jack didn't set much store by the observation but was instantly electrified when she lifted out the pen and glanced at him. "You should have left this and the glasses in the drawer Jack! If Constable Jolly opens it again and comments, I'll say I moved them!" She went to the wardrobe and examined Polly's clothes.

Jack didn't find his voice until Sarah took a button from one of the pockets. He began to say it was of no significance but again, with a frown, Terry shook his head and put a finger to his lips. Jack was irritated but complied. Whatever he thought, it appeared that the young man was another of Sarah's devotees!

In spite of himself he was impressed when, without hesitation, she connected it to the quarry road and he confirmed that Polly had found it there on their first visit. Okay, he thought – perhaps after all there is something in this psychic business, but who cared about a button? It seemed like a red herring to him. He watched Sarah's face as her eyes closed and saw it blanch.

She spoke in a low murmur, as if talking only to herself. "I see two people ... women, struggling! One, wearing a flowered head scarf, is dazed. A gash over her eye is bleeding ... she is falling to the ground, her arm swinging wildly, grabbing at her assailant's coat." Sarah, breathing heavily, leaned against the wall looking distressed. Jack moved to her in dismay, but Terry restrained him. Speaking to them directly and calmly Sarah described the scene at the quarry edge. "The older woman was overpowered by the other who wielded a heavy walking stick." The two men had no time to comment before her eyes closed and she lapsed again into a low monotone. "I see a body at the foot of a small cliff. The young woman, similarly dressed, but her dark hair now hidden by the scarf, stands above, with a bicycle – listening and waiting; I hear a car approaching; she starts to ride ..."

Jack exploded – unable to stop himself.

"Good God! It sounds like Irma – and her poor victim was Jean Webb! She waited for a vehicle, and then jumped into the ditch, throwing the bike in front of it. By the time the unfortunate driver stopped she was long gone! It wasn't an accident, it was murder!" Polly was wrong! Irma *was* in the village when Jean died – perhaps staying with the professor. If she felt threatened by Polly, Jack warned, Irma might murder again to ensure her silence! He put his hands to his head, not questioning now that Sarah was right ... he was desperately upset. "What am I saying? Please God don't let her come to any harm!" He looked at the others in horror. "Surely we can't be too late to save her!"

Sarah still felt convinced that Polly was alive but couldn't perceive where. "Perhaps because she doesn't know where she is herself," she mused! "She is immobile and weak – probably not conscious, I fear, because I'm getting no thought waves from her. She's known me long enough to try telepathy, if able to think."

They decided that their starting point had to be the professor, but alerting him would also warn Irma, so it would be better to go without Jolly. As a matter of courtesy they stopped at the constable's office on their drive to the farm. He agreed to stay put until contacted and gave detailed instructions how to find it. Reaching the wood it was clear, according to Polly's notes, that the professor's house must be about a quarter mile off the road, along the lane to their right.

Jack, who was driving, pulled in and suggested that he and Terry should investigate the house first. If he was at home they could pretend to be interested in the property; if he wasn't? Well!

"Are you suggesting we should break in?" Terry asked.

"Of course not," returned Jack. "If no-one is there, who is to say the door wasn't wide open?"

"I think the idea is okay, but I'll go alone. He won't know me but Irma may have pointed you out. We can't risk that. If I'm not back in twenty minutes, bring Jolly!" Terry was gone before they could argue ... Jack checked his watch.

***

Clarrie had a good trip to the farm as far as the weather and traffic conditions were concerned, but she experienced frequent waves of nausea. It was similar to travel sickness, yet every time she left the car it went. It was an unusual sensation and she wondered if exhaust fumes could somehow be getting to her. She drove on with the windows down, just in case, but even the fresh air didn't help much. On arrival her symptoms disappeared completely and in the excitement of meeting everyone she soon forgot the discomfort.

Gareth was eager to take her to see the cottage and laughed at her puzzled look. She had produced an oil painting of it and knew well what it was like. She had never told them that she knew what it looked like inside too! They knew nothing of the nightmarish visions in which she had witnessed a brutal murder – there had been no point in telling them; the murderer was himself dead. Now, Gareth was saying, he lived in the cottage. Her painting had made him realise it was worth renovating. "But you'll never credit what we found when the stone flags were ripped up! I would have kept the floor if it had not been so uneven. Anyway, underneath ..." he paused for dramatic effect, "were the bones of a woman!"

Gwen interrupted excitedly, the Welsh lilt in her voice more pronounced than ever. "Yes! You remember the girl I told you about, who we thought left to get married? Well, an autopsy there was, of course, and they were one and the same. So pretty she was, and pregnant too! The police searched for the man who'd lived here with her, but dead he was already, so her remains went back to her poor parents and that was the end of things. There's been no more haunting since Gareth moved in!"

"Well – so much for my news," laughed Gareth. "Come on, Clarrie, we'll walk over there while mum gets lunch ready. I'd like to know what you think of the old place now – and at least I'll be able to get a word in for a change!"

It was exactly noon as he unlocked the front door and with a proud flourish showed Clarrie his new home.

In Barr's Brook at the same moment, Terry was knocking on Professor Smythe's front door...

Chapter Twenty-Eight

There was no answer to Terry's knock. After trying again he walked to the back, keeping off the path, searching the ground with his eyes. The moss on the dirty paving was scuffed in several places. Someone might have walked there recently, but he couldn't be sure. The back door was rotting. It looked firmly closed but when he pushed it he felt it give slightly against the frame. There was a clean slash near the latch where a sliver of paint had recently broken away. He was tempted to put his weight against it but he was supposed to uphold the law, not break it, so he restricted himself to looking through the grimy windows. It appeared to be empty and it was difficult to imagine anyone renting it.

He hurried back to the car. It had been farther than he expected; his twenty minutes were almost up and he didn't want to worry them!

"Thank goodness," Sarah exclaimed as he came in sight. What would we have done if he had been five minutes longer?"

"We would have done as we were told," Jack said firmly. "A good officer has to be able to take orders as well as give them!"

Terry described the grim state of the house as they drove to the farm. He hoped the farmer would tell them about his tenant or even return with them to investigate. He thought they should be forthright with him – Polly was missing and they were trying to find her.

The farmer was at home. He and his wife were about to have their midday meal so he flatly refused to return with them. The idea that the missing woman might be inside his property struck him as ridiculous. How would she have got in there, he asked – Professor Smythe kept the place locked and it was hardly worth while her breaking in! He said Smythe was never in during the day; he went out getting material for his book – he was probably busy as his tenure was due to expire within a week. "Why don't you go and see him tonight? He'll let you in, but it stands to reason your friend isn't there, else he'd have found her already wouldn't he?"

While Terry and Jack were getting nowhere with the farmer, his wife was proudly showing Sarah her most recently acquired gadget. Outwardly, the appearance of the farmhouse was old and unchanged, but she had a modern, dream kitchen! "There's no room for sentiment," she averred, "when running a farm and feeding hungry labourers! They wouldn't use a hand plough would they?"

With half an ear on what the farmer was saying – aware that he was being unhelpful – Sarah said to his friendlier wife, "I believe the professor's place is actually for sale ... I wonder if it could be modernised with equal success?"

"Oh, I'm sure it could," was the eager reply. "Are you interested in buying it?"

"I am very tempted," said Sarah, "this is such a lovely part of the country. It's a shame I won't be able to see it in daylight, I'll probably leave early tomorrow – but from the outside it seems to need a lot of money spending on it."

The woman told Sarah conspiratorially that her husband was selling it very cheaply because it was leasehold and only twenty years left on it, which put people off. "I don't want to be rude but, at our age, twenty years is far enough ahead to look isn't it? And if it's basically what you want, why not have a look round?"

Sarah gave a non-committal shrug and glanced pointedly at the farmer. Within moments she was beckoned outside, where a key was pressed into her hand with the instruction, "If Mr Smythe isn't in, have a quick look. Leave the key at the post office when you've done – I'll collect it from there on Monday morning."

As they drove away Jack and Terry were commiserating with each other over their failure to persuade the farmer to accompany them. Jack was in favour of pushing in the back door ... if Terry was unwilling, he would do it himself; they had to see if Polly was a prisoner inside.

They were both astonished when Sarah waved aloft the key and in a state of high excitement they headed back to the isolated house. The narrow lane was not impossible to traverse by car, although it soon deteriorated to a rough track. Jack insisted on continuing; for Sarah's sake, the nearer they could get to the place, before walking, the better! They crossed two fields, opening and shutting farm gates, before the building was in sight. Beyond it, the lane widened again as it circled back to the farm but it was still a fair trek from the car. The men were worried but Sarah assured them she was quite capable of tackling it although she wasn't wearing flat heels.

Terry was extremely glad that, when no-one answered their knock, they didn't have to break in. He opened the door and went first with Jack close on his heels. Sarah followed and was drawn directly to the corner where Polly had lain helpless – she could not stifle a cry of dismay. Polly had undoubtedly been in the house and, although weak, had walked out. Where she had been taken Sarah still didn't know. In the meantime, Terry was scraping what looked like dried blood from the stairs into a plastic envelope.

Upstairs, they covered the same ground as Polly, with the same degree of bewilderment. There was now no female attire in the wardrobe but the presence of make-up seemed inexplicable, unless used for a disguise, Jack suggested, not quite clear why the professor should wish to use one!

Sarah lapsed into silence, concentrating so hard on Polly, trying to fathom what had happened, that her head was almost splitting. The pain began to overcome her and she staggered downstairs, into the fresh air. She inadvertently began walking off the path to a gap in the hedge and went through it. The distant village was just in sight; the agony was almost blinding until she guessed she was experiencing what Polly had suffered and almost instantaneously recovered.

Without a shadow of doubt Polly had come this way. She picked up Polly's confusion about her attacker but saw clearly that she was leaning heavily on a man. His face was not visible so she was unable to give Jack and Terry a description of him. Terry had already decided to have the professor picked up; he considered they now had enough evidence of foul play to put before his Chief, Alec Holmes. The Detective Chief Superintendent was an old friend of Sarah's, and she knew he would be willing to help in any way he could.

Before returning to the car, Terry walked over the rough ground in the direction Sarah had taken until he saw where it ended ... the lane behind the church. Once back on wheels, they found the spot where Polly must have been put into a vehicle, but there was nothing to discover there and, once again, Sarah failed to descry anything useful.

It was tempting to assume that Irma was involved, but ESP wasn't evidence! Even if the woman's fingerprints were among those Terry had just 'lifted' at the house, they would only prove that she had visited the professor. They were all convinced that Irma was tied to him somehow, why else would Polly have been considered a threat, but they had to find proof.

At the Lion, Terry risked contacting Alec at home. He was sure that as soon as he mentioned Sarah's involvement there would be no danger of recriminations for disturbing his boss's quiet weekend. He was right and grinned as he told them that he had permission to stay on the case for the following week if necessary. They differed about what to do next. Jack was in favour of visiting Margaret and assessing Irma's demeanour but Sarah felt they had much to lose and nothing to gain by confronting Irma before they were sure of Polly's situation.

Terry hadn't lost confidence in Sarah but was puzzled by her inability to discover where Polly was. "Perhaps when you try," he suggested, "you are dwelling too much on contacting her personally." He made wild circular gestures above his head. "Surely, there must be someone hovering around who is in a position to tell us!"

Sarah stared at him, first with amazement, then with respect.

"You clever man! You may have hit the nail on the head. It is always difficult when one is personally involved and, in my anxiety, I've been tackling the problem the wrong way. I'll go to Polly's room for a while and come to the bar afterwards."

Sitting quietly, trying to keep her mind empty, Sarah began to feel calmer and more composed than she had been since first learning of Polly's plight. She watched the sun's rays filter through the net curtains and allowed her eyes to follow the pattern on the carpet: unquestioning: acquiescent. After a few moments, a young man materialised. Sarah didn't recognise him but was struck by his likeness to Dan.

Dan's father was still alive – in his middle years, but his uncle, Polly's husband, had been much older and had died just before their daughter Jane was born ... it had to be him. His anguish was obvious and made worse by his inability to name the place of Polly's concealment. As his image faded he pointed dramatically and said clearly, "Thirty-two".

Sarah rang the bar and asked Jack to come up. "If Terry can get hold of a compass and a map and bring them to Polly's suite it would help. I'll wait here."

They agreed that 'thirty-two' was probably the range, in miles, in the direction he had pointed – in line with Shrewsbury. Evesham was about the right distance away. Terry had seen a Pershore address – which was only a few miles from there, on one of Irma's files, but couldn't remember the details. Jack also recollected Dewhurst saying something about Kleg owning property near Pershore. It was where Olive died; he had wound up the trust fund, so surely he would have the information they needed. When Jack rang to ask, explaining the urgency, Brian Dewhurst promised to go immediately to his office and call back from there but said the place had probably been sold years ago.

When he rang back he was apologetic. He had a bank reference only for Olive Kleg. The private letter she wrote had been destroyed. He remembered the name of the village though, because it was so strange ... Wyre Piddle! Terry was jubilant. Within the hour he had the actual address from the Pershore police and also discovered that the place was still owned by Irma. Moreover, the official call was followed by another from an old colleague, Sergeant Noel Cross, now on the Pershore force, who said he knew the house. He often walked his dog within a few hundred yards of it and in case he could be any help, being on the spot, he left his home number.

From him, Terry discovered that the cottage, Goad's Halt, had been vacant since Mrs Kleg died. She was a quiet, nervous woman, apparently dominated by her daughter who was regarded by the locals as 'stuck up'! They were convinced now that Polly was at Goad's Halt but needed irrefutable evidence – any application for a search warrant based on extra sensory perception would be laughed out of court! Eventually, Terry rang Cross and asked if he could take a close look at the place while was still roughly an hour of daylight, to decide whether it could have been visited in the last week and, if it had, how difficult would it be to get a look inside unofficially!

It was dark when Noel Cross called back. He had found the cottage gate shut but the ground behind it was scraped clear of debris where it had been pushed back. He was sure someone had used the path recently and also been inside the porch. The steps were scuffed and the thick cobwebs around the door frame were broken. He said it was impossible to look in the windows because they were all protected by padlocked shutters. He banged on them all but heard no response from inside. He advised applying for an official search warrant, if Terry had enough grounds.

Terry looked anxious – he knew they hadn't. He couldn't apply for a warrant when concrete evidence against Irma was non-existent ... but if Sarah was absolutely sure Polly was in the cottage he would ask Alec to pull some strings. Sarah began to feel panicky – knowing Terry's hands were tied. His promise to contact Alec was reassuring, but all this would take time and if Polly was beyond being roused by someone banging on the shutters, they had to rescue her quickly.

Feeling sorely in need of support, Sarah at last called Clarinda who was shocked and keen to leave immediately to join them, but when she heard Sarah's plan, realising that Pershore was closer, she agreed instead to drive there to meet Sergeant Cross. Together, they would return to the site of the highwayman's grave.

Chapter Twenty-Nine

Gwen and Bill Williams were disappointed when Clarrie left so suddenly and made her promise to return soon. She'd had a lovely, carefree day. Gareth had taken her out for an hour after lunch, to see views he knew she'd want to paint. They stopped for tea at one of his regular haunts where Clarrie met several of his friends including a young woman who eyed her sourly. After they left she teased him, and Gareth confessed that dark-eyed Blodwen was his current regular date ... he was, in fact meeting her later, for dinner. Bill, who had put in some time at the farm office, returned home soon after she and Gareth arrived and they had enjoyed a relaxing few hours before Sarah's call.

As Clarrie drove away, the delicious aroma of roast Welsh lamb was beginning to escape from the kitchen but her appetite had deserted her. Polly had never been merely their housekeeper. Since being a baby, Polly had always been there; looking after her in her parents' absence, bathing scraped knees and, later, comforting her through teenage tribulations. Totally uncritical of her early attempts at painting, she had encouraged her when her results fell far short of her father's.

During the drive to Pershore, Clarrie mulled over how much she owed to Polly's care, and when her previous waves of sickness began to return she suspected that, this time, they were caused by worry. It was dark when she arrived and without heeding its rating she booked in at the first hotel she found, hoping for the best, and lost no time in contacting Sergeant Cross who promised to join her within ten minutes. Clarrie then rang the Lion and learned that there was a fair chance of obtaining official sanction for a search, but precious time was passing; Sarah, fearing that Polly was in dire straits and might die before they reached her, had a plan. Clarrie was fascinated and only hoped it would work; she'd do anything to save Polly.

Cross walked into the crowded bar and picked out Clarrie straight away ... not only was she alone, but he said everyone else looked happy! She noted with relief that he was well over six feet tall, and broad shouldered; if she had to go to a deserted house at night to play her part in the drama, she'd just as soon go with a man who could be a professional wrestler!

As far as he knew, he was taking her to Goad's Halt to show her what he had already noticed ... he had no notion that her expectations were more specific. As she knew the missing woman, Cross advised that Clarinda should stay over until Monday. He had already arranged to be on hand when the cottage was entered and would like her to be present.

In his Land Rover they were able to take several short cuts over rough ground between Wyre Piddle and Upton Snodsbury. An even worse stretch, off-track northwards, brought them to the infamous crossroads where the gibbet had stood. Cross didn't need to tell her the story to make her hair stand on end. In the pale moonlight, when the sound of the engine died, an eerie quiet settled over the whole scene.

They approached the cottage gate on foot in order not to destroy some tyre tracks that Cross had noted on his first visit. Nothing had changed, he said. A distant owl hooted as they stepped through the gate and walked alongside the concrete path on a carpet of weeds. Cross indicated the long strands of old webs which, when intact, must have draped over the doorway. The same substance clung to a broken branch in the porch – it had probably been used to brush them away. They held their breath to listen. In the oppressive silence, Clarrie shuddered and tried to tune in to her mother's thoughts.

***

When Clarrie had 'phoned Noel Cross from Pershore it was eight-thirty. By the time he introduced himself to her in person, Sarah Jack and Terry were well on their way to visit Margaret. Irma answered the door and smiled sweetly at Jack. She stood aside for them to enter, gazing with undisguised curiosity at his companions. Sarah, after her first glance at Irma was staring beyond her. The low lighting in the square hall shone warmly on a wall filled with old maps and watercolours. It was not the pictures which held her attention it was the ghostly figure standing near a flower-filled table. Because of her likeness to her daughter, Irma, Sarah guessed it was Olive and sensed her extreme agitation. Through Olive's eyes Sarah saw Polly lying as if lifeless, and almost fainted with shock.

Irma was ushering Jack into the sitting room, where she and Margaret had been watching television, so Sarah whispered to Terry that they were right – Polly was definitely at Goad's Halt. Jack introduced Sarah and Terry as friends of Polly Bailey and Margaret immediately expressed her concern. "Oh, my goodness – has she still not been found? Irma, can't you help? Please do try, straight away!"

Terry accepted the idea with alacrity. "Well, yes, it would be interesting but we're not as worried as we were, because someone saw her leaving on the bus to Burford."

"And I know from past experience," Sarah added, "that Polly is very unpredictable. She probably took it into her head to visit an old friend! After all, she did ask for her room to be kept. We'll be leaving tomorrow – I expect I'll find a message from her when I get home but I must say, I am curious. How do we find out where she has gone then?"

Irma provided everyone with a drink as they settled down and Margaret switched off all but one light, informing them happily, "Irma's psychic power is amazing, you know. She has been such a comfort to me. It will help her to concentrate if we sit quietly for a few minutes."

Terry winked at Sarah as Irma rejoined them and stood dramatically in their midst. "Nothing may come through," she said, but I'll do my best."

The atmosphere was conducive to spiritual contact and Sarah almost slipped into a trance herself. Margaret was indeed surrounded by loved ones from her past. Without exception they viewed Irma with apprehension. Margaret's husband stood with a hand lovingly on her shoulder and the most recently departed, Jean Webb, pointed an accusing finger at Irma, confirming Sarah's vision of her brutal murder.

Irma closed her eyes and rambled on for a while about Margaret's parents and Grandmother Ermintrude being pleased with her – she was doing the right thing. Then she intoned, "Is anyone there who knows the whereabouts of our dear friend? Please reassure us that she is well." She paused and muttered as if in conversation. "I am told that the lady has travelled eastward and I do indeed see a coach ... but can't quite hear where she is at this precise moment." Irma sat abruptly and wiped a hand over her eyes. She said she was sorry she couldn't be more specific.

Sarah was fascinated. During the entire performance, Olive had been moaning and wringing her hands, begging Sarah to save Irma from damnation; she wasn't really wicked. She accepted the blame herself, for having failed as a mother. Instead of bringing her daughter a sense of security, her lies had given Irma an inflated idea of her own importance and finally led to total dissatisfaction with her lot.

Sarah visualised Polly in Olive's old home. If wrong, she knew she would receive a warning sign but none came. Instead, her certitude grew, and while the others talked she concentrated with all her will on Clarinda who must now be nearing Goad's Halt. The policeman with her wouldn't break in without a good reason and they were determined to provide him with one. Olive's features relaxed into a smile of understanding and she slowly faded away.

***

Cross, who had inspected all the shuttered windows again and found them secure, was ready to leave. He said there was nothing they could do tonight but, as soon as he had the 'go ahead' from Terry, he would pick her up at the hotel and they would return. Clarrie had no intention of leaving and asked him to listen quietly for just ten minutes more. Wondering if she was actually achieving anything, she stood and prayed hard for a miracle! Eight minutes passed slowly and Cross began to fidget, anxious to return home to his wife and children. He opened his mouth to speak and Clarrie's prayer was answered dramatically.

Inside the house, there was a tremendous crash!

Without waiting to discuss the cause, he dashed to the front porch and heaved his weight against the door. It gave slightly and his second charge almost took it off its hinges. The room, where Polly lay on a narrow cot, was bare of furniture other than a Formica topped kitchen table and four matching chairs. Only two were in place. The others, one leg-less, lay under a shattered window as if they had been thrown across the room; shards of glass surrounded them. There was nothing else to account for the noises they had both heard, but after taking one look at the half-dead woman, it was clear that she couldn't have been responsible. Cross was dumfounded. Leaving Clarinda to do what she could without disturbing possible evidence, he went to call for help. The rough terrain would shake Polly badly if she were to be transferred by ambulance so, with fingers crossed, he requested a helicopter; road accidents kept them busy on Saturday nights.

During the ten minutes it took for the helicopter to arrive on the adjacent field, Clarrie first wrapped her own coat over the unconscious Polly, who was covered only by a thin travelling rug and then took out her pencil. Needing to do something, she had decided to make a sketch of the room. Later, if her mother drew what she had seen in her vision of Polly, it would be interesting to compare them. Clarrie was used to having a sketchpad with her and was momentarily put out – of course, it wasn't with her. She looked around for something she could write on without destroying any evidence.

An old calendar still hung on the wall, displaying June 1979. She flipped the pages and as she expected, they were blank on the reverse, so she tore one off, to use for her sketch. As she tugged, the nail came away from the damp, crumbling plaster and the calendar fell open at April. She picked it up and gasped; there was a black line under the 25th ... incredible! Today's date! *'Mother died 9.40pm.'* was written alongside in the same crayon.

Clarrie glanced at her watch and felt her hair lifting from the nape of her neck – it was almost exactly a quarter to ten! She pondered over the strange coincidence as she sat at the table, still holding her pen ... the shine on the white paper seemed hypnotic in the low light...

Later, Clarrie moved as if through a bad dream while photographs were taken of the scene and the doctor examined Polly before she was carefully lifted to a stretcher. Cross and a uniformed constable looked around the rest of the house before they all left together. The next thing she remembered clearly was walking out of the front door and saying goodnight to the men who were fixing the door and sprinkling dirt over the path to cover evidence of all the activity. The pencil was in her purse but whatever she'd written or drawn wasn't with her – she wondered where it was.

Walking to the helicopter, Cross said he'd come to the hospital to take Clarrie's statement. They were sealing the cottage again – he'd have to consult Terry about the involvement of the house-owner. As Polly was too weak to talk, they lacked evidence for an immediate arrest and intended putting a watch on it hoping the abductor, someone as yet unknown, would return.

Grey Masque of Death

When Clarrie rang Dan from the hospital she assured him that although still unconscious and extremely weak, his aunt was expected to recover. Dan then made haste to join her, leaving Elaine to contact Riverbank. Dan, while rushing to throw a few necessities into an overnight bag, made sure that Elaine knew exactly what to say when she called Margaret. "When she, or Irma, tells you Jack is there, say – Clarinda sends him her love; she expects a full recovery soon. Thank God we didn't have to say the alternative!"

***

When the telephone rang Jack was telling Margaret that he had seen Dewhurst recently on business. She said Brian's son had been a friend of her husband's and was her financial adviser.

When Irma summoned Margaret to speak to Elaine, Sarah and Jack tried to curb their anxiety; Sarah sensed that all was well and gave him an encouraging nod. She commented on Irma's remarkable clairvoyance. Saying that palmistry interested her she asked to see Irma's hand and restrained a shudder as she touched it. Sarah's extra-sensory perception, which worked when she held inanimate objects, went into top gear as she touched Irma's cold skin; she discerned the woman to be full of malice. With an effort, and catching Jack's eye, she said Irma was unquestionably deserving of everything coming to her and dropped her hand quickly without being more specific! Jack nodded and Irma smiled in appreciation...

Margaret returned brightly with the message for Jack, which prompted Terry to ask if he might make a local call himself. Jolly had been waiting impatiently. He'd never before been on a big case with the CID! Terry asked him to contact Cross for a full report; he would ring again later. He rejoined the group in time to hear Sarah, examining Margaret's palm now, advising her against making any financial decisions until the next moon phase was over. Margaret was unimpressed until Sarah listed her past cycle of gloom and serenity. Sarah contrived to include a wily reference to a recent shock – the loss of someone close, a dear friend, perhaps? – And yet she was now happy and more optimistic about life. "Just remember, don't put money on anything for a week or two and you'll have nothing to worry about." Sarah finished with a laugh.

Irma was livid. The papers were still unsigned. So near to success, this interfering amateur fortune-teller was ruining her plans! Still, she reflected, she could probably put that right with another séance or two! ... It was only a minor setback. Now they had a witness to the Bailey woman's departure – and what incredible luck that was – they seemed happy enough. Things were definitely going her way!

Chapter Thirty

Sunday April 26th...

Clarrie spent the night at the hospital and Polly, although still very weak, recovered consciousness. She wept when she came round to find Clarrie holding her hand; she had given up hope of rescue and was resigned to death. "It was strangely comforting," she whispered. "I felt so alone and knew, if I passed on, the pain would go and I'd be free to come back home again. I'm sorry – had I tried to stay awake, it might have helped."

Clarrie repeated the doctor's words; complete immobility had helped her to survive the lack of food and water. She didn't burden Polly with an account of what was happening in Barr's Brook but said Sarah would come to see her soon.

Jack left the Lion after breakfast and went straight to Ethel's. Only she could foist herself on Margaret without causing comment and she had promised to leave her pets' care to a friend for a week or two. Someone must keep an eye on Irma and she had been elected by popular vote! It was Dan's idea. Ethel, after all, was the one who alerted them to the situation and he was sure she'd be eager to help.

Sarah waited for Terry who intended accompanying her when she visited Polly, hoping for a statement. He was still with P.C. Jolly who, assisted by Ethel, would keep a discreet eye on Irma. If she left the village he would notify other areas, enabling a complete network to go into action. Wherever she went, she would be under observation.

By the time Jack arrived at Stanton Harcourt, Ethel had already telephoned Margaret and was adding a few last-minute items to her two suitcases.

Ethel was so amused. "Margaret was flabbergasted when I asked if I could stay with her – but very enthusiastic, I'm relieved to say! She will expect me about tea-time tomorrow afternoon. I lied shamelessly – told her I have a pest problem – having the place fumigated. Even if true I wouldn't have had to move out for long, but I said I was nervous about the vapour lingering and she quite understood."

"I wondered what you'd say – you did well." Admiring her inventiveness, Jack smilingly added, "Even if she hadn't liked the idea she could hardly refuse." He would love to have seen Irma's reaction to the news.

"From what our dear foolish cousin said, I gather I shall be expected to join Irma's fan club!" Ethel frowned, "How can she believe such trash?"

Jack hesitated. He had felt the same before meeting Sarah. Deciding that it would be cowardly to remain silent in face of his sister's scorn, he tried to describe what he had himself witnessed. He ended by assuring her that in Irma's case she was entirely right, the woman was a fraud. Her object wasn't yet apparent but she clearly imagined she had a right to Margaret's money.

"When it's over, we must celebrate with a family reunion," Ethel said. "Mrs Grey and Polly included, of course," she added, her eyes twinkling. "Which one of them has taken your fancy?"

Ignoring her insinuation Jack reminded her that all being well there would soon be a Christening party. He refused a second cup of coffee and was soon on his way to Headington, where Elaine and Dan expected him for lunch.

Ethel's shrewd comment was on his mind; he had met few women for whom he would have exchanged his freedom. Now In his late sixties he had a comfortable home, was free to do as he liked and knew several ladies who enjoyed being taken out, without strings. He didn't seek a wife, but a woman like Polly could change his mind!

After arriving at Headington Jack called Dewhurst asking that, if contacted by Margaret, his son should delay any proposed monetary transactions without arousing suspicion and, in the event, would he please inform CID Sergeant Terry White...

***

Sarah and Clarrie were back at home before six-o-clock. They had decided not to stay with Polly as she needed complete rest. Making a statement tired her but, without it, Terry would have trouble explaining his actions over the past days. She was too vague about her attacker to incriminate Irma and, at one stage, even implied that Irma rescued her, which confused everybody!

They were both exhausted but Sarah noticed how Clarrie seemed to revive as soon as she left the car. "I thought several times that you looked quite green," she remarked. "I put it down to worry, but you seem fine now, thank goodness."

"I felt green," Clarrie confessed. "It's happened a lot lately. It can't be exhaust fumes or you would have been affected too. Anyway, I'll defrost something to eat before unloading the car." She shrugged dismissively. "I'll just lift my canvas out and take it upstairs later." Sarah said she would like to see the painting after dinner. Clarrie was pleased; she valued criticism, especially when there was still time to act on it!

While eating they discussed the week ahead. The memorial service for Jay was on Wednesday. Clarrie would go to Elaine's after dropping Sarah off. Clarrie would stay in Oxford and, if Polly was fit to travel on Friday she'd bring her back home, collecting Sarah on the way.

After clearing up together, while Sarah prepared coffee, Clarrie set up an easel in the sitting room. She deliberately concealed it until

Sarah settled down, and then also sat to assess her reaction. As Clarrie watched Sarah's face, her stomach tightened. She'd seen that expression often, but not in connection with her work. Thoroughly alarmed, she whispered, "Mother, what's wrong?" .

Sarah, trembling slightly, answered. "If I had known, I'd never have let you go alone. Why didn't you say anything? You must be aware of the evil that permeates that awful house!" Seeing Clarrie's dismay she bit her lip. "It's a remarkably good painting. Really," she added, "Miss Matthews will be delighted with it; take it to her straight away. I'm sorry Clarinda, but the sooner this commission is wound up the more pleased I will be. Do you *have* to go there again?"

Clarrie said she planned another session. Given good light she'd stay only one night. Hearing this, Sarah decided to accompany her. She also intended to be present when it was delivered. Miss Matthews suddenly loomed as an unknown factor and even her casual association with Clarinda filled Sarah with trepidation. Clarrie began to relate what she had heard about the family, but was silenced abruptly.

"I can do without the gossip dear," Sarah said. "If I'm to learn anything of value when I see the place, I must be sure I'm not being influenced by folklore!" Patting her daughter's hand affectionately she said, "Don't worry. I'll wait in the car while you paint. I'll take a book to read. Then we'll have lunch and enjoy the rest of the day."

Clarrie lay awake that night: not exactly worrying, but with Sarah's sensitivity to the supernatural, who could predict what she might see or hear there? Even she, less psychic, had seen a ghostly face at the window! She gradually became aware of movement downstairs. Thinking her mother had perhaps gone down for a hot drink she went to join her, it might help her to sleep.

To her astonishment when she reached the kitchen, Sarah was returning from the garage and, seeing her, gave a guilty start. She confessed that she had moved the painting from the house. "We might both be able to rest now," she said with a wry smile. "I just couldn't get the place out of my mind. I felt drawn into it, onto a wide stairway and then up a narrower flight into the gloom at the top of the house."

Seeing Clarrie's immediate interest she raised an inquiring brow. "So ... you've seen something there yourself have you?" Receiving a nod of confirmation Sarah continued without asking for details. She described a heavy wooden door carved with strange shapes opening into a dingy room full of books and dusty drapes. Sitting forlornly at the window was a child: a little girl, pale and thin. "I sensed no immediate threat, but I was in a dark past which, at this time of night in my present tired state, I can well do without. The painting can stay in the garage until it goes home!"

***

Grey Masque of Death

Margaret went to bed excited and happy, looking forward to Ethel's arrival. She was vaguely irritated by Irma's obvious lack of enthusiasm; it was no more trouble to cook for three than two! She supposed it was jealousy because Irma usually had her to herself but their little séances could continue, Ethel was bound to be impressed. It had been disappointing though – Irma's failure to locate Polly: such a shame!

Irma went to bed angry and was still lying awake, boiling with fury. There'd be no chance to discuss anything private with Cousin Ethel around. She would show Margaret the documents before Ethel came, if only she sat still long enough for an explanation! She wondered if she should leave them together – absenting herself to retrieve the body – but it might not be a dead one yet! Surely, the Bailey woman would be declared missing soon and searches would be made. The longer she delayed the more possible it would be to put it somewhere they had already looked, so there was no point in going for two or three weeks.

She had planned to put the time to good use; launching her new company, 'Heywood Haven', with a partner and chief investor! Her willingness to re-name it removed all Margaret's lingering doubts. But for having her fortune told, she would already have ratified their agreement and authorised the initial transfer of a hundred thousand. Still – she'd been waiting for years, why fret about an extra month?

By autumn, however little there is to show for her money, Margaret is bound to have parted with another lump sum and she will have signed a new will to protect Irma and the company!

Having to put shows on for Ethel might even prove to be amusing; she'd have to work up something really special for their guest!

***

Bertha wondered how the painting was progressing. Apparently it would be possible to make minor changes if necessary, but she thought it unlikely that she would want anything altered. Clarinda Hunter was undoubtedly a skilled artist. There was something else about her which even at their brief meeting had been compelling. In the past Bertha had known others with similar auras but this girl was unaware of the power within her. Perhaps she could be persuaded to stay over; there must be many local scenes worth painting. If they became real friends there were amazing things she could reveal to Clarinda, to develop her spirituality.

Bertha accepted that she'd never find a companion locally. Every misfortune, from unexplained illness to a plague of flying ants was blamed on her! It was positively medieval! If it were not so sick it would be funny!

As the days passed Bertha grew more fixated on Clarrie – it made it easier to shut out the hostile world. With her as a friend she could be happy again.

Chapter Thirty-One

Wednesday 29th April...

In spite of the sombre occasion, Clarrie and Sarah were light-hearted. Polly had made a remarkable physical recovery; even her grandchildren were allowed to visit her yesterday. Elaine had invited Clarrie to stay over, to be near Polly, so after dropping her mother at Amy's, Clarrie was going on to Oxford. Amy was delighted to hear that Sarah would keep her company at Oak Lodge until Clarrie returned with Polly on Friday, and pleased too when Clarrie declared Jay's photograph entirely suitable for copying in oils. She promised to complete the painting within a month.

Clarrie was shocked to see the changes Amy had made to the lovely home she recalled from childhood visits. Obviously designed and decorated professionally and expensively furnished, it now lacked character. Jay had probably taken no interest in such mundane things as furniture and decor and may have spent long hours working, but how could he sanction such changes to his family home! Clarrie left as soon as was decently possible. Sarah too was glad her own visit would be short but was gratified to find that regular walks had become a fixture during her absence; even Bobby looked fitter.

Although she had known Amy longer, she didn't empathise with her as she had with Dorothea and inevitably found herself comparing them. Dorothea, although she had good cause, never complained about her misfortune. Amy had always found something to moan about; politicians, the weather, even her own lack of fitness, although she knew the latter was entirely her own fault! Having lost a little weight, and with time to go shopping, Amy looked very presentable when they attended the memorial service. The church was packed and being the centre of attention, far from overwhelming her, boosted Amy's morale. It was as it should be; everyone assuring her of their willingness to help; she had only to ask, at any time.

Dr. Ellis had left a message asking Sarah to contact him so she telephoned shortly after they returned to the house. He was worried because, although otherwise fairly rational, Mr Johnson was refusing to eat. If he persisted, at his age, he'd soon die – would she talk to him? When Sarah said there was nothing she could do and advised against forcing the man to live when he felt he had nothing to live for, Ellis hung up in disgust. Sarah had half expected this to happen. It fitted in with John's incredible conviction that unless he died before Jay's – and his own – birthday, he would die on exactly that day to be reborn, presumably, as his own grandson! If their two souls did endlessly re-live those forty-six years – would everyone associated with them also be fated to do the same? Of course not! In going back in time, Jay, who idolised his mother, might well seek a wife who reminded him of Dorothea but it would not *be* her! ... Of course it wouldn't!

It was a pity John was not well enough to be confronted with the outlandish nature of his thinking. Sarah certainly didn't share his half-baked delusion, but although she tried, she couldn't dismiss the undisputed facts which supported the hypothesis. There had to be another explanation, but it was quite beyond her to find it. John would probably starve himself and escape the physical plane well before Christmas, let alone next Mayday! Sarah could only pray that after his earthly death he would find peace with his wife and son. The thought brought Sarah full circle. What was it that Dorothea had discovered which sent her into her final decline? In spite of all Sarah's probing, it still eluded her? She had covered every angle, she sighed, as she ultimately fell asleep.

After breakfast on Thursday, when Amy took Bobby outside, Sarah stayed to talk to Nettie. She didn't want to ask in front of Amy but what had Dorothea meant by, *'He couldn't have known'*? Did it tie in with John's reaction to Amy and her apparent familiarity to him? Nettie, an impartial observer, might unwittingly hold the key. She found Nettie in the kitchen and asked, "Do you remember Mr Jay's last visit to his mother?" Incredibly, Nettie did – because of the pullover! She thought it was gaudy and hadn't liked it, and she suspected that he didn't either.

Sarah was amazed that such a trivial thing had stuck in Nettie's mind, "He probably wore it to show her didn't he, because it was new?" ... but could Nettie know?

"Oh, I don't think so," said Nettie. "Mrs Jay told him to put it on because it was such a cold day! He gave me a funny look and I knew what he was thinking." Glancing into the garden where Amy was brushing Bobby, she commented, "We both knew his mother never liked him in green, but he did as he was told! It was always easier to give in than to please himself."

Nettie said she'd never forget that day. Mrs Johnson had collapsed immediately he arrived and he rang from the hospital to explain why he would be home late, if at all. Nettie had dashed home to cook for her own family and returned because Amy didn't like being alone. He never wore the pullover again until the night he died.

Sarah had only one more question. To Nettie's knowledge, had Amy ever visited Mr Johnson before Jay's death? The negative answer brought no comfort. She shied away from giving credence to the impossible, but she had to face two inexplicable facts... His only glimpse of Amy had been as a stranger at the end of the drive, seconds before he had thrown the fit that heralded his breakdown. He had not known of her existence, let alone been introduced – yet he had spoken her name under hypnosis. He had also known of her subsequent marriage to Jay, despite showing no other signs of awareness for most of his hospitalisation. Thirdly – when she walked into his room he knew her instantly, in spite of the radical change wrought in her appearance by the passage of twenty years! Could John have had lucid moments which no-one suspected? If so, was Amy discussed in his hearing? She thought not; even Dr. Ellis hadn't known about her before hearing the tapes. It was extremely perplexing but Dorothea had died before John apparently recognised Amy, so it could not have been responsible for her losing interest in life. No! Between Dorothea's last hospital visit and her collapse, something sent her over the edge.

Talking to Nettie hadn't provided the answer. Sarah would have to accept that she might never know! She had always been sceptical about re-incarnation and the idea of time travel had even less validity in Sarah's eyes. Time meant nothing in the spirit world but, even so, she had never quite grasped the concept, supposedly proved, that an astronaut in space aged less quickly than his twin on earth.

Time might well have been devised by man for his own convenience but travelling through it, at will, was far more fantastic to her than the afterlife, which she knew existed alongside her own. However, father and son were scientists. It was credible that they accepted the theory fully and discussed it at length. Perhaps they fantasised: hence the old man's obsession with 1945 on the tapes. To him, the dream had become reality. Sarah gave up and finally accepted that when Jay blew himself up the poor misguided man had actually expected to be taking himself back in time for a second chance ... how very sad!

The rest of the day passed slowly but Amy's lacklustre mood changed surprisingly. Now over the shock of losing Jay, with the ritual behind her, she was ready – almost eager – to embrace her changed lifestyle. Friday morning, Mayday, started sunny but the weather changed by the time Clarrie arrived with Polly, who was almost her old self. Rain came with them from Oxford and, being anxious to reach home before dark, they left immediately, promising to return soon with the portrait. Clarrie sensed that her mother's mood was troubled but didn't probe; when not talking to Polly, she drove in silence. To their surprise, as they pulled into the drive, the house was ablaze with lights and the door burst open. Pat came out to greet them. She hugged Polly and announced that there was a meal ready ... she hadn't liked to think of them coming home to an empty house, and they had both been so good to Auntie that it was the least she could do!

The household went back to near normal during the following week; Clarrie working in her studio nine hours a day, Sarah resuming her bridge mornings and Polly, albeit from the comfort of an armchair, mothering them both, whilst happily organizing Pat and the meals.

Overhearing Clarrie asking Sarah how soon she thought they could go to Mallwyd to finish the picture, Polly protested at their concern. She said she felt fine and they could go anytime, she didn't mind but Sarah wouldn't hear of it, if it meant leaving her alone in the house.

Polly consequently resolved to go to Jane's for a while to free them of responsibility. She was adamant, insisting that it would be fun to see her grandchildren again – as long as she could eventually come back to enjoy the peace and quiet! Polly meant it and in case Irma, or whoever was the attacker, escaped the net and came looking for her, she thought it was a good idea to move out until they were locked up!

They finally arranged to return to Wales at the end of the next week and with a wry smile Polly promised not to return alone – she'd had her fill of living dangerously. "And I've had enough of playing detective alone too! Don't worry, I know I'm not cut out for the job but I hope I don't have to hide for ever!"

They all wondered how long it would be before Irma made a move, but at least they knew where she was ... Smythe, if indeed he ever existed, had vanished into thin air!

***

Ethel's first week at Riverbank was going well. She had not expected to enjoy herself even though, because of her pets, she hadn't had a holiday for years. She made up her mind not to be so silly in future. Margaret appeared to relish her company and actually suggested she move in permanently. Ethel said she couldn't possibly give up her home but did promise to visit more often. They remembered playing Lexicon as children and Margaret unearthed an old pack. When Edna saw them having a game one morning she said it was like scrabble and volunteered to lend them her travel set. It was so successful that Irma was instructed to buy a 'proper one' next time she went to Burford!

Irma felt thwarted. Ever since her arrival, on Monday, Ethel had monopolised Margaret, always contriving to postpone any demonstration of her psychic powers. Margaret, however, was determined to hold a séance tonight, so Irma scrutinised the charred photographs for inspiration. There must be something about Ethel's mother she hadn't covered in previous sessions! As they were to be joined by an unbeliever it would have to be better than ever.

With three hours to go, Irma was putting the time to good use, rehearsing her part. Ethel was likely to be a harder nut to crack than her cousin but she relished the challenge. In one of the studies Helen wore a heavy gate bracelet – undoubtedly gold. Light glinted on the swinging padlock. The lower edge of the photo had burned away but in the singed area was a ring and with a surge of excitement, Irma identified it as the one Ethel wore most evenings. It was a pearl, encircled by small diamonds, which Ethel had obviously inherited; she might remember the bracelet even if she didn't own it.

Irma wracked her brains for anything her mother had said about Helen which she might use. She'd married someone called William – Irma couldn't recall telling Margaret that. When Olive went to the family in 1929, Helen had already left home and Jack was about five years old. She knew many stories about him and the twins, which Margaret liked hearing, but Ethel and her sister had been tiny and she was unlikely to remember those holidays. Still, it might be worth repeating a few.

Ethel, if not converted, might become hostile and create doubts in Margaret's mind. She too had been dubious at first and now believed fervently in the after-life.

Poor gullible Margaret!

Irma wondered momentarily how her victim was faring. She was a tough old bird; not many would have survived even the first wound. Dismissing the thought, she concentrated on her current, much more important task.

Chapter Thirty-Two

Friday May 8th...

Having been away so long and then leaving again so soon, the week had been busy for Sarah. She cleared up several outstanding tasks and, with Pat's help, prepared clothes for the trip. She had plenty of time to think. Although intrigued about Bertha Matthews' background, it was difficult to subdue her anxiety. If Clarinda had not had to go back to complete the painting nothing would have induced her to visit the house. Sarah had a healthy respect for the power of evil and would not ordinarily have courted danger by placing herself in close contact with it.

Sarah could not conceive of Clarinda going alone, she was less experienced and therefore more vulnerable but it would have been wrong to suggest that she should call the painting finished when it wasn't! Like any other client, Miss Matthews deserved the best picture Clarinda could produce and Sarah had no reason to think the woman herself was evil. However, her ancestors might not be so blameless!

Sarah had loved Stephen's family home but it was too large to maintain so she could understand the old lady wanting an oil painting as a memento. She had no doubt that Miss Matthews would be pleased with it, she thought, as Clarinda put the picture in the car. Not having seen it for almost two weeks Sarah was impressed again by the quality of her daughter's work; it seemed to pulsate with life. She was making a final security check when Clarrie called her to the studio. "Just a moment, there's something I want to show you before we leave. I almost forgot in all the rush."

Sarah went in and saw with pleasure that Jay's portrait was finished and drying on the easel. She admired it; Amy would be delighted. She assumed it was the reason for her being called, but Clarrie explained. "It was impossible to see the fine detail of his features – there was dust inside the glass, so I took the liberty of cutting the backing tape and removing the photo from the frame. How do you explain this?" She handed the mounted picture to Sarah with a puzzled frown. "It isn't a colour print as I thought; it is hand-tinted but very well done. Turn it over – there's a greeting card stuck to the back. I didn't try to pull it off in case it tore."

Sarah almost swooned as she read the message and recognised the writing – unmistakably the same as that on the front. She felt as sick and stunned as Dorothea must have been, seeing Jay wearing the distinctive garment in the photograph – the green sweater.

She told Clarrie to re-seal it in the frame ... to forget it and never speak of it to Amy ... and yes – of course – she would try to explain later! Explain... How? There was no explanation! Contrary to Amy's assumption, the photograph was not meant for her ... Even Jay might never have seen it. On the day he called on his mother, when the sight of him sent Dorothea into shock it was probably still packed away with the rest of the family albums, unseen for many years!

Of only one thing was Sarah absolutely certain – she would never be able to forget the message on the faded wedding card. The ink had yellowed but it was clearly written: *With love to my beautiful bride, my wife, Dorothea. September 1946.*

***

In mid-morning Irma announced that she was going to Burford and had their game on her shopping list. When she departed Ethel was on the phone within minutes.

P.C. Jolly answered and she said brightly, "Ethel here! How is the menagerie? Oh, good! Margaret and I are fine; I'm enjoying the change. We have just discovered Scrabble – Irma has gone to Burford to buy a box for us!"

"I understand, thanks," Jolly replied and rang off.

"Well I'm very grateful to you for taking care of my little family," Ethel nodded, smiling at Margaret who was nearby, "you have this number if an emergency arises and if you are quite sure, I'll stay here a while longer." Margaret laughed and said people would think they were in their second childhood, playing games.

Ethel reflected that her cousin played strange games with Irma but refrained from saying so aloud! She had gone along with the demonstration once and Irma's dramatic ability deserved an Oscar! Margaret's pleasure, when Irma, with closed eyes and frequent shivers of ecstasy – as if overcome by close contact with the long dead – spoke of Ethel's ring 'having once adorned the delicate hand of her beautiful mother'! It was sickening to note Margaret's gullibility but Ethel was aware that Margaret didn't have her own advantage of prior knowledge; Irma was an unscrupulous fraud.

She managed to sound overawed, but had avoided a repeat performance by saying that the idea of talking to ghosts unnerved her. It was pretty near the truth! According to Jack, there really were genuine mediums and the thought gave her goose-bumps! Irma returned directly from her trip and Ethel wondered how long it would be before she could resume her normal life in her own home ... however well she and Margaret were getting along, Irma's presence was disturbing.

***

Although it was late afternoon when they left, the drive began in sunshine. Clarinda drove well and Sarah relaxed, letting her mind drift back to the days when her husband had been at the wheel. They were so alike, father and daughter, she had been lucky. Her heart went out to poor Bertha, all alone. She would gladly help if she could, but her priority was to protect Clarinda. A light drizzle set in, making driving difficult. The screens, front and rear, were alternately rain splattered or streaked with muddy arcs as the wipers coped with spray from other vehicles. It was bad, but by the time they reached Welshpool the skies cleared again and the roads soon dried. They reached the inn after closing time – it was being cleaned. Sarah was gratified to see how warmly everyone welcomed her daughter's return. Whatever awaited them outside, inside they were safe and secure.

Early on Saturday, after a comfortable night, Sarah was sitting in the car, with her book and a pile of magazines that the innkeeper's wife insisted she would need. It was a beautiful clear day but as soon as her easel was in position Clarrie had her first shock. The corner of the house she had seen, and already painted, really was hidden by large bushes. The stones in her picture were not visible at all! The men in the bar were right! She hadn't told Sarah what they said, but wasn't sure now whether to repaint the area or leave it.

At her request, Sarah set aside her reading and walked over. After looking from the house to the picture several times she asked, "Did anyone also mention that it was an animal cemetery?" Clarrie nodded. Sarah shook her head sadly. "The child is there too!" Clarrie was chilled, evoking the small face at the window, and listened spellbound ... "As I look," said Sarah, "the bushes are fading. There's no sun – it is night. I see the stones you saw, but some are pushed aside revealing freshly dug earth. Two figures are standing over what I'm sure is the child's grave. Now they are rolling the stones back and walking to the house."

Sarah sank onto Clarrie's canvas stool and kept her eyes shut, breathing deeply. "One of the women is folding something – a black blanket which had been wrapped round the little body. It is patterned with tiny mirrors which flash in the moonlight." She opened her eyes wide in dawning horror. "I've seen it before – in our garage! How in the name of God did it get there?" Shocked by Sarah's extraordinary vehemence Clarrie described her encounter with Lofty and his light-fingered friend. Recollecting Len's nightmares she wondered if having it with her had also been the cause of her nausea while driving, but didn't say so – her mother looked worried enough!

Sarah came to a decision. "The innocent waif isn't at peace, we must help her. Leave the stones as they are and, I know it won't please you, but I'd like you to paint the little girl as you saw her, in the dormer window." Clarrie was astonished but, knowing from experience that her mother never asserted herself without good reason, didn't hesitate to do as asked. It was easy to transform the shine on the distant window to a face-like blur. There was no need for detail; the eye of the beholder could interpret the result in many ways: even as the reflection of a cloud. To anyone with imagination or inner vision it was the sad visage of a child.

Sarah watched as she worked and uttered murmurs of appreciation. "You have certainly inherited your father's skill with a brush but your work has something extra. He captured atmosphere of course, but you achieve an elusive aura for those able to see. Don't worry – I'm sure most auras are happy!"

Later, after the painting and gear were packed up, they walked to the copse for a closer look. The shrubs had obviously been planted deliberately to cover the stones. There would have been no reason to hide animal graves; the illicit burial of a child was a different matter.

Neither wanted to explore farther; they returned to the car.

The regulars at the inn who had seen the picture evolve from bare canvas were full of praise. It developed into a social event and Clarrie was glad; Sarah hadn't had much fun lately. Perhaps she should invite her on painting trips more often! Her thoughts were interrupted when old Gordy Bates, again occupying the fireside chair, beckoned her over. He asked if she believed in witches. Taken aback, Clarrie shrugged warily and sat with him, showing her willingness to listen.

"Now you don't have to go back there, I'll tell you," he said quietly, glancing about, ensuring he wasn't overheard, "My young brother 'ad a mate – nineteen this lad were and sweet on Miss Bertha. She were only sixteen but he'd 'ave waited – planned to marry her one day, but they two old witches laid down the law in that 'ouse and they'd not 'ear of it. Threatened him they did, if he didn't stay away he'd be sorry!" Wiping perspiration from his brow and, with no sign that he was other than deadly serious, he continued. "This boy were good looking enough – bright red 'air – and an honest 'ard worker, but only one arm he 'ad! They wouldn't let the girl marry a cripple. Time went on and he kept sneaking round to see her."

Clarrie was being called for lunch but Gordy clutched her arm. "Everybody warned 'im to stay away from the place, but he wanted 'er and gave no 'eed." She stood, but couldn't tear herself away without hearing how his tale ended. Hurrying, Gordy said, much louder than he had intended, "They turned 'im into a dog!"

Several people turned in surprise. Another old man laughed derisively. "Good grief, Gordy, you aren't bringing up that hoary old tale again, surely! The boy gave up when he saw he wasn't making headway. His parents said he'd gone north. Why won't you believe it? Filling this young lady's head with such twaddle, you should be ashamed of yourself."

Gordy wouldn't be silenced. Having begun he intended finishing. "The very day when that boy disappeared, a ginger three-legged dog turned up – scurrying between our 'ouse and 'is all day it were ... yowling! Where did it come from? As for 'is folks – it were funny, weren't it, the way they suddenly come into money and moved away." Clarrie smiled and assured him she was glad he'd told her. It was a really fascinating story... there were more things in heaven and earth etc. and who knew! Fairly mollified he returned to his pipe and newspaper.

Clarrie and Sarah discussed the yarn later. Neither gave it credence but Sarah, with John and Jay still at the back of her mind, felt bound to comment that they both accepted as natural, things which most people didn't. They believed in the kind of white magic which, with faith, sometimes worked. There were equally convinced followers of black magic ... the Yin and Yang. Allowing that a darker side might indeed exist, what made them so sure they knew the limits of its power?

After reaching home on Saturday night, Sarah fetched the blanket from the garage. Clarrie saw her fleeting expression of distaste and asked the cause. Pointing at the intricate floral design, as she carried it gingerly to the bottom of the garden, Sarah replied with a question of her own. "Can't you sense them? How can such vile images emanate from such beautiful handiwork?" They prayed as they watched it burn; it was almost like a funeral pyre for the long dead child.

The painting remained in the garage drying off. Clarrie, knowing her mother was anxious to get it off their hands as soon as possible, had finished it with a quick drying medium – it should be ready to take for approval within days, so she rang Miss Matthews and arranged to deliver it on the 16th – Saturday next.

Now able to put the strange house and its mysteries out of mind, Clarrie started on a new canvas.

***

In spite of everything, Bertha was happy. It was the middle of May and the weather was growing milder. More importantly – she had heard from Clarinda Hunter. The painting was ready and she would soon meet the young artist again. She cleaned and polished with more enthusiasm than for many months, excited at the prospect of entertaining. She actually sang as she hung her laundry out, until she heard scrabbling on the fence.

Billy's tousled head bobbed up as he clung to the top with his arms over. "You're evil! You shouldn't be doing that," he shouted. "Only wicked people work on Sundays!"

Utterly deflated, Bertha completed her task and hurried back inside. As she recovered, she clung desperately to the thought that Clarinda was coming. Surely, she would be her friend.

Chapter Thirty-Three

Rather than bring Polly home before Irma was under lock and key and as they would be away for hours when they delivered the painting, Sarah took over the housekeeping. She had forgotten how time-consuming it was, even without the manual work. She didn't mind cooking – shopping she could do without!

On Thursday, Elaine invited them for lunch with Terry and Jack. Terry reported on the situation in Barr's Brook. Ethel's presence was getting on Irma's nerves – she had asked for a day or two off next week to visit a friend. Jack suggested she could be going to the absent professor, but Terry had grave misgivings about Smythe. The only fingerprints at his house matched those found at Irma's. That might mean that 'he' had been to hers, but traces of Irma were found on the male clothing and forensics indicated only one wearer! If Irma had posed as the man, he had probably never existed at all. They needed a sample of Irma's fingerprints. In spite of everything, Irma might still claim innocence unless she eventually tried to dispose of the body.

He fervently hoped she would return to Goad's Halt. Depending on her reaction to finding her victim gone, she would have a hard time explaining herself. Polly, although confused about her attacker, was fairly sure that it had been Irma who had left her alone, without adequate warmth, food or water. Irma's failure to check on Polly's condition would certainly lead to a charge of attempted murder, even without proof that she was the Professor. He had not been seen since his tenancy agreement ended ... it all tied nicely together.

By leaving her at large, on condition that her every move was monitored, they might learn more, or make the case against her even stronger, Terry said, but Jack wondered what Irma must think of Polly's family and their apparent lack of concern over her disappearance. "Such things are usually splashed all over the media ... surely Irma must suspect we have already found Polly?"

Clarrie suggested with a grin, "Why don't you drop in at Riverbank, Jack, to update them all? You could hint that her daughter thinks Polly has a lover and wants to avoid publicity!" Amid the hilarity that ensued, Sarah protested that Jane, the daughter in question was unlikely to agree but it was good to be laughing again. Terry, having reasoned similarly, had already told Jolly to start a rumour – that they reckoned Polly was okay, having left of her own accord. In Irma's place, he would definitely bring the body back to Barr's Brook for disposal because the whole area had already been turned upside down looking for her; it wouldn't be searched again. She was most unlikely to bury it in her own garden! Satisfied that all was under control, he was content to play a waiting game.

Looking ahead, they were concerned for Margaret's future. When Irma went, she'd not only be lonely again, but would feel wretched, having been duped. Ethel couldn't stay forever. It had already occurred to Jack that Margaret might, when the time came, be willing to offer a home to Esther, daughter of the village postmistress, who was pregnant. He thought Esther might be pleased to keep house in exchange for a low rent. Her husband would be useful to have around too. Jack said it would be easy to sound out Esther's mother, at the shop, without revealing his ulterior motive or any connection with Margaret.

As Polly's car and suitcase were still at the Lion, Jack offered to drive Clarrie and Sarah to Barr's Brook when Terry gave them the all clear, so that Clarrie could drive the Mini back to Mapledurham. Sarah jumped at the idea – they could stay overnight in case there was anything they could do for Margaret.

***

When Clarrie rang Bertha on Saturday morning to confirm her visit she said that her mother would be with her as it was a lovely day for a drive. She hoped it wouldn't be inconvenient. Bertha was disappointed initially, having anticipated being alone with Clarinda but perhaps, initially, it would be better to aim at acceptance by them both. Her excitement returned and Bertha hummed quietly as she made a cake and prepared sandwiches for tea. When the car pulled into the driveway she went out to greet them, smugly aware that faces were peeping from behind curtains on all sides.

After they were seated and she had time to observe the older of her guests Bertha's heart sank. Mrs Grey was a psychic! They shared instant awareness of each other's medium-ship. Although astounded, Bertha suddenly relaxed, feeling strangely more at ease. They, at least, were likely to understand her. They might guess that her own roots lay along the opposite path but she had rejected her heritage and had nothing to hide. However, Bertha faced the bitter fact – the girl was lost to her; her mother was her guide and mentor. It was a set-back, but perhaps she would have two real friends instead. In retrospect, in view of her own upbringing, maybe the whole idea of an acolyte had been a bad one.

After some small-talk, a space was cleared and the painting positioned for Bertha's appraisal. No-one spoke. The spluttering of the fire was the only sound – as if they all held their breath. In her mind Sarah saw, re-enacted, that grim, moonlit scene but her eyes were on Bertha. Clarrie also watched their hostess, hoping she liked the picture but also anxious for a reaction to the changes she had made to the scene as it was now.

Bertha was lost in wonder; it was so real. She could imagine herself actually there. But something differed, surely: the river bank! Yet it really had been like that once, a long time ago ... when she was a girl. She raised her eyes to the top of the house and saw a child at the window of her old classroom – the hated place which she never entered again after going to a real school ... not until after her grandmothers were dead.

Who was the little girl? Definitely not herself! But how could there have been any other? Her eyes were drawn unerringly to the river bank – then to Sarah – and she immediately knew! Bertha was incapable of speaking, tears flooding her cheeks, but she nodded reassuringly at Clarinda who understood that the painting itself was not the reason for her distress. Eventually Sarah spoke. "We know the infant died in that room and is unable to find peace in the afterlife. Perhaps she is still seeking something she lacked on earth. I can't help her but I think you can, and I hope you won't regard my interference as anything other than an earnest attempt to help the innocent baby."

Their obvious sincerity overcame Bertha's reserve and her guard was down sufficiently to speak about her lonely childhood. She looked shrewdly into Clarrie's eyes and guessed that she had already heard the gossip. "The villagers shunned the house, you know, but we valued our privacy and were self-sufficient, except for the gardening." Older cousins of her parent's, three sisters, ran the house. Unluckily for Bertha she was the only child of her generation. Successively her elders died, leaving her quite alone in the world. Sarah and Clarrie sat in the growing gloom, fascinated by the story of Bertha – the last of the Matthews.

As Sarah's assertions about the child merged with her own thoughts and memories, Bertha shook with emotion. They had lied to her! And her mother sanctioned their deceit! Now she understood why her grandmothers had not been angry when they realised, even before she knew herself, that she was pregnant. They tended personally to her every need and how stupid she'd been, interpreting their actions as loving. They acted, not for her protection as she thought, but so that no-one apart from the family should learn about her condition. They said her baby would be accepted as belonging to a married cousin, the only one whose husband hadn't deserted their claustrophobic environment.

The boy she loved went away, so Bertha had no urge to rebel against her lack of freedom. His desertion upset her, but she was ashamed by the outcome of her short romance and relieved that she wasn't being punished. One fact cheered her, the only thing she clearly understood – she would have a baby to care for: a little replica of herself or the boy: her own child to love. Only her grandmothers attended her at the birth and as soon as the infant was born they removed it. She remembered as though in a dream the baby's cries, but when she woke hours later it was to the sound of her mother sobbing. She was told to forget the child. It was dead.

Gradually, Bertha regained control and told Clarrie, "I'm sure it was her face you saw. My poor little girl – how could I have known that she lived? Although just a child myself, I wanted her desperately. They said my baby was too weak to survive and it would be easier for me to put the whole ghastly episode behind me if I didn't see it, but they were wrong. I have always felt empty inside; a hollowness that nothing else could fill. If only they had allowed me keep her, my life – and hers – could have been happy. What wicked, wicked people they were!" Bertha couldn't stem her tears.

No wonder the child looked so sad, imprisoned in that small room. Her only contacts, those two awful old crones, having failed with their granddaughter, intended to bring up her baby in their own ways. There would have been no school inspector checking up on a child whose very existence was unknown to the world. Bertha didn't doubt that isolation and lack of sunlight contributed to the little girl's death. Her jailers were more interested in feeding her mind than her body! How could they have committed that heinous act? Now, they were beyond her vengeance and the child would never know her love.

"It isn't beyond your power to tell the child how much she was wanted and how you would have loved her if you'd had the chance." Sarah quietly answered Bertha's thoughts. "Your prayers can help her to accept what happened. She, in turn, can come close to you and help you to overcome your loneliness."

Clarrie watched the two women regarding each other warily, amazed as always by her mother's intuitive powers. Her own mystical experiences, now that they had passed, seemed insignificant and she wondered what it must be like, communicating directly with the spirit world – seeing and talking, almost at will, to people long dead!

Bertha was recovering from the shock. In fact, the revelation that she was still a mother albeit to a spirit or 'dreamchild' began to excite her. Other topics were broached but all gave way to Bertha's compulsion to discuss her past. It was cathartic talking through the whole sad affair with a sympathetic audience. She also told them about the way she was treated by the villagers and her despair of ever being accepted. The afternoon had long gone before her guests prepared to leave.

Sarah had some last words of encouragement. "We three were born blessed, or cursed, with special knowledge of two worlds. In both are two paths, good and evil, and we choose freely which to follow. To avoid being drawn into the ways of your forebears you struggled and won. Your baby escaped too, so don't be embittered. Time will heal the hurt you feel now."

After they went, assuring her that they were only a 'phone call away if she needed to talk, Bertha cleared up quickly, impatient to examine her new acquisition. Then, with curtains drawn against the hostile world, she found solace in the painting.

Mai Griffin

It hung opposite the fireplace. Illuminated by a standard lamp and the flaming coals, it vibrated with realism. She sat transfixed. Her thoughts drifted to the year she was sixteen ... she had been deliriously happy with the golden-haired boy. They dreamed of a beautiful future together. Orders to stay away didn't deter him. He came back to her silently and secretly, but the old harridans always knew, and were angry.

One day he went away without saying good-bye in spite of his promise that he would never desert her. She remembered the three-legged ginger dog and the wild stories ... people were so stupid; yet he didn't return! Surely they couldn't be right? Bertha dismissed the fleeting thought with a shrug. It was much more satisfying to think about their child. She had cried many tears thinking the baby dead. The old crones were a despicable pair, capable of anything if they could be so heartless!

The flickering light on the painting lulled Bertha into deep sleep in which she crossed the grass and went inside her old home. She walked without hesitation through the tiled hall and up to the second floor where she climbed the narrow stairs to the attic. As she entered, the tiny child turned from the window. The wan little face smiled; her thin arms lifted in welcome and they hugged joyfully. Wrapping the slender body in her arms protectively, Bertha repeated, over and over, the words of love and comfort she would have said long ago, if only she had been allowed the opportunity.

When she awoke, daylight filtered round the drapes. The light was still on: the fire, dead, grey ash. She felt amazingly refreshed. Although slumped against the arm of the settee she did not feel stiff. She'd actually had a better night's sleep than she remembered having for many months. Her dream had been so vivid that she still felt the warmth of the little body pressing on her breast and the silky smoothness of tiny arms wound round her neck... She suddenly felt less alone and dealt with her daily chores cheerfully.

Bertha looked forward that day and every following day to the long evenings, when she could sit quietly with her painting and lose herself in contemplation of what might have been....

Chapter Thirty-Four

Wednesday May 20th...

Irma was heartily sick of Ethel. In spite of her pretence, she was nowhere near as impressed by 'spirit messages' as her cousin and séances had been supplanted by scrabble every evening. When she did achieve a private word with Margaret, she found her no less enthusiastic about their partnership but she saw no need for haste. Irma decided to give up until Ethel went. Rather than waste time she would use it to dispose of her own unwanted guest.

The police were apparently convinced that Mrs Bailey had left the area, so bringing her back to the quarry for burial would be easy; she had already prepared a place. It had been something to do during the afternoons, while the cousins watched TV, reminisced and played games like children! Both were indifferent when she said she'd like to go away for a couple of days ... there shouldn't be much to clear up at the cottage but she must allow for unexpected developments and it wouldn't hurt for Margaret to miss her, and the attention she gave, for a few days.

Irma left the house immediately after breakfast and Ethel was on the telephone before she drove through the gate ... Constable Jolly relayed the information and then rang Terry. When apprised of Irma's departure, Jack picked up Sarah and Clarrie from Mapledurham and took them to Barr's Brook. They booked into the Lion at midday.

Irma confused her 'tail' by not going straight to Wyre Piddle.

She was observed shopping in Evesham, at a garden supplies merchant where a roll of plastic mulching strip and string were among her purchases. Then she had a leisurely lunch. She apparently had no intention of reaching her destination in daylight but as soon as they were convinced she was heading there, the police kept track of her and two policemen lay in wait, in the vicinity of the cottage.

They expected her to approach from the front and their Jeep was discreetly hidden in the woods, ready to follow when she left. Hearing the car in a field at the back, they knew they were in no position to keep track of it when she drove away ... they could only wait and watch.

Anxious to avoid being seen, Irma had kept away from all but the smallest lanes and although she didn't know it, evaded her pursuers soon after leaving Pershore. Carrying the plastic, to wrap the body, she pushed through a section of broken fence – the property had no rear gate into the field. There was little chance of being observed from the front, but even less at the back door.

Irma entered and switched on the light.

Illumination from the kitchen fell across the living room and the cot in the corner ... all seemed as she had left it. Then she suddenly realised it was unoccupied! Where was the body? Irma looked around fearfully as she approached the bed – almost expecting an attack, but how – from a corpse? No-one in that stupid woman's condition could have survived without care; it was beyond her comprehension. She saw something gleaming on the mattress – the torn calendar page – and was drawn to it, as if hypnotised.

The watchers at the front heard, but were in no position to follow when Irma ran screaming from the back of the house to her car.

They reported what had happened and hoped she would be picked up on the main road. Fifteen minutes later they received permission to relax – the subject was leaving the area at speed, in the direction of Burford. They were ordered not to enter the premises again, but to lock it up securely. Irma had been inside for only minutes, but it might be necessary to determine what she had done, while inside.

While Sarah and Clarrie collected Polly's case, Jack checked over the Mini and filled the petrol tank at the local garage ready for Clarrie to drive home. It was almost seven-o-clock when Terry joined them. His Chief agreed that it was highly likely that Smythe was purely an invention of Irma's and had issued a warrant to take her into custody. Terry had decided, in case Irma returned to Riverbank, that Margaret must be told what was happening. She would be terribly shocked otherwise, if he had to arrest Irma in front of her.

Jolly was stationed on the quarry road between Riverbank and Barr's Brook ... he had the drive gates in sight and was in touch with Terry by radio-phone When and if Irma arrived he would warn them, so Terry suggested that they should go to the house straight away. Jack and Ethel would be able to convince Margaret that they were acting in her best interests and Sarah, being Polly's friend, could verify that Irma was indeed responsible for her abduction.

Margaret was quite overwhelmed when her quiet evening with Ethel was interrupted by Cousin Jack, accompanied by what seemed like a crowd of strangers. She soon recognised Terry and Sarah but was puzzled by their presence. Ethel provided drinks for everyone while Margaret tried to take in the fact that Irma, far from being a kind companion, had not only tried to murder Polly but was probably responsible for Jean Webb's death too.

"I must be senile," Margaret moaned, tears of mortification spilling down her thin cheeks. "To think I trusted her! How could I be taken in by that psychic nonsense? ... But her knowledge was so detailed, she made the past live again for me. Who could guess that my family is as familiar to her as to myself?"

Terry would not allow her to dismiss the supernatural merely because of one fraudulent medium and informed her that if it hadn't been for Sarah, who was genuine and had helped the police on many other occasions, Polly would not have been found in time to save her life and Irma might have got away with her swindle!

Sarah motioned him to silence. "One individual's proof is useless to another ... I expect Margaret will keep an open mind in spite of Irma's having taken advantage of her." Turning to Margaret she said, "I think you often wondered why neither Jean nor your husband ever 'came through' during Irma's séances. I can only say that they are both here now, close to you, and will help you to get over this dreadful affair."

Margaret sniffed, not eager to be convinced, although she admitted it had seemed strange that those most recently lost to her were never among her ghostly visitors. Terry looked hopefully at Sarah, expecting her to say something to convince Margaret of her powers but Sarah merely smiled as she never went out of her way to prove herself.

It was dark outside. Ethel began drawing the curtains; Sarah stood abruptly and joined her, looking towards the road. Turning to Terry she declared, "She's coming, but she won't stop. Jean Webb is out there waiting for her; there's nothing we can do!"

Headlights approached. A car first slowed, and then suddenly hurtled past with a roar of acceleration, towards the village.

Sarah concentrated all her thoughts on Jean as she had seen her in her earlier vision, struggling for her life.

Irma drove through the night like one possessed.

The shock of finding her victim gone – her terror when she read the accusing letter in her mother's handwriting – and, finally, actually seeing her long-dead mother, pleading with her to repent – had unhinged her. She had reached Riverbank by instinct, but the spectre of Jean Webb, standing at the gate, ordering her away, protecting Margaret, broke her loose hold on sanity entirely; she tore past, recklessly.

With blinding tears streaming down her face she neared the place where she had waylaid Margaret's friend and screamed in terror! The woman was there again ... standing with her bicycle on the quarry edge!

Bursting with fear and malice, scarcely able to comprehend what was happening, Irma howled and steered straight at the grim apparition...

The only witness, Police Constable Jolly, later reported that her car suddenly swerved and soared off the road and there was a tremendous crash.

Irma died instantly.

When Terry joined Jolly at the site, they found a torn off calendar page beside her in the car and Terry recalled Clarrie mentioning that she had written something on one at Goad's Halt, but had lost it. He took it back with him to Riverbank where everyone was anxiously awaiting his return.

Clarrie instantly recognised the calendar sheet and was eager to discover what she had written. Sarah too read it before handing it to Margaret who had been waiting with barely concealed curiosity while Terry explained to her that Clarrie had penned it while in a trance.

Margaret's eyes widened, in alarm, as she began to read.

"But it's absolutely impossible! This was written by Olive! I could never mistake her flowery writing!" ...She dropped the page as if it were red hot.

"No, not impossible," Terry smiled, satisfied. "Reading it, Irma must also have known it was her mother's handwriting and regretted ever meddling with the dead!"

Ethel agreed to stay at Riverbank until other arrangements could be made. Margaret wasn't averse to having a young family living with her ... it was a big enough house to retain her privacy, but she'd have to get to know them first... Once bitten ... of course! Sarah and Clarrie were eager to return home to assure Polly that she had no more to fear, so they left early on Thursday morning. The remainder of the month was a rather dull anticlimax until Elaine's baby girl arrived on the thirty-first. Jack rang Polly with the news and also told her that he had found the photographs of Chaz ... still in the original frame in his bedroom, but they had been hidden behind a print, now removed.

He was giving the night-dress case to Elaine.

Polly rallied completely within weeks.

Only occasionally did either Sarah or Clarrie think of Bertha Matthews, content that she had not felt the need to call them.

Epilogue ...

As the year wore on, Bertha's past and present gradually merged. Her window drapes were drawn earlier and earlier as the weeks went by. Neighbours grew accustomed to them being unopened, sometimes for days on end.

Inside, Bertha and her phantom child played games and the cottage rang with happy laughter. Although only six-years-old when she died, Baby was able to recite long passages from the old books ... verses which Bertha herself had long forgotten and eagerly she learned the simple nursery rhymes that Bertha never tired of singing to her.

For the first time in her life Bertha was euphorically happy.

It was impossible to exclude the outside world from her sanctuary all the time and Bertha was impatient with anything which dragged her back to reality. She answered the door only when unavoidable and her reputation for eccentricity grew.

The children became bolder in their attacks on her privacy. Billy even came to the open kitchen door once, frightening her as she was carrying out the cinder tray to the roses. When the grey ash scattered over the floor, he roared with delight, ran triumphantly back to the fence and clambered over, into his own garden.

His friends were agog at his bravery!

From her cottage, Bertha watched. Billy was by far the most handsome. He had large brown eyes and the face of an angel, framed with dark silken curls ... but he had the heart of a devil.

The days grew dull and shortened with the coming of winter. Bertha was glad that the cold weather kept the children off the street; not that she wanted to venture out herself. She was content to stay at home with Baby. It was almost Christmas and she decided to decorate the room with holly from the hedge. There was a small tree in the garden too ... Baby would like a decorated tree. They could make tin-foil baubles for it and paint cardboard shapes together; it would be fun.

Then she began to worry... She should get Baby a present; every child should have a gift on Christmas day. Later, as she sat transfixed, staring at the painting, she had an idea ... she could solve two problems with one stroke. A stroke of sheer genius she chuckled. Baby must have a little pet.

Bertha wished she had kept the ancient volumes ... there was so much she had forgotten and even more, at the time, that she hadn't wanted to know. Contemplating the painting, she drifted again into a trance, visualizing the climb up to the attic. Her grandmothers were already waiting there, as if expecting her, smiling encouragement. They showed her the page they were studying. Her eyes followed the bony fingers as they pointed eagerly to the passages Bertha had been struggling to recall...

She woke at dawn, still slumped in her chair, her aching head spinning with fatigue, but now she knew, clearly, how to carry out her plan. It was Sunday morning, the ideal time. Billy's parents always attended church service, leaving him at Sunday school but he seldom stayed long. He preferred sitting on the fence, stoning birds with his catapult – threatening her windows to make her life hell – taunting and pulling faces, if he saw her!

There was no time to waste. His reign of terror was over!

The family would leave the house within the hour ... the Devil's spawn would sneakily return to their garden and see her back door, for once wide open. If inside there was something sufficiently intriguing, he wouldn't be able to resist a closer look. What could it be: something to see, or even hear? Perhaps he would hear a child's voice singing ... or a child calling his name? Yes! Baby would love to help Mummy!

***

It was a few days before New Years Eve. Clarrie and her mother were preparing happily for the celebrations ahead. Clarrie was going out and Sarah had friends coming in. They seldom spoke of Bertha but Clarrie tentatively suggested driving over to see her. Sarah refused and with a shudder explained. She was hardly ever troubled by bad dreams but confessed that after writing her greeting cards – one of them to Bertha – she had, on successive nights, suffered the worst nightmares of her life. She was trapped in that dusty attic – two menacing, shadowy creatures hovered over her, threatening her life.

Each time she woke in the dark hours her mind went straight to the card – still with the pile in the hall, ready for posting. Finally, she went down and tore it up.

The horrific dreams ceased and she wouldn't court disaster by renewing contact with the old lady. Miss Matthews had touched their lives briefly and knew where they were, if she wanted them. Clarrie and Polly were both astonished by her unexpected and very un-typical reaction but accepted that Sarah knew best.

The radio was on, but none of them was concentrating on it until the announcer referred to Hinney Green. "Listen, mother," Clarrie urged, "that's where Miss Matthews lives! A little boy has been missing from his home there, since just before Christmas – how terrible."

Hearing the boy's name, William Bonny, they looked warily at each other – it was Billy, the boy who had treated Bertha so cruelly. They hesitated to voice their thoughts...

Then Sarah said sadly, "How can his disappearance have anything to do with her, a helpless old lady? I can't imagine her committing an ordinary crime, although I'll bet she has heaped many a curse on his head!" Sipping her coffee she added thoughtfully, "It is awful to know that she is probably delighted to be rid of him, even if it turns out to be only for a short while! Anyway, there's nothing we can do either for the boy or her ... poor lost soul."

***

Thirty miles away, intense police action was underway – rivers and ponds were being dragged. When a house-to-house search through the village revealed no trace of Billy, members of the public were organised to comb the fields and woodlands.

His parents were numb and weary.

"As if things aren't bad enough," yelled Billy's father, "that damned cat of old Mattie's wails outside all night like a banshee and keeps creeping in here during the day! ... Look at it!" He sprang to his feet. "Here it is again... pestering!"

Bertha, standing in her garden, heard the cat being kicked out of her neighbours' door. It screeched and leaped over the fence where it stood – legs stretched, back arched – terrified.

She picked it up and carried it tenderly into her cottage – back to Baby. When she had found the little cat shaking and almost frozen stiff in her garden on Christmas morning it had been the answer to all her prayers ... a gift for Baby. Now, what should they call this little pet? ... A policeman had called earlier to tell her that the boy next door had

Grey Masque of Death

disappeared. "What a shame," she said. Bertha couldn't imagine a world with no Billy it. She would miss him...

With the ghostly child cradled on her lap she sat rocking gently in front of the glowing fire, one hand stroking the rigid back of the trembling animal... The glossy black fur stood on end and Bertha murmured softly. "Calm down, silly Billy, there's nothing to fear! You must stay with us and be friends. This is your home now! Hush...! There, there – we are going to be such a happy family... "

Mai Griffin

Grey Masque of Death

*If you enjoyed reading **"Grey Masque of Death"** the third book in the Grey Series, then look out for Book Four, coming soon...*

Haunting Shades of Grey

Clarrie is on a painting break, soaking up the atmosphere of the English Countryside, with her canvas at the ready, when she is senselessly attacked by a complete stranger... Her barely started painting is stolen from its easel and Sarah is left to put the clues together while Clarrie fights for her life on a hospital bed...

Mai Griffin

The Grey Series so far...

Deadly Shades of Grey
A Poisonous Shade of Grey
Grey Masque of Death
Haunting Shades of Grey *(Coming Soon)*

Sarah

As the wife of a successful artist, achieving normality for Sarah Grey was never going to be as simple as it is for most of us. But with the added impact of her extra sense, giving her the ability to see and hear the dead and the strongly telepathic living, 'normal' has always been a difficult concept. After her husband died, her loneliness was almost overwhelming as she felt surrounded only by the dead, but in the background there was always Polly, the Grey family housekeeper for many years, to keep her company. Soldiering on alone, as so many other widows have done, eventually allows her to assume a calm façade and a gradual acceptance of death when it comes so close to home.

Selling the old house and moving to a small apartment seems a good idea until her daughter is also widowed but her instincts are to go and live with her to help out. She has long suspected that Clarrie might have latent psychic powers and is concerned about what could happen if Clarrie tries to cope on her own. Once the grief has softened a little, she looks forward to having laughter back in the house...

Clarrie

As an artist's daughter it is, perhaps, not surprising that Clarrie grew up with a love for paint and canvas. Encouraged by her father to accompany him on his painting trips, she learned her trade from a master painter and plies it well. Now an up and coming artist in her own right, everything seems to have come together, until Tom is tragically involved in a crippling accident and she spends the final year of her seven year marriage nursing her paralysed and dying husband. After his death, devastated by her traumatic loss, Clarrie is grateful for her mother's suggestion so Sarah gives up her original plans to buy an apartment and moves into Clarrie's home.

Being able to immerse herself in her art proves therapeutic, but the immersion is so complete that Clarrie barely notices the changes in her perception of the world around her, often blurring the reality of the present with the realities of the past and that proves dangerous...

Having two psychics in the house is a recipe for trouble, even if one is trying for the "quiet life" and the other is in denial...

Deadly Shades of Grey by Mai Griffin
ISBN-13: 978-0955744709
UK Publisher: U P Publications Ltd

The horrific prologue, launches us straight into Mai Griffin's dramatic psychic mystery thriller "Deadly Shades of Grey". Reflecting the dark side of the mysteries that plague the day to day life of unwilling psychic Sarah Grey and her artist daughter Clarrie Hunter, it also marks the start of the Grey series.

As the plots twist and spiral around the edge of the reader's vision it is possible to see the dilemma of trying to live normally, when everything around you isn't.

Overcoming the temptation to live in denial of their unwanted psychic abilities, Clarrie and Sarah are gradually drawn in to help find a kidnapped woman and a child that has disappeared... and what does Clarrie keep glimpsing in her picture of an old empty cottage and why has she been driven to paint it?

No matter where she goes, danger keeps intruding into Clarrie's life and painting is not keeping it at bay...

A Poisonous Shade of Grey by Mai Griffin
ISBN-13: 978-0955744716
UK Publisher: U P Publications Ltd

Yet another twisting 'Grey tale'- the story starts with a rejected lover seeking to eliminate the competition by murdering the 'wife'. Carefully planned, and skilfully executed by someone who specialises in expediency and efficiency... what could go wrong?

Busy with her series of landscapes, Clarrie is refusing to be distracted from her various projects and leaves Sarah and Polly to their own devices...

Sarah is happy at home, until a spectral intruder invades...

All Polly has to do is help her niece, Elaine, in her last minute wedding preparations... including trying to track down a missing guest...

Mai Griffin

After a successful career as a professional international artist, travelling the world and painting portraits of Royalty, Heads of State and other prominent figures (www.maigriffin.com), Mai has returned to her first and all pervasive love of writing.

Although over eighty of her paintings hang in Palaces, Government Offices, Embassies and Stately Homes, Mai has never stopped writing whether her own work or ghosting and editing for others.

Deadly Shades of Grey was the first of the Grey series with 'A Poisonous Shade of Grey' the second. This book 'Grey Masque of Death' released by U P Publications Ltd before Christmas 2008 is the third and the fourth 'Haunting Shades of Grey' is due out early in 2009.

Mai now lives in Spain and between her painting commissions and art exhibitions is writing hard! She is delighted with the reception her books have received and has plans for more Grey stories in the pipeline.

U P Publications Ltd

Founded in 2003, U P Publications Ltd created and ran the Business to Business Magazine "Wising UP!" In 2005 the magazine moved to a wholly online format. In late 2006 the decision was made to move into book publishing and after two years searching for suitable material "Deadly Shades of Grey" was released in early 2008.

Wising UP! Is now only available online – www.wisingup.co.uk

Non-Fiction books planned for release by U P Publications in 2009 include an in-depth illustrated book on PSVs and "A History of South Kelsey" by Jean Collins

For more information on these books, the Grey Series and the other projects that we have in hand, please visit www.uppublications.ltd.uk

Grey Masque of Death

Reviews for 'Deadly Shades of Grey'

Publisher's Note - We sent out several review copies prior to publication. These are a few of the comments on **'Deadly Shades of Grey'** that we received from our first three reviewers:-

- 1 - I received the book at 5pm and started reading it that evening, I couldn't put it down and I certainly couldn't sleep, until I finished it at three in the morning!

- 2 - I usually read a book for five or ten minutes, last thing at night, before I go to sleep - I never have time to read in the day... but night after night, until I finished it, I found an hour had gone by, I was so absorbed...

- 3 - I thoroughly enjoyed this book, it kept me gripped til the end... I cannot wait until Book Two.

As publishers we feel that this book never loses momentum, every page is a cliff hanger and everyone who has read it has thoroughly enjoyed it... With Books Two and Three in the pipeline and already building a following, we are delighted we spotted Mai first! Available by order from all mainstream UK Book retailers.

A gripping page-turner, By Barbara Power (Spain)

The creativity of some artists, it seems, just cannot be contained or constrained within the limits of one particular medium, and so it is with the internationally-acclaimed painter, Mai Griffin. In the first of her series which introduces the Grey family, she has turned her artistic talent to the written word and proves as adept with her pen as she is with a paint brush.

For widow Sarah Grey, who only wants to live a quiet life, being psychic is a cause of much anxiety and discomfort. However, she knows that to maintain her peace of mind and sanity she must force herself to respond to the messages that haunt her. Adding to Sarah's anxiety is the fact that her daughter, Clarrie, seems to have inherited the same psychic ability, a situation which could lead her into terrible danger

Deadly Shades of Grey is a well-crafted mystery/murder novel with a gripping and taut plot that has intriguing twists and turns. It is a good and thoroughly satisfying read. Although Book 1 is a stand-alone novel, I cannot wait to get hold of Book 2 to learn more about this interesting family and what happens to them.